Stellar Praise for

Between,
Georgia

"[One of the] summer's hottest reads . . . The author's warm twang makes her novel about feuding Southern families resonate."
—*People*

"Adept at the kind of farce that requires characters to hide from each other in the bushes . . . she's also good at poignancy and at darker scenes of mayhem."
—*Washington Post Book World*

"Compulsively readable . . . brims with humor . . . cleverly explores the nature of family and belonging . . . [It] delivers the kind of sheer reading enjoyment that keeps bookworms up way past their bedtimes."
—*Christian Science Monitor*

"Quirky . . . a strong follow-up to her debut."
—*Atlanta Journal-Constitution*

"Colorful and evocative."
—*Sunday Express* (UK)

"By turns heartbreaking and funny, it is a powerful story."
—*St. Petersburg Times*

more . . .

"Accomplished . . . evocative and lovingly crafted . . . Jackson sweeps the reader away to a place where gravel crunches underfoot and the smell of corn bread wafts in the air . . . The plot is precise and sweet, and Jackson includes the perfect ingredients: quirky characters, a picturesque setting, and ample surprises."
—*Kirkus Reviews* (starred review)

"The author brings a whole new cast of riveting characters to life."
—*Birmingham Times*

"Jackson is a powerful writer."
—*Daily Mail* (London)

"A winner . . . you can't wait to finish it, but don't want it to end."
—*Library Journal*

"Uplifting . . . quirky and touching . . . Jackson has been compared to Fannie Flagg, and rightfully so; her characters are vivid and lovable, put in situations that are so hard to explain that it's just easier to pass the book lovingly along to a friend . . . even the most cynical reader will surely smile as the back cover closes."
—*Booklist* (starred review)

"A raucous novel, populated by wild characters, tenderly drawn. Joshilyn Jackson proves to be a wily guide who writes with wit and warmth about the complex nature of family, while handing down a beautiful and fierce new definition of motherhood."
—Julianna Baggott, author of *Girl Talk*
and coauthor of *Which Brings Me to You*

Also by Joshilyn Jackson

gods in Alabama

Between,
Georgia

JOSHILYN JACKSON

WARNER BOOKS

NEW YORK   BOSTON

For Bob before me and Sam after

Copyright © 2006 by Joshilyn Jackson
Reading Group Guide Copyright © 2007 by Hachette Book Group USA
Excerpts from *The Girl Who Stopped Swimming* Copyright © 2007 by Joshilyn Jackson
All rights reserved. Except as permitted under the U.S. Copyright Act of 1976, no part of this publication may be reproduced, distributed, or transmitted in any form or by any means, or stored in a database or retrieval system, without the prior written permission of the publisher.

Warner Books
Hachette Book Group USA
237 Park Avenue
New York, NY 10169

Visit our Web site at www.HachetteBookGroupUSA.com.

Printed in the United States of America

Originally published in hardcover by Warner Books.

First Trade Edition: May 2007

10 9 8 7 6 5 4 3 2 1

Warner Books and the "W" logo are trademarks of Time Warner Inc. or an affiliated company. Used under license by Hachette Book Group USA, which is not affiliated with Time Warner Inc.

The Library of Congress has cataloged the hardcover edition as follows:

Jackson, Joshilyn.
    Between, Georgia / Joshilyn Jackson.— 1st ed.
        p. cm.
    ISBN-13: 978-0-446-52442-1
    ISBN-10: 0-446-52442-5
    1. Women—Southern States—Fiction. 2. Self-realization—Fiction. 3. Southern States—Fiction.
4. Vendetta—Fiction. I. Title.
    PS3610.A3525B48 2006
    813'.6—dc22   2005023748

ISBN 978-0-446-69945-7 (pbk.)

ACKNOWLEDGMENTS

I have taken some liberties with Georgia's geography; Between exists, but I have never set foot in it. If its landscape and people resemble my version, then I will pray fervently that their Bernese moves far, far away, and state for the record that it *is* a coincidence. Also, in the forties and fifties, there was not a deaf day school within fifty miles, so I grabbed a corner of the Georgia School for the Deaf and pulled it east. I wanted Stacia to grow up with her family, but learn ASL in an environment that would value her resilient spirit. I promise I put the school right back after.

I've had untellable amounts of help from the Helen Keller National Center (especially Susan Lascek and Linda Collins) here in Atlanta, and all the deaf and deaf-blind people, interpreters, and CODAs who let me hang around them like a groupie. I am especially indebted to Bethany Jackson (she of the glossy brown hair), Jill Sheffield, Nancy Hold, Sylvia Primeaux, Darlene Prickett, and the fabulous Mariann Jacobson.

If you think a deaf-blind woman who came of age before feminism did couldn't be as strong and independent as Stacia Frett, then you need to come meet my friend Alice Turner. Although they are around the same age, Stacia is not anything like Alice in looks, personality, or spirit. But Alice showed me how to create a character with both a rich, fulfilling life and type-one Usher's syndrome. Alice is the president of the Georgia Deaf-Blind Association. She babysits her three small grandkids, bakes kick-butt brownies, and, when we go out to eat, *she* tells *me* where to turn by feel and timing. She was infinitely patient with my wretched finger spelling and generous with her time—thanks, Alice. Thanks for everything.

I am deeply in karmic debt to my agent, Jacques de Spoelberch, and my editor, Caryn Karmatz Rudy. If I could, I would kiss the living personification of Warner Books right on the lips. I have gotten such astounding levels of support and encouragement from every person in the building, including, but certainly not limited to, Jamie Raab, Karen Torres, the non–hell-bound Martha Otis, Jennifer Romanello, Penina Sacks, Emily Griffin, and the gifted Anne Twomey. Thank you, Beth Thomas, for tarting up the pages that still had bed head. I feel slavish gratitude toward fellow writers/readers Lily James, Jill James, Julie Oestreich, Amy Go Wilson, Anna Schachner, and the patient saints of the In Town Atlanta Writers Group.

My amazing family never ceases to support me and make life taste sweet in my mouth; Scott, you are my love, my partner, my best friend, and a dern good kisser as a bonus. Big love to Sam, Maisy Jane, Bob, Betty, Bobby, Julie, Daniel, Erin, Jane, Allison, Lydia, and all my family at PSFUMC.

CHAPTER

1

THE WAR BEGAN thirty years, nine months, and seven days ago, when I was deaf and blind, floating silent and serene inside Hazel Crabtree. I was secreted in Hazel's womb, which was cloaked in her pale and freckled skin, which was in turn hidden by the baggy sweatsuits she adopted so she would look fat instead of pregnant. Which was ridiculous, because who ever heard of a fat Crabtree? They were all tall and weedy, slouching around like wilting stems, red hair blooming out the top.

Hazel Crabtree was fifteen years old, and no one thought twice about her expanding waistline as she crept around the edges of rooms, watching her mother ignore her and ignoring me in turn as I kicked at her and spun and grew myself some lungs.

I never heard Hazel's side of the story. She birthed me but was never in any sense my mother. I heard an expurgated version from my aunt Genny; to hear Genny tell it, I frolicked blood-lessly into the world attended by singing rabbits. From Aunt

Bernese, I got raw medical data and a flat recitation of events in the order they occurred.

But my mother, Stacia Frett, told it to me as a love story, hers and mine. It wasn't a declaration of war to her, it was simply the tale of how we found each other. My mother's version, with every nuance communicated by her expressive face and flashing hands, dominated my imagination. Over the years, I interwove her story with what I had gleaned from Genny and Bernese, until I had an interpretation that felt like truth. It was as if my soul had been floating above the scene, watching, waiting to be sucked into my body with the air of my first breath.

I don't know why Hazel Crabtree went to Bernese for help the night I was born, and Bernese did not think to ask her. The why of things did not often trouble Aunt Bernese, but she was a master at discovering the how. Before agenting my mother's art became a full-time job, Bernese had worked in labor and delivery over at Loganville General. I like to think Hazel came to the Fretts because she knew Bernese was a former nurse and pragmatist savant who, beneath her bluster, had a kind heart. This was a distinct possibility: At that time Between, Georgia, had a population of about ninety people. Everybody knew everything about everyone.

But more likely, she was being practical. Bernese and her husband and their boys lived on the lot at the dead end of Grace Street. Her sisters, Stacia and Genny, lived together in the house next door. There wasn't another house on the block, and Bernese's backyard overlooked empty miles of Georgia pine trees. The only other nurse in town lived on one of Between's more populated streets; she had close neighbors. The last (although perhaps the most important) factor was that Hazel had to know going to the Fretts for help was a surefire way to piss off her family.

Bernese woke to the sound of someone banging on her front door a few minutes past four in the morning. She came down the stairs pulling on her robe, getting her gun hand stuck in the sleeve. Her husband, Lou, trailed behind her, saying nervously, "Is the safety on? Is the safety on? Hand the gun to me and then put your robe on, Bernese. Is the safety on?"

Bernese got herself untangled and tucked the gun into her armpit, barrel down, while she tied her robe belt.

"Is that the thirty-eight?" asked Lou. "Lord-a-mercy, why didn't you get your little purse gun?"

Bernese opened the door and there was Hazel Crabtree, holding a wad of her mucous plug cupped in both hands and saying, "This came out. Is this a piece of baby? I hurt."

Bernese said, "Holy monkeys! You're pregnant? Lou, call for an ambulance." Tiny towns like Between didn't have 911 service in 1976, so Lou went to get Bernese's emergency-numbers card from the drawer. But Hazel shoved past Bernese and grabbed at him, falling to her knees as she yowled, "No, no, you can't call anyone. My mother can't know."

Then she let go of Lou and said in a high, panicked voice, "Something's coming. Something else. Something bad is coming." Hazel scrabbled at her belly and crotch, frantic. Her sweatpants were soggy, and she shoved them down to mid-thigh. She wasn't wearing any panties. Then she tilted and tipped over, writhing on the foyer carpet.

Bernese looked up and saw all three of her young sons huddled in a clot on the stairs. They were clutching one another on the second-floor landing, staring down through the banisters with wide, horrified eyes.

"Never you mind," Bernese said to Lou. He was tugging at his earlobe as he watched Hazel flail and howl on the floor. He set the phone back down in its cradle on the hall table. Bernese said, "Get up there with the boys. Tell them something. I will fix this." Lou trotted obediently upstairs and picked up the toddler, herding the two older boys back toward their bedroom. Hazel's contraction subsided, and she rose up on her hands and knees, panting.

Bernese's front door opened into a carpeted entryway. A wide doorway on the right led to the den, and straight ahead was a long hallway to the kitchen. On the left, the stairs went up to a landing that overlooked the foyer. There was a heavy table, almost a sideboard, that ran the length of the staircase. The phone was on the edge of the table, close to the front door, and the rest of it was taken up by the huge glass terrarium that housed Bernese's beloved luna moths. The adult moths were awake, some fanning their wings as they posed on the perches and twigs. Others had paired off, attaching end to end to make the kind of desperate love that comes with an extremely short life span.

Bernese tried to step around Hazel, heading for the table so she could set down her gun and pick up the phone, but Hazel reared up on her knees in front of Bernese, crying, "No, you can't! No one knows I'm this way. No one can find out!"

She was grabbing for Bernese's arm, but she fell short and jerked at her hand, squeezing. The gun went off. The bullet whizzed past Hazel's head, smashing through the glass of the terrarium and burying itself in the staircase. Glass showered down, pattering onto the carpet and sprinkling Hazel's wild red hair.

Hazel and Bernese froze in the sudden silence, their eyes locked on the smoking hole in Bernese's stairs. From upstairs, Lou yelled, "Bernese? Bernese?" They heard his footsteps clattering across the upstairs hall, the little boys running in a panicked herd behind him.

"Stop!" screeched Bernese, and the footsteps stopped dead. "No one is hit, Lou. Stay with the boys."

"I asked you was the safety on," Lou called down, aggrieved.

Bernese hollered back, "Maybe you better put the safety on your mouth."

Next door, the gunshot woke up Bernese's sister Genny. Genny bolted upright, clutching the covers to her bosom. Her bedroom window overlooked Bernese's front lawn, and she saw the downstairs lights blazing and Bernese's front door standing open. Genny got up and ran on tiptoe down the hall to Stacia's room. She flipped the light switch and sat on the bed, shaking Stacia awake. Stacia sat up, her gray eyes opening wide, immediately alert. She held her fist up to her chin, thumb and pinky spread wide, asking by sign and her expressive face what was wrong.

Genny shook her head and signed back, *Heard gun.* She cut her eyes to the left to indicate Bernese's house, then signed, *Lights on, door open. What do we do?*

As soon as she finished signing, she moved her right hand to pluck at the fine dark hairs on her left forearm, tugging hard enough to lift her skin in points. One of the hairs popped out, torn root and all from the follicle.

Don't pick, Stacia signed. She gently peeled Genny's fingers away and gave her a bracing pat, then signed, *I'll handle it.* Stacia climbed out of bed and pulled on her robe. She tied the belt with savage efficiency, then spun on one heel and took off for the front door at a dead run. Her long black hair was unbound, and it unfurled behind her like a banner.

Genny stared openmouthed for a moment and then said, "Goodness grief!" She ran after Stacia, waving frantically in a futile attempt to catch her eye, signing, *Wait! Wait! Call police! Help! Wait!* at Stacia's implacable back.

She chased Stacia in this manner all the way across the lawn to Bernese's front porch. She stopped short of the stairs and leaned down and grabbed up a pinecone, ripping up a chunk of sod with it. She threw it as hard as she could past Stacia, through her line of sight. It thunked against Bernese's siding, and dust puffed out of it all the way around, like a firework going off. It left a black smudge on the porch, like an outsize thumbprint on the wood. Stacia paused to give Genny an irked look over her shoulder before she disappeared through Bernese's front door.

Genny stood a few steps outside the glow of the porch lights, tugging at her long black braid. Her nervous fingers climbed up, following the weave of her braid, all the way until she touched the fine hairs at her nape. She gathered two or three in a pinch and ripped them out, twiddling her fingers together to shake off the loose hairs and then immediately seeking out another pinch. A luna moth came fluttering drunkenly out the front door and wafted up, disappearing into the night. Genny watched it go, and then she scuttled up onto the porch. She peeked inside.

Bernese and Stacia were helping Hazel to the other side of the foyer, picking their way through shattered glass from the terrarium. Hazel was moaning and naked from the waist down. Her sweatshirt had hiked up over her grossly distended abdomen. The rest of her body was so skinny that Genny could see her ribs. Hazel's thighs were streaked with blood. Glass fragments sparkled in her hair, inappropriately festive. Three or four of the luna moths were dancing up around the light fixture, and one was fluttering in Hazel's wake, as if drawn by her bright hair. Genny saw the gun sitting by the phone on the sideboard.

"What's happening?" Genny squawked, jerking out another pinch of hair at her nape. "Is she shot? Was she shot in her pants?"

"No one is shot," said Bernese. "It's a baby coming, and it's coming now, very fast. Help me here."

Bernese and Stacia lowered Hazel back down to the carpet in the doorway to the den. They tried to get her to squat, but she flopped onto her back and lay there, thrashing back and forth as another contraction took her. Stacia signed rapidly, and Genny said, "Stacia wants to know, what do you need?"

"Boiled string. Scissors. Clean towels," said Bernese as Genny repeated her words in sign. "Hot water. A doctor, but that's not going to happen. I think this baby is coming now."

Stacia nodded curtly and ran down the long hallway into the kitchen. Bernese knelt by Hazel until the contraction subsided and she was still again. She was sobbing quietly on the floor: "It has to stop. Make it stop."

"It will stop," said Bernese. "We have to get this baby out is all. Genny, come sit by her head."

"Me?" Genny squeaked.

"Unless you want the naked end," said Bernese, staying beside Hazel. "Breathe," she said.

"Oh, oh, oh, oh," said Genny. She stayed right where she was in the doorway, rocking back and forth, her gaze flicking around the room, glancing off the moths and Bernese and the blood and the gun on the table, unable to light on anything. Her busy fingers sought hairs to pull as she rocked herself faster.

"Another one is coming," said Hazel. "Make it not come."

"You want it to come," said Bernese. "It will get this baby out, and then it will all stop. So let it come."

"No, no, no, I don't want it to come," Hazel moaned, but it came anyway. It came relentlessly, and she was helpless in it, with Bernese roaring at her to push.

Genny was weaving harder, panting, tugging at her hair. Bernese glared at her. "Quit that picking and get by this girl's head. Now. And quit panting. I don't have time to drag your big butt out of the way if you faint."

Hazel shook her head wildly back and forth, twisting her body as she fought the contraction. Genny, watching, dug her fingernails into her forearm hard enough to draw blood and then stared down at her arm for half a beat. The pain cleared her head, and she accessed the thread of Frett resilience buried in her, deep under her nerves. She stilled her hands and scurried over to kneel beside Hazel's head.

"There you go. You and her breathe together," instructed Bernese. Once Genny was in place, Bernese braced herself against the doorway and put the heel of her hand at the top of Hazel's belly. She leaned in to it, bearing down and saying, "And you, girl. Push hard from here."

Hazel shoved at Bernese's hand, weeping. She slumped again as the contraction ended, and Bernese said, "Next time you push like that at the start."

Hazel said, "I don't want a next time."

Genny reached out and patted ineffectually at Hazel's shoulder. Hazel grabbed Genny's wrist, looking up at her, beseeching, "Please tell her to quit it."

"Oh, honey," said Genny, pity softening her horror. "No one can make Bernese quit anything."

"I hate you," said Hazel to Bernese. "I hate you, you dumb whore."

"Why, this is Ona Crabtree's girl!" said Genny. "This is little Hazel Crabtree!"

"Course it is," said Bernese, a world of Frett contempt ripe in her voice. The two families had nothing in common and had long regarded each other with animosity. The Fretts were a proudly emotional bunch. No Frett lips ever touched liquor (they even sipped grape juice at communion), but their moods could sweep through them as fierce and fast as any drug. Their decisions came from the gut, and they didn't care one fig for what outsiders thought of their actions.

The Crabtrees, on the other hand, almost universally had the deadeye, and their emotional range ran from sullen right on up to enraged. Wary and canny, they felt nothing more keenly than the gaze of the disapproving world, a world that was out to get them. Their responses to feeling judged were shrugs and sneers followed by lashings of great, cold violence.

The Fretts were meticulous, order incarnate. The Crabtrees lived in unimaginable squalor. The Fretts lived within convention and tradition, while the Crabtrees spread like kudzu, generating chaos and more Crabtrees, generally without benefit of marriage. The Fretts had both money and the respect of the town. They were the royal fish in this tiniest of ponds, and the Crabtrees fed along the bottom.

This defied what the Crabtrees felt should be the natural order of things, because the Crabtrees, like everyone else in Between, were white. They were paper-white, pure Irish, most of them, maybe a little French or English or German blood in some of the branches. It was merely annoying when morally solvent white folks looked down on them, but it was maddening to take it from the Fretts, the children of a white father and a mother who was, as Ona put it, "half a damn squaw-Indian."

Hazel had closed her eyes for a moment, resting. Genny looked down at Hazel's pale eyelids, so smooth and dewy, and said, "Goodness grief, honey, how old are you? Bernese, you be sweet. She's a baby herself!"

Bernese said, "Apples don't fall off trees and land all the way downtown. She's almost sixteen, and I think her mama is my age."

"I hate you," said Hazel to Bernese, and then her eyes opened wide again. "Oh no, it's coming."

"This time you push," said Bernese.

"I don't know how to push," said Hazel, looking desperately to Genny. "Oh no, please do something. Do anything."

"Push like you're going number two," said Bernese, and Genny said, "Bernese! Really!"

"How many babies have you had?" Bernese barked, and Genny dropped her eyes. "So shut up and let me help this girl."

"Do something," said Hazel to Genny. "Talk to me. Anything. Sing."

Genny shook her head, but she opened her mouth and started to sing in her quavering soprano. " 'There's not a friend like the lowly Jesus . . .' "

Hazel lashed up at Bernese with one foot and screamed, "Oh fuck, please not Jesus." Bernese caught her thrashing leg at the knee and bent it back toward her abdomen. "Get ready," said

Bernese, anchoring the heel of her other hand at the top of Hazel's swollen belly.

"I'm not ready. Help me," Hazel wailed to Genny, and twisted on the floor while Bernese wrestled with her leg. "Help me. Sing. But not about Jesus."

Genny patted frantically at Hazel with her free hand and sang the first thing that came into her head. "'Sigh no more, ladies, sigh no more, / Men were deceivers ever . . .'"

Hazel thrashed and writhed. "It's here! It's here!"

Bernese bore down, saying, "Push, you hear me? You better push."

Genny kept singing. "'One foot in sea and one on shore, / To one thing constant never . . .'"

Hazel was shaking her head but pushing anyway. Genny saw my head coming out, slick with blood and slime, and she paled and felt her head getting light. Hazel's death grip on her arm was the only thing keeping her upright. She closed her eyes, weaving herself back and forth, and sang, "'Then sigh not so, / But let them go, / And be you blithe and bonny; / Converting all your sounds of woe / Into hey nonny, nonny.'"

"It's crowning. Where is Stacia?" said Bernese. "Genny, get between her legs and catch this baby."

But Genny had reached her limit. "'Hey nonny, nonny,'" she sang with her eyes squinched tight.

Stacia came in from the kitchen with a pan of hot water and clean dish towels, scissors, and string. She set them down and knelt between Hazel's legs as the next contraction hit.

Hazel pushed as Bernese bore down on her abdomen, and my head came out of her. I arrived faceup, staring into the light with my eyes open and angry. It seemed to Stacia that I was staring up at her. My eyes were puffed almost shut, slitted, but she thought my gaze was meeting hers. I looked aware to her, so angry and alive. My face was framed by the darkness that was eating the edges of her vision, and in that moment there were only the two of us. Not even Hazel existed.

Stacia dipped a finger into my mouth to clear it. As she did so, my eyebrows lowered and my lips opened wider. I looked like I was squalling, but it was airless and silent, my body still compressed inside Hazel. As Stacia stared at me, I spun slowly in the birth canal, rotating, turning facedown. Stacia cradled my forehead in her rough palm as another contraction hit. I came slithering out, slick as a fish into her waiting arms.

"Is it done? Is it done?" Hazel said.

"I think so, honey," said Genny, peeking. The skin around her eyes and mouth had turned green. "Oh please, please, I think it's over." Stacia looked across Hazel's prone body, and her eyes met Genny's. Genny signed one-handed, *Boy? Girl?*

Stacia slid her thumb down the side of her right cheek.

"A girl," said Genny, rocking herself and nodding. "That's good. That's not scary. Look, you have a sweet little girl."

"My cooter hurts," said Hazel.

Stacia stayed where she was, holding me with the cord trailing down into Hazel.

"Is it out?" asked Hazel. "Why is it coming again?"

"Again?" Genny squawked.

"It won't be half so hard this time," said Bernese to both of them, and she leaned down and grasped the cord, easing out the afterbirth as Hazel contracted. Genny shut her eyes and started singing again, "'Hey nonny, nonny, so weep no more, my ladies.'" Hazel relaxed, snuffling, and Stacia busied herself cleaning me up and tying off the cord.

"Genny, shut up that caterwauling," said Bernese.

"'Hey nonny,'" Genny sang, trailing off. "Please, is it over?" Hazel released her, and when Genny opened her eyes and looked down, she saw perfect red handprints braceleting her wrist.

"Who is Nonny?" asked Hazel in a puny voice.

"What?" said Bernese.

"She was singing 'Hey, Nonny.' Who is Nonny? Is that the baby?"

Stacia stood up, holding me wrapped in a towel. I was wide awake, staring up into her cloud-gray eyes, solemn and interested. Bernese had moved between Hazel's legs.

"You look good. No tearing. You want to hold your baby?" said Bernese to Hazel.

"No," said Hazel, and she turned her face away, looking at the shattered terrarium. A caterpillar had negotiated its way out over the glass and rubble and was oozing down the sideboard.

"It's a nice little girl, and she is looking much cleaner," said Genny. She sat slumped and exhausted, flat on her bottom on the floor by Hazel's head, faintly rocking herself.

Stacia looked up from me at last, and Genny signed that she should hand me to Hazel, but Stacia did not move. She looked at Hazel as Hazel said, "I don't want it," shaking her head petulantly. Stacia curled her lip and held me tighter.

"Maybe later," said Bernese.

Stacia stamped her foot to get Genny's attention and signed one-handed, cradling me in her other arm.

"Stacia says it's her baby," said Genny.

"Obviously," said Bernese. "Give the girl a minute. She'll take it."

Genny shook her head. "No, I mean Stacia's saying, 'This is my baby. I want her.' Stacia wants the baby."

There was a long silence as everyone digested this. Bernese looked from Stacia to Genny and back again and then snorted. "Don't be ridiculous." She tilted her face and bellowed up the stairs, "Lou, leave the boys for a sec and throw me down some sheets. The oldest ones we have. And any old towels you see in that linen closet."

"Stacia says, 'I am not being ridiculous. She came to me. She's mine.' I think she really wants this baby, Bernese."

"Oh good," said Hazel to Genny. "Take it. It can be y'all's Nonny."

"Let's get you to the hospital," said Bernese.

Hazel immediately said, "No hospital. They'll call Mama, and I'll never get away. She'll keep me. And she'll make me keep it." Her eyes filled up with tears. "Please, I'm fine. Just let me sleep a little and then I'll go away. Y'all can have that Nonny."

"You need to see a doctor," said Bernese. "You could have a complication and bleed out on my floor."

"I won't do that. I promise," said Hazel, and the tears spilled down her cheeks. "You said I looked good. And if you make me go to the hospital, I'll throw myself under a truck. I really will. I'll throw Nonny, too."

Stacia stamped her foot again, signing, and Genny said, "Stacia's insisting. She says, 'This baby is my baby. I know it. I don't know how to do it, how to keep her, but Bernese does. Bernese, you do it.'"

Genny got up and walked over, folding back the towel to look at me. "Oh, goodness grief, look at all that red hair. And the teeny feet."

"This is not like a hamster, Genny," snapped Bernese. "This is a person. A little Crabtree person."

Lou's pale face appeared at the top of the stairs. His brown hair, thin and gingery, was rumpled, and his comb-over was hanging down past his ear on one side. He had wrapped the sheets and towels into a bundle, and he tossed it over the banister to Bernese.

"Get back with the boys," Bernese commanded, and he disappeared. Bernese began gently packing the towels under Hazel's bottom to catch the fluids that were oozing out of her and soaking into the carpet.

Stacia was signing again, rapid and angry, her free hand flashing. Genny interpreted, and as she spoke, she got the rollercoaster look that she always got when she had to say things out loud for Stacia that she would not have said for a million dollars on her own account. Her eyelids lifted so high that the whites were visible all the way around.

"She says, 'Don't lecture me, and don't dare patronize me. I am telling you something real here, if you aren't too stupid to hear it. So shut up and help me.'"

Bernese ignored Stacia; she was still carefully arranging the old sheets and talking to Hazel. "Are you comfortable? You want some water?"

"Please don't tell," begged Hazel.

"Your mama's Ona Crabtree?" Bernese said.

"No," said Hazel.

But Genny said, "Yes, that's her mama." Over Hazel's head,

Genny's eyes met Bernese's, and Genny mouthed, "Drinks," then bobbed her head in a wise nod.

Bernese wrapped the afterbirth in the nastiest towel. She noticed Genny's hands creeping back up her braid and said, "Genny, for the love of Baby Jesus, get your hands off yourself. Don't start picking now when it's all over but steam-cleaning the carpet. Do you need a pill?"

Genny shook her head and rubbed at her forearm for a second, then went back to signing what Bernese was saying for Stacia. Bernese said, "Good, then make yourself useful. See if that girl won't nurse her baby. She should nurse it while it's awake. I am going to go get some trash bags, and I will call for an ambulance from the kitchen."

Bernese headed up the long hall, her arms full of filthy towels. Hazel watched her go, panting, and then she rolled over painfully and got to her hands and knees.

Genny said, "Honey, you should be still." Stacia, holding me, hesitated. She tried to hand me to Genny, but Genny, still dizzy and faintly green, did not take me. Stacia walked toward Hazel, holding me, and Genny followed, saying, "Honey, you need to lie down on this pad, you are . . . Oh my. You are leaking things."

Hazel crawled miserably across the foyer. She left the doorway to the den and crept back into the glass. It bit into her knees as she headed for the long table. Stacia followed, with Genny clucking and tutting along behind her. Hazel reared up suddenly on her bleeding knees and grabbed the gun off the sideboard. Stacia froze, and Genny almost ran into her.

Bernese was at the end of the hall when Hazel called, "If you go one step more, I will shoot you."

Bernese stopped and turned around. Hazel was so weak she

was swaying drunkenly from side to side, trying to hold up the heavy gun so she could aim down the hall. "I will shoot you if you tell my mama."

"Put that down, you idiot. I don't need more holes in my woodwork," Bernese said.

"I mean it," said Hazel.

"Spare me," said Bernese contemptuously. Blood was trickling out of Hazel, oozing in rivulets down her thighs. "You can barely stay erect. You couldn't hit me if I stood dead still and gave you all six tries."

"Fine," said Hazel. She twisted at the waist, bringing the gun around. Stacia was close behind her, and Hazel pressed the barrel into Stacia's belly, under me.

"Bet I can hit *her*," Hazel said.

Bernese became very still, and it was silent for a long, ugly moment.

"Jesus, help us," whispered Genny, barely above a breath.

"Will you stop with that Jesus? I told you!" Hazel's voice was shrill.

Stacia moved her free hand up very slowly to sign, making no sudden movements, and Genny managed to look away from the gun and focus on the familiar sight of Stacia speaking. "Hazel, Stacia wants to know where your sweetheart is," said Genny. Her voice was tinny and high.

Hazel looked in confusion from Stacia's slowly signing hand to her face and said, "My sweetheart?"

Genny was so afraid that all she could do was watch Stacia's hand and repeat after it, saying what Stacia's hand was saying, not looking at anything else. "You have a baby. You must have had a sweetheart."

Hazel sucked air in through her nostrils, loud. "I had a lot of sweethearts," she said. She shrugged. Bernese knelt down silently and set her armful of towels on the floor.

"I had a sweetheart," said Genny for Stacia, her eyes locked on Stacia's fingers. "Just the one." Stacia signed, her movements gentle and slow, as the luna moths fluttered up around the light and the barrel of the gun pressed into her soft belly. "His name was Frank. I don't have him anymore. He did something stupid, and I'm done with him. I thought I'd marry him and we'd live with Genny. Me and Frank and my sister, and I would have my own babies. But that's not going to happen now." Stacia kept signing, but her gaze lifted, and she looked over Hazel, meeting Bernese's eyes as Bernese stood and began creeping up the hall toward them, step by silent step. Stacia glanced back down at Hazel, at her trembling hand on the gun, and then back at Bernese. "Do you know what Usher's syndrome is?" Genny said for her.

"No," said Hazel. Her thin arms were trembling with effort, and Genny was terrified that she'd inadvertently pull the trigger. Genny kept her eyes on Stacia's hand and interpreted, hardly aware of what she was saying. The gun pressing into Stacia's belly was a black beast in her peripheral vision.

"It means I'm deaf," Genny interpreted. "I was born deaf. And it means my eyes are going. I'll be blind in another ten years, fifteen if I am lucky. The edges are closing in already. It's dark beside me, like shutters are being drawn. At some point my depth perception will go, and I won't be able to work anymore. I'm a sculptor; I make molds and cast dolls in porcelain. That's my work. So I've lost my sweetheart. And I'm losing my work. And here's this baby.

"This baby is mine. You brought her to this house, and she slid into my arms. No one is going to call your mama, because no one is going to take this baby from me. Frank is gone, my work is going, and I've been asking God, 'Why does my heart keep beating?' And you brought me the answer. Don't worry about Bernese. She won't do a thing to take this baby out of my arms. She's going to help me keep this baby. Once she sees my side—and she's seeing it now—she won't worry about what's practical or legal or even what's right. She'll make it happen. I'll take this baby, and you can go home. Home or anywhere you like."

Stacia looked hard into Hazel's eyes and signed, and Genny said, "But if you shoot me, Bernese is going to have to call your mama."

After a long moment, Hazel's arms dropped, pointing the gun down into the carpet. She sagged, and Bernese ran the last few steps up the hall and caught her before she slumped into the glass. Bernese peeled the gun out of her limp hand, flipped the safety on, then set it carefully back on the table.

"Help me," said Bernese, and Genny darted forward, panting, and together they lifted Hazel out of the glass and half carried her back to her pad of old sheets and towels.

"All right, then," said Bernese. "Let's make sure you haven't ruptured anything. What a mess."

Hazel closed her eyes. The sun was rising, spilling pale light across the lawn. Stacia turned and shut the front door. After a few minutes, Bernese got up from between Hazel's legs.

"You look okay," Bernese said. Her gardening shoes were sitting by the front door, and she slipped them on and crunched into the glass. She picked up the phone.

"Bernese!" said Genny. Hazel's eyes flew open and she started crying again, making piteous mewling noises deep in her throat.

But Stacia smiled and shook her head, meeting Bernese's eyes with a cool and level gaze.

"Don't get your pants in a bunch, Genny," said Bernese. "I'm calling Isaac." She added to Hazel, "That's my lawyer, so stop with that fuss. You sound like a kicked cat."

Bernese dialed from memory and stood waiting for the phone to wake up Isaac Davids.

"It's me," she said when he answered. "Yes, I know what time it is, but this is an emergency. You need to walk down here, quick as you can . . . I know, but pull some pants on and hurry down. Stacia needs us to help her steal Ona Crabtree's grandbaby."

CHAPTER

2

WITH SUCH A loud beginning, small wonder I grew up to be a person who studies silence. The Fretts and the Crabtrees spent the better part of my childhood chafing hard against each other at the point where they connected, and I was painfully aware of it because that point was me. I was barely out of diapers when Ona Crabtree found out I was her grandchild and appeared on our front lawn, drunk and howling for me. Bernese ran out to meet her with equal force and volume; I was only three, but their enmity was obvious, and I understood enough to realize I was somehow the heart of it. The brawl on my front lawn trained me to look for and interpret the subtler signs that told me how deeply my adopted family despised my birth family and vice versa.

I was raised in my mother and Genny's quiet, well-ordered house at the end of Grace Street, playing with my boy cousins and, later, the tagalong girl-child Aunt Bernese produced when I was nine. The Crabtrees, Ona especially, paced at the periphery of my life, staring hungrily in at me.

Ona Crabtree was half crazy, all mean, perpetually drunk, but she had a junkyard dog's sharp memory for injuries against her person. She'd hated all things Frett from childhood: Ona and Bernese first bonked heads when they met up on the jungle gym behind The First Baptist Church of Between. Genny, fresh off a Baptist summer-revival high and aching to fulfill the Great Commission, shyly invited Ona to come on in to Sunday school with them. Ona accepted, but Bernese eyed Ona's filthy sundress and added, "Run home and change first. We wear our nicest things to God's house."

I'm sure it never occurred to her that perhaps the sundress was Ona's nicest. Ona offered me that story ten thousand times as proof that Fretts were "fancy-pants faker Christians." She never stopped hating them, and after she learned we were genetically connected, she never stopped hounding me. No one ever had a clue who my father was. Not even Hazel, and she'd left town. If not for Ona, I'd have been a Frett free and clear. As it was, my mother and her sisters stood over me like she-bears guarding a shared cub, ever vigilant and suspicious.

The war that would tear up our little town percolated mostly under the surface, with an occasional minor skirmish cropping up here and there. Bernese routinely cut Ona dead in the market, and when I was growing up, the Crabtree boys egged the Frett homes every Halloween. (Or they did until the year Bernese spent all night crouched in her front bushes with a loaded shotgun. Those boys came sauntering down to the end of Grace Street just after three in the morning, and Bernese waited until she could see the whites of their eyes before she discharged the gun into the air, scattering them.)

At eighteen I moved an hour away to study anthropology at the University of Georgia, but my absence did not make the Frett and Crabtree hearts grow any fonder. I came home every other weekend, and after I graduated, my stays became longer and more frequent, so the wounds remained forever fresh and open.

The feud ebbed and renewed in a thousand small ways even during my absence, receding and resurging before it reached critical mass and exploded. The Fretts blamed the escalation on the Crabtrees, and the Crabtrees blamed it on the Fretts. And I, the only one who might have stopped it, was caught up in a battle of my own that was raging through the half of my life I lived in Athens.

Later, when I knelt in the ruins of Between, sifting through drifts of ash and bits of twisted metal and scorched glass, the thwarted archaeologist in me insisted that the only way I could have prevented the war would have been to strangle myself with my own umbilical cord before I pulled my first breath. I never became that archaeologist. My BA prepped me for grad school, but I didn't go, so I can't place much store in my findings. I ended up a sign language interpreter, but I'm a good one. I may not be able to reach into the past to reconstruct my family's losses, but I can read the signs around me and meld them into a single story. One I believe is kissing cousins with the truth.

The morning of the day it all went to hell, I don't know if it was Jonno or the phone that woke me up. Jonno was in the habit of groaning and muttering himself awake, and he went off at about the same time the ringer did. I looked at the clock and then rolled over and put one hand over his mouth. His eyes opened, and under my palm, I could feel his mouth stretching into a smile. We'd had our very last ever goodbye sex the night before. For about the twenty-second time.

"Morning, Nonny," he said cheerfully, his words muffled by my palm.

I said, "Do not talk or make any noise. No reasonable human being calls this early, so that has to be Aunt Bernese. She cannot know you are here. Understand?"

He nodded at me, and as I took my hand away, I added, "And don't smile at me."

He obediently made his mouth into a straight line, lowering his eyebrows as if taking me seriously. His dirty-blond hair was tousled and flopping in curls over his broad forehead. He looked beautiful, and he knew it. I rolled away from him, onto my side. I grabbed the phone off the charger and said into it, "I'm not driving over there today, Bernese."

"Who asked you?" she said. "You sound like you're still sleeping." Behind me, I could feel Jonno uncoiling, stretching like a big cat and rolling toward me, pressing his naked length against my back. I shoved my elbow at him, but he ignored it and nestled closer. His body felt warm and pliable, and his morning erection was nosing at my thigh.

I said, "I overslept a little. I have three jobs today, and I need to get going. I can't leave town and drive down there."

"You said that yesterday. But I thought you'd want to know that Stacia's been up next door pacing since before sunup. I can see her through the window, going back and forth, back and forth, all in a lather. Your mama's flat miserable."

I narrowed my eyes. "If Mama needed me home today, she

24

would have said so. I'm booked solid all week, and I have my court date on Friday. I'm coming Saturday, and Mama knows that."

Bernese went on as if I hadn't spoken. "She spent all day yesterday in her studio, digging around in her boxes of doll heads and humming and pacing and unwrapping and feeling all over the faces and then wrapping them back up and driving everybody rabid-dog crazy. And Genny! She catches your mama's moods like stomach flu, and I had to stop her from picking fifty times yesterday. This is going to end with her in bed for four days, if not in the hospital."

"Give Genny a Xanax," I said, shoving at Jonno's legs with my feet. He scooted away from me, but not far. I could still feel his body radiating heat behind me.

"She won't take a pill in case your mama chooses a doll head and is ready for her to start sewing the body and clothes. And she's already into the paranoid part. She wouldn't eat the applesauce I brought her because she said I had probably snuck her a pill in it."

"Which I am sure you had!" I said.

There was a tiny pause, and then Bernese said, "It's still paranoid for her to think that."

"No, Bernese, that's not paranoid. That's smart. You know, if you don't want Mama to be this unhappy and get Genny all riled, you could quit selling off her doll heads." Jonno started playing itsy-bitsy spider in the space between us, one hand fingerwalking down my spine.

"If you would come over here and help her pick one . . ." Bernese said.

I rolled over onto the spider, pinning it under my back. I gave

Jonno a look that could have withered a whole rain forest, but he grinned back at me, the tent in the sheet telling me he was completely unwithered.

"That's not going to happen," I said to Bernese. "There are a finite number of heads. Quit selling them."

Even as I said the words, I knew they were futile. Bernese had the artistic sensibilities of a handful of blackberries, and even if she had been gifted in that way, Mama and Genny were a perfectly closed unit of Artist and Craftsman. There had never been room for Bernese inside their doll-making process, so from the time they were young women, she had busied herself finding markets for their products. She'd used the appealingly tragic combination of Mama's talent, her deafness, and her incipient blindness as a hook. Exploitative, yes. Also effective. After a couple of years of traveling to doll-making and toy conventions on Mama's behalf, Bernese hooked up with an Atlanta lawyer, Isaac Davids, and together they negotiated a huge contract with Cordova Toys.

Cordova still mass-produced a popular line of dollhouse dolls that were based on Mama's work, and craft stores all over the country sold reproductions of her molds so hobbyists could cast their own dolls. At this point, there was no financial reason to sell any more of Mama's original dolls, and every doll she gave up seemed to take a bite out of Mama. But Bernese couldn't bear to pull her thumb out of any Frett pie, and stopping would sever her tenuous connection to Mama and Genny's work.

"It's for a museum," Bernese said sanctimoniously. "And anyway, did you see how much they offered? But Genny can't take this. She'll pick and then she'll chew and weave and bang until she knocks herself unconscious. And by the way, Fisher's mad at you, too. She sulked her way through her egg this morning."

"Fisher's naturally sulky. Tell her I'll be there on Saturday, Lord willing and the creek don't rise, and don't you call me again today unless you are personally on fire," I said.

Before I could hang up, Bernese was talking again. "Wait one second. Fisher was hoping you'd show yesterday, so you better talk to her if you really aren't coming."

Jonno lay quietly beside me with his hand still trapped beneath my back. I asked, "And who told Fisher I was coming home early?" But I already knew the answer.

"Let me get her," said Bernese, and thunked the phone down hard enough to make me pull the receiver away from my ear. I hammered my heels into the mattress in frustration; I would happily have hung up on Bernese, but never Fisher. My earth revolved around that child's sun. Fisher's mama was Lori-Anne, Bernese's tagalong girl-child. Lori-Anne had Fisher at sixteen and almost immediately crapped out on motherhood. Bernese and Lou were raising Fisher, but I felt like she was at least a third mine.

As a baby, Fisher was colicky, and Bernese had needed a break from the daily four-hour screaming sessions. Mama was immune to screaming, but Genny couldn't bear it, so Mama would take Genny to their studio while Bernese and Lou were off working at their store. For six months, I spent every Saturday and Sunday afternoon walking Fisher back and forth at Mama's house. The doctor recommended swaddling, so I would wrap her tightly in blankets until she was a roly-poly tube with a round, angry face on one end. She reminded me of one of Bernese's caterpillars, wailing and squirming, a limbless bundle of rage trying to flip itself out of my arms.

Mama's house was built in a circle around the central staircase. The foyer flowed into the living room and then the big eat-in kitchen. An archway in the kitchen led to the dining room, and the dining room opened back onto the foyer, closing the loop. I would walk baby Fisher around and around, as if the downstairs were a racetrack, while she screamed magic screams that seemed to require no pause for inhalation. After a few hours, she'd switch to bleating, breathless screams that sounded like an enraged goat. Toward the end, she did a series of short, coughlike screams, one after another, and the pause in between made me think every time maybe she was finished, and then another would come, and another, until I was ready to throw her off an overpass.

But I fell in love with her every afternoon when she at last wound down and dropped into a boneless sleep. I would stand swaying to the music of silence, Fisher a solid string of limp weight in my arms. I would loosen her swaddling clothes and then lie down beside her and curl inward, becoming her protective shell. I was mesmerized by the grassy smell of her baby sweat and the way her fingers would clutch my shirtfront or my finger as she slept. I couldn't stop rubbing my cheek against the skin of her fuzzy head.

By the time she'd outgrown the colic, I was addicted to her. I doubled my twice-monthly visits home and brought over a third of my clothes from Athens. I hung them in my childhood closet beside a goodly portion of Fisher's pink and yellow wardrobe, and then I blew a couple hundred on a prime portacrib. Jonno's band was booked solid most weekends, and Saturday was Bernese's busiest time at her store. It suited everyone for Fisher to spend her weekends with me at Mama and Genny's, so Fisher had grown up as addicted to me as I was to her, and woe betide me if I did not show up on days when Bernese told Fisher I was coming. Days like today.

I heard a rustle and a click, and then Fisher's dour little voice filled the line. "Hey, Nonny."

Jonno chose that moment to finally pull his hand out from underneath me. He sent it wandering across my hip to my belly.

"Hi there, Woolly-Worm," I said. I sounded breathy. I cleared my throat and pulled ineffectually at Jonno's wrist. "What are you up to?"

"Grampa is about to walk me to the bus stop," Fisher said. "Grandma said you were coming over today?"

"Grandma made a mistake," I said into the phone, and then I looked at Jonno and added to both of them, "It's not happening today." Jonno ignored me and slid his arm around my waist, pulling me closer. I smacked at his hand. "I wish I could come, if only to see you. But I have a lot of work." I put one hand over the mouthpiece and hissed at Jonno, "Go pee that thing down and get your clothes on. Out!"

Fisher was saying, "Nonny, but please can't you? We could go to Henry's store and us both could get books. In the window, Henry has this new book about what's inside frogs. It shows half a frog."

Jonno grinned, unrepentant, and rolled away from me. "You have to hang up sometime," he said softly, and got out of the bed.

"Who is that?" demanded Bernese. "Is that a man talking?"

"Bernese?" I said, and flapped my hand at Jonno, frantically trying to shush him.

"Yes," said Bernese. "Fisher's on the walk-around phone. I'm on in the kitchen."

Jonno said, "I thought Fisher had the phone."

Bernese said, "You do have a man over there! Nonny! You are still married, you know."

29

"Until Friday," I said.

"So today it's adultery. And on Friday it will be fornication. You can go to hell for either, last I checked," Bernese said tartly.

"Fisher, hang up," I said, as Fisher said, "What's formication?"

"Hang up, Fisher," said Bernese.

"Okay, Grandma," said Fisher, and I heard the click of a disconnect. Jonno chuckled, gathering his scattered clothes. I grabbed my pillow out from under my head and half sat to hurl it at him. He dropped his jeans and caught it. He set it gently on the foot of the bed, bowing and running his hands over the pillowcase like a maitre d' smoothing a tablecloth, mock-fussy and officious. I flung myself onto my back and stared up at the ceiling.

"Who's that over there?" Bernese demanded.

"None of your business," I said.

Jonno said, "Tell her it's me and get her off your ass. Even a Southern Baptist will let you do it with your husband."

"That's Jonno!" Bernese crowed triumphantly. "I recognize his voice! You're back with Jonno?"

"No," I said.

"Sounds to me like you are," said Bernese.

"Goodbye, Bernese."

"Wait, Nonny. If you're back with Jonno, you don't have to be at court on Friday, so there's no reason not to get on home. I am telling you, your mama is in a deep need, and there you sit, hardhearted as Pharaoh."

I said, "Mama's not on the other end of this phone asking, Bernese. You are. And Jonno and I are still getting divorced." I sat up, my free hand clutching the covers up over my chest. "On Friday. Four P.M." I fixed Jonno with a steely gaze as I said it, reminding him. He held up his hands in surrender and went into my bathroom.

"I'm done having to be quiet, huh?" he said, and released a mighty pee that went thundering down into the toilet bowl.

"Aunt Bernese, I have to go get ready or I'm going to be late."

"Give Jonno my love," said Bernese.

"No," I answered, and clicked off.

Jonno flushed the toilet. His back was framed perfectly in the doorway. Jonno, damn him, was delicious from most angles, but he looked particularly good from behind. I groaned and slipped one leg out of bed, fishing around on the floor for my T-shirt. I clutched it with my toes, pulling it up into the bed with me.

Jonno turned sideways, offering me his Roman profile as if it were a present, and gumming up my toothbrush in exchange. He was still outlined by the door, but this was due more to the ridiculously tiny size of my bathroom than any planning on his part. Probably. I pulled the T-shirt on over my head and got up.

"Shove over," I said, and crammed into the bathroom with him. I pointed at my toothbrush. "I need that."

He obediently passed it over. I stuck it in my mouth and brushed while he leaned around me and spat. When I looked up, I could see him watching me in the mirror, grinning smugly, his arms folded across his broad chest.

"What?" I said.

He shook his head, raising his eyebrows innocently. "Not a thing."

I spat and rinsed. "No, what?"

He gave me his patented naughty-little-boy look and said, "You're going to cancel those jobs and go see your mama today, aren't you?"

"No," I said. "Get out of here. I have to shower."

He took a half step forward and wrapped his arms around my waist from behind. I'm a tall girl, but Jonno easily topped six-three, and he had to bend deep at the knees to nuzzle the back of my neck. He started chanting, "You're going to Betwee-een," in a soft singsong to the tune of "Nanny-nanny-boo-boo." "You're going to Betwee-een."

"Stop it," I said, but his warm breath was stirring the hairs at the nape of my neck, and I was already leaning back against him. He bent deeper, one hand dropping to my inner thigh and running up to cup me between my legs while the other went foraging under the T-shirt. "You're going to Betwee-een."

"I said I'm not. Stop that singing, you brat."

He stopped singing, but he didn't stop touching me with one hand, opening the bathroom drawer with the other and fishing out a condom. He tore the wrapper with his teeth, and as he was rolling it on, he whispered, "I heard what you said, but you'll give in and go see your mama."

"Why do you say that?" I asked. His hands were back on me, and I was bending with him, into him, my eyes drifting closed. Jonno lifted me, sliding into me from behind.

"Because you always do," he said. He seemed to have a thousand hands, and he smelled so familiar. The little red Crabtree who lived in my blood had woken and was running wild under everything the Fretts had tried to raise me to be. Jonno had infinite appeal to that muffled beastie. I braced my arms against the bathroom counter and said, "Stop talking."

He stopped talking, and it was good, for a while. He had always been good at this part, the seduction, knowing exactly what my body wanted. But once we were well into it, I found my eyes opening again. When I looked into the mirror, his eyes were open, looking at us, too, and against the background of my pale blue shower curtain, the angle of our bodies seemed staged. He saw me watching and moved one big hand up from my hip to my face, tilting my head back until the line of my neck was a curve that echoed the curve of my hip. Our reflection was a moving photograph, perfectly composed.

We worked our way through our lexicon of positions, moving from the bathroom to the bedroom floor to the bed. He was getting the job done—he always got the job done—but I knew that if someone walked in on us at any point, he would look beautiful. He moved with me in a way that was externally lovely, almost poised. It was the kind of sex you want to film; my orgasm was inevitable, and his arrived precisely ten seconds after mine while he made a Hollywood-approved facial expression.

He rolled off me and sprawled on his back, completely at ease, while I lay beside him wondering what the hell was wrong with me. Last night I'd fallen off the wagon after almost two months of Jonno-less propriety, and I couldn't seem to get back on that wagon this morning. Then I looked at the clock and panicked. I leaped up and ran all over the room, trying to get myself cleaned up and reasonably presentable in fifteen minutes. Jonno watched me scramble into underpants and thrash around in my closet. I pulled on a brown and gold knit dress that was long enough to wear without hose.

"X. Machina has a late gig tonight. We don't start playing till midnight," Jonno said. "Mind if I stay here and sleep a little longer?"

"Fine," I said, rolling my hair into a wad at the back of my head and securing it with a clip.

"We're playing the Rox Box. You want to come?"

"No."

"Oh, right," he said, grinning. "I forgot. You'll be with your mama in Between."

"Shut up, Jonno," I said. I'd had on brown sandals the night before, and normally they would be in slot three of my shoe rack. Last night he'd played reverse Prince Charming and taken them off me, pausing theatrically to kiss my ankles and my arches, then flinging them away. I traced my memory of their trajectory and found them under my dresser. I stuffed my feet into them. The clip was already slipping in my slick red hair, and I looked wild-eyed and pale beneath my freckles. I didn't have time for makeup or contacts. I got my glasses out of my bedside table drawer and shoved them on, cursing my Crabtree genes. Every Frett but Mama had 20/20 vision. "I'm not going to Between."

"Yuh-huh," said Jonno. "If you don't go, come hear us play. I'll take you for eggs after."

I paused at the bedroom door and said, "I don't want you to take me for eggs. I don't want you to take me for anything. Be gone when I get home, lock up behind you, and the next time I want to see you is Friday at four P.M. sharp, in court. This was really the last time."

"Yuh-huh," he said. I turned to go, and he added, "Hey, want to drive to court together on Friday? I could pick you up, take you for eggs after."

By way of an answer, I slammed the bedroom door hard, and I could hear his laughter following me all the way out of the apartment.

CHAPTER

3

I COASTED THROUGH my first two jobs, interpreting back-to-back anthropology lectures on the UGA campus. Student Services often called my agency and booked me as an interpreter when a deaf student enrolled in an anthro class, since I knew the professors and was familiar with the terminology. Channeling a lecture wasn't like interpreting a conversation; communication moved in only one direction. And since I'd heard this particular lecture three times before, I don't think my clients realized how distracted I was.

My last appointment was at a local restaurant, interpreting a job interview. I was still off-center as I pulled my ragtop Mustang into the parking lot behind Bibi's Real Ice Cream. I sat for a moment, turning the air-conditioner vent to blast my overheated face. I opened the file. My client, a deaf man named James Leeds, had applied for a part-time job there. According to my sheet, the manager, Amber DeClue, had asked for me specifically, so I was betting I had interpreted for James Leeds before. The name wasn't ringing any bells, but I would probably remember him when I saw his face.

I was a good twenty minutes early, so I pulled the rearview mirror to face me and put contacts in and powdered my nose, put on lipstick and mascara. I took my hair down and brushed it out, but even in my narrow rearview, I could see it still had an obvious rumpled-by-sex look. I shoved it back into the clip and checked my cell phone for messages or missed calls. Nothing. I'd turned off my phone while I was working, but Bernese had made everything sound so dire, I'd almost expected to find a message from Mama. I knew what her doll heads meant to her.

The first dolls my mother ever made were explorers, sent as emissaries to find her own mother's past. My Frett grandmother died before I was born, but by all accounts, Jane Frett had been one hell of a woman. After Mama was born, she taught herself to drive so Mama could attend a school for the deaf. It meant almost three hours of driving a day, but Jane would neither allow her child to board and lose her connection with her family, nor let her remain uneducated. It was a phenomenal decision to make in the forties.

But Jane Frett's life seemed to have begun with her marriage. If Mama or her sisters asked about her childhood, her family, their shared heritage, Jane feigned a deafness of her own. Bernese the pragmatist shrugged and let it go, and Genny was too diffident to press, but Mama wanted some connection to her past. Her genes had given her clever hands and deafness, a bone-deep understanding of shape and color and form paired with vision that she had known from childhood would not last through middle age. All this had to have come from Jane. Mama grew up knowing her father's family—solid, warmhearted folk of German descent—but there was neither artistry nor Usher's syndrome in that family tree.

Jane Frett was half Seminole, but she was the most assimilated Native American to ever draw breath, a devout Baptist whose only language was English. Her heritage was the proverbial smelly elephant in the drawing room; it was there, but it seemed like bad manners to mention it. All my mama knew of Indians was what she read in her *Little House* books. While the adults of the town never spoke of Indianness to the Frett sisters or their well-respected father, they surely must have been talking at home. Genny and Bernese were teased at school, called Injuns, whooped at, the usual casual cruelty of children sniffing out differences.

Bernese, built low and solid and fearless, squelched her share of teasing early on by tackling the loudest bully and hitting him in the face until his nose was bleeding and he was weeping for mercy. Mama didn't meet a lot of prejudice at her deaf day school, but she lived it vicariously through Genny. Genny, nervous from birth, was a natural school goat. She could always be counted on to dissolve into entertaining tears or, even better, rip out little chunks of her hair.

Prowling through her mother's drawers and closets, Mama found no birth certificate, no family Bible, nothing that would open a path into her mother's past. But when Mama was eleven, she discovered that the bottom of her mother's jewelry box lifted out. Beneath it she found a photograph of a man, a decidedly Native American man, sitting with a white woman and a little girl. The girl had Jane Frett's face, and she was holding a white girl's china doll in fancy dress. The doll's neck was wound with loops and loops of Seminole beadwork.

Mama made her first doll the very next day. She formed the

head out of salt dough and dried it overnight. Genny, already her willing craftsman, hand-sewed a limbless body that wasn't much more than a stuffed cone of red silk. My mother tried to make the doll's head look like the one in the picture, but she didn't have the skills. So she practiced. She read every book on dolls and doll making in her school's library, then begged Jane Frett to buy her more. She moved into working with clay and got better, then started making molds and casting porcelain slip. She made the same doll over and over again as a way of asking her mother a question that was never answered. Decades after she'd successfully reproduced the doll from the picture and had gone on to other faces and forms, years after her mother's death, all the way up until her world went dark and she was no longer physically able, Mama had been asking.

Each of the delicate porcelain heads she had cast when she was sighted had a name, even the animals. The heads that had never been made into completed dolls, more than a hundred of them, had been packed away, the molds wrapped in cotton and paired with her best cast, then sealed into individual boxes. Each box was labeled with the doll's name in English and Braille, and even now, over twenty years after her vision had narrowed to a pinhole and then winked shut, she could run her hands across the label and describe the porcelain face that went with the name.

Mama's dolls were a tangible link to her work, her heritage, her mother, and her sight—to all her deepest losses—and she always wanted me to come home and be with her when Bernese sold one of them. But I had no trouble guessing why she hadn't asked me this time. Mama wanted my divorce to go through probably more than I did. She knew that when it came to getting shut of

Jonno, I was easily derailed. If she called me home to Between, I might waffle there until I had good and missed my court date.

I needed to talk to her. Phone conversations with my mother were usually unsatisfying for both of us, but I had to try. I couldn't be distracted and risk misrepresenting James Leeds to his potential boss: I could cost him the job. I unclipped my cell phone from my purse and dialed 711. It rang twice, and then I connected to the relay service. I punched my way through the automated response menu, choosing voice service and inputting Mama's number.

A female voice came on the line and said, "This is CA 75857, dialing your number now."

"Thanks."

After about a minute the CA said, "Your call has been answered with 'Hello.'"

I said, "It's Nonny. Bernese called me. Is everything okay at home? Go ahead." I could hear the soft click of the keys as the CA typed my message out for Mama to read on her Braille display.

There was a long pause, too long, and then the CA said, "All fine here. Go ahead." Which meant absolutely nothing. I had no idea if Mama was being so short because she was irritated with Bernese for calling me, with me for calling her, or because she was simply typing the truth in the most expedient language possible.

"Did you choose a head? Go ahead," I said.

"Not yet. Go ahead."

"Maybe you shouldn't. You don't have to give up any of them at all if you don't want to. Go ahead."

"Choosing is hard, but I like to think of my dolls in museums. Smile." The CA paused and then said, "I can't read this. Looks

39

like she typed J-N-N-O. J-N-N-O sleep your house? Still set for Friday? Go ahead."

So Bernese hadn't waited a minute to tell Genny and Mama that Jonno had been at my apartment early this morning. Too early. I said, "All fine here. Still set. I only called to see if I should come home and help you. Just for today. Go ahead."

The CA said, "Do not come before Saturday. Go ahead."

"Because you don't need help choosing? Or you do but you don't want me to miss the hearing? Go ahead."

The CA's voice was flat as she read, "How many times would you like to ask me? Smile. All fine here. Signing off or go ahead."

I needed to see my mother's hands. I would know exactly how "fine" she was by how her fingers moved, wiggling cheerfully as she touched her thumb to her chest, or twitching in a quick dismissive flicker.

"Signing off," I said.

The CA said, "The connection has been closed at the other end." I thanked her and ended the call. It was the best I could do. Mama at least knew I was available. I flipped the phone back open but paused before I hit the power button. I usually kept the phone off when I was working.

I had a reputation in Athens for being a meticulous interpreter. When I was at a job, I tried to stop thinking and become a conduit, a bridge that let conversation flow between deaf and hearing cultures. If I wasn't focused, getting it exactly right could be tricky, especially since not all deaf people use ASL. Some rely on finger spelling or signed English or their own invented system of home signs or combinations of all these things. To complicate matters, ASL is not at all structured like English. In fact, a hearing person given a flat word-for-word interpretation would probably think the deaf speaker was uneducated. Literal translations are about as user-friendly as those instruction manuals that come with some Japanese electronics, because ASL isn't a way to speak English.

It's a separate language with its own structure and idiom, a whole-body language that relies as much on physical nuance as it does on signs. Interpreting ASL comes very naturally to me, because it is my native language as surely as English is. It's the language I learned first, signing with my mother months before I said an intelligible word to anyone else.

Instead of turning off the phone, I set the ringer to vibrate and clipped it back on my purse. Knowing Mama could reach me might let me forget about what was going on at home long enough to do my job well. I sat in the car for a moment longer, breathing in the comforting, familiar smell of my Mustang's ancient leather seats. When I felt centered, I turned off the car and got out, walking around to the front door of the ice-cream parlor.

Bibi's was decorated in cutesy retro kitsch, with a few red leatherette booths and a lot of small round tables surrounded by wire chairs with heart-shaped backs and puffy red seats. Two boys in candy-striped jerseys and caps were working behind the counter, and they had a good-size lunch crowd waiting in line. A blackboard menu by the ice-cream case listed a small selection of soups and sandwiches. The place was full of UGA students; it seemed like a bad time of day to schedule an interview. I was standing inside the door wondering if I should knock on the EM-PLOYEES ONLY door at the back or go ask one of the boys where I could find Amber DeClue when I felt a light touch on my arm.

The girl standing beside me looked like another college kid, a skinny, doe-eyed thing with golden-brown hair that fell in random waves past her shoulders. She was so daisy-fresh and dewy she was practically dripping. She had long tanned legs, as thin and awkward as a fawn's, and she tipped her weight from one to the other, swaying as she sized me up.

I said, "Ms. DeClue?" as she was saying, "Are you Nonny?" She flushed and added, "I mean, Mrs. Overmilk?"

"Frett," I said.

"What?" She took a tottery step backwards.

"My last name is Frett."

She tucked her hair behind one ear and said earnestly, "But I specifically asked—I mean, I requested Nonny Overmilk."

"That's my married name," I said. "I go by Frett now."

"Oh! So you got divorced?" Her big eyes widened.

"Where is . . ." I glanced down at my sheet. "James Leeds?"

"Oh, not here yet. Maybe we should go sit and wait a little?"

"So you're conducting the interview?" I asked. She seemed too young and too uncertain to be given the responsibility, but she nodded and then turned around and began threading her way through all the tables, working her way across the room. I followed her. She was wearing a short, sleeveless linen dress, expensive-looking. It wasn't something I would wear to scoop ice cream. Her arms were so thin that her elbows looked bigger around than her biceps. We sat in an oversize booth in the back. A yellow leather backpack sat as a placeholder on the table.

She stopped in front of the table, and I slid into one side of the booth. She didn't sit, but moved so she was standing in front of my bench, blocking me in. I had to look up at her when she spoke. "Nonny. That's an interesting name. What's that short for? Wynona?"

I shook my head. "It's not short for anything."

"Oh. So that's, like, your whole name? Nonny?" She picked up one foot nervously and then set it down again in exactly the same place.

"Yes." I glanced at the time display on my phone. It was just past three o'clock. "Shouldn't you sit down? So you can see when Mr. Leeds arrives?"

"Oh. Sure." She sidestepped and then slid into the booth across from me.

Her habit of prefacing everything with a breathless "oh" was starting to wear on my nerves, which caused me to feel irritated with myself. Athens was a college town, so I worked with a lot of college kids, and I usually liked it. Nothing that was bothering me today had anything to do with Amber DeClue, and I knew I shouldn't take it out on her.

She was looking at me with moist brown eyes, nervous and diffident. I shifted in my seat. Her expression was expectant, almost encouraging, as if she had sallied forth with the whole "Is it short for Wynona?" bit and was waiting for me to do my part to maintain polite conversation. I looked away, watching the boys behind the counter scoop out double-dip cones and grab wrapped sandwiches from a cooler behind the counter.

After a couple of minutes, Amber said, "So that seems like a pretty neat job, translating for deaf people."

I said, "I like it."

"Does it pay okay?"

"It's fine," I said. I did not look back at her, but in my peripheral vision, I could see her big eyes focused on my face. I didn't want to be rude to her, but I also wanted to avoid forming even a tenuous social bond. If she got comfortable chatting with me, she would be far more likely to address herself to me rather than James Leeds during the interview.

After another few minutes, she spoke again. "Overmilk. That's a weird name, huh? Is that why you went to Frett? Except that's kind of a weird name, too. So, but you didn't say you were divorced?"

"No, I didn't say," I said. "I'll wait another thirty minutes, but if he isn't here by then, I'm going to have to go. You can reschedule through the agency if you still want to interview him."

Her eyebrows came together. I waited, but she sat looking helplessly at me, her hands coming together to fiddle with an alarmingly large diamond solitaire on her ring finger. At last she asked, "So you think I should call him or something?"

"I'm not really supposed to advise you," I said. "I'm only here to interpret."

She turned sideways in the booth, scooting down and hanging her legs over the side. She crossed them at the knee, dangling her sandal off of her heel and swinging her leg. The sandal swayed hypnotically, balanced on her toes. Her toenails were painted seafoam green.

"I'm not going to call him," she said at last, turning those giant eyeballs back my way.

"All right," I said. I sat another few minutes. Normally I'm comfortable with silence, but she never seemed to look away from me. Her gaze was earnest, and her little body was so restless, bouncing on the edge of the booth, her leg swinging more and more violently until the sandal was clapping against the sole of her foot. She was probably the owner's daughter, or maybe fiancée—the solitaire was on the proper hand. Either way, she was dressed more like a princess than a junior manager, and I suspected she had never conducted an interview before. Or perhaps she had but was nervous about interviewing a deaf person.

I said, "This is going to be easy. When James Leeds comes, pretend I'm not here. Talk to him, not me, and ask him all the things you asked the other applicants. I'm sure you'll do fine."

She shrugged and said, "So, if you're not divorced, why are you going by Frett now? Because of, like, feminism or whatever?"

"No," I said. We sat for another few minutes.

"I don't think he's coming," she said. She clambered out of the booth and stood at the end of my long seat, blocking me in again. "You're not really allowed to talk to me? Is that it? I mean, even though he didn't show up, you're supposed to sit there totally silent?"

While she was talking, my phone began to vibrate, purring insistently against my purse. I held up one finger and looked at the display, expecting to see Mama's number. It wasn't a number I knew, but I could tell by the area code that the call was coming from Between.

"Could you excuse me for a moment?" I said.

She shrugged, annoyed, then took a step backwards and turned to the side, showing me her ski-slope nose. She was still standing close enough to block me in. I shook my head and then answered my phone.

"Nonny?" It was Bernese, but her voice was so hard and desperate I almost didn't recognize it.

"Bernese? Are you okay?" I said. "Is Mama okay?"

"Stacia is going to be fine," said Bernese. "It's Genny, and may those Crabtrees rot in hell. It's Genny. It's our Genny."

"The Crabtrees?" I said, confused. "What do the Crabtrees— Bernese, what happened?"

"The Bitch got out," Bernese said. "That Crabtree Bitch got out, and she ate your Genny up."

CHAPTER

4

IT WAS NEVER a question of *if* one of the Crabtrees' Dobermans would get loose and go after Genny. It was *when.* Those animals were just this side of wild and mean straight through. They had been trained as guard dogs by Ona's oldest boy, Lobe. He'd employed some half-assed Crabtree methodology, probably a booklet found among the impulse items they kept by the register at the Loganville Piggly Wiggly: *30 Days to Deadly Dogs.* Add in general Crabtree carelessness, and apply these factors to a swinging gate held closed by a long chain that had to be wrapped three times around the posts before it was padlocked. It was the algebraic formula for doom.

Genny was deathly afraid of any animal that came up higher than her knee. She was especially afraid of big dogs. Of course, she was also afraid of hospitals. And loosely wrapped Halloween candy. And crosswalks and Jehovah's Witnesses and self-serve gasoline pumps and anything with more than six legs, particularly squid. But the acrid smell of her fear was probably the thing that sent the dogs into apoplexy whenever they caught a whiff.

And it was only Genny they didn't like. The dogs didn't mind even Mama, and she was Genny's twin. Fraternal, but they had become more and more similar as they aged. Genny had always been prettier, but the differences had faded over the years, especially after Mama became completely blind and Genny started choosing her clothes. After their sixty-plus years of living together, a stranger would have a hard time telling Eugenia and Eustacia apart. They were short, plump ladies with strong Native American features that looked somewhat incongruous in their small, pale faces. Every day Genny put their black-and-white-striped hair up into identical tidy buns, powdered their noses, and pinked their cheeks with liquid rouge.

It boggled my mind to consider how tiny the delineation in their genes must be, and yet my bold mama, who had the soul of a pirate, came into the world stone deaf and with eyes that would fail her soon after she turned forty. Genny, on the other hand, was physically healthy but so timid and racked by nerves that I doubt she would have left the womb at all if Stacia had not gone first. But externally? They looked practically interchangeable.

The dogs, however, had no trouble differentiating, especially the alpha dog. The female. The one Aunt Bernese had christened "the Bitch."

Bernese had called her the Bitch for so long that the whole family had picked it up, in spite of the fact that the Fretts usually only cussed if it was biblical. That is to say, they'd use "hell" to mean the literal place and "ass" to mean donkey. They'd all say "whore," especially if it was followed by "monger" or "of Babylon." None of them would dream of calling a person a bitch, or even use the word as a verb, but they'd refer to the Crabtrees' alpha dog as the Bitch while standing in the vestibule of The First Baptist Church of Between.

The whole town was so inured to it that not even Pastor Gregg raised an eyebrow when we used that word in relation to that particular dog. Nervous little Genny had a spun-sugar heart. Her standard-issue Frett Steel Spine was bogged down in taffy. She was the pet of the family, if not the whole town, and any dog who didn't like Genny was a bitch, and God already knew it, so there wasn't much cause to ease up on the language.

Those dogs, the Bitch especially, more than didn't like her. The Bitch wanted her dead.

The day the Bitch got out, Mama and Genny spent the morning on Between's town square, up in Mama's studio. The studio was on the second floor of a large Victorian house, the downstairs of which Bernese had turned into a museum featuring Mama's dolls and her own prized caterpillars. The rest of the upstairs was storage where Mama kept her boxes and boxes of porcelain doll heads lined up neatly on bookshelves. Mama was in the storage room, running her fingers across the Braille labels, still trying to pick one. Genny was in her sewing area, getting fussier and hungrier by the minute.

Bernese had built that studio for Mama and Genny long before Ona Crabtree ever thought about owning guard dogs. At first Bernese had planned to tear out most of the wall that faced the landing and replace it with plate glass. That way, tourists who were visiting the dollhouse portion of the museum could come up the stairs and watch Mama work on the kind of outsize, tactile sculptures she currently favored. But the very idea had activated the fragment of Frett gumption at Genny's core, and she'd put her little fat foot down.

"You've already got mile-high pictures of us downstairs, Bernese, and that's about enough," she said. Her voice got higher and higher as she spoke. "Stacia and I won't sit in a cage and scratch like monkeys for whatever philistines come here to nose-pick and google."

Genny signed rapidly into Stacia's hands as she was speaking, and before she had gotten too wound up to stop herself, Stacia's own hands were churning the air. Genny added, "And Stacia says if you put that window in, she and I won't work here. Period." That ended it. The wall stayed a wall, and the staircases were roped off with velvet cord.

Now Genny was wishing there was a window. She'd been drooping around the studio all morning, and the air was beginning to taste stale and used. She went to the storage room and signed *Lunch! Lunch! Lunch!* until Stacia agreed to stop head-hunting. They gathered up their handbags, and Genny slipped her shoes back on. She had high blood pressure, and her feet tended to swell, but she wouldn't give up her size-six shoes.

The front door of the museum was kept locked; tourists paid admission at the store, and Bernese personally took them over. Genny and Stacia let themselves out onto the square, and Genny relocked the door behind them.

Between's town square was the working definition of pictur-esque. It was so tidy and bright, with a burbling center fountain surrounded by riotously colored flower beds filled to bursting with seasonal blooms. Beyond that, a thick green lawn of preter-naturally healthy grass grew in cheerful spikes. A cobblestone walkway ran in front of all the shops and crossed to the fountain on the diagonal.

The square was lined on three sides by rows of connected shops, all fronted in warm, peachy brick with crisp white trim. The First Baptist Church of Between sat on the corner closest to the highway. It was a textbook country Baptist church, with a tall steeple and bells that tolled the hour in happy tones.

The other three corners each sported a large Victorian house. The first one contained Bernese's museum, and next was the Marchants' bed-and-breakfast. On the last corner, Isaac Davids lived in a buttery-yellow house with tons of gingerbread and pale lavender trim. His law offices were downstairs. Laughing gargoyles peeked out over the eaves, and a tower on one side was topped by a weathercock.

It would have been faster for Mama and Genny to cut across the square. Grace Street began catty-corner to the museum. But Genny had an errand, and they wanted to see what was cooking at the diner, so they made their way around the square's perimeter. They passed the Dollhouse Store; they could see through the big front window that Bernese was with a customer.

Henry Crabtree's bookstore was in the shop right beside Bernese's, and Genny and Mama stopped there. Genny had ordered a book of quilt block patterns, but Henry told her it hadn't arrived yet. He was one of the few people left in town who were around my age; most residents of Between were over fifty. Henry was my close friend, and he was good to my family and watched out for Mama and Genny on the weekdays when I was in Athens. Genny, who was often twitchy and diffident around men, flat adored him. He was soft-spoken, and his low-pitched voice was like balm on her nerves, soothing and cool. Mama liked him, too, so they paused to chat, telling him I was expected in town on Saturday instead of Friday.

"Because of her divorce, you know," Genny said in a confidential tone, her eyes gleaming. My mother released Genny's signing hands to send her forefingers shooting triumphantly away from the corners of her mouth.

"'Finally!' Stacia says," Genny interpreted. She gave her hands back to Stacia, so Stacia could feel the conversation. "I know divorce is wrong and all, but just between us and the little birds? We're glad. We don't like that boy," Genny said, signing at the same time.

Henry straightened his immaculate cuffs and quirked one black eyebrow at them. "Me neither," he said.

They said their goodbyes, and Genny and Mama continued on to the diner. The special was written on a blackboard sign by the front door. Genny signed to Mama that it was Trude's god-awful Turketti.

Mama made a sour face and signed, *Soup at home?*

Genny hesitated, trying to choose between the evils of walking by the dogs and Turketti. At last she nodded her hand and they walked on, past the row of three kitschy antique marts and then Isaac's house.

Crabtree Gas and Parts was directly across from the square, on Philbert. The gas pumps and the dilapidated country store faced the square, and beside it two mechanics' bays yawped open like black mouths. The parts yard was behind the store, and humps of twisted slag metal and junk were visible over the store's low roof. Philbert Street was the border that separated the town square from the Crabtrees' squalid holdings. It was a different world across the street, and Bernese was not alone in thinking the complex was an eyesore.

Genny and Mama left the square and crossed to the corner of Grace and Philbert. The gas station was on their left, and there wasn't anything to the right but a sloping shoulder that led into a ditch full of kudzu. Beyond that was nothing but rolling Georgia wilderness awash in loblolly pines and scrub. The sidewalk ran parallel to the fence that surrounded the parts yard. My two little squashy marshmallow ladies, joined at the hip, stepped up onto the sidewalk and went tootling down the length of the fence.

Mama held Genny's elbow in her left hand, her right hand swinging her cane to check her path. Genny took three teeny bird steps for every long, careful stride of Mama's, and the white cane tapped out the rhythm of their walk. In their print dresses and orthopedic shoes, they were completely innocuous. But as they walked, the male dogs appeared, one slinking out from under an old Chevy, the other easing his head from behind a rusted-out refrigerator.

The Bitch came out of nowhere. Genny did not see the dog until she loomed up beside them at the fence about halfway to the gate. The Bitch bared her teeth in a menacing parody of a grin, and the males growled so deep in their chests that Genny felt it as a vibration of the air more than she heard it. They moved like sleek black birds in formation, the two big males flanking the sinewy female. The Bitch let her breath out, something between a growl and a hiss.

Stacia could smell the dogs, and she felt Genny's arm trembling. She stopped walking and began their pet argument, one as old as the dogs themselves. She tucked her cane under her arm and signed that they should walk home on the other side of Grace Street, to give the dogs a wider berth, then reached for Genny's hands so she could feel the answer she already knew by heart.

Genny signed, *You know there's no sidewalk. We'll end up in the ditch with every hip we've got smashed into fifty different pieces.*

They started walking again. Mama knew she would never win the argument, but the ritual of asking seemed to soothe Genny.

The dogs started walking when they did. The hair on the Bitch's spine rose, and her legs stiffened so that her usual lithe gait became eerily mechanical. All three flattened their ears so tightly against their sleek, elongated skulls that they looked like evil seals.

They came abreast of the gate. The Bitch, as always, tried to stuff her narrow head through. This time, however, the chain had been wrapped only twice, and as she levered her snout into the narrow crack, the gate gave.

Mama felt the muscles in Genny's arm tighten. She stopped walking and reached for Genny's hand just as it was opening, the fingers spreading into rigid lines. Then Genny was gone and Mama was pushed, staggering and falling a long way sideways, landing hard on her shoulder on a wide surface so nubbled and unyielding that she knew she was in the street. She felt her body bracing futilely as imagined cars came speeding toward her, and she lay there waiting to be dashed to pieces in the road.

After an endless moment, she realized she was still in one piece, and she tried to collect her wits. Her head was swimming, and the wind had been knocked out of her. She was dizzy from not breathing. She had to struggle to pull in a mouthful of air that was acrid with the smell of dog and road oil.

She rolled onto her stomach and got gingerly to her hands and knees, trying to feel her way to Genny or her cane or the curb.

But she had lost all sense of direction, and the street spread itself out flat and smooth under her hands. She smelled the bright copper of fresh blood mixing with the pollen of the May air, and she could feel it coming from her shoulder and arm. There seemed to be a lot of it. She did not know where Genny was, and she started pushing her air out in deep vibrating shoves. She pushed air out, hard, again and again, because years ago, when they were children, Genny had taught her that was how to make screaming happen.

Mama, deaf and blind, disoriented, didn't know if the dogs were out or if a car had hit them, but Genny had seen exactly what was coming. To her, it had looked like the gate was giving birth to something evil. The Bitch's face came shoving through first, stretched tight with the lips pulled back and open and her eyes showing a quarter inch of white. Then her head popped free and she got one shoulder through, her claws raking at the concrete. The two males barked violently, cheering the Bitch on. For an endless fraction of a second, it seemed she would stick at the second shoulder, but she braced her powerful back legs and shoved, twitching her shoulders back and forth, working herself out. Genny watched her long narrow hips slither through easily, and in two bounds, the Bitch was on her.

The dog hit Genny at an angle, knocking her into Mama. Genny clutched at Mama, but her hand was ripped open by Mama's weight as she fell. Mama's cane sailed away in a high arc and then clattered and rolled in the street. Genny was falling, too, feeling hot breath and then the slide of the dog's teeth against her skin as they missed a spine-snapping hold on the back of her neck. She turned in midair with the dog still on her, and she hunched her shoulders up high, shoving uselessly at the dog with her little fat seamstress's hands. The two of them landed together, the dog's weight slamming into her stomach. It got its teeth in her, puncturing the meat of her upper arm and then releasing and digging into her at the shoulder.

The Bitch shook her head back and forth, jerking at Genny. The pain was immediate and awful but very welcome, because it was stronger than the fear. Once the pain started, she could think; she could clinically feel her flesh tearing away and the smoky heat of the dog's body bracing into hers. Genny thrust her forearm in the dog's throat and began beating at the Bitch's back with her other hand, shoving herself along the sidewalk with her feet. She could feel the concrete tearing her dress and the skin of her back as she wormed away. She didn't care. She had to get out from under, because she knew when the two big males came, she would be dead in a matter of seconds, and she absolutely could not be dead. She heard Mama screaming, and in her very center, in some calm place that was watching with mild interest as the dog killed her, a voice said, "Oh, that's probably a good idea," so she started screaming, too.

Henry Crabtree was trying to sell a Dennis Lehane on tape to a trucker who had stopped in to see if the bookstore carried any decent porn. Henry made a lot of sales this way; the truckers who paused in Between to gas up generally took to him. There was something a bit dirty about Henry that belied his crisp white shirts and fine-boned face. It lived in the hollows of his severely cut cheekbones or maybe in the permanent dark circles that made his eyes look deep-set and older than the rest of him. It was hard to pin down, but Henry seemed like he might have an opium pipe or an ivory-handled knife in the back pocket of his tailored khaki pants.

He had the trucker all but sold when he heard my mama start screaming. At first he couldn't identify the source of the wail; it didn't sound human. He looked quizzically at the trucker, who shrugged.

"Steam whistle?" the trucker said.

Then Genny started screaming, too, and Henry said, "No," and vaulted the counter, knocking the big trucker aside and sprinting out the door. Bernese had come out of her store already and was puffing past, her stocky legs pumping as she ran toward her sisters. Henry passed Bernese easily, and as he went by the diner, he yelled, "Call 911" to Trude, who was standing open-mouthed in the doorway. She disappeared back inside.

The Bitch already had Genny by the time Henry could see them. The male dogs were practically scraping the skin off their heads trying to get through the gap in the gate. Stacia was crawling down the center of the road, keening. Henry didn't stop; he was afraid that at any moment the Bitch would burrow down deep enough into Genny's neck to tear open an artery.

Henry threw himself onto the dog, trying to lever her mouth open with his hands. His long black hair escaped its leather tie and got into his eyes, blinding him, and in that moment the dog released Genny and clamped down hard on his forearm.

Ona Crabtree came loping around the corner from the front of the gas station with her graying red hair slopping out of its bun. She was calling, "Here, dog, got-dammit, here, dog, here, got-dammit, here." The Bitch ignored her, but the males froze immediately and slunk away from the fence. Lobe was at Ona's heels, red-faced and sweating in his coveralls. He came bearing down on the scene with a choke chain and a grim expression, his bushy orange beard bristling fiercely.

Bernese huffed up and peeled Stacia up out of the street, then led her to the side of the road. Stacia was signing in frenzied bursts, and Bernese, who had never learned ASL, was trying to capture her hands and manually spell out "OK" into them. She was so flustered that she was actually signing "BK, BK, BK" over and over again, and Mama was slapping at her and trying to sign at the same time.

Together with Henry, Lobe managed to wrestle the choke chain over the Bitch's head. He jerked back on the chain, putting his weight into it so that the choke cinched and the dog was pulled off of Genny, who immediately rolled over and began worming her way up the sidewalk, weeping.

Ona Crabtree arrived and went at the Bitch with her bony bare feet, kicking so violently that her housedress flipped up, showing her varicose veins. "Piece of shit! Piece of shit!" she cawed, and the dog dropped to her belly and cringed like a meek puppy, her mouth still foamy with Genny's blood.

Without a word, Lobe turned and started dragging the Bitch back toward the gas station. Ona opened the combination lock and began rewrapping the chain that held the gate. She got it shut properly and then marched off after Lobe. The sidewalk was freckled with small puddles and spatters of blood, both Genny's and Henry's. It was a fake bright Hollywood red but was already drying to brown at the edges. Ona had walked through the worst of it, and her right foot left four red prints, one after another, growing sketchier as she stomped back around the corner to the gas station.

Henry pulled off his shredded shirt, crouched down beside Genny, and pressed the shirt hard into her shoulder to stanch her bleeding, ignoring his own wounded arm. Genny was only semiconscious; she'd crept off the sidewalk into the strip of grass beside the fence. Henry pulled her up into his lap to try to elevate her wounded shoulder, still applying pressure.

Isaac Davids had come out of his law office and was making his way down Grace Street as quickly as he could with his cane. Trude from the diner followed with her arms full of paper towels, as if she planned to clean up the street. Behind them, Mr. and Mrs. Marchant were toddling as fast as they could from their bed-and-breakfast, their daughter, Ivy, and Amy Bend from the Sweete Shoppe urging them on. The doors of the antique marts were opening, and worried faces were peering out.

Bernese had given up trying to communicate with Stacia, and Stacia was breathing like a steam engine, red-faced and trembling, silently demanding Genny in their shared language.

Henry could hear the sirens of the ambulance coming to Between from Loganville, and just as it seemed things would calm down, that moron Lobe kicked the cringing Bitch out the back door of the station, back into the parts yard. The minute the back door shut, the Bitch untucked the stump of her tail and charged at the fence, growling, hackles rising. Genny heard her and struggled with Henry, trying to sit up, screaming as the dog's leering face came up against the fence not two feet from her own. Trude went into gratuitous hysterics, but at least she gave Bernese someone to slap.

When the ambulance arrived, it was all chaos with Lobe and Ona Crabtree taking turns screaming profanities out the back door, trying to quell the dogs by sheer volume. Genny was wailing, Henry was bleeding and dizzy, and Trude was hollering at Bernese, who was clearly itching to slap her again. Everyone else was milling around wringing their hands and tracking through the blood and generally getting in the way. Mama's back was bleeding from where she'd scraped it in the street, and she was reaching out with both arms, trying to touch something, the fence or the side of a car or a person, anything that would help her orient.

The EMTs took one look at the scene and started waving needles and threatening to sedate everyone who wouldn't shut up. The warning worked as well as any medicine could have, and the crowd's hysteria dropped by a dozen decibels. The medical personnel then methodically made the rounds to see who was bleeding and who had only rolled in the blood. The sheriff arrived, and more ambulances, and cool, efficient people who were accustomed to carnage got everyone sorted out and the injured were carted off to Loganville General. It was nominally over.

I pieced it all together later, questioning everyone who had been there, getting the details separately like puzzle pieces I had to put together in both time and space to get a clear understanding of what had happened and when. It was strange, the odd bits that stuck with different people. No one but Bernese had any idea what the male dogs had been up to. Isaac Davids was the only one who noticed Ona's trail of bloody bare footprints. And Henry told me that while he was fighting with the dog, that trucker walked out of his bookstore with about five Dennis Lehanes on tape.

"It's terrible to be robbed, of course," Henry said to me later. "But looking at the bigger picture, perhaps I've created a reader."

I added the trucker to the scene. I saw him, a big man, thick through the chest with long, meaty arms, looking across the square. He squinted to see down Grace Street where the dog was tearing up Genny. I watched him choose not to help, instead grabbing whatever he could reach and then dashing for his truck in the lot behind the church. I could not forgive him.

I couldn't forgive myself, either. Mama had needed me to help her choose a head, Genny had needed me to soothe her nerves, and Fisher had simply needed me, like always. But I had been unwilling to lose one of the last days left that I could rightfully call Jonno mine. I'd been simultaneously afraid that if I so much as looked away, Jonno would find a way to gum up the works and stop the divorce himself. Maybe I'd wanted to prove to them all that I wasn't such an easy dog to call. Whatever my motive, the result was that I found myself in Athens, staring into the vapid honey-brown eyes of Amber DeClue with a cell phone clamped to my ear, listening as Bernese told me everything I'd failed to avert.

CHAPTER

5

T HE BITCH GOT Genny?" I said into the phone, and for a dizzying moment, I thought Bernese was telling me Genny was dead. Amber was still looming over me, blocking me into the booth, or I might have thrown the phone and gone running pell-mell crazy for home.

"She's in the hospital," said Bernese. "Serious but stable. She lost a lot of blood. The Bitch tore her up and down."

"The hospital?" I was suddenly so afraid that I couldn't bring myself to say it. I helplessly said, "Bernese, Bernese," while Amber's eyes got bigger and bigger in her pointed kitten face.

Bernese chose that moment to be intuitive for the first and last time in her life. She said, "No, no, she'll be able to sign just fine. It didn't get her hands at all," and I could breathe again. Bernese continued, "It went for her throat, but you know podgy Genny doesn't hardly have a throat you can get to."

I heard the low tones of a male voice in the background, and then Bernese apparently covered the mouthpiece with her hand.

61

I couldn't make out anything my uncle Lou was saying, but I could have heard Bernese braying through a brick wall. "Yes, it's long-distance—it's Nonny. Nonny is long-distance."

I heard the rumbling male voice again. Bernese overrode it and snapped, "You act like I'm sticking a monkey up your nose. I'm just making a phone call."

"Aunt Bernese, where's Mama?"

"She's in the hospital over to Loganville. I couldn't make her understand what was going on, and she was flushed and flapping around, ill as hornets. Then she went paper-color. The EMT took her pulse, and no one could talk to her. He was worried she'd stroke out, so he pumped her full of Ativan. They admitted her right alongside Genny. Stacia won't wake up for at least another four, five hours, not with the dose that EMT put in her. Hell, she's likely to sleep through the night. But I can't be for sure."

"I'll be there before she wakes up," I said. "I'm on the way now." Already my brain was ticking back and forth like a metronome, flipping between horrified listening and a to-do list to get myself on the road to Between as quickly as possible.

"Don't go leaping in the car all harum-scarum and blast over here and have to go back tomorrow because you didn't get your work squared away. Genny's not going to be able to do for herself, and when that dog knocked your mama in the road, she scraped half the skin clean off her back. She needs you, Nonny. I have to go."

"Wait a sec. What aren't you telling me, Bernese?" I said.

"Just do what you need to do to be able to stay over here with us. If you can't get here by eight or so, tell me now. I can hire that mealy-faced worm-boy to drive over from Atlanta and interpret. Someone has to tell Stacia what happened when she wakes up."

For the ninety-seven millionth time, I silently cursed Bernese for not learning to sign, but the Fretts' system of communication had been in place for decades and was ingrained and habitual. Genny and Mama were twins after all, and as toddlers they had made up their own sign language. When Mama started school, Genny picked up ASL almost by osmosis, and to the rest of the family, there was no recognizable transition. Mama had always spoken by gesture, and Genny had always interpreted. The pattern was set.

"I'll be there before Mama wakes up," I said.

Amber was bobbing in my peripheral vision, trying to get my attention. When I looked up at her, she mouthed, "Is everything okay?"

I waved her off, but instead of leaving, she slid back into the booth across from me, sinking into the leatherette upholstery. She folded her legs up into the seat after her, crumpling up into a wad with her knees poking up over the table. She looked about twelve.

I heard Uncle Lou talking in the background again, and Bernese barked, "She needs to know what all is happening. Can you clamber on down out of my butt, please?"

"Good grief," I said. "Don't take it out on Uncle Lou."

There was a slight pause, then Bernese said, "That's not Lou. He's in Loganville."

"Wait a minute, then. Who are you yelling at?" She didn't answer me, and I remembered the number on my cell phone had been a Between number, not Loganville. "Where are you, exactly? Why aren't you at the hospital?"

"I'm going over there soon as I can," said Bernese, then didn't say anything else.

63

"Bernese," I said. "You better get straight with me right now. Where are you, and where is Fisher? Is she okay?"

"Oh, take a pill, Nonny. Your uncle Lou is picking Fisher up at her little friend's house. She had a playdate set for today after kindergarten, praise Jesus in heaven, or she'd have been there with me and seen the Bitch eating up Genny."

"Then who is that man I heard talking?" I said.

I could hear Bernese drumming her fingers, impatient and annoyed. Finally, she said, "That's just Thig."

"Thig Newell? Sheriff Newell? Are you pressing charges against the Crabtrees?" She didn't answer me, and my spine began to straighten, elongating involuntarily, until I was sitting up as stiff and taut as if I were being inflated. "Bernese, quit dancing with me and tell me what the fuck is going on." Amber's eyes were as round as quarters, and I got dirty looks from a young couple spooning ice cream into a baby at the next table.

"I'm a little bit arrested," said Bernese primly. "And I wish you wouldn't use the F-word."

I sank back down in the booth and covered my eyes with my free hand. "Arrested! What did you do?"

"I did the only thing I could and still look at myself in the mirror, Nonny. What do you think I did?"

I took a deep, cleansing breath that didn't leave me feeling any cleaner. I lowered my voice and said, "I think you stood there until everyone left for the hospital or went back to the square, and then I think you pulled your illegally concealed pistol out of your purse, and I think you shot the Bitch dead." Amber gave a little gasp, her shoulders jerking up. I turned sideways in the booth, away from her. "Please, please, tell me I am wrong."

"Two to the head," said Bernese, and her voice was creamy

with satisfaction. "I would have got those boy dogs next, but they took off running and got under the junk cars when I started shooting."

"Oh, shit, Bernese. Shit! Are you crazy?"

"Watch your mouth," Bernese snapped. "I know what I'm doing."

But she didn't. She didn't have a clue. She'd gone up against Ona before, but she'd used lawyers and paperwork and police, all parts of the civilized world that the Fretts inhabited, a world that cowed the Crabtrees. Now she had opened with violence, and that was a language the Crabtrees spoke fluently. I suddenly felt so scared I couldn't get a breath in. I wished I could simply fold myself up and slide down under the table and hide. "It's a war, Bernese. It's going to be an all-out war."

Bernese snorted rudely into the phone. "Well, I didn't start it. My devil dog didn't eat a Crabtree."

I had to get home. Not only to see Mama but to intercept Ona before she retaliated. My brain ticked back over to my to-do list and paused. I had several jobs scheduled that my agency would need to get someone to cover. I should probably give up the an-thro classes altogether, since the semester was ending in a few weeks and I had no idea when I'd be back. Friday afternoon I was supposed to be at the courthouse, getting my divorce, but I couldn't leave Genny and little Fisher and my injured mother to the nonexistent mercies of angry Crabtrees. I'd have to gauge Ona's emotional state before I'd know if I could come back for the hearing.

Maybe I could call Jonno and ask him to go on Friday and get us a new court date. I'd have to beg. As it was, I'd needed to take his hand and lead him through our breakup, showing him where to sign and ferrying him to and from our lawyer's office. Honestly, he was so disconnected from the process that had he owned anything but a 1987 Chevy Impala, I could have robbed him blind. Even more honestly, there were moments when I had been so angry I probably would have.

I was tired of patting him along through the jocular dissolution of our marriage. Jonno had treated our initial visit to the lawyer's office like a field trip, a mildly interesting peek at how divorce worked, like going behind the blue door at the donut factory. I was willing to admit that he might take it more seriously if I stopped sleeping with him, but when I was around him, my desire to murder him usually got sublimated. My hands were magnetically drawn toward him; they longed to wrap themselves inexorably around his lovely throat. They would cramp and twitch as I fought to hold them into flat, unthreatening pancakes at my sides, and then in the next breath, they'd be climbing him, never quite making it up to strangle him before I found myself on my back.

"Nonny?" said Bernese. "You got quiet. You're not bothered about the Crabtrees, are you? Because they can go to hell. This is about our family, about Genny and your mama."

I glanced over my shoulder. Amber was leaning forward straining to hear, her pretty face avid and her eyebrows lowered. When our eyes met, she looked away fast, turning her whole head so that all I could see was her profile.

"I'm not thinking straight," I said. "I need to get going. I'll bail you out if Uncle Lou hasn't collected you by the time I get there."

She said goodbye and I hung up.

My busy brain added "Find Jonno" to the running list in my head. I had to try, even though the chances of his actually showing on Friday were slim. After our shared lawyer had filed my petition, Jonno had never returned to sign the acknowledgment. I'd set up three appointments for him, and then he'd missed two and I'd missed one. I'd had our lawyer mail him a copy that he never mailed back. I decided to pay for the sheriff's office to send a process server, but before they could serve him, he'd disappeared on a cross-country bar tour with his ska band. When he did arrive home, I was waiting on his stoop with the acknowledgment and a pen, and the second after he signed it, I fell into bed with him. After that, I'd personally driven it to our lawyer's office, scared that if I left it in Jonno's mailbox, he'd help it find its way back out and into the trash. It was highly unlikely that he'd spring into helpful action now.

I grabbed my purse and stood up. Amber stood up, too. I glanced at my watch. "I'm going to have to call this a no-show," I said. I walked across the restaurant, weaving my way quickly between the tables.

Amber trailed after me. "You're leaving?"

"Yes. Call the agency if you want to reschedule."

"You said you would wait thirty minutes. It's only been a little more than twenty." Her voice was strident with outrage. "What's going on?"

"Family emergency." I was almost to the door, but she ran around me, trying to block me.

"What happened?" she asked. "Is it bad?"

I sidestepped around her and went out, not answering. She followed me outside; I could hear her clicky-clacking along behind me in her ridiculous, strappy sandals. She stopped as I picked up the pace and dogtrotted to the parking lot. I unlocked the Mustang and got in. As I pulled out of the lot, I could see her standing by the entrance, her backpack a bright blotch of yellow at her feet. Her eyebrows were lowered, and she had her cell phone out, one stiff finger violently punching at the numbers. Calling her daddy-or-fiancé to complain that I left six minutes early, no doubt.

Well, she could ask the agency to send someone else next time. I hoped she would. Her thrilled and horrified face would be forever linked in my mind with this awful day, the awful dog. I would be as happy as whole herds of clams to never see her face again.

Jonno had left my apartment by the time I got home. I called his house, but no one answered. They sometimes turned off the ringer when the band was practicing and then forgot to turn it back on for days. I told myself that the urgency I felt to find him was so I could try to get him to schedule us a new court date, but I wasn't sure I was buying my story. My hands were shaking as I dialed, and half of me wanted nothing more than some arms to put around me.

I hung up after nine rings and dialed Ona Crabtree at home, but I got her machine. The sooner I could talk to her, the more likely it was that I could preempt whatever mayhem she was setting in motion. I left my cell phone number and added, "Please don't do anything, anything, until you see me." I tried her at Crabtree Gas and Parts but got only her youngest son, Tucker. He promised to have Ona call me back, but I wasn't counting on it. He sounded stoned out of his tiny mind.

I called my agency and cleared my work schedule and then went next door and enlisted my neighbor's teenager to take care of Lewis, the cat. Lewis was technically Jonno's, but much like the size-twelve red Converse high-tops under my bed and the pair of

Jockey briefs in my top drawer, Lewis hadn't quite moved out of the apartment yet.

I called Jonno again as I got ready to go, but no one picked up. I knew he had that late gig at the Rox Box, but I needed to be on the road well before then. I went down to my car, made sure the top was securely up, and got in. I meant to drive straight to the highway, but on the way to 78, I found myself making a turn that would take me to Boyd's house.

Boyd was X. Machina's percussionist. Not the drummer. He got cranky if you called him a drummer. Jonno had been crashing at Boyd's for about a year now, ever since I kicked him out. At this point it was safe to say he was living there. Jonno's Impala wasn't parked in front, but I stopped anyway. I made my way up the rickety porch steps and rang the bell.

No one came. Boyd's moped was on the porch, chained to the rail, but he could be off with Jonno, prepping for the gig. I stepped over and peered through the window.

The windowsill was lined with Chianti bottles and plastic toys from Happy Meals. Boyd was twenty-eight years old, and he lived on Happy Meals and Chianti. The bottles blocked half my view, but the window above them was clean enough to see through. This was probably due to Jonno, who had been known to wave a bottle of 409 around. But the place was decorated in a style best described as Early Piles of Crap.

The floor was littered with drifts of folded laundry and boxes of CDs. An amp was sitting in the middle of the floor next to a giant brass hookah that had been used as (among other things) a candleholder. It was coated in multicolored wax drippings all down its tarnished neck and belly. The only light came from a forty-watt bulb screwed into an ancient floor lamp with a stained-glass shade. The TV was off, and I couldn't see any light coming from the kitchen or the back hall.

The dimness mixed with the clutter made the house seem exotic to me. All the quasi-dank places Jonno frequented had an air of mystery about them; when I was growing up, the cans of soup on the lowest shelf of the pantry had to stay in order, and the door to my room had to be closed unless it was "fit for company." All the Fretts were meticulous to the point of mental illness, but Genny and Mama had, by inclination and necessity, taken it further, until order was a religion.

Nothing ever changed in their house. I knew that when I walked in their door in a few hours, the same square table would be by the front door, with the same dusty blue vase in the same spot, still sporting a decades-old spray of plastic gerbera daisies. A willow-pattern china bowl sat empty beside the vase. When I brought Mama home, she would immediately drop her keys in it.

I straightened up. I was anxious to be on the road, but I couldn't quite bring myself to leave without seeing Jonno. I decided to give him fifteen minutes. They might be out on a quick clove-cigarette run for Boyd.

There was a permanently damp upholstered love seat on the porch. I sat down, immediately sinking a good eight inches. I rooted under the cushion next to me for one of the coverless paperbacks Jonno shed like cat hair wherever he went. I found one near the back and pulled it out. *Zen and the Art of Motorcycle Maintenance.*

I scrunched down to read in the fading afternoon sunlight, but I couldn't get my eyes to focus on the words. I pulled in a deep breath, my first since I had talked to Bernese. The porch smelled of Jonno. Not like him personally, but like the air around him. It smelled like a place Jonno would be. I wanted him there so badly, although if he did show up in the next few minutes, I wasn't sure what I would say.

Except that was a lie. I knew what I wanted to say. I said it anyway, even though he wasn't there. "I'm so angry," I said. "I'm so angry, so angry," and saying it at last made me able to feel it. Down in the pit of my stomach, I could sense how it had grown beneath my initial panic, creeping along my bones like a vine, filling me and twining down through all my limbs, spreading up through me and binding me.

The anger was a living thing, separate from me but so deep, so basic, that it had been working its way through me as unnoticed as my blood, circulating to its own fierce rhythm. The words on the page wavered and danced. I threw the book down beside me so my hands were free to beat at the sagging cushions. I uncurled, drumming my feet hard against the porch.

Out loud I said, "It was an accident, a stupid accident, the dog got out by accident," but the anger burst out through my skin, enveloping me, and I wanted to tear up Ona Crabtree, all the Crabtrees, even though I knew anger this hot and violent was coming from the genes I shared with them. I wanted to pull their careless arms off, rip at their throats. Tears were coursing down my cheeks, and if I was right, if it was war, I was at least very clear about which side I was on, even though no one had intentionally set out to hurt Genny, and Bernese had with malice aforethought shot that hell-spawned dog.

It quieted as quickly as it had come storming through me. My stomach unknotted and my limbs stilled. I gulped, scrubbing at my eyes and panting. I sat a moment longer, letting it recede. I could feel the anger in me still, contained and waiting, as much a part of me as my freckles or the need for neatness I had learned at Mama's knee. But I was so spent I could not have gotten up and walked away if the porch had been on fire.

I wished I could simply lie here, paralyzed, until Jonno came home to pet my hair and touch me. I didn't know what to do with this body, so angry and so limp. I did not know how to sit or stand or run in a way that would let me be this frightened and grieved, this angry, and so exhausted by my anger that my vision was wavering. I needed Jonno to appear and artfully arrange my limbs into an appropriate pose. As I imagined him bending me, shaping me, I could feel the ghost of something sexy trying to rise in me, and for a moment I was absolutely certain that he would come, that my need for him was strong enough to summon him.

So I still hadn't given up the fantasy: Jonno as he should be. And me as well. An almost-me. A me that wasn't. The woman I could have been if I had been born a Frett instead of being an adopted Crabtree, if I hadn't married so young, if I had taken the scholarship offered me and gone on to graduate school in North Carolina, if Mama and Genny and, later, Fisher hadn't needed me so close.

I could never be her. She would be my age now, thirty, but established and professional, with her black hair secured in a braided bun. Mama's biological daughter would have a lovely wide mouth and half-moon eyes, and she would have to wear heels so her colleagues did not tower over her. She'd be in a museum somewhere, far away from dogs and Crabtrees and divorces. I saw her in my mind's eye, poring over thick books, picking through the Civil War relics she'd unearthed. She sorted them into clean, cotton-lined boxes. Then I saw Jonno arrive, and he was a grown-up. He had grown-up things like a suit and a basic sense of personal responsibility. He took her in his arms.

They moved together and became unbridled together. They forgot how pretty they were. They lost time. They lost the world around them. They fell to the floor in between the regimented rows of glass display cases. There they became a melded heap of beast: panting, sweaty, unbeautiful.

It was crap, absolute crap. I could flop here in a pile all night if I let myself, weeping over woulda-coulda-shoulda, but half the things I so regretted were things I could not change. I'd been born what I was, and if I had been her? That other woman? Then I never would have picked Jonno in the first place. What Frett would choose a baby in a lovely man's body who treated sex like art and her like crap? Once he left the bedroom, the chaos Jonno spread was beauty-less and anything but clean. But the fantasy had managed to survive ten years of marriage and a year's worth of on-and-off divorce proceedings. And here I was, shaking myself into exhaustion with a violent rage and then running for solace to a man who was all manner of bad for me.

It was exactly what every other Crabtree would have done.

I was instantly disgusted with myself. My family needed me, and here I sat. I couldn't get the hell away fast enough.

Literally.

As I boosted myself out of the depths of the love seat, I saw Jonno's Impala making the turn around the corner. My heart leaped up into my throat and pulsed wildly, practically hitting my gag reflex with every beat. He would see me any second, and before I could think it through, I put one hand on the porch railing and jumped it, tumbling into the loamy earth behind Boyd's scraggly hedges. I squatted there, panting.

The only thing I could imagine that could be worse for me than seeing Jonno would be having him see me crouching like a lunatic stalker in his bushes. I gathered the skirt of my long dress and crept around the corner of the house, scrabbling along the base of the wall like a rodent.

I sat up and pressed my back to the wall of the house, then peered back through the bushes, poking my nose out around the corner. I had a clear view of my Mustang, parallel-parked across the street between two other vehicles, almost opposite Boyd's front door. If Jonno noticed it, he would recognize it instantly as mine. He thought it was hilarious that I was so in love with a restored muscle car when the Frett in me drove exactly three miles over the speed limit and never put the top down.

The Impala turned into the driveway and pulled up on the other side of the house, disappearing from view. I prayed that Jonno and Boyd would not notice my car. The big houses on this street had all been hacked up long ago into apartments, and the junky student cars lining both curbs were good camouflage.

I heard the doors of the Impala opening and slamming, and then a jumble of male voices. They sounded like they were arguing. As they came around to the front of the house, Boyd was saying, "No, because if we end on the G, it's an upswing, like this hopeful half step up."

"Hope sells," said Jonno.

"Whatever, dude, that's not what the song's about. If we end that way, it's a contradiction. It's like the music is saying they might make it."

I heard their boots clomping against the wood of the porch and held my breath.

"Maybe they will," Jonno said.

"Dude, come on," said Boyd, and then the door banged shut behind them.

I stood up abruptly and noticed I still had Jonno's book clutched in one hand. I let it fall into the dirt. I struggled out as silently as I could from between two of the bushes and headed for my car, running away, running toward home.

CHAPTER

6

THE EXIT FOR Between was about five miles before the Loganville exit on Highway 78. Between is built around that highway, midway between Athens and Atlanta. There's nothing there except the town square and a couple of small neighborhoods. The whole town probably would have died out by now if my mama and Bernese hadn't been born there. The Fretts (especially Bernese, who managed Mama's finances) had practically created Between's economy. Their tithe paid the lion's share of the pastor's salary, and their taxes paid our part-time ornamental sheriff. The shops and restaurants on the square survived because Bernese had also turned Between into the creepiest tourist attraction in the South. Her museum, half devoted to her exploitation of my mother's work and half to her own interest in butterfly farming, was highly rated in all of those offbeat travel books for weirdos. In one book, her museum got more stars than the Cadillac Ranch.

In spite of Bernese, Between didn't rate its own hospital.

Genny and Mama were at Loganville General. But I got off onto Philbert Street anyway and drove past the square to turn onto Grace Street. I needed to check on Fisher, and I also wanted to make sure Uncle Lou had been able to get Bernese out of jail. It was not yet seven; Mama would still be wrapped in a soothing blanket of Ativan.

The sun was going down, and all the downstairs lights were on at Bernese's house, spilling out of the windows onto the immaculate lawn. Bernese lived in a blue-gray frame house shaped like a saltine box. A rocking-chair front porch was tacked on like an afterthought.

In the fading daylight, I could see Fisher squatting down in the grass by the gravel drive as I pulled in. I knew Lou or Bernese would be checking on her, watching from the window, but it made me nervous. She looked so small, a living ball of everything dear to me, exposed and alone outside.

I didn't think Ona would want anything to happen to my Fisher. But if Ona was mad enough and drunk enough to call her brother or his crazy-ass sons over from Alabama, she'd be unleashing something on my town and my family that I doubted she could control. Surely she wouldn't call them. Not without talking to me first.

I parked in the driveway. I didn't know if Bernese was inside or still down at the jail, but I took a moment to dig down to the bottom of my purse and make sure I had my empty bottle. It was an amber plastic cylinder, safety-capped in white. If Bernese was home, I might need it.

I climbed out of my Mustang and shut the door. Fisher didn't look up as I approached her. She stayed staring down at the lawn, resting on her short, sturdy calves. She was wearing her favorite pajamas, yellow with butterflies on them. She'd built a cairn of white driveway stones in the grass and put a fat magnolia leaf on top. She was meditatively poking the leaf with a frayed toothpick.

"Hey, Woolly-Worm," I said. She still didn't look up. She poked again at the leaf, rocking on her haunches. "Does anyone know you're out here?" She still wouldn't answer, so I tried a different tack. "What are you doing with the leaf there, Fisher?"

"I'm playing Dr. Splinter and the Human Body," she said, monotone. Her stumpy toes clutched at the grass.

"You want to come in with me?"

She finally deigned to raise her head. Her straight black brows were lowered. "Are you staying even one minute?"

"Not right now," I said, and she dropped her head again. The sharp points of her bobbed hair fell down, obscuring the top half of her face, but I could see her lower lip poking out. "I'll be back, though. Probably not until tomorrow, so don't you go night-walking. No one is going to be next door tonight."

Her silence was noncommittal.

I said, "I mean it, Fisher. Stay in your bed. I'm going to be in town for a long time, and you can stay with me over the weekends like always. Okay?"

She made a small formal motion, more of a head dip than a nod. I decided to take what I could get. "Did your grandma get home?"

Fisher peeked out from under her bangs, studying my face. She lifted one shoulder in a shrug and dropped her head again. "Grandma is inside, measuring my supper. Grampa can see me out that window. I'm not going in the road."

"*Making* your supper," I corrected. I ruffled her hair and she suffered it politely, bowing her neck like a well-mannered cat accepting a pet from an unwholesome stranger.

"Okay, Fisher, I get that you're mad. I'm sorry I haven't been around much this month. I've missed you, too, you know." She didn't answer, so I headed up toward the house.

I was two steps up the walk when she said, "My friend Tia at school is a Methodist."

I looked back. She was prodding the leaf again, and I wasn't sure if she was talking to me or just talking. She went on, "I'll be so sad when she's in hell. Like one thousand sad."

I put my hand to my forehead. "Fisher, Tia's not going to go to hell for being a Methodist."

She didn't answer, and I stood staring helplessly at the back of her head. "She's not going to hell for being black," she said at last, as if challenging me.

"Of course not," I said.

"So why is she going to hell?"

I said, "God does not send little girls to hell. Ever. Trust me on this one."

She stabbed savagely down at the leaf, and the toothpick broke through it. She twirled the toothpick, making the impaled leaf revolve, and a few of the stones fell down. She muttered, "Well, I'm not going in the road."

"Good girl," I said. She hunched her shoulders up around her ears, still squatting over her rock pile with her back turned squarely toward me. I waited, but she didn't say anything else. Fisher was part mule. She would be mad at me until she was good and ready to stop.

I went on up to the front door and paused for a moment, girding my loins for battle. Bernese had been running a guerrilla campaign against me for almost a year, ever since I'd told her I had kicked Jonno out. According to Bernese, neither Baptists nor Fretts got divorced. Her flurried attacks had stepped up considerably as my court date approached. And she always found a way to prang me. I couldn't expect her to cut me a break simply because my mama and Genny were in the hospital; my divorce was like Rome, and all of Bernese's conversational roads led to it.

I had my bottle with me, though, tucked down deep in my purse. If she pushed me hard enough, in the mood I was in, I might bounce it off her head.

I passed through the foyer, pausing to peer into the terrarium where Bernese had laced branches and twigs from her dogwood trees. Yellowy-green and pink caterpillars were climbing all over, and here and there I could see a few cocoons. Bernese now did all her butterfly farming at her museum, but she'd long ago replaced the terrarium my birth mother had shot to pieces. It was Fisher's now—she shared Bernese's fondness for the little bugs—and it looked to me like Fish was raising Azures.

I went down the long hall toward the kitchen, passing the archway to the den and then another that led into the formal dining room. It was so pristine in there, you could safely perform open-heart surgery on the big table. The dust-free china gleamed in orderly rows in the cabinet. I'd never actually eaten off any of Bernese's wedding china. She served all her meals on plain white Farberware.

Bernese had recently updated her kitchen. She'd replaced her avocado-green appliances with brushed steel, and they looked overly large and shiny against the faded daisies that drifted down her wallpaper. The walls were covered with pictures of Bernese's three boys and their families. There were several gaps where the wallpaper glowed brightly in the shape of the frames that used to hang there. Bernese had taken down all the pictures of her youngest child, Lori-Anne, and was slowly filling in the holes with portraits of Fisher.

Bernese stood in her kitchen beside her gigantic gleaming fridge, facing the counter with her back to me. She was already dressed for bed in a terry-cloth robe and her house shoes. Pink foam curlers were lined up in a neat row on the top of her head, revealing a hint of silver at the roots of her otherwise dead-black hair. She had her cutting board out and was slicing half a cantaloupe into four equal slices.

"I thought that was you," she said, glancing over her shoulder. "I called over to the hospital a little while ago. Genny's stable, they say. Doing good. They got her on a drip for pain and to put antibiotics straight into her blood. They said she's going to spend the next day or two pretty much sleeping, but Lord, that just proves they don't know Genny. If she's upset enough, she'll fight off any drug they think to give her, and God help them then. Stacia is still solid out."

I nodded. "I told my agency not to book me for anything. I'll stay at the hospital until we see how Genny's going to do."

Bernese set down the knife and turned to me, saying, "You'd best lean over here and give me a squeeze."

I put one arm around her in a sideways hug, bending low to drop a peck on the front curler. Bernese's waist felt strangely squishy. I was used to the packed feel of her body after it had been subdued by her cast-iron foundation garments.

"I'm too done in to make a real supper. I can heat you up some of these leftovers, though, and there's fresh fruit."

81

I shook my head. "I need to get going. I wanted to make sure you had gotten home. I see Fisher's in a mood."

Bernese released me and turned to the fridge. I took a step back so she could get the door open and pull out a couple of Tupperware containers. "That girl. She's a grudge holder." She lifted the lid on a container and grunted at the green beans in it, then walked past me to put it in the microwave.

"She says she's worried about her little friend Tia going to hell. Did you say something to her about Methodists?"

Bernese blew air out between her lips. "I didn't say Methodists were going to hell. Fisher wanted to visit her friend's church over in Loganville for some picnic day they had. I was telling her she didn't want to fall in with them. Methodists think everybody who's born is already bound for heaven or hell and there's nothing you can do about it, like there's no grace and Jesus don't matter."

I shook my head. "You can't say that kind of thing to Fisher, Bernese. You know how she is. And if you mean predestination, that's not the Methodists. That's the Presbyterians."

Bernese shrugged. "Well, the Methodists believe something stupid or else they'd be Baptists. Anyway, if you want to know why Fisher's ill as hornets, why don't you look in the mirror, Miss Busy Divorce. She's used to you being here every week. She counts on you."

There it was: salvo one. I ignored it. "Did you get things straightened out at the sheriff's office?"

Bernese opened the other Tupperware. Egg salad. She gave it a sniff and nodded, satisfied. "Yes, for now. Lord, Thig is such an ass. I sicced my lawyer on him."

I rolled my eyes. "Bernese, Isaac wrote up Thig's will. He's everyone's lawyer. You probably want to go to Loganville and get someone who knows some criminal law."

Bernese shrugged. "Isaac's always done me fine. And you know nothing's going to happen. I pretty much own Thig." Her lower lip poked out, and she suddenly looked like a giant, swollen version of Fisher. "I better get my gun back, too."

She took her linked measuring cups out of the junk drawer and scooped out a level half-cup of the egg salad. There was a plate sitting out on the counter, and she upended the measuring cup so the salad fell onto the plate in a little mound. "Check the microwave, see if those green beans are hot?"

I opened the microwave and pulled out one of the limp beans while Bernese rinsed the measuring cup.

"They're warm enough," I said, and handed her the container. She measured out a half-cup of the beans and dumped them into a heap beside the egg salad. She picked up her pepper mill and began grinding it over the beans until they looked freckled. I narrowed my eyes. "You're making this plate for Fisher?"

"Mm-hm," said Bernese. She grabbed a slice of the cantaloupe off the cutting board.

"Why are you measuring Fisher's egg salad?"

Bernese put the fruit on the plate. It looked like a sad face, with little round piles of egg salad and beans for eyes and the lonely cantaloupe slice making a long, curved frown. Bernese picked up an open book that had been lying on top of the bread box, closed it, and held it up so I could see the cover. It was called *Get Fit, Kid!* and underneath the title it said "Help your kids win the war on the obesity epidemic."

I shook my head. "Fisher isn't overweight."

"Have you looked at her?" said Bernese. "She's as squatty as a brick."

"That's how she's shaped. She isn't fat."

"She's pretty thick." Bernese paused and turned toward the hallway. She raised her voice and bellowed, "Lou? Get Fisher in here for supper."

I heard a faint "All righty" float down the stairs.

Bernese put the book back on top of the bread box. To me she said, "And if she's not fat now, then this book says it can make sure she won't go that way. Have you seen her mama?"

"No. Have *you* seen her mama?"

Bernese set Fisher's plate on the kitchen table, keeping her back to me. I walked around the table so I could see her face. "Was Lori-Anne here?"

Bernese shrugged, her mouth pinching up into a little wad as if she were preparing to kiss a mortal enemy. Then she said, "Yeah. She came by on Monday. You never saw anything so fat."

"What'd she want?"

"Not to see Fisher. She came by during school hours, and her bad luck, it was a teacher planning day, and there Fisher was. Lord, Lord. Lori-Anne wasn't sure what to do with herself, and Fisher was trying to climb straight up her like she was a big, fat tree. Wanting to get in her arms, crying, 'It's Mama, it's Mama,' and Lori-Anne was barely standing it. Gritting her teeth and giving me the pointy eye like I planned to have Fisher home. Like I magically knew she was going to drag herself over here to try and borrow money again. She wants to get that gastric bypass."

"What'd you tell her?"

"What do you think? It's like pouring money down a black hole. So she got sorrier and sorrier with me and said, 'You are making me gain fifty more pounds, because if I do, the state will pay for my bypass. You want to make me gain fifty more pounds?' I had to laugh out loud. I said, 'Girl, I couldn't even make you brush your teeth when you were seven. If I could make you do anything at all, you got to know your butt would be in church this living second and you'd be praying to Jesus to take you back.'" Bernese went back to the hallway. "Lou? I said I need Fisher for dinner. Now," she hollered.

I took a deep breath. "It depends on when they release Mama and Genny, but maybe tomorrow after school, I can take Fisher down to Henry's. She wants some book about the insides of frogs."

"Don't encourage that mess," said Bernese. "I got enough talk about blood and organs when I was nursing to last me. And Fisher is always after me about what's inside a person and what a kidney does. A kidney doesn't do anything pleasant to talk about, that's certain."

I opened my mouth to respond but closed it again as Fisher came trailing in. She flopped into her chair at the kitchen table and stared balefully down at her supper.

Bernese started running warm water, adding a little dish soap and dropping in the dirty Tupperware.

I took a deep breath and stayed over by the table. I said, "To-morrow I need to go out for a little, so if they release Mama, I may leave her here with you. You know those drugs can make a person woozy for a day or two, and I'm not sure she should be alone."

"Where on earth do you have to be that's that important?"

"I have to go see Ona Crabtree."

Bernese froze at the mention of Ona's name and then turned

slowly around. "I hope you're going over there to kick her bony old butt."

Fisher seemed oblivious, deep in a staring contest with her pitiful supper, but I said, "You're going to get Fisher expelled, teaching her that ugly talk."

"How can you even look at Ona after what they did to our Genny?" Bernese said.

"I don't have a choice. You made sure of that. I already tried to get her on the phone, and I'll be trying again as soon as I check on Mama. Those boys of hers are wild, Bernese, and their Alabama cousins are over here all the time, and they are more than wild. They are criminals. When Thig drops the charges against you and lets you get clean away with shooting that dog, and you know he will, there's no telling what they're going to do."

"If they don't like how Thig handles it, they can call the real police over in Loganville," said Bernese.

"Crabtrees don't call the police. Half those boys are on parole."

Bernese glared at me and then began meticulously scrubbing at the edges of her measuring cups. "That dog getting out was Crabtree carelessness, if they didn't do it on purpose. They hate me, and they wanted to hurt our family. The dog was a weapon, so I took their weapon away." She glanced over her shoulder. "Fisher, eat your supper."

Fisher picked up her fork and gave the egg salad a halfhearted prod. As soon as Bernese wasn't looking, she set the fork back down, centering it carefully on her folded paper napkin.

Bernese said, "Well, if you're going, you might as well take Ona a message. Tell her she better get those other two dogs put down. They're a menace." She stared down into the dishwater, implacable, running the sponge around and around the half-cup's edge. "If Ona won't do it, I'll get Isaac to get me a court order, and Thig can. And if Isaac and Thig can't get it done, I will shoot those dogs myself. Fisher, are you eating?"

"My dinner is sad," said Fisher, and Bernese wheeled around on her.

"Eat it," she yelled. "You have to eat this list of food exactly for the book to work."

Fisher looked mutinous. Her hands stayed in her lap.

"Pick. Up. Your. Fork," said Bernese.

Fisher shoved her hands under her thighs and slumped. "It's too sad for eating."

Bernese came roaring down the length of the kitchen looking murderous. I hurried around and got in between them, leaning over the table by Fisher. "It's not sad," I said to Fisher. I picked up the cantaloupe and turned it over so its points curved upward in a cheerful arch. "It's happy. See?"

Fisher stared down at the plate for another moment. "Okay," she said. She picked up her fork and dutifully stabbed some beans.

I turned around to Bernese, who was standing behind me, blowing like a bull. "Are you all right?" I said to her. Bernese had a temper, but I'd never seen her loose it upon Fisher so quickly.

"You riled me," she said.

I held up my hands. "I'm sorry I brought it up. We can talk about Ona later. I need to get on to see Mama now."

Bernese moved her tongue around inside her mouth, shifting her jaw as if sucking on something nasty. "All right then." She went deliberately back to her dishes.

I kissed the top of Fisher's head. "See you tomorrow." She kept her head lowered, mechanically forking up food. "I'll let myself out, Bernese."

I was almost into the hall when Bernese added in an oddly formal tone, "Thank you for coming."

I paused, surprised, and said, "You don't have to thank me. She's my mother."

Bernese said, "It's hard to know how seriously you take your family these days. Technically, a husband is family, and look what you're doing to yours."

Hot blood rushed to heat my face, and I found myself clutching my purse, with the nails of my other hand digging hard into my palm. But Fisher was between us, sitting with her head bent earnestly over her supper, and there was nothing I could say.

CHAPTER

7

I STOPPED AT the nurses' station to find out Mama and Genny's room number. They were up on the second floor. As I came out of the elevator, I could hear Genny's piping voice coming down the hall. She was yammering in spurts, and as I got closer to her room, I heard a calm male voice speaking soothingly in the pauses. I followed the sound to room 214. The door was open, so I went in without knocking.

Mama was tucked into the bed by the window. She was still sound asleep. The curtains between the beds were open. Genny was in the closer bed, her shoulder and neck swathed in bandages. She had the blanket pulled over her legs. Her mouth looked tiny and puckered in her round face, and it took me a moment to realize this was probably the first time in years I had seen her without a cheerful slash of pink lipstick. Her long white hair was down, thick and still streaked liberally with black.

Henry Crabtree was sitting in a visitor's chair, pulled up close beside her bed. As I came in, Genny saw me over his shoulder, and her eyes lit up as she squawked, "Oh, Nonny, you came!"

Henry stood immediately and turned toward me, smiling. He was built low, close to the bone, and his unbandaged forearm, corded with muscle and prominent dark veins, looked incongruous emerging from the rolled cuff of his shirt as he held one hand out to me.

I took it and squeezed, saying, "I'm so glad you're here." Then I bent down and dropped a kiss on Genny's forehead. "Of course I came, silly widget." To Henry I added, "Has Mama stirred at all?"

He shook his head.

Genny blinked, so long and slow I thought she had dropped into sleep, but then her eyes sprang open, and her hands came fluttering up like drunken birds. "Oh, Lordy, Nonny, why isn't Stacia awake? Is it a coma?"

My eyes met Henry's, and he mouthed, "Morphine," tilting his head slightly to indicate the IV drip.

"It's not a coma. She's sleeping."

"You don't know," Genny said. "It might be a coma." I caught her hands and set them gently back down on her stomach, but the moment I took my hands away, she bent her arms at the elbow again, lifting her palms toward the ceiling. "Is she breathing? Poke her a little."

"She's fine. Your Nonny's here, and you can sleep now, widget. I'm going to fix it all." I caught her hands again and pushed them gently down, and her eyelids lowered with them.

"Those dogs," she said. Her words were slurred. "I smell their breathing. My shoulder hurts."

"You need to sleep now," I said, soothing and soft. "Does this button make the morphine come? Let's push it." I put the box in her hands, and she gave it a tap.

"I can't sleep because of those doctors. Who knows. And those dogs. What if they get loose? They could track me. They could track me to here, and I'd be sleeping, so I wouldn't know to run," Genny said.

"I won't let them," I said.

"Uh-oh, am I falling down?" Genny said, and her hands relaxed under mine. I eased backwards. I thought she was asleep, but then she said, "What if I'd died, Nonny? What would happen to dear Stacia? You mustn't let me die, because what would Stacia do?"

"You didn't die, and you won't die," I said.

Genny didn't say anything else, and after a moment even her pursed mouth relaxed and she was truly out.

I turned to Henry. "Did they admit you, too?"

"Not at all. That dog took out a chunk of me, but all I needed was a stitch job and a shot of antibiotics that they kindly put right into my ass. I went back home to clean up and make sure the store was locked, then came back here to check on Genny and your mother."

"Has Genny been picking?" I asked.

"No. Fluttering and fighting sleep, but she hasn't tried to hurt herself," he said.

As I straightened up, Henry and I were exactly eye to eye. He was wearing one of his millions of white button-down shirts. This one looked buttery soft and expensive, a leftover from his stint as a software developer in New York. It was tucked neatly into khaki pants that had a crisp seam running sharp to his oxblood loafers. His shoulder-length hair, something else he'd brought back from

New York, was gathered and bound into a neat ponytail behind him.

"Do you think you'll be able to open up your store tomorrow?"

"I think so. On the other hand, I don't think anyone has ever died from not getting a book," Henry said.

"Thanks for coming back and sitting with Genny and Mama. You didn't have to do that."

He raised his eyebrows and looked at me over the lenses of his small round glasses. "Sure I did, Nonny Jane. We're almost not unrelated."

I grinned back at him. This was our running joke. Henry was a transplant from the Louisiana branch of the Crabtree family tree. A couple of years ago, while Fisher and I were hanging out with him at the bookstore, we had tried to work out exactly how we were connected to each other. We'd ended up pulling out a long string of register tape so we could make a flowchart. The Georgia Crabtrees often had babies before they had high school diplomas, and after tracing our way back through their short generations and his family's longer ones, we figured out we were fourth cousins, three times removed. On paper, anyway.

I'd never said it out loud to him, but I didn't think we were related at all. Henry's father, Reau, was your typical Crabtree: red-haired, freckled, tall, pale. When he was a young buck in Lafayette, Reau got into trouble and was given the choice of jail or the army. He took the army, which was an odd choice for a Crabtree. The general Crabtree consensus was that you got better drugs in prison.

The army turned him into a mechanic, and he liked it. On pass in Lafayette, he fell in love with a young woman who already had two divorces behind her. He married her a month after their first date. She came with a lot of baggage, including a world-class case of manic depression and a reputation for taking her marriage vows lightly. She was a sloe-eyed Cajun with a junk-French accent so thick it had to be at least partially fake. She never lost it, and even Henry had retained a bit of a Cajun slur to his S's.

Henry, half a head shorter than any Crabtree ever born, looked like her if she'd been painted one shade darker. She'd been sallow, but he was olive-skinned. Her eyes had been milk chocolate, but his were almost black. His younger sister was as redheaded and weedy as her daddy, though there wasn't even a lick of Reau visible in Henry. But since Reau had buckets of the legendary Crabtree rage and a gun collection, folks didn't exactly line up to point that out.

Henry had been seven when Reau opted out and moved the family to Between. Reau worked for Ona as a mechanic, and Henry's mother bought space on the square for her bookstore. Reau, who had both enjoyed a stint in the army and married a book lover, was considered the Crabtree family loon. Which really, there's so much irony there, you could mine it for years and never have the vein run out. But when Henry was about twelve, Reau proved he was a true Crabtree after all: He got drunk as a goat with some of his buddies, and they decided to hike out into the woods with twelve-gauge shotguns and vaporize some squirrels. Reau leaned his gun up against a fence post, and as he was climbing through the barbed wire, he knocked the gun over and blew a large and unforgiving hole in himself.

Henry's mother moved her abbreviated family into the apartment over her store. That was after my aunt Bernese had opened her museum, and Between was becoming a must-stop spot for the kind of people who liked to pack up a camper and go see freakishly large balls of tinfoil and Mary statues that wept blood on Easter. The tourist traffic kept the bookstore alive, and since they lived over it, they managed to scrape by even without Reau's salary. I think Ona may have helped them some.

Growing up, Henry and I weren't close. He was a good four years older than me. But I spent my allowance at the bookstore and my afternoons at his house, playing with his sister, Lily. Henry was a constant presence, reading or tinkering with one of the old computers he was always dragging home. I didn't mind him being around, but I never crushed on him or anything, in spite of the fact that he looked like Johnny Depp. As a teenager and young man, he hadn't quite grown into himself. He was quiet, introverted, and his face was so fine-boned he was almost beautiful. These things rendered him asexual to me.

When I went off to UGA, Henry was still living at home, taking care of his mother and working freelance as a computer programmer to keep the bookstore afloat. His income meant Lily could say yes to her partial-scholarship offer and escape to Savannah State.

My junior year, Henry's mother died. Her liver quit on her. Next I heard, he'd left Between. Bernese was irritated because he wouldn't sell her the bookstore so she could expand. He wouldn't even sublet, although the move looked permanent. He had up and married a woman he met over the Internet, some kind of an art dealer who lived in New York City.

Bernese got to see her before I did. "Pretty thing, but weird-looking," she told me.

"Like dressed weird?" I asked, curious.

"No. Dressed nice. I bet you her shoes cost more than my car. But she was mutty-looking." Then she added in hushed tones, as if telling me something dirty, "I'm not sure, to look at her, but I think she might be part black."

"Good grief, Bernese, who cares," I said.

"Well, none of *us* do. But how do you think that's going to fly with Crabtrees?" Bernese said.

I saw her point.

Two years later, Henry came home pulling a small U-Haul trailer behind his car and quietly reopened the bookstore. He didn't go back to New York, and his wife was never seen in town again. Rex Gentry, Between's lone mailman, told me—told everyone, really—that letters and fat envelopes came and went between Isaac Davids's law office and a practice in New York. Then the letters stopped, and then Henry took off his wedding band.

In the years after his divorce, Henry and I had drifted into a close friendship. We both were obsessed with good novels and good coffee. Fisher adored him, and I had come to depend on Henry's companionship on my long weekends home. I should have known I would find him here, taking care of Mama and Genny.

Mama stirred, and I quickly moved to sit in the chair beside her bed. Her hands flew up into the air, exactly like Genny's had. I reached over and drew a heart on her shoulder. I always did that when I came into a room she was in, so she would know that I was there and it was me. She made my name sign, questioning, still half asleep, and I drew the heart again. She exhaled in obvious relief and said my name out loud.

My mother rarely spoke, and when she did, when she said my name in her high-pitched, scratchy voice with the vowels drawn out long so that it sounded like "Nah-ay-nay," it flooded my stomach with immediate, visceral love.

Her hands were reaching to find mine, and so I gave them to her. My mother had lady-shaped hands, small with tapering fingers, but her nails were kept short and plain and her palms were callused. I signed, telling her everything I knew she'd want to know, first of all that Genny was going to be fine. I told her where she was and what had happened, and that I was here and Genny was in the next bed sleeping, and that Henry was here as well. As I signed, her quick hands skimmed over and around the shapes my hands and fingers made, reading me like Braille.

When I told her Bernese had shot the Bitch, she lifted one shoulder in an eloquent shrug and signed, *Good.*

She had questions, of course, so I gave her my hands and answered them, interpreting what both of us were saying for Henry as I signed, so that instead of thinking in English or ASL, I thought between them. Mama made me go through what had happened several times, reconstructing it from her experience and questioning Henry, who had witnessed it.

"At first I didn't realize it was the dogs. I could only think, 'I am being killed.'" When I spoke for Mama, I did so directly, in first person, but there was rarely any confusion about whether I was speaking for Mama or myself.

Mama felt down the side of the bed to the control buttons and jacked up the bed until she was sitting. She signed, *I was sure I was going to die, and I thought what would Genny do. I was so afraid. What would Genny do if I had died?*

You didn't die, and you won't die, I told her.

What about the other two dogs? Mama signed. *Did Bernese shoot them?*

I shook my hand no, and Mama's lips compressed. *Tell her to go back and shoot them. She'd better, or we'll never get Genny home.*

I did not interpret this exactly for Henry. I said only, "She's worried about Genny, Henry. Excuse us for a second? I need to talk to her." Henry nodded and went to sit in the other chair. He didn't bother to look away. Henry could slowly grind out the alphabet and sign a few phrases, but he didn't know enough ASL to follow the conversation. I stopped interpreting for him and signed to Mama, *I'm taking care of it. I am going to go talk to Ona Crabtree.*

And say what? Mama demanded. *Genny is going to be gobbling Xanax and picking herself bloody until she feels safe.*

I started to outline my game plan, but my hands stilled. Ona Crabtree was in the hospital hallway, as if mentioning her name had somehow conjured her. She stared me down with a flat gaze as she walked slowly past the open door. Fear trickled icy cold down the length of my spine, and Mama felt the pause in me. She was signing before I could pick up the conversation, asking me what was happening.

Henry, sitting by Genny's bed, had his back to the door. By the time he turned to see what had caught my attention, Ona had disappeared on the other side of the doorway.

What? What? Mama signed impatiently, shaking my quiet hands. I wanted so badly to lie, but I couldn't lie to her. That was Genny's rule. If it happened in Mama's presence, if it happened in the room with her, Genny insisted that we never hide it. Bernese still refused to get that, and 80 percent of our ugliest family fights began with Bernese saying, "Don't say this to Eustacia, but . . ." While she was saying it, Genny would be simultaneously signing, *Don't say this to Eustacia, but . . .* into Mama's hand.

I signed, *Ona Crabtree is here.* I spelled out Ona and used our name sign for Crabtree, snapping one hand in a quick pinch like a claw and then dropping it in the same movement I would use to sign "low." It was more complicated than a usual name sign, and it carried a negative connotation. We never used it to refer to Henry. It didn't bother me; the fact that my mother had so named them was only more proof that she thought of me as wholly her own. I looked at the doorway. Ona was passing again, going the other way.

Henry said, "What is it?" I shook my head at him; I did not want Ona to hear me talking about her. Mama started to respond, but I told her I would be right back and stood up. She didn't let go of my hand.

With her free hand, she signed, *Why is Ona Crabtree here?*

"What's happening?" said Henry.

He was quick enough to have seen Mama and me spelling out "Ona." I brought my free hand up to put my finger to my lips, hushing him. For Ona's benefit I said, "Mama is wanting a drink; will you pour her some water?"

Henry gave me a long, level gaze that said more eloquently than words that he knew I was full of crap. Then he said, "Certainly," and went to the table between the beds where a small plastic pitcher of ice water sat along with two cups. Ona Crabtree passed the door once more. She was like a shooting-gallery duck, appearing and disappearing, reversing and appearing again.

To Mama, I signed, *Let me go find out.*

She let go of me, and I said to Henry, "Can you stay a few more minutes? I need to go see when they'll release my mother."

Henry nodded, giving me another assessing gaze. He was trying to hand Mama the water, but since she hadn't actually asked for it, she was surprised by its sudden presence in her hand.

I went out the door, leaving it open. Ona was moving away from me, down the hall. I followed her. She looked over her shoulder to make sure I was coming and then picked up the pace. She rounded a corner, and I hurried to catch up, my heartbeat increasing and my hands shaping themselves into fists. The coiled anger I had felt on Jonno's porch was unfurling again inside me. I felt like a predator going after a stringy beast made of tendons and gristle. When I turned the corner, Ona was waiting right there for me, and she clamped my arm in a bony grasp. I started, and before I could speak, she turned and began dragging me urgently up the hallway.

"You could have come in the room," I said, but I let her tow me along.

"I don't want to talk with Henry right now. I want to talk with you," she said. "And what's Henry doing here? Those Fretts didn't get enough with you, they have to put a claim on Henry, too?" She didn't wait for me to answer but toted me back past the bank of elevators, then into a recessed alcove that held vending machines. She let go of me, but I still felt pinned under her twitchy gaze.

"Whicha one of them got bad bit?" Ona said. She was wringing her rough hands. "The blind one or the crazy one?"

"It was Genny," I said. Ona looked at me impatiently. I glared back at her. "You know which is Genny."

"So not the blind one," Ona said. "That's good. I swear, I didn't want it much to be that blind one."

I said, "You're talking about my mother."

Ona lifted her upper lip, baring her teeth like a nervous horse. Her teeth were gray around the edges and oddly flat. My front teeth had been flat like that before braces.

She was in her early sixties, and she had lived every one of those years hard. She still lived hard, and her face showed it. But I could see my face under it, in the good high cheekbones and the narrow jaw. I had her nose, too, long and skinny and a little crooked, and about a third of her freckles. She was shorter than me now, hunched with age, her shoulders curving inward, but in the pictures I had seen of her as a young woman, she had my body, leggy and long-waisted with not enough on top. I didn't say anything, and she relaxed her mouth and looked away, turning her head to the Coke machines.

"What happened?" I demanded. "Why did it happen? Who screwed up closing the gate?"

She shrugged. "I think it might well could have been Varner." Varner was the most recent in her long chain of common-law husbands. "We got into it pretty bad the night before when we was closing up the station. He went stomping out the back. He was pretty drunk."

"Why do you even have dogs like that? They're dangerous if you don't get them properly trained. And you had to know they hated Genny."

She shrugged again. "They's good dogs, Nonny. Cost me more than four hundred apiece as puppies. Maybe I knew they had a little mean to them, but you want a guard dog to have some mean. You got to know I never thought they'd eat nobody. Not unless somebody came in the parts yard that wasn't supposed to." We stood there silently looking at each other. She added, "Not like you ever ast me to get rid of them."

"I told you I thought they were a menace."

She couldn't quite meet my eyes. "You never said get rid of them."

I turned my back on her and took two steps away, then faced her again. "I don't think I can talk to you right now." But I didn't leave. I couldn't leave until I knew she wasn't going to call her brother over in Alabama, assuming she hadn't already. I had to know my family was safe.

She lowered her eyebrows and looked up at me from under them, thrusting her chin out. At last she jerked one thumb at the Coke machine and said, "You got any change?"

"I know you didn't come to check on Genny," I said. "Why are you here?"

She thrust her chin out even farther. "I came to see you. I knew you'd come running here for them, like always. This machine will take dollars if you don't got the change."

I narrowed my eyes. "I don't feel like giving you a dollar right now, Ona."

She started rummaging in her pocketbook. At last she pulled out a crumpled bill and started fussing with the machine, trying to thread the dollar through. The machine spat it back out, and she immediately tried to stick it in again. The rollers inside made a tinny, mechanical buzz as they sucked at the bill.

She said, "I bet Bernese is already at home, isn't she? Shot my dog on the public street with the same kind of gun that put my boy Tucker on probation." She shook her head as the dollar bill came whirring back.

"Bernese is home on bail," I said. "Thig did arrest her."

"Bernese owns Thig Newell, and you know it," Ona said. "It was wrong what she done, shooting my dog." The machine spat the dollar back at her for the fourth time.

"Oh, for heaven's sake." I snatched the dollar and stretched it tight between my hands, rubbing it back and forth across my thigh to straighten it. "No one is saying Bernese should have shot that dog. Even Bernese probably knows it was wrong." I put the dollar in the slot, and it stayed in. I pressed the Coke button, and the can clattered out at the bottom. "She was overwrought. We all are. Genny's hurt. She really got hurt in all this. I hope you see that."

When I looked back at her, I could see she wasn't listening. She was staring at me with a lost and hungry look, avid and familiar. She'd been watching me that way since I was three. That was the year Hazel Crabtree, my birth mother, ran off with a roustabout she met at a traveling carnival. She hadn't been heard from since. But she left a note, and in it she told Ona what an awful mother she had been and detailed the horrors Ona had driven her to. As a parting shot, she'd explained exactly why Stacia Frett's adopted baby had such wild red hair.

My first memory of Ona may well be my first real memory. I was lying in my toddler bed, and I heard a sound like the shrieking of the damned. It was coming from below me, from the front yard. It was Ona Crabtree, beyond drunk, waving her daughter's Dear Mama note and howling, "Bring me that baby, you bitches. That baby is my baby, and you better bring her out to me before I light your fucking house on fire. I'll burn you Frett bitches out and take her!"

I got out of bed and ran to look out of my window, down into the yard at the screaming creature with wildfire for hair. She was so pale and thin that her flailing arms looked like they were made of bones. I started crying, sure she had come to chew me open and eat my guts while she dragged me away into the black night.

Then the light flipped on and I saw Genny in my doorway. And I saw my mother, hurrying to pick me up and hold me, tucking me close against her. She carried me away from the window and sat down with me on my bed. She tilted my chin so my face was directly in front of hers, within her narrowing field of vision. I looked up into her eyes, gray and calm and reassuring, and she began signing.

That was the first time she told me the story of my birth, our love story. I don't remember the specifics of that particular telling, swaddled as it is inside the memories of the thousand other times she told me. I do remember the comfort offered by her hands as they moved for me, telling me that I was safe, that I was Nonny Jane Frett, that I was hers and no one else's. She may have been trying to tell me who I was, or only who she wanted me to be, but either way, the thing I understood most clearly was that I was so, so loved.

As she signed, I could hear people yelling. It was probably Bernese and Ona trying to outscream each other on the lawn. My mother's voiceless assurance, silent but so eloquent, drowned them both out, and then her moving words were bathed in flickering lights coming through the window, flashing red and blue, as the police came to restore order and take Ona away.

Now I felt Ona's gaze on my skin like greedy fingers, and I knew, for her, this conversation we were having was not about Genny, and it wasn't about Bernese shooting her dog. This conversation was twenty-seven years older than that. I felt the terrible force of her love closing in over me. It was fierce and hopeless, close to unrequited.

Some of my anger was pressed out by the palpable weight of her longing. I knew then, in a deep, real place inside of me, that the dog getting out had been an accident. It was just one of those things, and Ona hadn't called her brother or his crazy sons, demanding violence. Not yet, anyway. She had come here to see if I was blaming her, if I hated her. She'd lost me on so many levels; I could feel how deeply it still mattered to her.

Deflated, I said, "Genny's going to be fine, though. They say."

"I looked in on y'all in that room, and she seemed plenty perky to me. She was sitting up and making that witchy-poo hand talk," Ona said.

"Genny was sleeping in the other bed. I was talking to Mama."

Ona eased closer to me. "That's good, then. I was worried maybe the dog got at her voice box. What's the blind one doing in the hospital when it was that other one got hurt?"

I tried to hang on to my patience, but it was her genes that had left me with such a short supply. "My mother's name is Stacia Frett. You know her name is Stacia, not 'the blind one.'"

"But she *is* blind," said Ona, defensive.

"Yes," I said.

"And deaf, too," said Ona.

"Yes. She was born deaf."

"How can that be a mother," said Ona. She wasn't speaking angrily; in fact, she sounded like she was musing, but I could tell by the way she refused to meet my eyes that she was riled. "She can't see what you're up to, or hear you, and it's a miracle she didn't drop you on your head and make you pure retarded."

"Maybe she didn't drop me because she was sober," I said.

Ona's breath came out in a sharp little cough. I flexed my hands once, twice, trying to keep them from fisting.

"Make peace," I thought to myself. "Give her what she wants so she won't call her brother, so she'll get rid of those other dogs." What did it matter, as long as Genny felt safe? All I had to do was make peace and I could go home, get divorced, and get the hell away from Athens and Jonno forever. There was plenty of interpreting work in Atlanta, not an hour away from my family in the other direction. Maybe I could even have Fisher for part of the summer, get the two of us away from Between with all its Fretts and dogs and bloody-minded Crabtrees. We could go to Centennial Park and sit by the fountain and eat some damn peaches.

I saw how easy it could be, in this moment, as Ona peppered me with starving glances. She was desperate for some sort of connection, and it seemed possible that if I would lean forward, give her a hug, give her something, maybe we could be done with this. But it was so hard to lean in that direction. I didn't know how to offer affection when I didn't have it, especially since she wanted me to prove I cared by talking trash about my own mother.

I tried for some warmth of tone. "All I'm saying is, please keep in mind that you're talking about my mother."

"My girl carried you in her body. That's a mother," said Ona, her back still up. "I'm your granny by blood."

"I know what you are," I said flatly, and we stood together in the alcove with all our history hanging between us.

After Hazel spilled her guts and fled town, Ona had tried to win custody, but Isaac Davids squelched that. He'd finally agreed to let her have limited visitation with me when I was five, probably to keep us out of court. I'm not sure Isaac's rushed adoption job was 100 percent kosher; Isaac would breeze cheerfully around the closest of legal corners when the client was Bernese.

The visitation did not last long. I remember a few strained outings with Ona, sitting shy and silent in her truck while she drove me to Tastee-Freez and asked me question after question. Was I doing well at school? Did I have friends? Were "those people" feeding me properly?

The open, angry way she talked about my mother and the rest of my family made me squirm. At five, I did not know what to say when she handed me a soft-serve cone and said, "You're being raised up by thieves."

She called Bernese by the same name Bernese would later give Ona's alpha dog. She probably hated Bernese more than she hated Mama and Genny put together. Ona wasn't stupid. She knew who had done the legwork. In fact, if there was a person on God's green earth Ona Crabtree hated more than the Fretts, it was their lawyer. The Fretts never would have been able to take me without Isaac. Bernese may have married Lou Baxter, but Isaac was her good right hand. Uncle Lou always seemed dragged to me, as if tumbling along haplessly in Bernese's considerable wake; it was Isaac who walked beside her, and Ona knew it.

After what would be my last unsupervised visit, I came out of Ona's front door and down to the sidewalk where my mother and Genny were waiting to walk me home. I kissed Mama, and then I turned to Genny and said, "What's a faggot Jew?"

I was fluent in ASL, but my spelling skills were not yet up to asking Mama about words I did not know how to sign. Genny blanched and then told Mama what I had asked.

Where did you learn that word? Mama signed.

I had watched Genny's hands and could now answer her. I signed, *Ona calls Mr. Isaac the faggot Jew of Between.* Mama turned so I could not see her hands and erupted in a flurry of violent sign to Genny.

Then she turned back to me and signed patiently, *Ona doesn't like it that Mr. Isaac is Jewish. That's his religion, like we are Baptists. And it also means he was born Jewish, like you were born Irish and we were born German and Seminole. Some people don't like peo-*

ple who seem different from them. That's a stupid way to be, and we Fretts are not stupid.

The other word . . . is not a nice word. Don't say it. In our house, we call men who have never married "bachelors." Do you understand?

I nodded. She gave me a kiss and then marched us all immediately over to Bernese's house. Bernese deployed Isaac again, and within a few days he was knocking on Ona's door with more paperwork. After that, our visits were supervised. That meant my mother and Genny would take me to meet her at a park or the Loganville McDonald's. Genny and Mama would sit down side by side, hips touching, a few feet away from Ona and me. They sat as still as if they were the two main components in a wall, watching Ona with daggered eyes and hostile posture.

Now they were lying hurt in a room down the hall, and Ona was visiting with me frighteningly unsupervised. "What does that mean, you know what I am? I'm blood kin to you, and you ought not side with Bernese Baxter against me."

I took a deep breath. "I have tried to make Bernese see your side of things, Ona. You should know that. I had a long talk with her, and I am sure that here, in the light of hindsight, she's sorry about shooting your dog. Just like I am sure you're sorry about what the dog did to Genny. She's not going to ask you to help pay for Genny's treatment here at all. Genny's going to be here a couple of days more, and she had to have over forty stitches."

Ona huffed and then got the Coke out of the bottom of the machine. She stared at the can and said, "This is plain old Coke. I was gonna get me that vanilla kind."

"You know, a lot of people would sue over the hospital bills. I think that shows how sorry Bernese is." I hated the wheedling note in my voice, but I forced myself to smile and step in closer.

Ona rolled her eyes. "Bernese sleeps on a big old pile of money, and it don't mean shit to her." She popped the tab on the Coke and took a swig. "I tell you what, if she's going to let bygones be, then I can, too."

"Thank you, Ona. I was worried you might call your brother. You know his oldest boy, Billy, has quite a temper," I said in what had to be the understatement of the decade. "I hope you won't get them all riled up and coming over this way."

Ona shrugged. "Them boys can get into some trouble, though, can't they? But right now I think me and you, we can work it out between us."

I swallowed and added, "I was also hoping you might consider finding new homes for the other two dogs. Maybe one of your relatives could take them. I have to tell you, Ona, I'm scared of what might happen if the dogs get out again. Bernese wants to have them put down, but I can convince her to let that drop, too, if you can move them somewhere."

Ona nodded almost agreeably. "I got me a second cousin, Clint, who might would take them." She sidled a step closer to me, so close I could smell her breath, the sweetness of the Coke masking an undersmell, something faintly rotten. I held myself still beside her. "He's been wanting some good dogs, and he's all the way over to Baton Rouge."

"I'd really appreciate that." I reached out and gave her upper arm a quick squeeze. "I need to get back and check on Genny."

I started to go, but Ona jumped toward me and clasped me in her bony arms. I went rigid, almost recoiling, but immediately forced myself to relax and put one stiff reciprocal arm around her.

She let go of me and stepped back, and I knew that she had felt my involuntary pulling away. Her throat moved, swallowing, and her eyelids ticked, twice. I watched her watery eyes ice up, hardening over pain. Then her eyelids dropped, and she said, "So as soon as I get, let's say, eight hundred dollars, we'll forget the whole mess."

"Eight hundred dollars?" I repeated.

"Yeah," said Ona. "Them dogs is pure-blood Dobie. And that bitch was the pick of the litter. She was worth the four hundred I paid out, easy. And I'll need two hundred apiece for them other two. Since my cousin will have them, it don't seem right Bernese should pay full price for me giving them up."

I wasn't sure what I had in the bank, but I could get the eight hundred from Mama, no question. Mama was as pragmatic as Bernese but with only half her temper. She'd pay it to be sure Genny was safe, which was all that mattered to her. The war would be halted with no more blood spilled, which was all that mattered to me. "That seems reasonable. I can bring the money over."

"Bring it Friday night, why don't you. Ain't seen you in a age of Sundays. I'll make us a roast."

I nodded vigorously. "I'd love to have dinner with you. That would be great. Eight hundred. Fine. I'll see you later, then."

I was headed back up the hall, almost giddy with relief, when Ona came out of the vending alcove and called after me, "Don't bring cash. I can't have cash like that around the house. You know Tucker moved back home for his probation, and if he gets aholt of it, he'll drink it up."

My heart stuttered. I turned back to her and said, "Maybe I can bring it to you Friday morning, while the banks are open."

"Naw, you just come on to supper. You can bring me a check." She smiled at me, her yellowed eyes leveled on me with a gaze as cunning as any fox's. "Bernese's check. And if she felt like it, she could write 'sorry' down in the space where you write what a check is for, but I don't absolutely have a demand on that. Her check. Signed by her. That's sorry enough. Soon's I get it, I'll move them dogs."

I opened my mouth to answer her, but she quickly lifted the Coke can in salute and said, "See you Friday."

CHAPTER

8

"OVER MY DEAD body," said Bernese. "Over my bloated, rotting, double-dead body and the bodies of my executors."

"Lord, help me," I said to the ceiling. I tried again. "Do you mean that? Because Ona's nephews might take you literally."

I was helping Bernese restock the display shelf at the front of her store. The counter and the register were against the opposite wall, with the display window and a big play table in between. Behind us were aisles filled with dollhouses and kits and furniture and molds and doll-making supplies. This bank of shelves was nothing but dolls. Reproductions of my mother's dolls.

They looked blankly down at me. Each doll was centered in its own box, and all the boxes lined up in uniform rows that stretched from floor to ceiling. My mother's dolls were lovely, but here there were simply too many of them, perfectly aligned like beautiful, stoic soldiers. The whole wall was like a shrine to OCD. A shrine with eyes.

"Hand me up the frogs," Bernese said. She was balanced on top of a rickety stepladder, restocking the animal dolls on the highest shelf. My mother had made a series of long-faced foxes and portly bears, neckless frogs and sloe-eyed cats, all with furry hands and delicate feet, arched and pawlike. Genny had sewn them into upright bodies, like people, and dressed them in stuffy Victorian finery. I started passing up boxes from the open crate beside the stepladder, wincing. I was sore from spending the night in a chair between Genny's and Mama's beds. They hadn't released Mama until this morning.

Bernese put the frogs up on the highest shelf, her thick body balanced precariously on her tiny feet. All the Fretts had ridiculously short, wide feet. Paddle feet, Genny called them. She said I had ski feet because they were so long and narrow, the tops dotted with pale freckles.

"So the Crabtrees want my money. There's a shocker," said Bernese. "Ona should pay me to not sue her and take her stupid gas station. I could put in a BP with a decent toilet. She's got some long hairy hanging ones to even ask."

"Good grief," I said, cutting my eyes at Fisher. Mama and I had picked her up at kindergarten after lunch, and now they were playing together with one of the open dollhouses on the play table. Bernese had assembled two huge houses, back-to-back, mostly for Fisher, but also for customers' kids. There was a box of battered furniture and about twenty dolls that had seen better days. Mama and Fisher had picked a family from the box, and they were deep in silent conversation about the dolls' imaginary lives.

"She's not listening," said Bernese, and Fisher immediately looked up.

"Yes, I am," she said, and with the acrobat mind of a five-year-old, she continued to sign the life story of the daughter doll into Mama's hands while saying to us, "Do they still have Jews?"

"Who are 'they'?" said Bernese, her eyebrows lowering.

Fisher shrugged. She put the baby in Mama's hands, and Mama felt her way to the third-floor nursery and set him down in his crib. She was slumped in a folding chair that Bernese had dragged out of the storage room, and her hands did not move over the house with their usual surety; she was on painkillers for her scraped shoulder and bruised side. She was lucky she hadn't broken a hip when she fell. The pill damped her down and muted her colors. She was usually such a presence that I could get a palpable feel for her mood whenever we were in the same room. Today she looked older and smaller than herself. Or perhaps it was just that she was sitting alone; I almost never saw Mama without Genny. But Genny was still in the hospital. Mama and I had stayed with her until we had to pick up Fisher. Genny had dozed off and on, and when we'd left, she was solidly asleep.

Fisher was rearranging the second floor now, making a music room where the daughter doll could practice her tiny violin. She said, "Like in Bible times, they had dinosaurs, but they don't have dinosaurs anymore. Do they still have Jews?"

"Methodists," said Bernese darkly. "You see the sort of crap she brings home when she goes over to Tia's church?"

I said, "Of course there are still Jewish people. You know Mr. Isaac, your grandma's lawyer? He's Jewish. But dinosaurs weren't really around in Bible times, Fisher. They were a long time before that."

"If you believe in evolution," Bernese said. "Which we don't." She placed the last animal, a duck with extravagant yellow curls

113

peeping out from under her mobcap, and then turned back to me and said, "You think I should pay off Ona Crabtree, don't you? Holy crows, Nonny, whose side are you on?"

"This is hardly choosing a side. I'm telling you what Ona said because I'm scared, Bernese." I gave her my hand, and she came down off the ladder.

"Horse poop. You think I should pay, and that's taking her side." Bernese glowered.

"I think paying her would make things safer for *our* side," I said.

"You go back and tell her—"

"I don't think that's a great idea."

Bernese picked up the empty crate and carried it to the back of the store. A door there opened onto a storage room and her office. The office was a neat cube with a desk and two tall filing cabinets stuffed with receipts and tax forms and customer files and orders. The files were arranged by category, subcategory, and sub-subcategory, some alphabetical, some chronological, and some in mystical Bernese order, depending on the file type. To anyone other than a Frett, it probably looked like chaos, and indeed, except for Bernese herself, only Isaac Davids could reliably pull a file without needing three hours, a Sherpa, and a fistful of Prozac. In the far corner, stairs led up to a two-bedroom furnished apartment. Bernese called the upstairs her rental property, though she had never actually rented it out.

I followed her to the doorway. "Going back and forth between the two of you like this—she thinks I'm on your side, and you think I'm on hers. The two of you will end up madder at me than you are mad at each other."

"Not possible, unless you drop to all fours and personally chew

Genny's other arm off," said Bernese. She opened the door and hurled the empty box back there for Lou to break down later. "You tell Ona if she doesn't get those dogs gone, I'll show them the way to hell myself." She bulled her way past me, heading back toward the counter.

"I wish I was a Jew," said Fisher mournfully.

"No, you do not," Bernese snapped, not breaking stride.

I bit back a laugh. Fisher hated to be laughed at. She was already angry with me, and I knew if I so much as smiled, she would shut me out all day. I followed Bernese to the front of the store. "Can't you write the stupid check?" I said. "What happened to Genny and Mama—I'm as upset as you are, but at least I can understand that it was an accident."

"I do, too, want to be a Jew," Fisher called after us.

"No, Fisher, you want to be a Baptist. And you are. So get happy," Bernese said. She looked at me. "Why is it my job to smooth down Ona Crabtree's ruffled butt plumage when she's the one caused all this?" She bent down behind the counter and began organizing the shelves, realigning the already tidy rows of paper bags.

Fisher waggled the father doll back and forth and said in a deep, officious voice, "The Jews are God's chosen people!"

Bernese glared at Fisher over the counter, her cheeks reddening slightly and her breath coming faster. "Well, the Jews are going to hell. You want to go to hell?"

"Bernese!" I said. "That's a hair shy of child abuse. Not even."

Fisher stopped signing with Mama and stared up at Bernese with solemn eyes. "Mr. Isaac is going to hell?"

"No, of course not," said Bernese.

"Right. God only sends people to hell if you don't personally approve of them," I said, pitching my voice down low for Bernese's ears alone. "What's gotten into you?"

Bernese shot me a venomous look and said to Fisher, "No one really knows who is going to hell but God, Fisher. But if you were Jewish, you couldn't have Christmas. And you couldn't go to church with us on Sunday. Wouldn't that be sad? You'd still want to go to vacation Bible school, but you couldn't."

Mama tapped at Fisher's hands, and Fisher turned away from us, resolutely setting her blocky shoulders. She signed, *Grandma won't let me be a Jew,* into my mother's left hand.

My mother considered this and then felt along the second floor until she found the daughter doll. She picked her up and put her into Fisher's hands and then signed, *This girl is Jewish. She's a real little girl. Her name's Anne Frank.*

Does she play the violin? Fisher asked, and then my mother immersed her in the story. In minutes the two of them were busy helping Anne and her family set up house in the attic. In Fisher's version, Anne Frank went into hiding with several fathers, her violin, and a baby. The mother doll was pressed into service as a Nazi.

The bell on the door tinkled, and a young couple came in. Tourists. They had that rumpled look you get only from hours in a car wearing clothes that came out of a suitcase. The man was carrying a toddler with pale, angelic curls, maybe three years old. Bernese looked up and smiled, baring all her huge, square teeth at them.

"Babies!" the little girl said, pointing at the doll display.

"Yes," said her mother, wilting under the onslaught of staring doll eyes. "That's a lot of babies."

The father was holding a guidebook, *Southern Car Tours.* That was the most mainstream guidebook the Dollhouse and Butterfly Museum appeared in, and it did a shamefully poor job of preparing people for the realities of next door.

"The sign on the door said we get museum tickets here?" the father said.

"That's right," said Bernese. "Five dollars for adults, and your little friend there looks to me to be free. She's under four?"

While Bernese was ringing him up and exchanging pleasantries, I tried to get the mother's attention, but she was engrossed in watching Fisher sign into Mama's hands. I watched for a moment, too. Apparently, Anne Frank had joined the Powerpuff Girls and was headed downstairs to beat the crap out of some Nazis.

I gave a discreet cough, and the mother looked up. I tilted my head toward her daughter and then gave my head a shake, trying to indicate that the museum might not be the best place to take a toddler. She misunderstood me and turned away from Mama and Fisher, blushing a faint pink. She said, "I wasn't trying to be rude. I've never seen that, what they're doing."

Bernese stepped in before I could get my mouth open. "Now, if you folks follow me, I will let you in next door, and then you can wander as long as you'd like."

"Good luck," I called as they followed Bernese out, helpless ducklings who'd accidentally imprinted on a carnivore.

Bernese shot me a dirty look and said, "After you tour the museum, be sure and come back and shop. We have all kinds of—" Then the door closed, and I couldn't hear any more.

"Why are they taking a little kid next door? Are they stupid?" Fisher asked me without looking up from her game.

"They don't know any better."

A moment later, Bernese bustled back in, her mouth curving

into a wide, smug smile. "Early in the season for tourists," she said. "But I've been getting quite a few this week. Not even a weekend!"

"You left them alone?" I asked.

"Lou's over there, cleaning the frass out of the terrariums. He's got an eye on them."

"While you're in a good mood," I said, "with this Ona thing—could you think about bending?"

She snorted. "Bending over, you mean. Don't hold your breath. And I am dead serious about her getting those dogs gone. You tell her."

I threw my hands in the air.

The bell went off again, and Bernese whirled, unleashing the big dog-in-the-litter-box grin she kept at the ready for tourists and customers, but it was only Henry this time, poking his head in.

"Coffee?" he said to me, raising his eyebrows.

"God, yes," I answered. "Give me a sec."

He let the door close. I went and knelt down on the floor by Mama, drawing my heart on her shoulder to get her attention, and told her I was going over to the bookstore. She wanted to stay and play with Fisher, so I told her I would bring her some supper back from the diner. It had been a long day, and I didn't want her wearing herself out cooking.

Before I could stand up, Fisher gripped my forearm. She leaned in to me from the other side and whispered into my ear, "When I grow up to be a Jew, I'll let you come to my Jewish church. Even if I'm not allowed to come to yours."

Her breath stirred the tendrils of hair at my nape. It was warm and smelled of SweeTarts. Mama must have been slipping her candies. I looked at her, as serious as she was.

"I know you would," I whispered back, and she lunged at me,

banging her bullet-hard head into my teeth, then tilting to stuff her face down into the corner where my neck met my shoulder. She clutched me, a fisted bundle of muscle in my arms, and then relaxed, suddenly pliant. I squeezed her tight, my teeth buzzing from the blow.

She let go of me abruptly. I didn't let her go until she wormed backwards out of my arms. As I released her, she gave me a bracing pat, as if bucking me up, before returning to Mama and her dolls.

I stood up, rubbing my mouth. On my way out the door, I said, "I'm getting Mama's supper while I'm out. Want me to bring y'all something?"

Bernese, back behind the counter, said, "If you're going to the diner, get us two meatloaf specials, extra gravy."

"Fisher won't eat that," I said.

"It's for me and Lou. Fisher's eating from that book."

I said softly, "You need to quit with that. Fisher's still a baby, and her body is working hard to grow. What would happen to all your caterpillars if you stopped feeding them?"

Bernese answered back almost as quietly, "Don't get in my way on this, Nonny, especially not in front of her."

"Something's not right with you, Bernese. You're not yourself with her right now. What's changed?"

Bernese didn't answer me, just glanced at Fisher. "Bat ears," she said.

I looked over at Fisher. Her head was bent down over her dolls, but her spine was straight and stiff and her body was held motionless. She was listening intently, even while her hands moved dolls about and signed with Mama.

"I'll take it up with you later," I said to Bernese, and left.

CHAPTER

9

S TEAMED MILK OR demitasse?" Henry asked, grinning over his shoulder at me. He'd made himself a double shot of espresso. It was sitting on the counter, so thick and black it was practically a solid; Henry was a purist.

"Double shot, please. With lots of steamed milk. If you have any sugar, put that in. And if you have any opium, a heaping spoonful of that, too." Henry's register was at the front, by the door, and the rest of the counter had been converted into a coffee bar. I was slumped on one of the stools, my head cradled in my hands.

"I have vanilla opium," said Henry, holding up a bottle of flavored syrup.

"Sold," I said, and he upended the bottle over the largest-size paper cup he had.

"Keep it coming," I said.

"That bad?"

"Mama's going to be fine, and the doctor said Genny will be

fine, too. She's drugged to the hilt. Bernese, however, is going to give me an aneurysm." I shook my head.

"It's going to get worse before it gets better," said Henry. "Ona's ready to go on a tear."

He handed me my latte, and I took a long, searing gulp.

"Bernese, too. And it isn't only this mess with the Crabtrees. My whole family is out of sorts. Bernese is like an upset hamster mama. She's going to chew off Fisher's head. That's if she doesn't starve the kid to death first. Something is bad wrong there all of a sudden, and I can't put my finger on it. She's making Fisher moody. Moodier. And Mama's lathered because Bernese sold another one of her original heads," I said.

"Why does she keep doing that?"

"Because she's Bernese. Last night at the hospital, Mama asked me to pick out the head for her," I said. "She doesn't feel up to it, and she says she doesn't even want to know what one I pick. I think she's too distraught over Genny to think about it, but as sure as God made little green apples, that will bite me in the ass later. I'll pick the wrong head. Whatever one I pick, it'll be the exact one she can least stand to lose, because she can't stand to lose any of them.

"Meanwhile, Ona Crabtree is demanding that Bernese pay for the Bitch's funeral, and worse, she's making me come to her house and eat roast this weekend, and I hope to the Lord God Almighty you can get yourself invited to that dinner, too, or I will probably stroke out, and my divorce is Friday afternoon, assuming I can even go, and how is that for a giant dump of horror in your lap." I was surprised to find that I was near tears.

Henry regarded me solemnly and then said, "I don't think I've put nearly enough opium in."

121

"Not by half." I gulped down more of the coffee drink and then looked up at him from under my lashes. I tried to give him my best wheedling smile in spite of the tears. "I don't suppose you'd be willing to talk to Ona for me? Try and get her to see reason."

Henry shook his head. "Am I wearing a name tag that says 'Hello, my name is Sisyphus'? I am going to stay out of the middle of this. And you should, too."

"Except I was born there," I said morosely. "The middle is my damn birthright." I polished off my drink and stood up to throw away my empty cup. We looked at each other across the counter, eye to eye, exactly the same height.

He said, "Unfortunately, I have very little influence in this matter. I was seen consorting with the enemy at the hospital." I watched him turning his demitasse cup around and around, his movements measured and precise. He had square hands with long, blunt-tipped fingers, and he kept his nails cut very close. His hands were a little too large for his wiry frame. At last he said, "Come on. I'm having a slow day, so I'll help you pick out the head. It's about all I can do."

He left the demitasse cup on the counter. On the door, he had one of those reversible signs with a paper clock on it. He flipped it around so that the "closed" side was showing, and set the hands of the clock to show when he would return.

We walked back down the cobblestones, past Bernese's store to the museum, waving at Bernese through the window as we passed. I could see the top of Mama's head over by the play table.

The young couple was just coming out of the museum. The little girl's flower-bud mouth was trembling, and her eyes were rimmed in pink. The mother was pale, and the father glanced at me and then quickly away, his mouth drawn and angry. He put his arm around his wife, herding her sideways to give Henry and me a wide berth as they walked toward the parking lot.

"I tried to warn them," I said, shaking my head.

Henry laughed. He had a great laugh, throaty and low. He'd gotten it from his mama, along with the faint edges of his Cajun slur. "Got your key?"

I nodded, and we went up the stairs. A sign on the front door said WELCOME TO THE DOLLHOUSE AND BUTTERFLY MUSEUM. It listed the hours and instructed visitors to buy tickets at the Doll-house Store next door. I unlocked it and we went inside, locking up behind us.

A staircase led up to a landing overlooking the entryway. It was roped off, and the upstairs entry was bolted from the inside when Mama and Genny weren't there working. "We need to go around to the back stairs," I said.

On one side of the staircase, a sign that said BUTTERFLIES pointed patrons to a doorway on the left. On the other side, a DOLLS sign pointed right.

"Let's play tourist," said Henry. "Pick a path."

"Dolls," I said immediately.

"Then I'll go butterflies. Meet you at the back." He headed left. The downstairs rooms were built in a big circle, connected by wide arching doorways. Along Henry's path were all of Bernese's terrariums, filled with caterpillars and cocoons, and above each hung a plaque with information about the species and pinned adult specimens that Bernese had chloroformed and mounted herself. There were no live adults. When butterflies emerged, Bernese released them into the gardens on the square. The Baptist Ladies' Gardening Club kept butterfly-attracting flowers blooming in the square's beds all through spring and summer.

In the first room off the foyer, I heard Henry greeting Uncle Lou. Caterpillars are essentially eating machines that spend every moment changing food into frass, and Lou had the charming job of cleaning up after them.

I obediently followed the arrow on the DOLLS sign. It led me into a large open room that was devoted to my mother. Some of her earliest dolls were on display, including the remains of her first salt-dough doll. Most of the face had crumbled away, but the basic shape of the head and the red silk body were still intact. On the right-hand wall, mounted plaques told an abbreviated version of Mama's life story and explained Usher's syndrome. The plaques were interspersed with pictures of Mama and Genny at different ages, mostly working on dolls.

On the left wall, a single long frame housed the picture and every written page of the article that had appeared in *Life* magazine when my mother was in her early twenties. That was the article that had helped Bernese and Isaac land the contract with Cordova Toys. In the picture, my mother stood next to Genny, who looked shyly away, but my mother stared boldly into the camera, her gaze direct and level. Genny's hair was pinned up in a bun, but my mother's hung in a long, loose braid over one shoulder.

Mama was a few pounds thinner than Genny, in the face especially. Her cheekbones and jawline looked sharper, and I could see the Seminole in her. Her eyes were shaped like half-moons that had been tipped over to stand on their points. The shape of her eyes made it seem as if she was smiling, but her wide mouth remained closed and solemn. Beside her, Genny looked like a carbon copy, paler, prettier, and blurry around the edges.

The caption read "The dying eyes of the artist look into the camera, unafraid." Bernese wrote that crap, and they used it.

I hated this room. Nothing in it was actually about my mother. It was all about Bernese, a celebration of her chutzpah and marketing savvy. It was a shrine to exploitation, and the thing that got to me about it every time was that when I looked at the dolls themselves, I could see that my mother was better than this. She was too good an artist to need to use her blindness as a hook, but Bernese had done it anyway. I had always wondered what Bernese took away from Mama by marketing her this way, if she had undermined Mama's self-assurance or her belief that her vision, while it lasted, had had both clarity and distance.

I walked on into the next room. Here, the mounted plaques walked visitors through the process of casting porcelain, and some of my mother's original molds were on display. But the room was dominated by a huge glass case in the center. Inside were the originals of my mother's last series. The animal dolls. Cordova had scaled their versions down, but the originals were all about twenty inches tall, lions and mice alike.

They were posed on and around a miniature carousel, a work of art itself, hand-carved and -painted to look like the old wooden carousels my mother remembered from the carnivals of her childhood. If you put a dime in the slot beside the case, the horses would go up and down and it would spin and play a tinny, thin version of "The Carousel Waltz."

I paused to look at the animals. Bernese the literalist could never see it, but I knew the animal dolls had all been modeled on the people in my mother's life, people from Between. Mama had done herself as a brown bear, standing with Genny, a sweet-faced panda. Genny had dressed both of them in steel-gray silk. Trude was a duck, the Marchants were deer, and I could see Crabtrees in the thin-faced red foxes. One little fox girl stood by her pony, and from beneath her cherry-red skirts, brown bear paws peeped out, a quiet love letter from my mother to me.

Bernese was there. Mama had cast her as, of all things, a moth, her insect eyes bugged wide and long, fierce porcelain antennae coming out of the top of her head. Genny had made the moth a short, stiff body, too fat for flight, and bound it tightly in a dress of black bombazine. A gray cloak suggested the wings, and Mama had gotten around trying to sculpt and cast moth feet by putting her in buttoned boots. Lou sat on the horse beside her as a ginger-colored mousie. Isaac, a long-headed, elegant grasshopper, stood on Bernese's other side.

I had always questioned this choice of totem. Though Bernese loved moths and butterflies, she seemed far too carnivorous to be properly represented by an insect. But the moth, sitting stiffly on its carousel pony, was undeniably Bernese. And if Mama had still been sighted when Fisher was born, I was certain that her doll would have been a caterpillar. I could imagine that perfectly, a pale green caterpillar with a short, sturdy body and an earnest face.

"What animal would I be?" said Henry, reading my mind. He had not spent much time learning about the life cycle of butterflies; he'd come all the way around through the back room to meet up with me here.

"I don't know," I said. All the Crabtrees were foxes, but that didn't seem right for him. A lynx, maybe, dappled deep brown and gold.

We left the carousel and went into the large room at the back of the house. This was the place where the two halves of the museum collided. On the far wall, we would find a locked door with a STAFF ONLY sign. It opened onto the back stairs, and I had a key. But we couldn't see the door because of the huge blue velveteen box that practically filled the room from side to side and was only six inches lower than the ceiling. It was made out of a frame of PVC pipe, jointed and squared off, and thick velveteen drapes hung from the pipes all the way to the floor. It had a dense blue velveteen roof as well; it was probably safe to develop photos in there.

Facing us was a pipe-and-drape hallway that led back into the box. The entrance glowed faintly purple with black light. "Want to?" said Henry.

"Not even a little bit."

"Come on. I haven't been back there in years." As he smiled, I could see the wickedness that lived somewhere under his tailored clothes emerging, daring me, like a young man who wants to take a girl into the fun house at the county fair.

"It creeps me out."

He grinned at me. "One minute. You wimp. Come on. If we go, you can put off choosing a head." He grabbed my hand and tugged me along, toward the mouth of the pipe-and-drape tunnel. I allowed myself to be drawn in.

The tunnel doglegged almost immediately, so the opening and its friendly rectangle of sunlight disappeared. Glowing footprints on the floor and a string of tiny black-light bulbs strung along the wall led us to the entrance into the box. I'd seen Bernese's masterwork hundreds of times, but I found myself clutching Henry's hand tighter anyway.

At first glance, it seemed innocuous enough; a large display case held a fully decorated dollhouse surrounded on both sides by a miniature forest. It seemed perfectly ordinary except for the lighting. The black lights made the furniture gleam oddly, and the white portions of the papered walls and the sheets on the beds glowed with purple phosphorescence.

A family of cheap plastic dolls lived in this midnight world, mass-market reproductions of some of my mother's work. A mommy stood by the stove in the kitchen, the black lights emptying her smile and eyes of anything human. The daddy had fallen over, and he lay stiff and silent in the yard, his white golf sweater spotted with flecks of black like a Dalmatian's coat. Two identical boy dolls were sitting quietly on identical rocking horses in the third-floor playroom. A freckled baby lay in its crib, alone in the nursery on the second floor. And in the living room, a spotty little girl with my face sat stiff and wary on a rocking chair.

As our eyes adjusted, we began to sense an undulating movement within the house, within the woods surrounding it. Something shifted, caught at the corner of my eye, and I saw one of them in the nursery, pale green and glowing sickly in the light. It pulled itself along the back edge of the baby's crib. Then I saw another, rearing up to bump its black-tipped head twice against the little girl's shoes. Its sticky leg-buds attached to her calf and it began to climb her, half disappearing as it went questing under her skirts.

Once I had seen those two, they began appearing all over, coming into focus as they moved. In the black lights, they bore no resemblance to the busy little bugs that Fisher loved. Here, their segmented bodies oozed through the woods and crept around the furniture, their black heads seeking a path. In the playroom, behind the silent boys, a long cocoon stretched from the ceiling to the floor, attached by webbing at both ends. Through the paper-thin casing, I could almost see the thing inside twitch and spin as it morphed.

The family glowed pale and still in their polka-dotted clothing, and the caterpillars crept all around them and over them, endlessly shitting. The furniture was spotted, too; Lou was behind on his cleaning. The scale, the size of the caterpillars as they skulked past these children and their vacant, grinning parents, made the whole scene monstrous. The worms lurked and loitered in the night landscape, eventually cocooning and then fighting their way free to mate and die in the glass box.

On the roof I could see three of the adult moths. One perched, unmoving, the pale eyespots on its yellow-green wings glowing fiercely like purpled eyes, its long hind-wing tails quivering. The other two were attached end to end, and as I watched, they flailed into motion and bounced together off the back of the house. I couldn't blame them. They were on a schedule. Luna moths emerge with no digestive systems, so they mate and die in a matter of days. Bernese did not release all the adult lunas. They'd lay their eggs inside paper bags Bernese had hidden behind the woods, and the caterpillars would come out and cocoon and morph, cycling endlessly in the constant nocturnal springtime she'd created for them.

"What a freak show," Henry said. I had almost forgotten he was there. As I stared into the box, he'd been reduced to a warmth and pressure on my hand, grounding me. I turned away from the dollhouse to look at him. The whites of his eyes and his teeth glowed iridescent. He was still staring at the luna moths' doll-house terrarium, fascinated. "Bernese really has no idea?"

"Nope," I said. "It seems obvious to her, like basic math. She enjoys raising moths and butterflies, she's built her life on dollhouses, so obviously, she ought to be able to put them together somehow."

Henry stared into the case for another moment and then shuddered and averted his eyes as well. "Maybe. But this is not the way."

"You know who else likes it? You won't believe this."

"Who?"

"Jonno," I said. "He loves this thing. Thinks it's 'kicky.'"

Henry let go of my hand, squinting at me from behind his glasses. "Kicky?"

"That's what he says."

"Okay," said Henry. "I guess I can see that about him." Then he was silent, looking at me too long, too intensely.

"What?" I said.

"Are you going to go through with it?" he asked. "Divorce him?"

"Yes," I said. "Why does everyone keep asking me that? I have a lawyer. I have a court date. Even Jonno acts like this is some silly whim I'm going to get tired of sooner or later."

"It doesn't seem believable that you could get a divorce and be done with Jonno. Not that one naturally follows the other, but that's the idea of the divorce, isn't it? To be done with him."

"Why is my divorce so fictional? Yours was real enough."

"Not to me," he said. "I didn't believe in it until months after it was over."

We carefully held each other's gaze so as not to look back at the dollhouse. One of the moths fanned or flew, a slight flutter of movement in my peripheral vision. I kept my eyes on Henry. "I believe in it," I said.

His teeth flashed in the black lights. "You never met her, did you," he said.

"Your wife?" I shook my head. I'd seen her once, though, when she and Henry had visited Between briefly to settle some business of his mother's. She was exceptionally pretty, with yards of black hair that fell in perfect rumpled waves down her back. But she also had something beyond beauty. Charisma, maybe, or an excess of style. She moved as if she were covered in tiny, invisible bells and her walk was designed to make them trill. Seeing her made me interested in knowing him better, because I was being tugged along in the wake of something equally charismatic. Henry knew what it was like, this thing with Jonno and me.

Now I said to him, "I'm sick of not being believed. The only person who believes me is Bernese, and she's probably pretending so she can lecture me about the sanctity of marriage. But I'm deadly, earnestly, seriously done with him."

Henry tilted his head to one side, as if weighing my words. His eyelids lowered; he was looking at my mouth. "Your lip looks swollen."

"Oh, right. Fisher banged into me." I touched my upper lip, then let my hand drop. Henry was still looking at my mouth. He seemed oddly still, and in that moment I became aware that there was something between us. It was like a tiny green thing pushing its head up through rocky soil, so pale with newness that I had not noticed it before.

Before I could examine it, he took one step in to me and put his mouth over mine. It wasn't a friendly kiss or a social kiss. It was too long for that. But it was so static that it seemed uncomplicated, like a cool drink of water meant to clear the taste of Jonno from my mouth.

Then it changed. It was only his mouth fitting itself against mine, but he eased in closer. Our bodies weren't touching, and our hands were at our sides, but I could feel heat radiating off his skin, and I became aware of his body almost at the cellular level, feeling its differences.

He was much broader than me at the shoulder, a little narrower at the hip. He smelled of coffee, clean linen, and clean paper, and something under that, a warm and living smell that had the tang of copper in it. It was the smell of some lithe predator, toothy and dangerous. Then he moved even closer, his body meeting mine as he kissed me, hip to hip, breast to chest, his head turned left to my right, his mouth opening and opening mine.

He was kissing me like no one had kissed me but Jonno for over ten years. But it was not like Jonno, nothing like Jonno. Jonno was a wall I leaned against, a wall with a hundred hands, each hand studied and sure, doing its assigned job with expediency. That was Jonno, and this wasn't him. This was Henry, wiry and sleek, with one hand resting lightly on my hip and the other reaching up to twine into my hair, tilting back my head. The hand at my hip snaked around my waist, bending me in to him.

It seemed to me I teetered on the brink of sinking back into something, the arch of my foot a fulcrum, no familiar ground under my heels. My eyes were closing, but I saw it again, that tiny shift, the flutter of wings to the side of me. I put my hands on his shoulders and shoved at him. He released me, and cold air leaped into the space that opened between us, touching my skin with chill. I jerked away from that coldness and overbalanced. I took one giant step backwards and immediately thought, absurdly, "Mother, may I?"

We stared at each other in the purple light.

As soon as I had breath back in me, I wanted to ask him, casually, lightly, "What the heck was that?" Standing by the terrarium, he seemed himself, unchanged, and I wanted in that single breath to match his mood. But when I opened my mouth, what popped out was "For fuck's sake, Henry. I'm married."

We faced each other, breathing hard and in unison. After a moment Henry straightened his immaculate collar and lifted one shoulder, trying for levity. "So, you see, 'Are you done with Jonno?' is a valid question," he said.

I didn't smile back. I stared at him big-eyed, shocked with myself, my hand coming up again to touch my sore lip. I traced the ghost of his presence against my mouth.

Henry said, "Maybe I should . . ." But he trailed off, and I didn't have a way to finish his sentence for him. I shook my head helplessly. At last he said, "My mistake," and he backed away from me and then turned, walking down the corridor of pipe and drape. He came to the corner and disappeared around it, heading toward the square of sunshine that would lead him back into the outside world.

CHAPTER

10

WHEN I GOT back to the store with everyone's supper, it was almost six, and Bernese was closing up. She told me Mama had gone to lie down in one of the bedrooms in the rental property upstairs. Fisher and Lou had gone home, so I passed Bernese the bag with their dinners in it.

"I got Fisher a kid-chick plate," I said.

"You better eat it." She dug out the top box, sniff-tested it for chicken nuggets, then set it down on the counter. "Fisher's got to have a boiled egg and carrot sticks tonight, with a fat-free yogurt."

"This is verging on mentally ill, Bernese," I said, but she waved me off, saying, "Get that food up to your mama while it's hot. Lock up tight behind you when you go."

I went back through the office and up the stairs. I set Mama's dinner down on the table in the square kitchen. As I came into the front bedroom, Mama was slowly pushing herself up into a sitting position. I drew my heart on her shoulder and sat down beside her on the bed.

Dinner smells good, she signed.

It's a lucky day for specials. Trude's meatloaf. Want to eat here or go home?

Here. So hungry, and that meatloaf is always good. I dreamed about those dogs. Did you talk to Ona Crabtree? Is she having them put down?

No. She is going to have her cousin drive over from Louisiana and get them.

When?

I'm not sure.

But you are sure she is doing it?

Pretty sure. I let my impatience stiffen my hands as I signed, *I am working on it.*

Mama started to get up, then sat back down on the bed. *I better have one of those pills with supper.*

Your back is bothering you?

A little. And I bruised my hip, falling. Did you pick out a head?

Yes. I had actually taken down three or four boxes at random, unwrapped each head, and then one by one put them back. Each one seemed impossible for Mama to part with. Then I'd picked out three or four more. Lather, rinse, repeat. I'd finally pulled out the first head I had grabbed and shoved it into my purse without upwrapping it or looking at it again or thinking. I remembered her, though. She was a flapper girl, and my mother had given her marcelled hair, tinted black and glossy. Her hands and her delicate arched feet were slender and luminous, solid pieces of porcelain. The head itself was hollow, so that her skin and hair glowed translucent and fine.

Who did you pick?

I started to spell *Josephine* into her hands, but as I got to the H, she pushed my hand away.

Not Josephine, she signed.

I tapped at her leg, and she grudgingly put one hand over mine. *You asked me to pick—*

She pushed my hands away again. *Not Josephine.* Her mouth was set in a mutinous line. Her hand drew a forceful slash through the air, closing the subject. *I'm hungry. I need my pill.*

I gave up. I put one arm around her, careful of her injured shoulder, and helped her to her feet. I walked with her to the kitchen, letting her lean on me on her bad side. We walked to the table and I stayed beside her, supporting her until she found the chair back with her hand. She felt her way to the front of the chair and eased herself down into it. Her hands drifted lightly along the table's edge and then crept their way carefully up onto its surface, mapping the placement of her fork, the Styrofoam box with her supper in it, and her fountain drink. She felt along the top of the cup to see if I had already put the straw in, then picked it up and put her hand out for her pill.

I'd gotten her prescription filled for her, so I had the bottle of Percocet in my bag. I got her one, and when I put it into her hand, she swallowed it, then put her hand back out.

I put my hand in it and signed, *You only take one.*

She compressed her mouth and demanded the bottle.

You can only have one every four hours.

I can tell time, she signed, annoyed, her index finger making an audible thump as she tapped at her wrist. I handed over the bottle, and she stuffed it carelessly in her pocket.

I told her I was going downstairs, and she nodded her hand.

She didn't like to talk at meals because she couldn't easily chat and eat at the same time, and she hated it when her food got cold.

I went back down to the store to make sure Bernese had turned the front lights off. She'd left the Styrofoam box with the chicken nuggets sitting out on the counter, either for me to eat or as a message to butt out of her plan to have Fisher bloom into anorexia before she turned ten. Probably both. I hadn't gotten myself anything. Between choosing a head and trying not to think about Henry kissing me, I hadn't felt hungry. There it was again, Henry kissing me. I was doing an indescribably bad job of not thinking about it.

I wasn't sure how to take it. His comment afterward seemed to indicate he'd viewed it as some sort of litmus test, as if he'd licked the inside of my mouth so he could stand back and observe the chemical reaction: If my tongue turned blue, it would mean I'd tested positive for Jonno.

I wasn't sure why I had never thought of Henry as anything more than, well, Henry. I'd somehow neglected to be affected by his beauty or notice his interest. I'd been married, but I hadn't been dead. Maybe it was the Crabtree connection? But even if, by some miracle of previously untapped black-eyed and swarthy recessives, Henry was genetically a Crabtree, fourth cousins three times removed was such a distant link it didn't count.

Except for his last name, he was everything my family would want for me. Mama and Genny already adored him for his manners, his book smarts, and his common sense, even his devotion to laundry starch. I realized he actually had a lot more in common with the Fretts than with the Crabtrees. Hell, his bed probably had hospital corners. I felt my cheeks flushing at the thought of his bed.

I dunked the chicken nuggets in Trude's overly sweet barbecue sauce and tried to shelve Henry for now. The last thing I needed was another man when I wasn't at all sure I was shut of the first one. But then I realized that the actual last thing I needed was to lose Henry's friendship.

I threw away the rest of Fisher's rejected dinner and went upstairs to get Mama. I could tell she was feeling low. As if her bad mood weren't hint enough, her movements were languid, and she took the stairs one at a time, favoring her bruised hip. I offered to run home and get my Mustang and come back and drive her, but she insisted on walking.

We set out together, me in Genny's normal place beside her. She wanted to cut straight across the square. Usually, she stuck to the cobblestone walkway, but she was willing to trade a paved surface for a shorter walk. She leaned on me a bit more than usual across the springy grass, but her steps were sure, and she'd said she didn't need me to carry her large handbag. She had it slung over her uninjured shoulder.

We paused to rest at the crosswalk, then crossed Philbert and passed the Crabtrees' gas station. As we came even with the corner of the chain-link fence surrounding the parts yard, her pace slowed and she paused again.

I stopped as well. She let go of my elbow and took three long breaths, shifting her weight to her unbruised hip and leg. From behind a rusted-out Dodge, the two big male Dobies appeared. They came slinking down to where we were standing, regarding us with their blank and soulless eyes from the other side of the fence.

I turned to look at her as she signed, *I smell them. Are they barking?*

No, they seem very calm.

It was always only Genny.

Let's get you home. Can you keep going?

My mother gave her head a quick shake and then dug her left hand into her pocket. Into her other hand, I signed, *You can't have another pill for at least three more hours.*

My mother's eyebrows went up, and her mouth shaped itself into a concerned O of surprise. The hand in her pocket came out holding nothing but the cap to her Percocet bottle.

"Oh, good grief," I said out loud. I signed, *Did you take it out again at the apartment? Did you take another pill?*

She shook her hand in a firm no. *Go find the bottle. I'll wait here.*

I'm not leaving you here by these crazy dogs, I signed. She was so close to the fence that she could have reached out with one hand and touched it.

Those dogs never minded me for a minute. I won't be able to sleep without another pill. Go find them.

I tried to get her to come with me, but she drooped by the fence as if she had taken root there. I finally let go of her and backtracked across the street, my eyes scanning the ground. In the middle of the road, I saw one of the pills and picked it up. I saw another in the gutter. The bottle, open and empty, was lying a bit farther on, and near it I found a third pill, almost completely hidden in the thick zoysia.

Mama had apparently been leaking pills all along our walk, like an outsize Gretel with narcotics instead of bread crumbs. If I was willing to be Hansel, I could follow them all the way back, and tomorrow Bernese could cook me up in Mama's kiln.

I had found only a few of the pills, but I didn't want to leave my mother standing between those dogs and the street for a second longer. Mama was never careless with physical objects, and the fact that she had casually stuffed the bottle in her pocket to begin with should have alerted me to how off she was feeling. I'd found enough pills to get her through the night, and in the morning I could take on the exciting project of calling Dr. Crow and telling him I needed a refill on a controlled substance because my mother had sprinkled the first batch into the long grass. He would probably say, "I see! And I suppose the check is in the mail? And your little brother ate your homework?"

I looked over and saw my mother still standing in the same spot, her weight on her good leg. I hurried back and drew my heart on her arm, then stood beside her so she could get out her cane again and grasp my elbow.

We picked our careful way home, and I made a mental note to drive her to and from the square until she was back up to snuff. Once through the front door, my mother dropped her keys into the blue bowl and plopped her handbag down beside it. She pulled in a long breath through her nose, catching the scent of home, and then released it in a long, satisfied sigh. Her spine straightened, her chin came up, and all at once she bloomed into her vivid self, her presence palpably filling the room.

Can you call and check on Genny? I think I'll make orange pound cake, she signed. She headed briskly toward her kitchen, one hand trailing along the wall. I followed her, passing through the dining room. As soon as she reached the kitchen counter, I tapped at her shoulder. I suggested that since we had spent the last twenty minutes creeping home like wounded mice, it might be better if she went to bed.

But you didn't get me any dessert. Go call about Genny and quit worrying.

There was no stopping her, so I picked up the kitchen phone and called Loganville General. The charge nurse said Genny was doing fine, and that Dr. Crow had come by earlier to check on her. I didn't get to talk to Genny, who was asleep again.

I sat at the kitchen table and succumbed to the pleasure of watching my mother baking in her own house. She got four sticks of butter out of the fridge and chose her midsize mixing bowl. She unwrapped the butter sticks and dropped them in, then set the bowl in her microwave. She ran her fingers lightly along the Braille buttons, programmed it to run for a minute on a low setting, and hit start.

I loved watching the surety of her movements as she rambled about, sifting flour and salt together and humming. She often hummed when she was home with no one but family. She said the vibrations in her chest felt good. High-pitched, coming in tiny random spurts, her humming was a noise that might startle a stranger, but it gave me a feeling of peace because it meant my mother was home and happy and at ease in the middle of her world.

She'd made this cake for me every year, for my birthday. One of my first memories was of her making it when she was still sighted. She missed only one year, the year I turned eight. That was the year she stopped working in porcelain. Her vision was failing, and she left Genny and me for seven months to stay at the Helen Keller National Center in New York and learn how to live blind.

I hadn't wanted her to go, and Genny had been in a state of nervous prostration. We'd both wept and clung and fussed and

141

tried to keep her, but she left us anyway. She said to me, *I can leave you now for half a year, and come back knowing how to be your mama, or I can stay here and never know, and very soon you'll have to be mine.*

She poured the batter and put the Bundt pan in the oven, wincing as she bent. She stood up and leaned on the counter, finished, so I gave her the update on Genny, and she nodded her hand, satisfied.

Then she added, *This week I am going to start a new piece. I've had it in my head, but I wasn't sure what I was trying to say. It came clear while I was mixing. It's going to be called* The Bones of Dogs, *and I will make it in many pieces, very smooth, very long, each one knobbed on the end. I'll fire them separately, and each piece will be so smooth it will be like butter, firm and cool. After they are fired, I'll take a hammer, and I'll hit some of them in places. Not exactly in half, although some will go in half. Some will need the ends smashed off into powder, and some will be in three or four pieces. They'll have to be fitted together in a way that feels right to me, I think upward, leaning against each other like the spines of a tepee. So to feel it properly, you start at the base and follow the long pieces up with your hands, and it will be very smooth and beautiful, inviting you higher, but then it will become sharp, jagged, and that will happen mostly where the pieces intersect. Although some shorter pieces won't make it up to the main intersection. They will lean on taller ones. It is going to be a very angry piece. You'll like it.*

I knew better than to try and talk her out of working until her shoulder had more time to heal. When Mama was ready to sculpt, you couldn't stop her if you tied her to the bed. *It sounds wonderful,* I said. *But you are going to wear yourself out. Why won't you go to bed? I'll get your cake out for you when it's done.*

Because I want cake now, she said.

Why are you so cussed and strong-willed? For "cussed," I used one of our home signs, shaping the letter B beside my right temple and then shooting it forward, fisting my hand with my index finger extended. A more perfect and literal interpretation was probably "Bernese-ish."

Because my mama taught me I had to be, she said. Her eyebrows knit together, and she tapped at my wrist three times with her index finger. After another pause, she added, *So did your mama. Why aren't you?*

I am, I signed, and she chuckled at my irritation.

I know you are worried about what those Crabtrees might do. And Bernese is giving you a hard time. But I hope you won't use these things as excuses and miss your court date on Friday. You need to get your divorce. Then maybe you can go after the things you really want. Or will you find some other bad thing to pin you down and keep you busy so you can't?

You're making me angry, I signed. *You say that like I know what I want.*

You know. And I know what I want, too.

What do you want?

I want to make glaze for this cake. It smells beautiful. She gave my wrist a final tap, and I told her rather huffily that I was going to bed.

Without cake? she asked, raising her eyebrows, mock-innocent.

I signed a terse good night and stomped upstairs, hard enough so she could feel the force of my footsteps through the floor. But the reverberations I felt came from her almost silent laughter following me up the stairs.

CHAPTER

11

MY EYES SPRANG open. I was breathing hard in the darkness, with the echoes of an unidentified noise dying in my ears. The digital alarm clock by my bed said 3:26. I lay in the dim light coming through the slats in the blinds, but the noise that had woken me up was not repeated. It took me a moment to orient.

A damp ridge of heat was pressed into the small of my back. I half sat to look. Fisher. She was sleeping in a curl with her arms up tight against her chest, and she had pressed her bowed spine into mine. Her bangs stuck up in two sweaty tufts.

I shifted, turning onto my side to face her and propping my head up on one arm, my elbow grinding a hole into the ancient feather pillow.

She was such a pretty thing, asleep. Her lashes were thick and dark on her faintly pinked cheek, and her mouth, relaxed, retained the rosebud pout of a baby's. I leaned down close to smell her hair: Johnson's baby shampoo, and under that, the cut-grass angry scent that was Fisher. I leaned farther and dropped a kiss beside her mouth. She had one hand stuffed under her cheek, and her breath was as sweet as a cow's. Apparently, her temper with me had shifted up a generation and sideways to Bernese.

Whenever Fisher got mad at Bernese, she went night-walking. Sometimes she'd move down the hall to Bernese's guest bedroom, sometimes to the sofa in the den. If she was really angry, she'd break into Mama's house and sleep in her own toddler bed or climb in with one of us. Twice she had set off down Grace Street alone in the dead of night, all the way to the Dollhouse Store. She had let herself in with the spare key and gone to sleep upstairs in Bernese's rental property.

Bernese would have a duck when she woke up and found Fisher had gone on another night walk. I was debating whether I should try to move her back to her own bed or simply go next door and leave a note for Bernese when I heard it again, the mystery thunk that had woken me up. It was coming from outside. I slipped out of bed and went to the window, which faced front. I could see a pickup truck I didn't know parked across from Bernese's house. It was facing away from the dead end; someone was planning a quick getaway.

Uncle Lou's car was under the carport, and Bernese's was pulled up behind his in the gravel drive. As my eyes adjusted to the moonlight, I saw the slight figure of a man or a boy slipping between Lou's car and Bernese's, bent low. I narrowed my eyes. The moonlight was too dim to show me his face, but I could see he was built long and scrawny. I put my money on Ona's youngest boy, Tucker Crabtree.

I was wearing nothing except my Braves T-shirt, so I picked up my folded jeans off the ottoman and pulled them on. I jammed my feet into my Adidas sneakers without bothering with socks. I walked quietly out of my room and crept down the stairs to the front door. I slipped out into the night and padded silently across the lawn to Bernese's gravel driveway.

The boy was on the other side of Bernese's car now. He was still bent over, creeping, so I couldn't see him. On the side of the car closest to me, I could see that both of Bernese's tires had been slashed. Not just punctured but cut open in long slices, so that the side of each tire was now three or four connected ribbons. I glanced over at Lou's car and saw that his tires had been decimated as well. I could hear the hiss of air as a knife plunged into one of the tires on the other side.

"Tucker, you moron, is that you?" I whispered.

The boy straightened, looming up across the hood from me. I found myself staring into the face of a stranger, a skinny kid with greasy brown locks and dreadful acne. His mouth was hanging open.

"Shit!" he said, and I said it, too, at exactly the same time. We stared at each other, and even though he had the knife, I was uncertain who was more frightened.

He hissed, "Come on, come on, come on, let's go!" and started sprinting for the pickup.

"Hey!" I said, but he didn't stop.

Like an echo, another female voice said, "Hey!" in tones as softly outraged as my own. "You better not leave me!"

The kid's accomplice was sitting on the ground, on the other side of the car. As the boy scrambled into the truck's cab and slammed the door, she lumbered to her feet. She was a mountain of a woman, pale, gelatinous; her upper arms, as big as thighs, wobbled and trembled in the moonlight. Her head was bent so I couldn't see her whole face, only a splash of smeared lipstick around her mouth.

"That dumb-ass," she muttered, and I recognized the voice. It was Lori-Anne, Fisher's mother. She weaved forward once and then back. The truck started and went zooming away with the lights still off. "I think I'm going to puke."

I said, "Lori-Anne? Are you crazy?"

"Shut up, Nonny. You snot." She had both her hands braced on the car, holding herself upright. I hadn't seen her since January, when she'd driven by to drop off a stuffed bear in a Target bag for Fisher's birthday. She'd left her car parked at the curb with the engine running, and a strange man had been sitting in the passenger seat. Bernese had not asked her to stay. She had gained another twenty or thirty pounds since then, and her face was so puffy that I wasn't sure she could get her eyes completely open.

"Lori-Anne, you know better! You cannot go crashing around out here, drunk, slashing tires. Your mama keeps guns. Do you think she'll pause to see who it is that's messing with her car before she opens fire?"

Lori-Anne bent double and disappeared behind the car again, and I heard the unmistakable sound of someone gagging up a solid quart of liquor. The smell of soured peach schnapps followed in a wave, and I took a step back. A few moments later, Lori-Anne reappeared.

"You caught me," she said. A string of glossy saliva was hanging down from her lip. Lori-Anne had big eyes, Billy Joel eyes; she always looked sad to me even when she was smiling. Now streaks of smeared mascara accentuated their natural down-tilt, and she was so pale that she practically glowed green in the moonlight. Her hair was matted and frizzed into a high crest that had gone flat on one side.

"What were you thinking?" I asked.

She waved one hand, dismissing me, and then stomped ponderously out from behind the car, crunching her way down the gravel drive toward the street. She muttered something about "damn nosy bitches" as she lurched past me in her high-heeled boots. I followed her.

"You better come over to Mama and Genny's place and sleep a little. Or I can drive you home."

She flapped that hand at me again and kept walking. At the end of the drive, she headed up Grace Street. I followed her.

"What are you going to do? Stagger all the way back to Loganville?"

She looked sideways at me and then briefly stuck out her thumb in hitchhiker position and jerked it back and forth.

"That's a great idea, hitchhiking, if you want to get raped and killed."

"Shut up. Run go wake my mother up and tattle on me."

"Lori-Anne, who was that boy?"

She shrugged. "Just some good ol' boy I hooked up with at this bar. I went out and got to drinking. I was feeling lowly, and I was telling him about Mama and what all, and he said he knew a way to fix her. It seemed like a good idea at the time." She finally stopped walking, and we stood in the middle of the road, staring each other down.

Of all Bernese's children, Lori-Anne was the one who looked the most like her. The boys all favored Lou, built slope-shouldered and hippy, just as ginger-haired and diffident as he was. They were spread out all over Georgia, busy leading what Bernese called "productive lives." By which she meant they were married and working and spawning great herds of ginger-haired, diffident children. But Lori-Anne was female, tall for a Frett, and as black-haired and ornery as her mother.

Her full lower lip began quivering. "Are you going to tell Mama on me?"

"Oh, good God," I said. "You're twenty-one years old. I think it's illegal for you to even think that, much less say it."

"I don't feel good," she said.

"What on earth possessed you?"

She was weaving on her feet again, faintly. "I don't know. I see Mama and I get crazy in my head and then I do stuff. It's like she makes me do stuff. Please don't tell her I was here."

"When are you going to grow up?" I asked. "You can't keep acting like a stupid kid. You have a daughter."

We were almost to the Crabtrees' parts yard, and she let out an abrupt bray of a laugh. "Naw. I do not."

"Yes, you do," I said. "You have a child, and you should probably know that your mother isn't doing a great job raising her right now."

Lori-Anne sat down suddenly and settled onto the curb. "She's not mine. I guess Mama didn't tell you?"

"Tell me what," I said.

"Mama termintated my rights," she slurred, and her smeary raccoon eyes filled up with tears.

"Terminated your— What do you mean? Your parental rights?"

Lori-Anne nodded. "Fisher belongs to Mama now, and I got nothing. That slick lawyer of hers, that Isaac, he sat me down and talked nine kinds of shit in my face, like, 'Blah, blah, if you can't take responsibility, at least be responsible enough to admit it.' Then he made me sign this long thing, and I had to go to a court and admit I'd signed it, so now I don't have any say in what happens to Fisher. She isn't mine anymore. So don't you tell me what I have and don't have. I don't have nothin'."

"Oh, Lori-Anne," I said helplessly. "When did this happen?"

"Couple weeks ago."

I sat down beside her on the curb. "I told you when you were pregnant, Jonno and I would have taken her. In a heartbeat. I still would."

Lori-Anne shook her head. "You know Mama wouldn't let that happen. She has Fisher squelched down under her thumb so's I almost feel sorry for the little shit. I lived there my whole life, and she's never going to get out from under that. She's as fucked as me, just too dumb and little to know yet. There wasn't nothing I could do, and then Mama screwed me, Nonny. I gave her my kid, and what did I get? Shit-all, that's what. And she won't help me get my bypass. Mama and her lawyer set up this trust for me, but I can't get at it. It's my money, she said it would be my money, and I signed his stupid papers. But it comes trickling out in bits, and even the bits go right on past me to pay my apartment and phone and shit. I can't touch a lick of it, even when it's going past. Only Isaac Davids can get at it, even though it's mine. Mama said no gastric bypass, so he said no bypass, and if I don't get this bypass, I am going to kill myself. You tell her that."

It was hard to make out what she was saying through the tears and slurring, but one thing was clear. She'd sold Fisher to Bernese, and it sounded like the only regret she had was that she hadn't gotten enough money out of it. I stood up and started walking back up the street, afraid that if I stayed beside her, I would start beating her about the head and shoulders.

I stopped a few feet away from her and didn't look at her at all as I asked, "Does Fisher know?"

Lori-Anne didn't answer me. But of course Fisher didn't know. I would have seen it in her. Fisher took her first bottle lying in my arms, and she learned to say her prayers with me. She whispered her birthday-candle wishes to me and showed me her hiding spots. She brought me every cut and scrape for kissing, circling the spot with a marker to show me the place if it healed before I came. I knew Fisher through and through, and deep in her tough little body, she held a secret longing for her mama. She wanted a mama who swung her up high and called her a dumpling, and these baby hopes were hopelessly pinned on poor Lori-Anne. If Fisher knew, it would break her.

I started walking again.

"Nonny, don't you tell my mother it was me slashed her tires," Lori-Anne called after me.

I hesitated. Part of me wanted nothing more than to go wake Bernese up this moment and drag her in her nightgown and her curlers down to see her shipwrecked daughter on the curb, but I couldn't. Bernese would lay into Lori-Anne, and that would be satisfying, but tomorrow, when Lori-Anne was back in Loganville, there wouldn't be anyone to take the blame but Fisher. I saw all too clearly the way things were working in Bernese's thick head in the aftermath of the sale: Lori-Anne had gained weight, but it was Fisher who was being starved for it.

"I won't tell her, Lori-Anne. Just get out of here, okay?"

"Thank you, Nonny," Lori-Anne said. "You swear?"

"I swear. But don't thank me. Just go."

I trailed up the street toward home. I didn't look back.

Fisher slept with her nose thrust deep into my pillow. I sat beside her and stroked her hair lightly, so as not to wake her.

She had wound herself up in my blanket, and as I touched her, she stirred and turned, unfolding. Her compact body retained some of the swaybacked shape of toddlerhood. She was all belly, with a short, sturdy back and narrow hips. One of her feet was sticking out. She had the Frett feet, so wide that her toes looked slightly splayed. She used to have fat pork chops on the ends of her legs, hopeless things, obviously not made for anything more than being waved around, possibly gummed. But somehow they had changed their basic nature and realigned themselves into perfectly good working feet, without me noticing. And now the process was complete.

CHAPTER

12

THE NEXT TIME I woke up, I could hear Mama and
Fisher rattling around in the kitchen, and my cell phone
was buzzing like an angry wasp against the leather of my purse. I
got up and answered it.

"Is Fisher over there?" Bernese barked before I was halfway
through "hello."

"She's here," I said, rubbing at my face.

"Get her butt home." Bernese hung up.

So she'd seen the tires already, and Fisher would get royally
chewed out for taking a night walk. But the lion's share of the
blame, I knew, would land flat-smack on the Crabtrees, and there
wasn't anything I could do to shift her mind. She would never
buy that this was random vandalism. The only way she'd absolve
the Crabtrees would be if I served up Lori-Anne on a platter. I
wouldn't mind, except right now the Lori-Anne platter came with
a side of Fisher, and Fisher was in enough trouble.

I threw myself into some clothes and headed downstairs.

Mama was washing her breakfast dishes, and Fisher was still eating her cereal. Mama was already dressed, her hair in a loose braid over one shoulder. With Genny still in the hospital, Mama didn't have anyone to do her face. I realized how much the powder softened her strong features and the cheerful lipsticks Genny favored drew the focus away from her cheekbones, still fine and high.

When I asked Mama if she wanted a pain pill, she shook her hand in breezy negation, the movement brisk and sure. *They make my brain tired. I took a lot of Motrin,* she signed. *I want to go see Genny soon. Will they release her today?*

I didn't know, so I called the hospital. Genny was awake and eating breakfast. I assured her that Mama and I would be by to see her as soon as we could get away. She was nerved up, but she swore to me she wasn't picking.

While I was talking, Fisher brought her bowl to the sink for Mama to wash. She was already dressed in a bright yellow shorts set and sandals, so as soon as Mama put the clean bowl in the drainer, we were ready to go.

The three of us went trooping across the lawn to Bernese's house. As we passed, I glanced at her car with its three shredded tires. They looked even less salvageable in the butter-cool light of early morning.

As we came in the front door, Bernese slowly came down the stairs to meet us, stomping as if the stairs were covered in tiny Crabtrees she was smashing in effigy. We stopped in the foyer, and I could see Fisher's face beginning to set in mutinous lines. Her bottom lip poked out. Her eyes narrowed, and her spine stiffened as if she were bracing herself. I bent down to rub her back and whispered to her, "It's not you, baby. You need to stop with the night-walking. You know that. But Grandma is mad about something else today."

Mama folded her cane and put it in her bag, then reached for me, and I gave her my hands so I could interpret for her. Bernese stopped on the second step from the bottom, where she was tall enough to look down on all three of us. Her eyes blazed hot and bright, and I almost expected her to say, "I am Oz! The great and terrible!" I was startled to see her glaring gaze come to rest on Fisher. It was Fisher after all.

"Go upstairs and get your piggy bank," Bernese said. Fisher stood solidly beside me, clutching the leg of my jeans, and then wrenched away from me and ran up the stairs, flattening herself to avoid touching Bernese as she slid past.

As soon as Fisher was gone, I said, "Good grief! She was right next door with me and Mama."

Bernese abandoned her post on the stairs and headed down the hall toward the kitchen. She threw a terse "Follow me" over her shoulder. Mama and I trailed after her, puzzled.

A full laundry basket was sitting on the kitchen table. Bernese rummaged around in it and pulled out a pair of Fisher's Cinderella panties. She held them up, stretched between her hands so I could see the picture of the pumpkin-turned-carriage, and then she dramatically flipped them around, showing me the seat.

At the top, along the elastic waistband in Bernese's square hand, were the letters FFB, for Fisher Frett Baxter. The initials were written in black laundry marker. Under that were long, wavering black lines; the entire seat was covered in uneven stripes and crossbars. It took me a moment to realize the lines were forming huge kindergarten letters. I couldn't quite read them. I could make out an M or an N, and Fisher's familiar version of a

J, with the top line crossing through the vertical as if it were a lowercase T.

I looked at Bernese and shrugged, trying to describe the panties to Mama at the same time.

"It says, 'I'm a Jew.'" Bernese rummaged in the laundry basket and pulled out another pair, then another and another, flinging them down on the table so I could see the scrawly lines all over each of them. "She has written 'I'm a Jew' on the butt of every pair of underpants she owns. Every single pair. And she's used my Sharpie, which is strictly a forbidden pen, and she knows it. I could wash these underpants in pure bleach from here till Jesus comes, and they would still come out saying 'I'm a Jew.'"

Mama's mouth dropped open, and her hand fluttered, shaping a fast H to a fast A, laughing. I felt laughter bubbling up in me as well, but one look at Bernese's face, flushed a hectic red, told me laughing might get me shot. I squelched it, pressing my lips together, my cheeks pinking with the effort. I squeezed Mama's hand and then shook my hand no at her, signing, *Hush, she is going to have a stroke.*

"I don't think this is what you're really angry about, Bernese," I said when I felt I could safely speak.

Bernese's eyebrows lowered thunderously and she said, "It's not? What the hell else did Fisher do?"

I realized, horrified, that she had not seen her tires yet. My mouth opened, but nothing came out. At last I said, "Nothing. Nothing. She night-walked and slept over with us, but you know that."

Fisher was coming down the hallway, dragging each foot behind her in a funeral march. She was carrying a small, silver-plated pig with a slot in his back. He broke apart in the middle for easy access. I'd given him to her when she was two. Last year Fisher had covered him in scratch-and-sniff Hello Kitty stickers and then scratched and sniffed them relentlessly until they tore and fuzzed over and began to look like a skin disease.

She set the pig silently on the tabletop near Bernese and then stood staring down at her toes.

"Sit down and eat your breakfast," Bernese said. On a plate at Fisher's place was a small mound of cottage cheese, a turkey-bacon strip, and half a peach.

"I ate with Aunt Stacia," Fisher said.

Bernese turned her reddened eyes on Mama. "You *fed* her? I told you! What did you feed her?"

Mama spelled *Loop Fruit,* and I staunchly interpreted that for Bernese as "cereal."

"No! She's supposed to have protein in the morning. Protein! Not a bunch of carbs and sugar! You're going to turn her into a worthless chunk of fat like her mother!"

"Bernese!" I said, and Fisher stared up at her, stricken.

Bernese snatched up the piggy bank and said to Fisher, "We're buying you all new panties with your—" Then she stopped, puzzled, and stared at Fisher's leprous pig. She gave him a shake. Nothing. She popped him open and upended the two halves. Nothing came out. "Where is your money?"

Fisher shrugged, looking back down at her toes.

"You've been saving up your allowance for weeks for that game you wanted. Where is your money?"

Fisher would not meet her eyes. "I put it in the fountain."

Mama signed, *You better stop them,* but I wasn't sure how. Part of me believed Bernese would at any moment revert to her usual self, ruffling Fisher's hair and saying, "You'd best do better next time." Surely she could not be as angry as she seemed over some underpants and Fisher's habitual night walks.

"The fountain? The fountain in the center of the square? Why on earth?"

"For a wish," Fisher said.

"Maybe you should take a break, Bernese," I said, but it was as if I hadn't spoken.

"You put over fifteen dollars into the fountain? Even the bills?" Bernese's voice was pig-iron cold.

Fisher nodded again. "It was a big wish."

"What in God's green meadows did you wish for that costs fifteen dollars?"

"Okay. That's it. You really need to stop now," I said, but Bernese flapped one hand at me, simultaneously dismissing me and telling me to shut up. She never took her eyes off Fisher.

Fisher's shoulders curved inward in a protective hunch. Her voice was barely audible. "If I tell, it won't come true."

"If you don't tell, a big spanking is about to come true." Bernese's voice stayed low and dangerous, with none of her usual brash good cheer.

There was a breathless pause, and then Fisher's shoulders straightened again. Her pout flattened into a hard line, and she looked up. The amount of sheer animal will in the room thickened the air as their eyes met, but she was barely audible as she said, "I wished you would die. I wished you dead and for my real mommy to come and get me."

A long, hideous silence followed. Bernese was looking at Fisher as if she couldn't quite understand what she had heard, as if she couldn't quite believe it. Then her mouth crumpled in, her lips all but disappearing, and her eyes widened, the pupils dilating as if she were in physical pain. It was as if all the air had been kicked out of her. There was dead silence for another endless five seconds. She got her breath back, and I remembered what I had learned from Lori-Anne the night before. Bernese, wounded to the core, was about to tell Fisher. I could see it. She was about to tell Fisher that she'd been sold by her own mama. I could not allow it. I would kill Bernese before I let those words come out of her mouth and rip into my girl. I stepped forward, pulling Mama with me so that the two of us were standing like a wall between Bernese and Fisher.

"Don't say it," I yelled to Bernese. "Do not speak. Fisher, go upstairs and brush your teeth. Go. Go. Go now. Do you hear me? Now. Go." I kept yelling it, louder and louder to keep Bernese from speaking over me, and, almost violently, pouring it all out into Mama's hands. I yelled at Fisher to go until I heard her run for the stairs and then pound up them. Then I stood blocking the doorway and said to Bernese in a quieter tone, "You think a minute. You think a minute and take a deep breath. That's a baby up there. That's a five-year-old baby, and you will not unleash whatever's in you on her. You will not."

Good girl, Mama signed, and then again, *Good girl, good girl.*

When Fisher was all the way upstairs, Bernese drew in a shuddering breath, and then she said, "Excuse me," and tried to push past us, out of the kitchen.

"Let her alone," I said.

"I'm not going up to Fisher," she said. Her face looked gray, set in exhausted lines. "I need to go sit down."

I stepped aside, and she walked down the hall and into the den. Mama and I followed her. Bernese went to her plaid sofa and sat down, her back to the bay window. I put Mama's hand on the

159

back of the matching love seat across from Bernese, and Mama felt her way around it and sat. I sat beside her to interpret.

Mama signed, *What's gotten into you? You didn't used to be this way with Fisher. What has changed? You are damaging that child.*

Bernese was listening to me, but her eyes were on Mama, and it was as if I weren't in the room.

"She didn't used to have such a mouth," Bernese finally answered, but her heart wasn't in it.

She's just giving you your mouth back, Mama signed. I interpreted, but then I added, "And Bernese, she's growing up. You keep on like this, you're going to break her."

Bernese turned a baleful eye on me and said, "Why don't you use that great flapping hole in your face to interpret for my sister? No one has asked your opinion, Nonny. You don't get to judge me. You haven't been here. Half of Fisher's problem is she depends on you, and you've been too busy screwing up your life to notice how bad she's pining. She misses you like nuts, so she acts like a brat. And I get stuck with that."

"You are the one—"

I heard Lou loudly clearing his throat at the top of the stairs, and I fell instantly silent. Mama started to sign, but I interrupted her, signing, *Wait. Fisher is coming down.*

Behind Lou, Fisher took one stair at a time with her eyes downcast. She was practically dripping sorrow from every pore, her posture a sharp contrast to her cheerful yellow shorts set covered in orange slices and the bright green frog-shaped backpack she had slung over her shoulders.

Lou said, "Hon, I'm going to walk Miss Fisher here to the bus stop."

"Don't forget her lunch," said Bernese.

Lou trit-trotted to the kitchen and got Fisher's brown-bag lunch out of the refrigerator. Fisher waited in the foyer, not looking at any of us. He unzipped the frog backpack, slipping the lunch into it, and the added weight pulled the backpack down so it drooped from her shoulders like exhausted wings.

Everything in me wanted to go to her, pick her up, and squeeze her tight, but Fisher hated to be touched when she was unhappy. I knew if I tried it, she would go stiff in my arms, like a cat does when you pick it up against its will. With Fisher, I had to wait until she was ready, and then she would come to me.

As she went out the door, I could not help but call after her, "You have a good day at school, Woolly-Worm."

She darted her eyes at me, and I was rewarded with a faint upward twist of her lips. Then she was gone.

The second the door closed, I was ready to pick it up right where I had left off, but Mama felt my hands begin to move as I was readying to speak, and she shook her hand no, quieting me.

Let me, she signed. *Tell Bernese that I know it was a bluff. I know she never expected Lori-Anne to call her on it.*

I wasn't sure I knew what her point was, but that wasn't my job. The interpreter in me kicked in, and I spoke it to Bernese exactly as Mama had expressed it.

Bernese seemed to sag down even deeper into the sofa. "Of course it was a bluff. Lori-Anne wouldn't talk to me at all. She was eating and drinking herself to death, drugging, too, I bet you. All those men. Any man who'd have her. And then when she did finally come to talk to me, it was to ask for money. Again. I only said it as a wake-up call. I thought it might jolt her into seeing what she was doing. I never thought for a second she'd really trade all her chances to ever have Fisher for some money."

Don't you talk now, Mama signed to me. She must have felt the tension in my hands. *This is not your conversation.*

I shut my mouth, and Bernese went on. "I can't let it happen again, Stacia. I know I may seem hard on Fisher, but she and Lori-Anne are of a piece. Lori-Anne was that same kind of sullen, willful thing, and I never knew what she was thinking. My boys never gave me a lick of trouble. But Lori-Anne growled and stomped and fought me six ways from Sunday. And then when that didn't work, she nodded and said, 'Yes, Mama. No, Mama. Oh, I see, Mama,' and then she'd lie and sneak. She got into a thousand times more trouble than all three of the boys put together. Now, Lori-Anne is going to keep on till her heart bursts or she drives drunk off a road into a tree, and there isn't a thing I can do except make sure Fisher won't go that way."

Even if it ruins her? Mama asked.

Bernese wasn't listening. "Isaac understood Lori-Anne better than I did. He set up the trust to protect me and her both, while I stood there like God's biggest fool swearing to him up and down that he didn't need to write it up. I said we only needed a wad of paper with a lot of small print that looked legal so's I could wave it at her. I said it didn't matter because she wouldn't ever terminate her parental rights."

Fisher has to be protected from this fight.

"I haven't told her a thing about it!" Bernese protested.

Maybe not, but she can tell something has changed.

A little color came back into Bernese's stone-gray face, and she said, "Things *have* changed. She's my responsibility now, forever. Lori-Anne's never going to straighten up and be her mama, so it's all on me. I got three good sons just like their daddy, and then Lori-Anne happened, which I never planned for or expected.

That girl was born wayward. Got pregnant at fifteen like she wasn't raised right, and to this day she hasn't told me who Fisher's daddy is. Doubt she knows. And you three sit all comfy next door and say what I should and shouldn't do. Bunch of aunts, clucking and tutting like dern-fool chickens. But I can't be that way, not anymore. From here on, I'm all the mama Fisher's ever going to get. And I can't fail her."

I couldn't keep my mouth shut anymore. I said, "Don't act like we've abandoned you or stuck you with Fisher. You picked this before she was born. Lori-Anne wanted to give Fisher up from the get-go. You bullied her, even though me and Mama and Genny and Lori-Anne herself told you loud and clear that she wasn't ready to be a parent. And when you said you couldn't stand to farm your grandchild out to strangers, I told you Jonno and I would take her—"

Mama was frantically shaking her hand no even as Bernese interrupted me. "Yes, and if we had done it your way, Fisher'd be in the middle of your divorce."

"Okay. Let's make you killing Fisher's spirit about my divorce. Everything else is about my divorce, why not you abusing Fisher, too?"

You are exasperating me, signed Mama.

I didn't answer Mama. Interpreting was easier than trying to have a three-way conversation, and once I had started speaking for myself as well as Mama, it was all I could do to say what was needed and still keep Mama in the loop.

Bernese was talking again. "I'm not 'abusing' Fisher, and no matter how crazy she makes me, at least I'm not going to ditch her. She knows she's mine, no matter what."

"That's probably what's upsetting her," I said.

"At least I'm not going to toss her away like you're tossing your husband. I know what family means."

It was so hard to stay seated. I sorely missed Genny. Her nerves held us all hostage to decorum, and I missed her constant presence beside Mama, interpreting. Without her, I had to think in nine different directions while taking on Bernese, and I couldn't stand up and scream loud enough for Bernese to hear what I was saying. I stayed where I was, letting all my pent-up rage out through my hands as I savagely signed what Bernese was saying to me. My interpretation was baldly accurate but with none of my usual detachment.

I said to Bernese, "You sit here judging me, pointing at my speck, though how you can see it what with all the beams sticking out of your eyes is beyond me. And you don't seem to give two craps that maybe it sucks for *me* to be in the middle of my divorce, and that maybe my marriage failing is not entirely my fault."

You are letting her change the subject, Mama signed. *This is not about you, it's about Fisher.*

I signed, *Bernese needs to hear this,* then said, "Do you know you have never asked me once why I'm divorcing him? You just assumed it's some sort of childish whim of mine. Oh, ho-hum, what a drab spring, think I'll toss my marriage away."

This won't do any good, Mama signed.

Bernese said, "Because it doesn't matter why. We don't get divorced."

"It does matter why," I said, and even though Mama answered me by signing, *This is a diversion,* I signed back, *Hush, I am showing her.* Mama threw her hands up, then mimed washing them of me, but I went and got my purse anyway. I dug around in it until

I found the empty amber bottle I had carried with me for a year now. I set it on the coffee table with an audible click, and then I sat back down by Mama and gave her my hands again.

"What's that?" Bernese said.

"That's why I'm getting divorced," I said. I sounded very matter-of-fact, almost abrupt, but looking at it, this innocuous cylinder of brownish-gold plastic, safety-capped to protect the babies I didn't have, almost undid me.

The bottle had been full the night I ended my marriage. I was holding it in my hand when I heard Jonno's keys in the door. I stuffed it in my pocket as he walked in. It was three A.M. or so, and he was fresh off a standing gig X. Machina had at McGoo-Goo's on Thursdays.

I sprang up from the sofa where I had been grinding my teeth and weeping myself into a redheaded state where all control went out the window and there was nothing of the Frett family in me at all. I was a frothing mass of Crabtree rage. I ran at him and kicked savagely at his shins, making him dance backwards out the door. He tried to come in again, and I screamed at him word-lessly, holding my hands up in claws, ready to take his face off.

"Gig," he said. "What's wrong?" That made it worse. He called me his Gig, the one thing he'd always show up for, when things were good. If he didn't realize things weren't good, then I hadn't kicked him hard enough.

The apartment had built-in bookshelves right by the front door, and I grabbed a paperback and hurled it at him, pegging him dead center. He said, "Oof," and bent over a little, and the next book beaned him in the head.

"What, what the—" he said. I grabbed an armful of paper-backs off the shelf and followed him into the building hall, hurling them at him, driving him toward the stairs. He held his trumpet case up in front of him, trying to block my shots, and I aimed lower, pinging books off his knees and thighs.

"Quit it," he said, finally sounding a little angry. "What gives?"

I had one book left. I stuffed it under my arm and answered him by reaching in my pocket and pulling out the rattling bottle of penicillin. I didn't have to say anything else, because I could see he already knew, and that made it worse.

"Oh," he said. "Yeah." He dropped his gaze, his long golden-brown lashes brushing innocently against his cheekbones. "I've been meaning to talk to you. I mean, I wanted you to see a doctor. You needed to, and I was worried, but I wasn't sure yet how to put it. You know? Gig? How to put it?"

I snatched the last book out from under my arm and reared back with it, readying for a hard throw. He ghosted sideways around the corner. I heard him thumping down the steps and the bang of the building's front door. I didn't see him again for months. He called a couple of times, but I hung up on him before he could hit the O in "hello," so I suppose he lacked the courage to come around. And that was good. I had to wait six months for my second HIV test to come back negative before I could calm down enough to be able to think.

Waiting to take that test, I knew I was done with the marriage. After I got the results back, then I could see him, though I shocked myself by falling so immediately and with such relief into his bed. But even in the middle of that reunion, I knew. While I was unwrapping the oh-so-necessary condom, rolling it onto him, I knew that whether I loved him or not, there was no way back from that level of careless betrayal. The next day I got both of us out of bed and dressed by nine A.M., and I drove us downtown so we could meet with a lawyer.

Now, looking at the bottle, I didn't think I could say it all again, but Bernese was looking at me expectantly. "What's that supposed to mean, that bottle?"

"It means he cheated on me."

There was a long silence, and Bernese's gaze on me was speculative, as if she was sizing me up. She blew air out between her lips like a horse and rubbed one hand across her mouth. Finally, she said, "Grow up."

I leaned forward, certain I must have misheard her. "Excuse me?" I said. To Mama, I signed, *I think she just told me to grow up.*

Mama answered, *Sounds like her, yes.*

"I said, 'Grow up.'" Bernese's face was carved out of implacable wood.

"He cheated on me," I said.

"I got that," said Bernese. "So he cheated. It happens. It happens all the time. In almost every marriage, it's going to happen. You don't get divorced."

"Yes, you do," I said, and then my eyes widened in comprehension. I leaned forward even farther, and my voice softened. "Aunt Bernese? Are you saying . . . Do you mean that Uncle Lou—"

She interrupted me with a rude snort. "Lou? Please. I didn't mean it happened to me. Don't be an idiot. But it happens, I am sure, to other people all the time. That doesn't mean you let some whore win and take your husband. You drag him home and make his life a walking festival of hell until he wishes he'd cut off his own man parts before he let them go wandering."

Mama's hands felt stiff around mine as I interpreted, no doubt tense with the huge effort of not saying that she had told me so.

I said, "When you're married, there's a trust there. There's this vow. If you break that, if you let yourself get intimate, in whatever form, with another person—"

My voice cut out abruptly. Over Bernese's shoulder, through the gauzy sheers that covered the bay window, I could see Henry Crabtree advancing down Grace Street. He was too far away for me to read his face, but he was moving fast, with long, purposeful strides, and his shoulders were set forward and braced. His sinewy body, thin as a blade, was probably whistling as he sliced through the air.

"I've been married over forty years, Nonny. I have a notion of how it works." She didn't seem to notice my abrupt silence as anything more than a place where she could easily interrupt. "Did you even try to bring that dog to heel?"

"He doesn't love me," I said. As Henry came closer, I could see his jaw was set and rigid. I tried to keep my eyes on Bernese, because I couldn't imagine a worse time for the man I had kissed—in, by the way, strict violation of my still-standing marriage vows—to come storming up on some romantical mission.

"Don't be such a schoolgirl," said Bernese. "Love-schmove. This is your husband."

I shook my head. "I don't mean he's not *in* love with me. This isn't about romance." I glanced at the golden-brown bottle and then back up to her face, carefully not watching Henry's resolute progress toward the house.

Mama was signing again, *Forget this. You are supposed to be talking about Fisher.*

I signed back, *I'm going to talk about Fisher, but until I settle my divorce with her, she won't hear me on any other subject. She always drags it back to this.*

Mama subsided, unconvinced.

"Why do you keep looking at that bottle? What's that got to do with anything?" Bernese asked. She picked it up off the table and read the label. "Penicillin? What has penicillin got to—" The nurse in her kicked in then, and I saw her put it together in her head.

I said, "If he'd cheated, yeah, maybe there's a way back from that. But he didn't use a condom with her. With all the hers, for all I know, even though we'd stopped using them at home."

Bernese flared her nostrils like a bull and said, "Why were you using condoms in the first place?"

I said, "Because the pill makes me crazy, and we weren't ready to have a baby."

"And you stopped?"

I felt myself flushing, and when I spoke, my voice came out barely above a whisper. "Because I thought we were ready. I don't see a way back from going to your doctor's office and being told that no, actually, you don't have a urinary tract infection from all the sex you've been having, trying to conceive. You have syphilis."

It was hard to meet Bernese's eyes, but I forced myself. Over her shoulder, I could see Henry Crabtree drawing closer and closer. But then he turned abruptly, veering off to my left, and I realized he was heading for Mama's front door, not Bernese's. In four more long strides, he was out of sight.

I blew out a relieved breath and turned my full attention back to Bernese and signing for Mama. Of course he had no way to know I was over here. I would catch up with him later. Maybe he had been coming to say that the kiss was a mistake. To apologize.

169

To restore all our old ease. I needed that so badly right now, his friendship, but I didn't believe it. He had moved with the unwavering gait of Prince Charming preparing to broach the witch's tower.

Bernese, meanwhile, was suffering some sort of internal drama. Her cheeks had reddened, and she threw the pill bottle down. It skittered across the coffee table and dropped to the floor. "That rotten piece of stinking meat," she said. "And you didn't know a thing until you went to your gynecologist?"

"No," I said. It had been awful. Syphilis, of all things. Practically a dead disease. Jonno couldn't bring home some regulation rampant campus animal like the clap or crabs. It had to be some bizarre throwback of an illness, one my gynecologist hadn't seen in ages. "I wonder if we'll get a rash of it now," she'd said, considering me speculatively, and I had flushed at the implication.

Mama, who knew all this, patted my leg while Bernese regarded me with worried eyes. "Nonny, tell me you're sure that is all he gave you."

"I'm sure," I said. "I got tested. Twice."

Bernese nodded, relieved. Her gaze flattened back into anger, and she said, "I can't believe you're going to divorce him." I boggled at her until she added, "You need to track his sorry butt down and shoot him. Put him in the ground."

Henry reappeared and headed back up Grace. But then he pivoted and paused, staring speculatively toward Bernese's house. He started moving in our direction again, looming larger and larger in the bay window.

Bernese had launched into a long anti-Jonno diatribe, threatening all manner of biblical vengeance. I tried twice to break her flow, but she overrode me. I signed to Mama, *Bernese is on a tear, and Henry Crabtree is coming up to the house. I have to talk to him.*

Then you should go. Because this conversation is worthless.

Yes. Bernese is talking at me, but she isn't saying anything interesting, I signed. *I'll have to let her wind herself down. Do you want to go home, or stay here, or come with me to talk to Henry?*

Henry reached the bottom step of Bernese's wide front porch. He hesitated there. I could see his eyes burning with a bright blackness, as if he were trying to incinerate the front door with the intensity of his gaze.

Mama seemed to be thinking over her options, so I signed, *Bernese is going on about how Jonno should be taken out and hanged with a loop of his own intestines, and you were right. I shouldn't have let her divert me. Now it won't be about the divorce, it will be about why I don't kill him. It's all smoke, because she doesn't want to deal with what she's doing to Fisher.* I was signing to keep Mama abreast of the situation, but also so Bernese would think I was still interpreting and therefore probably listening to her.

Henry was standing completely still, his eyes on the door, and I tried to think of something softening to say to him. But honestly, considering everything that was going on with our families, the trouble between us was nothing. It was just a kiss. He was being ridiculous. I felt a stab of irritation. I didn't have the energy for romantic drama today.

At last Mama said, *I will stay here and have a lie-down on Bernese's sofa. My hip is bothering me. Let me rest, and then we can go to the hospital and check on Genny.*

I nodded my hand in hers and then stood up abruptly while Bernese was in mid-sentence. Henry, frozen on the porch, caught the movement through the sheers. He peered through the window and then came toward it, and our eyes met.

I understood immediately that whatever his mission was, it had zero to do with romance. He hadn't been standing immobile at the door because he was feeling at all uncertain. Henry Crabtree was angry. So angry he was practically vibrating. I saw his shoulders shudder, as if he were shaking a weight off his back. He pointed a savage finger at me and then jerked his whole hand back toward himself, telling me by gesture, "Get your ass outside."

CHAPTER

13

HENRY STOOD IN the driveway, staring at Bernese's tires. It had taken me a few minutes to extricate myself from the derailed conversation with Bernese and then get Mama settled on the sofa. In that time, Henry had become contained, if not calmer. He waved a hand at the tires. "Those are shredded."

"Yeah. It's a mercy Bernese hasn't seen them yet."

His head jerked up, and I watched some of the fury leach out of his black gaze.

"Henry, what's going on with you? What were you doing standing on the porch steps for so long?"

"I wasn't sure I could see Bernese yet without beating the living shit out of her," Henry said. I raised my eyebrows, puzzled, and he stared back at me. At last he said, "Come and see. Because you won't believe me if I tell you." He started stalking back up Grace Street.

"Henry?" I called after him.

"You have to see it," he said, pausing to wait for me.

I trotted to catch up. "I can't be gone long. I need to take Mama to the hospital soon. Genny's going to get nerved up if we aren't there when visiting hours start."

He nodded curtly, and we walked up the street side by side until we came up even with the fence that surrounded the Crabtree parts yard. The dogs didn't appear, and when I looked ahead, I saw that the chain was swinging loose and the gate was open.

I stopped, staring. "Holy crap! Are they out? Henry? Did someone let them out?"

Henry responded by grabbing my hand and pulling me on to the gate. We went inside. I hadn't been in the Crabtree parts yard in years. Not since I was a child. Even then I never spent a lot of time there. In the brief period when Ona had unsupervised visitation with me, I'd been told at home that on no account was I to play in the yard. Genny said it was a death trap filled with rusty sharp things that dripped tetanus. The refrigerators and chest freezers looked to her like suffocating coffins, even after Ona went out there with a hammer and broke every latch so that the doors gaped open obscenely on the uprights.

From what I remembered, it looked very much the same. Rusted-out bodies of cars and partial cars, heaps of old lawn mowers, fridges, gas stoves, and chunks of various engines lay in disarray. A narrow path wound through the mountains of gears and scrap metal and spark plugs. Henry led me toward the other side, near the back entrance to the gas station.

The two male dogs were there, lying together in a stiffening heap in front of a wall of used tires. Their eyes were open and glassy, and their mouths were ringed with white foam. All eight of their legs were stiff and curled, and their spines were bowed, making them look like they were in midleap, though they were lying on their sides. A large fly with a swollen bottle-green abdomen was marching across the closer dog's face. It walked straight out onto one of the open eyes. I flinched, but of course the dog did not.

"She was going to get rid of them," he said, almost to himself.

"Oh, no. Henry, has she called her brother or his boys? Are any of them coming?"

Henry shook his head. "I think I've talked her out of calling them in. So far."

I put my hand on his shoulder and said, "I know what you're thinking, but you're wrong. Bernese couldn't have done this."

"I know," he said. "I was so sure it was Bernese. I came down to see you so you could stop me from killing her. And then I decided to go straight to her house and kill her anyway. But then you told me she hadn't seen what they did to her tires yet."

"Wait," I said. "You thought she'd killed the dogs because of her tires? How did you know about her tires?"

"I saw Lou at the diner this morning. He was telling Trude about the tires. I thought he was hiding out because Bernese was in a rage, but I guess he just didn't want to be the one to tell her. Can't blame the man. I got home from breakfast and my phone was ringing. It was Ona calling and asking me to come down to the parts yard. She was a wreck."

I cursed under my breath. If Lou had moaned to Trude, then everyone knew. Everyone except Bernese. And finding out last would do nothing to soothe her when she finally did clue in.

The whole town, including Henry, must be assuming one of Ona's sons had slashed the tires. I was about to tell Henry about Lori-Anne's nocturnal visit, but he started talking before I could. "If she hasn't seen the tires . . . And Bernese isn't a poisoner. She

would have marched up here in broad daylight and shot them."
At last he met my eyes, genuinely baffled. "So who did this?"

"I don't know," I said.

Henry's shoulders were set and tense as he stared at me from
behind his glasses. "Ona cried. She's the toughest old bitch. But
she cried when she saw them. I never saw her cry before. When
she's drunk, she'll bray like a donkey over country songs, but her
eyes stay dry. It doesn't mean anything. This was different. She
was silent. She was trying to suck it up, but fat tears kept falling
out of her eyes. She wouldn't look at me."

I let my hand drop from his shoulder. "You love her," I said. It
came out wrong: I didn't sound surprised so much as accusatory.

His brows came down. "Of course I love her. What do you
think?" he said.

"How?" I said. He looked incredulous and angry, and I held up
one hand, rushing to speak before he could. "No, I meant it sin-
cerely. How? She wants me to love her. She's wanted it so badly
since I was little. But I was scared to death of her. Her house was
dark and filthy, and who knew what lived under the sofa. She sat
around in all this squalor watching me, so hungry. I thought she
would eat me. So, yeah, I am asking how you can love her, because I couldn't. I still can't. And now I can see why. She's this
horrible old racist drunk. She's as mean as a bag of snakes. She'll
say awful things out loud, anything that comes into her head.
She's had seven or eight common-law husbands since I've been
alive, and none of them treated her children any good. She let
them stay around anyway, being crappy to her kids, having more
kids with them, so yes, how? How on earth?"

"You love Bernese," Henry said.

"Not today I don't."

Henry went on as if I hadn't spoken. "Bernese and Ona are practically the same person."

"That's crazy," I said. "Fretts and Crabtrees are like two entirely different species. I don't think they even share a genus."

Henry snorted. "Bernese is nothing but a dead-sober Ona with an outsize scoop of ambition and some money. She keeps her nasty parts yard in a black-lit terrarium and calls it a hobby, but squalor is squalor, Nonny. They both shoot before they think, and they'll both do anything that needs doing for their families, no matter who or what is in the way."

I stared at him with my mouth hanging open, and then I shook my head. "Are you on crack? Bernese has been known to take a moral shortcut, but that's not the same as not having any morals to cut across. I admit that Bernese is not the easiest person to love some days, but she isn't like Ona. Anyway it's not like I have a choice. She's family."

Henry regarded me blandly. "What's my name?" he asked me.

"Yes, but . . ." I said, floundering. "But you're not really like them. You aren't a crazy, awful redneck racist with less self-awareness than a pill bug. You read for pleasure, and I'm not sure more than half of them can even read the want ads. You have things they don't even know exist, like ethics and table manners. You're kind to them, of course you are, but you aren't really one of them. You never have been. You don't even look like them, and I seriously doubt you actually are—" I stopped abruptly, horrified by what I was in the middle of saying. "I didn't mean to imply anything."

"Yes, you did. And you aren't the first." His eyes were cool now, unfathomable. "I get this shit all the time from my relatives. Sideways comments about my mother's habits, my dark skin. All the time. Never from you before, though. And never, by the way, from Ona Crabtree."

"I wasn't thinking," I said.

"Who do you think of as your mother, Nonny? Hazel Crabtree or Stacia Frett?"

"You know who my mother is," I said in a low tone.

"Yeah. Because Stacia did the job. That's all that counts. I know what I look like, and I know what people say. But Reau Crabtree did the job. He was my father. And that means Ona Crabtree is part of my family."

It had never occurred to me that Henry might be fighting to feel like one of them just as hard as I was fighting to distance myself. I'd never thought that anyone could want that. "I'm so sorry, Henry. I was out of line."

I felt as if I had killed something, the small green thing that had been growing imperceptibly between us. I must have looked as miserable as I felt, because his expression softened, and he said, "Ah, screw it. You didn't mean anything. We're both under some pressure right now. Let's forget it, okay? We have bigger problems." He stared down at the animals' bodies, stuffing both his hands in his pockets. "No one but Bernese makes any sense."

"I know," I said, relieved to be back on ground where we could stand together. "But Henry, she would never. I can't imagine Bernese being clandestine."

"Maybe you're underestimating her," Henry said.

"All I can think is, it must have been an accident. Did Lobe or Tucker put down any rat poison recently? Or maybe some old engine is leaking antifreeze."

"That would be quite a coincidence, wouldn't it? If it wasn't

Bernese—" I started to speak, and he quickly said, "I see your points, but who else could it be?"

All at once it came to me. I put my hand over my mouth to stop myself from speaking. Bernese would not have done this. It wasn't her way, but there was someone else.

Henry took one look at my face and knew I'd figured it out. He stared at me intensely, and then he leaned back, understanding dawning. "I'm an idiot. Of course not Bernese. It was her lawyer, wasn't it." It wasn't said like a question, so I didn't answer. He took my silence as confirmation, adding, "I should have seen that. She either sent Isaac Davids or he did it for her on his own."

I kept my hand over my mouth, my eyes wide. I wanted to answer him, but this was a war, and I was beginning to understand that Henry Crabtree and I were on different sides. He was part and parcel of everything I was fighting, and half a kiss didn't make me his family. It didn't make me his anything. I wanted to hurl myself at him and weep and put the answer in his lap to get his help. But I couldn't. He'd made it clear where he stood, and anything I told Henry could be used as ammunition against my family.

I couldn't even tell him about Lori-Anne and the tires, because he might relay it to Ona. And wouldn't Ona love that? Wouldn't Ona love to be able to say to Bernese, "No, it wasn't me or mine. It was your own child, your own child attacking you, and who could blame her?"

"You need to talk to Isaac," he said. "I'm going to keep working on Ona. I'll try to make sure she calls the police instead of her psychopath nephews."

I nodded, grateful. Ona would have to do something. She

didn't take things lying down. But the police were a cakewalk compared to the Alabama Crabtrees.

"Good," I said. "I have to go."

"Nonny, wait," he called after me.

But I didn't wait. I turned and ran, leaving him in the jungle of old cars and junk stacks, sprinting full out as if running away from Henry Crabtree were a competitive event and I was training for the Olympics.

Once outside the gate, I ran up Grace toward the square, heading across Philbert and into the butterfly gardens. I dropped to my knees beside the cobblestone walkway, searching, thrusting my fingers deep into the grass. I crawled, backtracking all the way across the square to the fountain, heading toward Bernese's store. I found only two Percocets, melting in the morning dew.

Isaac, my ass. If Bernese had sicced Isaac Davids on Ona, he would have put on a tasteful navy suit and a power tie and knocked on the gas station's front door. He would have brought a court order and some folks from Animal Control, not poison. It wasn't Isaac. And it wasn't Bernese.

It was Mama. And worse, I had helped her. I'd brought her the big plate of Trude's meatloaf, extra gravy, and while I was downstairs in the store, she must have been loading pain pills into the meat. She'd probably wrapped it in her napkins and shoved it down into her giant handbag.

Walking home, she'd dropped a trail of a few pills and the empty bottle, giving me something to do so she could make me leave her by the fence surrounding the parts yard. Once I was gone, she'd reached out and put her fingers through the fence, fearless, and dropped her bombs. The dogs, trained haphazardly at home by Lobe—who didn't have enough personal discipline to hope to teach it to an animal—would have been happy to eat up the meat. Every bit.

Half of me wanted to run home and ask her, "Why, Mama? Why would you make it worse? You knew I was working to get those dogs moved, working to keep Bernese from doing anything violent and permanent. Why would you?"

But I knew why. I didn't have to ask. She had been certain my methods wouldn't get the dogs out of there before Genny got released from the hospital, and Mama couldn't have that. She wouldn't be able to bear Genny coming home, so hurt, to spend days or weeks picking herself bald, chewing holes in her skin, banging her head into the wall.

Genny in one of her bad phases could find the slim thread of the Frett willfulness that lay mostly dormant beneath her pretty face and fluffy heart. When fear was driving her, she could refuse to sleep, could fight off Xanax and soothing music. She would stretch rigid in her bed with all the blinds drawn, refusing food, refusing water, until she was so tired and dehydrated she was hallucinating.

But Mama didn't have to search so hard for that thread; she was Bernese's sister, after all, and a world-class pragmatist in her own right. She'd quietly found her own way to make the world tell lies, and say that it was safe.

CHAPTER

14

DRIVING MAMA TO see Genny was an exercise in not plummeting off the highway to our doom. She liked to chat in the car, which meant I was steering with my knee half the time. But we didn't talk about the dogs.

I waited until we were safely parked in the visitors' lot at Loganville General before I signed, *Do you need me to ask Dr. Crow to write you another prescription for Percocet?*

She shook her hand no, signing, *They make me fuzzy.*

I sat beside her for a moment longer, not sure what to do. I knew what I knew, and what could she possibly say? The ugliest bits inside me were glad the dogs were gone, whatever the method, however much the cost. Arguing with her or even asking her about it was pointless, but even so, I couldn't help but sign to her, *I guess the pills already served their purpose.* Mama stilled, a beat with a total absence of movement, and I added, *They let you sleep last night. Right?*

Mama eased her shoulder forward, stretching her hurt back,

and then she signed very tersely, *I never think that you are cute when you are being coy.* She opened the door of the car and unfurled her white cane, feeling her way out and then shutting the door behind her with a little more force than was strictly needed.

When we got to Genny's room, we found her sitting up in bed, pleating and unpleating her sheet. She had distressed eyebrows and a trembling soft mouth. I could see she'd been picking. Her good arm was dotted with reddened patches where she'd ripped the hairs out by the roots. The bed itself was a wasteland of crumpled tissues that were spotted red with her blood, so I knew she'd already moved on to chewing the inside of her mouth. The blood made her nauseated if she swallowed it, so she blotted her small wounds incessantly with the tissues. When she saw Mama and me coming through the doorway, she smiled and then burst into a quick flurry of tears.

She was already reaching toward Mama with her good arm, and to me she said, "Dr. Crow came by and told me they'll send me home tomorrow!"

I walked with Mama to the chair by the bed and guided her hand to the back of it. "I'm going to go talk to the doctor right now, widget," I said. I tried to keep my voice calm and even. I could see Genny was already more than halfway into the maelstrom of a bad phase, perhaps too far in to be drawn back. I wondered why on earth no one had given her a Xanax or some Ativan, but Genny could spiral down so fast. I walked toward the door, saying, "Maybe I can get them to let you go home today."

Genny shook her head. "No! You can't! I can't come home!" She shuddered with another burst of short, racking sobs. Mama worked her way around the chair and sat, then reached out to find the edge of the bed and Genny. As soon as Genny's hands met Mama's, Genny began signing frantically to her, talking to me at the same time.

"Those dogs are right by home. They are waiting for me, those awful dogs, and what will happen? I hate it here. I'm so lonely, and I hurt, and those dogs will kill me if I go home. They know I am coming, and they'll—"

Mama closed her hands around Genny's, stilling her, then began signing, soothing her. Mama said nothing to me, did not turn even a millimeter toward me, but her posture radiated with "I told you so," even though she had told me nothing.

Standing in the doorway, I couldn't see her face, and her hands were mostly hidden by her body, so I wasn't sure what explanation she gave Genny, but after a few moments Genny was fairly glowing with relief. To me she said, "Nonny, find out if they will let me go now. I hate it here. This room smells like beets." She was simultaneously signing into Mama's hands.

"Beets?" I said.

Genny nodded vigorously, and then her mouth scrunched up as the movement hurt her torn shoulder. She went on, "Can't you smell it? Like overcooked beets that got scrubbed down with antiseptic, and Nonny, they are threatening me with a new roommate. It will be someone I don't even know! Who can sleep like that? I'll get hives. What if it's a man? Would they put a man in here?"

I said, "Let me go see when they'll release you." I turned to go, but Mama squawked, stopping me. I walked back over toward the bed until I could see Mama's hands.

Mama was signing to me, *But even if they release Genny today, you're still going to Athens tomorrow, right?*

Of course she is, Genny signed. *I won't need Nonny if you'll be home with me.* To me she said, "You wouldn't miss your court date just because of me." Her mouth was trembling again. "Because I could stay here if you even think for one second you would have to miss it because of me. It's not so very awful here." She stiffened up her rounded shoulders, wincing.

"Don't be silly, widget," I said. "We all want you home. Now, let me go talk to the nurses, please." I darted back out the door and up the hall so fast it was shamefully close to running.

I had slipped into an odd comfort zone, assuming that Genny's and Mama's injuries meant I would have to miss the hearing. As bad as the last few days had been, and as much as I wished the Bitch had never escaped or even existed, it had been something of a relief to shove Jonno to the back of my mental closet. Our divorce was the last thing of any substance that would take place between us, and it was comforting to pack off the moment to a misty afternoon in an undefined future. I wanted the divorce with all my heart. I did. Only I wasn't sure I wanted it tomorrow.

It seemed like it might be easier to wean myself off Jonno in slow stages instead of trying to quit him cold turkey. Although some people—my mother, for example—might say that I'd had a year to wean myself. Then she'd ask how that was working out for me.

Dr. Crow did want to keep Genny another day, but I reminded him Bernese was a retired RN who lived right next door. He agreed to let Genny go home. There were two women sitting at the nurses' station, and their faces lit up when he said I could take Genny. I was sure the minute I was around the corner, they were giving each other high fives. Genny in a bad phase was a handful and a half, and I had no doubt she'd all but kept her thumb permanently clamped down on the call button since she'd woken up.

I drove back to Between with Genny reclining in my cramped backseat. Just from being with Mama, Genny's color was better. Mama had one hand wedged back between the seats, touching her. This wasn't only because Genny was hurt; they were usually in physical contact, even when they weren't talking.

Mama home alone with me had been a little disconcerting. I was so used to seeing Mama and Genny, Genny and Mama. I was struck now by how tiny they seemed, how frail, in their bandages, gingerly holding hands. Watching them made both their extraordinary connection and their simple human frailty more real to me than it had ever been, and I felt a flash of longing for someone who was mine like that. I didn't want to be so alone.

There had been something real growing underneath my friendship with Henry. It had been there when he kissed me, but I hadn't been truly aware of it until I killed it in the junkyard. I'd mortally insulted him, and he had made it clear that he was on the other side of this ugly war. And that left me what?

Jonno? There was always Jonno. It seemed there always had been. I had a dizzying desire to skip the hearing tomorrow and then blatantly not reschedule. Jonno would be happy to drift with me in this limbo and see what happened. Drifting along and seeing what happened was practically Jonno's middle name. Looking at my mama and Genny, I was reminded that Jonno, whatever his faults, had always understood what these women were to me.

Jonno had known—we both had—that a day would come when there would be only one of them, and no matter who was left behind, she would immediately come to live with us. It wasn't negotiable. I couldn't bear to think of Genny living afraid, or for Mama to be isolated inside her own head.

When I left the acceptance letter for my scholarship to graduate school, two states away from my family, sitting unanswered until the deadline for accepting it wandered past and escaped me, Jonno hadn't judged me or said I was too dependent. He never minded that I left him every weekend, sometimes three- and four-day weekends, to be with them. And with that thought, the longing for him was wiped away as quickly as it had come, leaving behind the beginnings of a bleak headache. Jonno probably never minded because it had made me very easy to cheat on.

If it didn't happen tomorrow, I would have to get another court date, one I might even show up for. I would divorce him, and then I could settle down to live the rest of my life, alone, probably, because what man wants a thirty-year-old woman with one and a half mothers, one deaf-blind and the other so neurotic she was less than four baby steps from flat crazy. After Mama and Genny both passed, I would shuffle around in my house shoes, living on Cream of Wheat so I could afford to feed all nine thousand of my cats, who would no doubt eat me after I died. But hey, at least my mother up in heaven would be happy I had finally gotten off my ass and done something definitive. If I couldn't murder dogs with cheerful abandon, I could at least follow through on my divorce.

I wasn't in the best frame of mind to spend the day playing step-'n'-fetch-it for Genny, who was hurting and out of sorts. Mama went to her room, and I could hear the clack and clatter as she pounded the Braille keyboard on her TTY. She was probably on the phone talking smack about me with one of her friends in Atlanta.

When the typing stopped, I wanted to go to her, but Genny didn't give me a moment to breathe. She needed me to pet her hair, she wanted to eat only the kind of soup we were out of, and the remote for the TV in her bedroom started acting squirrelly. I was up and down the stairs hunting new batteries and screwdrivers, and when my minor surgeries had failed, I stood by the TV flipping through every channel five times, hunting for *Trading Spaces*. Then Genny realized she had the remote set to VCR. She switched it to TV and settled in to channel-surf. I went to make her some tea to keep from strangling her.

At about noon, we heard Bernese out in her driveway bellowing, "Lou! Lou! Bring me the stinking walk-around phone." I leaned over Genny's bed to peer out the window. Bernese was standing by her car, staring down at the mutilated tires. When Lou did not appear, Bernese remained rooted in the driveway, howling, "Phone! Phone!" with the O drawn out into a primal howl, as desperate for it as if she were Marlon Brando and the phone, Stella.

"What's happening?" said Genny.

"Nothing good."

I helped Genny sit up, bracing her back with pillows so she could watch out the bedroom window. I went and got Mama. She sat by Genny, who gave her a play-by-play as the drama in Bernese's driveway unfolded.

Lou must have crept home while I was picking up Genny, and he had apparently decided to pretend he hadn't noticed the tires and let Bernese discover them on her own. Now he appeared with the phone, and she snatched it from his hand and dialed, then stood in the yard yelling into the mouthpiece. Lou orbited her like a panicky satellite.

After a few minutes, we saw Isaac Davids come walking elegantly down from his Victorian on the square, swinging his cane.

Moments later, Bernese's pet sheriff, Thig Newell, drove up with his lights flashing, and five minutes after that, two cops from Loganville showed up. The menfolk all milled about in the yard while Bernese paced around and around her car in a posture so predatory it looked as if she were stalking it.

Mama signed, *You should go check on her.*

I was spared that, because just then the crowd dispersed. Lou went in the house, the Loganville cops left, and Isaac and Bernese got in the sheriff's car with Thig and drove up Grace Street toward the square.

That afternoon, when Mama had gone to have a lie-down and Genny was exhausted to the point of tears, Lou came by and added Fisher to the mix. He asked me to keep an eye on her so he could go run some errands for Bernese.

"How are you going to run errands with seven slashed tires?" I asked him.

"Oh, and Bernese said to ask you can I borrow your car." Lou looked flushed and pop-eyed, so I took pity on him and passed over the keys.

Fisher was grumpy and hyper all at once. She couldn't be still, and she wouldn't stay out of Genny's room as long as I was in there. She kept banging into Genny's bed and jarring her until I settled Genny in with *Days of Our Lives* and a smoothie and took Fisher downstairs to color while I cleaned the house. But Fisher wouldn't stay at the kitchen table, either. She followed me from room to room, tangling herself in the vacuum's cord and getting between my feet, tripping me.

She said, "Can I sleep over?" After I somehow managed to swallow the words "Sweet Lord, no!" that were trying to burst out of me, I managed to say, "You know Grandma won't let you on a school night."

Fisher didn't answer, just kicked at the banister.

I added, "And you need to stay in your bed tonight, wormy. Okay? Grandma has had a very hard day, with the cars and all, and you don't want to upset her any more."

Fisher gave the banister another good whang with her foot. "Maybe you should take me to my grandma now. She's with Mr. Isaac. He could teach me secret Jewish things, and then I wouldn't tell you." Her lip was sticking out so far, a good-size bird could have perched on it and ridden to town.

"Fish, your grandma's having kind of a hard time lately. You know how she's been extra cranky?"

Fisher gave me a vigorous nod. She knew.

"I'm trying to fix that, okay? I'm going to try and get her to stop being so cranky and act like normal, but I need your help. I need you to not do things you know make her crazy. I don't want her to come check your bed tonight and see you gone."

"That's dumb. She knows I only go downstairs or next door."

"Sometimes you walk all the way down to the square and sleep upstairs at the store."

"It's not far to the store," Fisher said.

"Fish, it's not safe. You have to walk right"—I stopped myself abruptly and finally said—"near the exit from the highway. And cross the street by yourself. Grandma sees your empty bed and panics. If you won't panic her tonight, then I promise you, I will help your grandma not be so cranky all the time. And you can stay over here with me all weekend like always, and tomorrow we'll rent movies and stay up really late, okay?"

"Grandma says I can't stay with you probably at all tomorrow. She says you have to go to Athens and you won't be back till late."

I took a deep breath. "I don't think I'm going."

She peeped up at me sideways from under her bangs. "We can get any movie I want?"

"Any PG or G," I said.

"And eat kettle corn?"

"Until we're sick," I said, flipping Bernese's *Get Fit, Kid!* lunacy a mental bird. "But only if you help me by being sweet and not freaking out your grandma."

At last she said, "Okay."

Genny was calling me again. Fisher and I trailed back upstairs, and the afternoon wound endlessly on. Lou came back at about five, no doubt sent to snatch Fisher before I could feed her any actual dinner. Bernese probably had a nice plate of raw bran steeping in carrot juice at home. Mama and Genny were both sleeping.

"Do you think you and Fisher could stay here?" I asked Lou. "I want to let Mama sleep, but someone needs to be around in case Genny wakes up first and needs something. And Lou, I really need out of here."

"Sure thing," Lou said.

I stuffed the book I was reading into my purse and practically fled the house before Lou could change his mind. I thought I would head up to the diner and get some dinner, read a chapter or two, maybe take a walk after.

It felt strange to walk past the parts yard and not have the dogs come charging toward me. I still had that familiar wobble of unease in my belly. I kept expecting to see them materialize in my peripheral vision.

191

As I passed the gas station and came up to the crosswalk that would lead me across the street and onto the square, I saw Bernese stomping down the cobbled walkway past the Marchants' bed-and-breakfast. At the same time, Ona Crabtree emerged from one of the antique marts and walked up the sidewalk toward the diner. Directly across from me, on the other side of the center gardens and fountain, Henry came out of Crabtree Books.

He turned around and saw Bernese and Ona about a heartbeat before they saw each other. They were walking in opposite directions, on opposite sides of the square, and as their eyes met, I felt it as a reverberation that spread up from the earth's core and made the ground shudder under my feet. Neither of them stopped moving, but neither of them took her eyes off the other.

On the surface, it was simply two ladies of a certain age glaring balefully at each other across the green expanse of the square's lovely lawn and butterfly garden. But for me, it was like watching two icebergs pass each other. Under the surface, shelves and blades of ancient ice ground against each other, splintering as they passed. Bernese was radiating her fresh rage over Genny's injuries and this latest assault on her tires. Ona's gaze dripped pure, cold poison, fueled by her ancient bruises as well as her recent losses, laying thirty years' and three dead dogs' worth of blame squarely at Bernese's splayed feet.

They moved forward, eyes locked, each on her own side of the square. They came even with the center fountain, and at the same moment, they slowly turned their faces forward and continued past each other. I realized I had stopped breathing, and I sucked in a huge gulp of air that tasted oddly frigid, in spite of the fact that it had to be 80 degrees outside. Ona went into the diner, and

Bernese saw me and cut the last corner, coming across the lawn and then to the end of the crosswalk to meet me.

"You going to get some supper?" she said.

I nodded. "Lou and Fisher are sitting with Genny."

"Glad to see you're getting out. I know Genny's probably driven you bat-crap." She continued past me up Grace, heading for home.

My eyes met Henry's across the square, and by unspoken assent, we started walking toward each other. I crossed the street and walked directly across the grass, meeting him by the fountain.

"Want to come back to my place and get drunk?" said Henry Crabtree.

"God, yes," I said.

CHAPTER

15

HENRY LOCKED THE front door of the bookstore behind us. The overhead lights were off, and we wound our way through the stacks using the fading sunlight that was coming through the display window. By the time we got to fiction and literature, I was having trouble seeing where I was going. I put one hand on Henry's shoulder and let him lead.

At the back of the bookstore, in front of his office, Henry had put in a seating area where shoppers could relax and read and have a cup of coffee. There was a wide sofa covered in stripes of rose and gold velvet, the nap soft and worn through in patches. Two pale gold corduroy chairs flanked the sofa, turned to face each other so the three pieces formed a conversation pit around a low coffee table. Henry stopped walking, and when I let go of his shoulder, he went behind one of the chairs and turned on the floor lamp.

"Take a load off, Nonny Jane," he said. The lamp had a beaded burgundy shade that dampened the light coming from the low-watt bulb. Without the overheads on, it was a cozier, more intimate place than Henry's apartment.

I sank into the sofa, and Henry disappeared into his office for a moment. I heard him thumping up the stairs and then back down. He returned bearing a half-full bottle of Jameson and two rocks glasses.

"I could make Irish coffees, but I assume you'd rather skip the niceties and get right to the Irish?" he said.

"Let's not screw around."

He nodded his assent and sat down beside me. He lined up the glasses on the coffee table and poured a generous shot into each.

"Skoal," he said, and we each picked up a glass and downed it. It burned a righteous path all the way to my empty stomach.

I set the glass back down, and Henry poured again, first for me, then for him. He touched the rim of his glass, tracing it with his forefinger, then starting talking, picking up right where we had left off in the Crabtree parts yard.

"In some ways, Reau Crabtree was my only parent. You know Mama had some problems."

"I remember," I said.

"After my dad died, she got worse. Stayed in her pajamas most days. I was thirteen and practically raising Lily, giving my mother her meds, running the store. So many times, I was ready to head to Highway 78 and put my thumb out. Ona always knew. I'd be twelve seconds away from walking. Ditching Lily. Letting Mama drown in her own juices. And right then Ona would drag in. She'd be drunk. Or she'd be so hungover that the first thing she'd do was go have herself a good puke in our toilet. Then she'd make Lily and me some eggs. Pack Lily's lunch. Give me a roll of quarters and tell me to skip school, spend some quality time at the Loganville arcade.

"I'm not blind to what Ona Crabtree is, but before she's any of the things you said, she's my family. There's no way for me not to love her."

I reached for my glass, and Henry reached for his at the same time. "Skoal," I said, and we threw the second shot back. It went down easier than the first. I banged the glass down on the table and then tilted my head back and closed my eyes. I heard the click of Henry's glass coming to rest beside mine, and then I heard him pouring for us again.

I said, "You don't have to explain them to me. If there's a human alive who truly understands the meaning of the phrase 'family obligations,' you are looking at her."

"I'm not apologizing. I'm telling you something." He paused and I opened my eyes. He was rubbing his long fingers against his forehead, as if trying to press whatever was in his brain down and out through his mouth. "Tucker slashed Lou and Bernese's tires. He was bragging about it to Ona. Skoal."

He downed his shot. I was feeling a little dizzy, so I left mine sitting on the table. I wasn't sure what he was presenting me. A peace offering? Or an equal exchange of information from one hostile side to another? Maybe it was the whiskey, but I thought I felt again the presence of the thing that had been growing between us, and my heart started banging like a fist against my rib cage. I hadn't realized how much it meant to me until I thought I'd killed it.

I looked him dead in the eye, and I let the little green thing between us bloom. "Tucker didn't do it. He must have been lying to score points with his mama. Lori-Anne slashed the tires. I saw her. Skoal." I picked up my glass and tipped the shot down my throat. I set the glass back down and then looked at him, big-eyed with nerves. "And if you tell Ona that, you will have mightily shafted me."

"And if you tell Bernese that Tucker is claiming he did it, she'll have him arrested. Ona will know it came from me."

My hands were shaking. "So why did we do that? Whose side are we on?"

"Not Bernese's," he said.

"I'm not on Ona's."

"I know." He capped the whiskey and turned to face me squarely. "I've decided to be on yours."

"My side is Bernese's," I said, a little muddled from three shots and no dinner. I clamped my trembling hands together in front of me, trying to still them.

"It shouldn't be. Bernese is in the wrong. Not alone there, but she's wrong. You know it."

"Then whose side should I be on?"

"I hope you'll be on mine. Ours. Be on ours." He moved down the length of the sofa until he was right beside me. He was deliberate and slow, and I watched him, unmoving, with my heart beating so hard that I felt its pulse from throat to knees. I didn't look away. I didn't even blink. He reached up slowly and took my head in his hands, burying them in my hair on either side of my face, and then he kissed me, and I closed my eyes and let him.

Again I felt that odd sense of slipping backwards, of falling into something, and this time I didn't fight it. I had been fighting it before I was even aware it was there, and for what? For Jonno? To hold up my side of a vow that was so eroded it was sand slipping through my fingers? I grabbed Henry's shoulders and let myself fall. He fell with me, and the kiss changed radically, immediately, and Henry Crabtree was all over me.

His hands were fumbling at my clothes, desperate and clumsy, and my hands were doing the same to his. My fingers felt swollen, as if they were filled with too much blood. My pulse beat in every joint as I plucked helplessly at his buttons. I gave up and jerked his shirttail out of his pants so I could run my hands up underneath and feel his heated skin. Then he pulled my hands away, and I was briefly blinded as he wrestled my T-shirt off over my head.

"Freckles," I whispered, embarrassed for a moment to be tearing at Henry Crabtree's clothes in my jeans and my tatty bra, but he said, "I love freckles," and his voice was thick, and I believed him. He was kissing my collarbone, his fingers busy with the bra's clasp. I got most of his buttons undone and engaged in a desperate, thick-fingered battle with his belt buckle while he was tugging down my jeans.

Underneath the pull of the strange gravity that was drawing us down and down into the depths of the velvet sofa, I felt strangely relieved; Henry wasn't very good at this. He hadn't studied. He didn't know me like a book and he wasn't reading me from some lofty height, bending my body to his practiced will. He only wanted me. He wanted me so bad he couldn't get my jeans off fast enough, and whatever he was doing to me, thank God, thank God, it wasn't pretty. He didn't care if it was pretty, and I didn't care, either. I only knew I wanted him to, and he did.

But then he pushed himself away from me, saying, "We have to stop."

"No, we do not," I said, emphatic, and I sat up and reached for him again.

"I don't have anything," he said.

But I did. Of course I did. I'd put my purse beside the sofa. I grabbed it and dumped it out, mostly onto the floor. Change went tumbling across the Berber carpet, my lipstick rolling under the coffee table. My contact solution bounced once and skittered away. I rooted past my keys and a pen and grabbed one of the little packets that were always in my purse these days.

"Oh. Good, then," said Henry Crabtree, taking it, too intent on using it to question why a married woman carried such a thing. He pulled my body back to his. My teeth banged into his chin and I clutched at him awkwardly, tilting my head back farther to kiss him until we were in free fall again.

And then we were together, my jeans still twined around one ankle, his shirt still mostly on. We melded into something private, externally unbeautiful, but from where I was, beneath him and then open-eyed above him, watching us from inside the moment, it was perfect, perfect, perfect.

Afterward we lay enmeshed on the wide sofa, breathing in unison, face-to-face on our sides, grinning foolishly at each other. My back was pressed into the sofa's back, and I had something digging into my ribs. I rooted around underneath myself and pulled out the canister of pepper spray Jonno had given me a year or so ago after a rash of muggings near the UGA campus. I tossed it over Henry and heard it ping off something on the floor and roll away.

"So this is what adultery is like," I thought. No wonder Jonno had been such a fan. I pushed the thought away. No one wanted Jonno in the room right now.

I sat up and untwisted my jeans, finding my panties stuffed way down inside one of the legs. Henry began putting himself back together, too, as well as he could. I couldn't stop smiling at him. I had never seen Henry looking so rumpled. His Dockers were draped over the lamp, and they had survived almost unscathed, but his shirt hung open, hopelessly wrinkled. At some point I had pulled off the leather tie that held his hair back, and hurled it away. His hair was all one length, dead straight, thick and black, and it hung to his shoulders. He was barefoot, his glasses cast aside.

Henry's face was fine-boned, and the combination of severe cheekbones and a cut-glass mouth gave him an ascetic, almost androgynous beauty. The effect was heightened by his wiry build, his deep-set eyes, his long, elegant hands. But now, disheveled and grinning at me, ringed with the glow of good sex, he'd slipped into the skin of the dangerous thing that lived in him. It was an edge I had always sensed but rarely saw. I liked the few strands of slate that were mixing in with his black hair. I liked how the skin crinkled up beside his eyes as he smiled.

Henry found his glasses and then helped me gather up all the crap that had tumbled out of my purse. Once we had it all packed away, he handed me the purse, and we stood awkwardly together.

"You know I have to get home," I said.

"Are you okay to walk?" he said, and I realized I was buzzing from the whiskey.

"Crap. I need a Velamint," I said. There was nothing but rubbing alcohol at Mama's house, and Bernese had kept the same bottle of gin in her medicine cabinet for twenty years. I assumed she used it to sterilize needles, because Lord knows I never saw anyone drink it.

"You need a meal," said Henry. He listed right as he walked back to his office, and I realized he was not entirely sober himself. I followed him. He opened his desk drawer and pulled out a giant Otis Spunkmeyer orange muffin, still in its plastic wrapper.

"Eat this on the way home," he said.

"I think I better leave by the back."

Henry walked me through his office, and we stood by the door for a moment while he straightened my clothes and I ran my hands through my hair, trying to look like a girl who hadn't just had the best sex of her life on a semipublic sofa.

There was no such thing as a town smaller than Between. If I came weaving and hiccuping around the corner from the rear entrance to Henry's store with a bed snarl on the back of my head, everyone in town, including my mama, would know about it before I could finish my five-minute walk home.

"Will I see you tomorrow?" I asked.

"I thought you were going to Athens," said Henry.

No one had wanted Jonno in the room, but there he was anyway. I swallowed hard, looking away.

"Unless . . ." Henry trailed off, and he swallowed, too. "Oh. You're not going to Athens."

"Genny came home today," I said hurriedly. "I forgot to tell you. But I'm going to try to work it out so that I get to go. It depends on Genny."

"Right," Henry said.

"And you saw Ona and Bernese. On the square? That's a flame and a fuse getting awfully close to meeting up with each other, and I'm the only water in town."

"Right."

"I swear, I am going to try to go to Athens. And I meant what I told you before," I said.

"You told me you were done with Jonno. Then you said, 'For

fuck's sake, Henry. I'm married.'" His voice was calm and level, and his eyes met mine, dead earnest. "I know I've jumped the gun here. Either I don't listen or I don't learn. But I need to know. Which is it?"

After a long time I said, "Both."

He started smoothing his hair back. He'd found his leather tie while we were packing up my purse, and he tilted his head down to look at the floor as he gathered his hair and bound it.

"Okay, then," he said. He moved to open the door for me, but I blocked him, not sure what to say.

"Henry? I won't say anything to Bernese about Tucker, or anything you tell me."

"I know that." He sounded distant and slightly exasperated. Then he bundled me out the door and closed it behind me.

I walked home, eating the muffin as I went, wishing I were flexible enough to kick myself in the head. What was I doing? Earlier that same day, driving home from Loganville General, I'd been crazy-weepy because I thought Henry wouldn't ever speak to me again. Not five minutes after that, I'd been questioning whether I wanted a divorce at all. Either way, I had no business tumbling onto a sofa under Henry Crabtree. Maybe I had the exact marriage I deserved. I was no better than Jonno; Jonno had only gone first.

And then two minutes ago, I had vehemently sworn to Henry that I would try to go to Athens. I'd meant it, too, but dammit, I had already promised Fisher that I wasn't going, that we could have movie night. But Genny was definitely expecting me to go and would make herself ill with guilt if I didn't. Bernese had all but offered me one of her wide selection of firearms so I could skip the divorce and make myself a widow.

And then a lightbulb went off in my brain. Hadn't I also told Ona Crabtree I would come to her house for dinner on what was turning out to be the most overbooked Friday of my life? Yes, I had. And I had told her I would bring her a check, written by Bernese, for those dogs.

Of course, that was before Mama killed them. I doubted a check could fix anything now, unless it was signed with Bernese's heart blood and came in a box with her head. If I didn't find a way to soothe Ona, she would call in the Alabama Crabtrees, and I held little sway with them. Whatever awful thing they took it in their heads to do, there would be no way for me to stop them. I couldn't let it come to that.

Everyone wanted something from me, and I hadn't a clue what I wanted myself. But I did know there was one person who was absolutely on my side, first, foremost, and no matter what. Mama. Mama could help me cut through all the crap in my head and decide what had to be done.

That night, once Genny was settled and Lou and Bernese had taken Fisher home to bed, I went into Mama's room and drew my heart on her shoulder. She was already in bed but awake. She started and then smiled as she signed, *Sorry. My mind was far away. Are you going to bed?*

In a minute. I sat down beside her.

She found my face with her hands and traced its shape, leaned in and kissed my hair, but then she jerked away from me as if she had been stung. She signed, *Did Jonno come here? To Between?*

Of course not.

She cocked her head to the side, and then her body relaxed and a slow grin spread over her face. *You have a sweetheart!*

I started to protest, but she pushed my hands away and signed, *Don't lie to your mama. I know. You have a sweetheart. Is it Henry?*

I nodded hesitantly into her hand.

Finally! she signed, shocking me a little.

I'm still married, Mama. Shouldn't you be giving me a lecture?

She shooed her hand at me, as if whisking off the peskiest of the Ten Commandments with an airy wave. *If it takes this much sin to get your head straight, so be it. You need a sweetheart.*

I don't know if I would call Henry my sweetheart, I signed. *I don't know what he is.*

Mama was close to laughing. *Don't try to fool me! I had a sweetheart myself. It was a long time ago, but I still have a nose, and you don't forget. Henry is your sweetheart.*

I felt bright heat bloom in my cheeks, and my mouth dropped open. Genny always signed "sweetheart" to mean "boyfriend" or "husband." I had not realized until this moment that when my mother used the same sign, it was a euphemism.

Frank? I signed to her. I remembered his name from the hundreds of times she had told me the story of my birth. *Frank was your sweetheart?* And this time I was using the sign the way she meant it.

She nodded her hand. *Not when we were in school, after. When we'd graduated. I loved him so much. I thought for certain that we would be married, and so it didn't seem that bad to do things out of order.*

I signed, *But when it came down to a choice, you picked Genny.*

She shook her hand in a vigorous no. *Never! I would never have chosen anyone over Frank. I loved him. He was my husband in my head and in my heart.*

I put a question mark into her hand because it didn't make sense to me.

Mama didn't answer me. I started to say something else, but she waved my hands away. She was thinking. *In the end, I came to realize that he didn't love me,* she signed at last. *I thought we would be together, the three of us always. But he said it was him or Genny. I didn't choose Genny over Frank. I only stayed with the person who loved me enough to not ask me to choose.*

I thought about that while my mother lay back on the pillows. I tucked the blanket up higher on her, and then I put my hand in hers and signed, *What about Genny? Did she ever have a "sweetheart"?*

No, of course not. Don't be silly, my mother signed, and then laughter welled up in her so hard it made her shake, and she barely managed to sign to me what was so funny before it dissolved her. *You know Genny is afraid of big animals.*

I laughed, too, so hard we were shaking the bed. When we stopped, I took her hand again and asked her, *I know it's been a long day, but can we talk for a minute?*

Yes. I'm glad you came, Mama signed. *I've wanted to ask you how angry you are with me.*

I started to answer her, but she stilled my hands with her own.

I realize that isn't really the question. I think I want to ask, Do you think what I did was a sin? She added, *The dogs.* But I had known what she meant.

You'll have to ask God, Mama, I signed. *I can't answer that. I do know I wish you hadn't done it. I know why you did. But I wish you had trusted me. You knew I was working on it. You know it wasn't right, or you wouldn't be asking me about it at all.*

Mama compressed her lips, mulling, and then signed, *It wasn't right. But I would do it again the same way.* Her expression shifted, became patient, loving, and she signed to me so gently, *You do not have this thing that's in me. The thing inside Bernese. I am not sure what to call it. Will or evil, or maybe it is only that we see things through.*

I can see things through! I signed, emphatic, and she patted my arm and shook her hand. *I can,* I insisted.

You never have before, she signed, still gentle. *Genny was too afraid to come home, and I couldn't trust that this would be the moment that you would pick to grow into yourself. I know you will. But there have been things you knew you needed to do before, hard things, and you folded in and waited and hoped either until something outside came along to make you or until it was too late.*

I knew what she meant. She'd seen it in me when I had never followed up on the scholarship offer, even though I'd spent months writing my application essay and collecting recommendations. I'd stayed in my safe interpreting job in a town less than an hour from my family. And tonight I had come to her because I didn't know where I would go tomorrow, and I was wanting her to push me to Athens or hold me here, to move me in a direction because I did not know how to move myself.

Maybe she sensed that, because she had just made it impossible for me to ask her.

As for the dogs, she had done the best she could. Maybe not the best thing there was to do, but the very best she could.

I know who you are, Mama, I said, as gentle as she had been. *You're the lady who steals babies and poisons dogs, and you are the exact mother I would have picked for myself had anyone asked me.*

I leaned in to kiss her, and her arms came around my neck and she clung to me, burying her nose in my hair, breathing me in. I held on to her, too, waiting for our usual peace to settle in between us, but it didn't happen.

When I drew back, she signed, *I know you, too.*

She looked so small and tired in her bed. The lines around her unmoving mouth drew it downward, as if she were sad. *I know you, too.*

CHAPTER

16

────────────────────────────

M Y PLAN WAS to go to sleep and let my subconscious work everything out. I would have deep, meaningful dreams about riding a train through a tunnel to a city called Jonno, France. Perhaps a highly symbolic storm would come and tear the city down, pound the bricks to red dust and churn the glass to sand. Hurricane Henry or only Hurricane Me. Strangers, passing by on their way to Cannes, would never know a city had been there at all. Or the storm would pass, and I would spin like Julie Andrews across its weather-beaten streets, singing about home. I would wake up refreshed and clear-eyed, knowing what I wanted and, more than that, knowing what was right. Maybe even how to get there from here.

I am sure it would have happened exactly that way if only I had managed to get fifteen consecutive minutes of REM sleep. But Genny had a bad night. Dream dogs chased her up through layers of Xanax and Vicodin. Every time I drifted off, she would begin whimpering, flailing at her covers. I lost track of the number of times I went up and down the hall from my room to hers and back again.

Finally, I gave up and climbed into bed with her. I stayed beside her, petting the inside of her wrist and humming softly until she was deeply asleep.

My presence in the bed seemed to help, but at four she woke us both up with a shriek, and when I touched her forehead, it was slick with cold sweat. I turned on the TV for her, and she clicked around with the remote until she found a station that ran old movies with no commercials. She sat up, propping herself on a stack of pillows, and we held hands. I dozed, fading in and out as she watched the back half of *Bringing Up Baby.*

I woke up as the clock downstairs was chiming seven. A different movie was playing, some old Western I didn't know. I blinked, scrubbing at my eyes. If I'd had any dreams, I didn't remember them.

Genny appeared to be sleeping hard beside me, but as I sat up, her eyes opened and she said, "I'm a silly old thing, aren't I? How do you all put up with me?"

She sat up, too, carefully, shame-faced, twisting her fingers together. I saw the worst was over. Her eyes were bright and birdlike, and some of the tension seemed to have drained out of her round shoulders. Mama and I had succeeded in turning her back from the bad day we'd seen starting up at the hospital. I was hugely relieved; unchecked, a bad day for Genny could last weeks.

"Don't worry, widget. You know we adore you," I said, yawning. I leaned over Genny to check the other side of the bed. Fisher wasn't there.

Genny nodded. "I do know. But it's silly to flap and panic

when I know those dogs are so far. And don't think I'm not grateful. It really makes me in some ways think better of her."

"Of who?" I said. I got out of her bed and stretched.

"Ona Crabtree," she said, and I made a mental note to find out exactly what pacifying lie my mother had told her frail sister, and to be sure the rest of Between knew the expurgated-for-Genny version.

I thought giving Ona the credit was pretty big of Mama, considering. But perhaps it was only pragmatic. She could tell Genny the dogs had left the state, but she could not so easily spirit Ona away. Genny needed to think of Ona as, if not benevolent, at least not actively plotting to do her harm.

On the way back to my room, I glanced in on Mama. She was still sleeping, and she was alone. My room was empty, too. So Fisher had stayed in her own bed. Good. Bernese needed to calm down a notch before I could hope to get her to see the connection between her anger with Lori-Anne and her twisted obsession with *Get Fit, Kid!*

All that morning, I felt like the house was holding its breath. Or maybe it was Mama. She stayed out of my way. I heard her clicking away on the Braille typewriter as she talked on the TTY. When she emerged from her room, she seemed very much herself again, brisk and busy. I knew she was eager to get to work on her new sculpture, but she stayed at home, caring for Genny so I didn't have to, creating dead space around me so I could think.

I did think, as time ate away at the day and I mulled through all the promises I had made and did nothing toward fulfilling any of them. If I didn't go to Athens, I couldn't say it was because I was worried about my family's safety. Even though things were the worst they'd ever been between the Fretts and Crabtrees, this was the one day it was safe for me to leave town; Ona was expecting me for dinner. She wouldn't have called her nephews in tonight.

Whether I went to Athens or not, there was no way I was going to make it to Ona's. Fisher was much higher on my list of priorities. But Ona didn't know I wasn't coming. If I waited to cancel, it would be too late for her to mobilize her troops. When I did call, I would make sure to reschedule immediately, and I could ask her to stay her hand until she had spoken with me face-to-face. Henry was working on her, too.

When I thought of Henry, I discovered a cheerful pocket in my head, foolishly colored pink and stuffed full of belief that he would give me a call this morning. If I could talk my decisions for the day through with him, I might figure out what on earth was causing me to waffle.

He didn't call.

Maybe he was waiting for me to come by the Dollhouse Store so he could talk to me in person. That was how we usually connected; I couldn't remember him ever calling me. Of course, I also couldn't remember him ever having sex with me on random pieces of the bookstore's furniture, and it seemed to me that if he could so easily change that one, he ought to be able to pick up the damn phone.

Genny felt up to coming downstairs for lunch, and after we ate, she and Mama went into the den. They sat side by side on the sofa, in silent chat. I curled up in an armchair nearby, pretending to read and obsessively checking my watch. There would come a time, in a couple of hours at most, when, by not deciding, I would have made a decision. I wouldn't have time to get to

Athens before my slot on the docket. Mama kept feeling her Braille watch, too, but she didn't bring it up.

I gave myself a deadline; I would know what to do by the time Lou got back with my car. He'd borrowed it again, since his car and Bernese's were both at Firestone getting new tires. He was in Loganville buying potting soil, and since he was already in town he was picking up Fisher, but one o'clock came and went and he still wasn't back. I was beginning to get concerned when the front door opened. "That you, Lou?" I called.

"Nope, it's me," said Bernese. She stomped through the foyer into the den. "Lou's minding the store for me, and he's got Fisher with him."

"What are you doing here?" I said.

"I'm here to sit with Genny and your mama so you can go to Athens and get shut of that syphilitic testicle you married."

I gaped at her. This was one of the many reasons I hadn't gone into detail about why I was divorcing Jonno. Jonno had been permanently and publicly renamed. Worse, Bernese was such a behemoth that I often forgot that when she did decide to turn, she could do it on a dime. And heaven help the people standing in her path when she decided to go in the new direction.

"Lou came straight over from school with Fisher and parked in the lot behind the church, so you'll need to walk down there. I don't know why he didn't park here and walk himself. He knows I can't drive a stick shift. But this way you can pop your head in and explain to Fisher when you'll be back. She's already in a froth, but I told her to quit sulking. Y'all can do your movie night tomorrow. Here are your keys—you better get going."

I was still sitting in the chair with my mouth hanging open, catching flies. Mama was signing, but I couldn't peel my eyes off

Bernese, so Genny interpreted. "Bernese? Stacia says to tell you to keep your big butt out of it."

I glanced their way in time to see that Genny's cheeks had pinked, and she was signing as an aside to Mama, *Do you have to talk ugly?*

"Someone's got to make the girl see sense," said Bernese.

Mama signed, *Nonny? Forget Bernese. Forget what I want, too. You decide.*

"What's she saying?" Bernese asked Genny, but Genny had seen that I was watching Mama's gracefully arching hands and had not interpreted.

"She was talking to Nonny, not you," Genny said primly.

"You make me crazy," Bernese said. "You tell Stacia every stinking thing that happens in a room whether someone is talking to her or not, but now you won't tell me what she's saying to Nonny?"

Genny said, "No one's stopping you from learning to sign."

Mama was rapid-fire signing to me while they argued. *This isn't like the dogs. I can't do this for you. If you don't want the divorce, then say so. If that's true, you still need to get on the road to Athens. Go get Jonno and fight for him. But don't act helpless and pretend it isn't a choice. Pick—either finish it or make him treat you better.*

"Nonny, what is she saying?" Bernese demanded.

I ran to the sofa and knelt by Mama, signing into her hands, *I am done with Jonno, but maybe today is not the day. There is so much going on here, Genny's still very hurt, Ona Crabtree's on the warpath, and there's Fisher and Bernese. I can get the court date rescheduled—*

Mama pushed my hands away, shaking her hand no.

"Are you weaseling out?" Bernese said. "Are you seriously thinking about keeping that diseased piece of crap?"

"Shut up, Bernese," I said. I reached for Mama, but she pushed my hands away again.

Mama signed, *Do you think I care about this stupid day in court? This is about you. You were "working on" moving the dogs when the dogs needed to be gone, period. And now you are "working on" getting shut of that man. And tomorrow you'll be "working on" helping Fisher. You can't change Bernese, you'll say. But I know you can. Maybe you will, maybe you won't, but don't say you can't. You are welcome to throw happiness away with all your hands and stay with Jonno until you dry up and die or until he brings something home that will kill you. It's your love life. But how much longer can Fisher wait while you "try" and "work on it" and fuss around not doing anything? How long before Bernese breaks her?*

She folded her arms and stuffed her hands under them. She had said her piece, and she wasn't giving me the opportunity to explain my way out from under her gospel.

"I hope she's telling you to get your butt on the road," Bernese said, and then the doorbell rang.

I immediately thought, "Henry," and ran to get it.

"Nonny!" Bernese called after me, but I ignored her and flung the door open. It wasn't Henry. It was a girl I didn't know, although she looked terribly familiar. She was slim and big-eyed, a dewy little thing in peach capri pants and strappy sandals, standing nervously on the porch, wringing her hands. When I opened the door and she saw my face, she stared at me and her expression changed from nervousness to sheer, ugly rage.

"Are you kidding me?" she screeched. "You are actually here?"

When her mouth twisted up, so angry, I knew her. I didn't see how I could have forgotten that hateful face, watching me so avidly when Bernese called to tell me Genny was hurt. She'd been sitting across from me in a red leatherette booth at Bibi's Real Ice Cream, enjoying my life as if it were a daytime drama. I searched my mind for her name and found it. She was Amber DeClue, the girl who had booked me through my agency for an interpreting job that had never quite happened. Now she was standing on my mother's doorstep in Between, glaring at me with the same expression I had seen when I drove away and left her poking viciously at her cell phone.

She reached up and grabbed handfuls of her long hair, one hunk on either side of her face, and clutched at it. "Jonno said you'd be here. Jonno said you'd never give him the divorce. But I thought for sure you couldn't possibly be such a bitch."

"Jonno?" I said to her, my eyes narrowing.

Bernese came into the foyer, Mama and Genny trailing behind her. Mama was following the wall with one hand while Genny signed madly into her other.

"Who's this?" Bernese said.

Amber DeClue answered before I could. "I'm Jonno's fiancée."

Bernese raised her eyebrows. "Jonno has a fiancée *and* a wife? How very modern."

"He isn't supposed to still have a wife, now, is he?" Amber snapped at Bernese, and then her gaze flipped back to me. "But here you sit, blocking him again."

"Me?" I said. "*I* am blocking *him*?"

"If you don't show up this time and finally get your mess all finished, what am I supposed to do? Huh? Our wedding is this weekend."

I took a step back, off balance, as if she'd pushed me. "Married?" I said. "Jonno can't get married this weekend."

"He can, too," Amber insisted. "My mama's lawyer worked it out, and we got the license. Our minister will sign it if Jonno brings the proof he got divorced."

"Stop talking," I said, holding up one hand. Things were starting to make sense. Of course she was somehow rolled up with Jonno. There had never been an interpreting job. She probably didn't even work at that ice-cream parlor. All she'd needed to book me was a valid credit-card number, and then she'd gotten to scope out the wife in neutral territory at a time when I didn't have my guard up. I could feel my lip curling. I had known something was off. Her expensive shoes and jewelry, her oddly pushy conversation, her endless questions about why I was using my maiden name.

"Calling my agency, booking me like that, I don't think that's even legal," I said.

She rolled her eyes. "My three best friends in all of life and my hateful cousin Jeannie have each spent four hundred bucks on apple-green taffeta bridesmaids' dresses. And what's my mother going to do with two hundred plates of dilled salmon? It's not like I had a choice."

"I could sue you. I could maybe have you arrested," I said. "That has to be some kind of fraud."

"You got paid," she said. "As for the rest, I don't care, but can you wait, please, and sue me on Monday? I kinda have a lot going on this weekend. And P.S.? I don't care if I have to drag you back to Athens by your hair. I love him with all my whole heart. You have to accept that he loves me and not you, and do you have any idea what my dress cost? It's Vera Wang, okay?"

Staring at the tiny, angry creature who was now shrieking about the nonrefundable deposit at the reception hall, I didn't know whether I should sink to the floor and laugh myself sick or slap her upside the head and start a cataclysmic catfight.

Bernese snorted. "If you think Nonny is the only reason the divorce is taking so long—whoa, has that man got you snowed."

"Oh yeah, blame the victim," Amber DeClue said. To me she said, "Are you coming peacefully? Or is this going to get ugly? You have to leave right now and drive like hell or you'll miss it. My daddy doesn't even know Jonno was ever married, much less still is. You have to come fix this or I will have to kill you, because Jonno has to be divorced or a widower by six P.M. on Saturday, do you hear me?"

I glanced over at Mama and Genny, standing together in the doorway to the den. Genny's eyes were so round I could see white all the way around her irises, and her hands were a blur as she speed-signed. Mama's face was closed, unreadable.

"X. Machina," I said.

Amber DeClue looked at me as if I had lost my mind.

"Jonno's band?" Bernese asked.

"Yeah, that's his band," I said. "It's slang, like a pun I don't get on 'deus ex machina.'"

"They're changing it," said Amber. "I told him that was a dumb name. They're going to be called Kicktown now."

"Shut up," I said.

"Why are you babbling on about Jonno's band?" Bernese's voice was sharp with impatience, but Mama didn't ask. I'd had an hour-long conversation with her once, trying to explain the band name, and she knew what I meant.

"It means 'god in the machine,'" I said. "It's a device from

Greek theater, and they used it when a play got too complicated to ever work itself out. An actor dressed up like a god would come down on a machine and fix everything with magic and end the play."

Bernese jerked a thumb at Amber. "And that's her? She's the god in the machine? Because I think that sounds a little bit blasphemous. This is more like 'adulterous whore in the machine.'"

"Hey!" Amber said.

"No, it's not her. It's more like her being here at all." I was talking to Bernese, but I was looking over at Mama. She was perfectly composed, her hands reading Genny's flashing signs as Genny tried to keep up. Then Mama was nodding.

"Are you going to go?" Amber demanded.

To Genny I said, "Tell Mama this doesn't mean I'm going to let Fisher down. Tell her to please trust me and not do anything drastic."

But Mama signed, *You can't choose to get a machine god. One happens or doesn't.*

"What does Fisher have to do with this?" Bernese said.

Amber stamped her foot. "You are going to miss it if you don't go right now."

"I'm coming," I said to Amber. "But you're driving me."

"Me?" said Amber.

"You want me to go?" I said, and she nodded. "Then you are driving me. I'm not done with you. I haven't even started with you. And yeah, okay, I'll go to Athens now. Maybe by the time we get there, I will have decided if I'll walk into that courtroom, but you don't even get that unless you take me there. I get this hour with you. Nothing's free."

Bernese was already opening her big mouth to argue with me,

but I cut her off. "Try to make it right with Fisher for me. I won't have my car, so it might be past her bedtime before I can get home." To Genny I said, "Tell Mama I am choosing this," and I watched her sign it into Mama's hands.

Mama knew I was watching, and she signed directly to me: *You aren't choosing. It's a push. You're just falling over.*

And then, comfortable with the pacing in her own home, she let go of Genny's hands and walked back into the den, her fingers trailing lightly along the wall as she traced her path.

CHAPTER

17

I F I COULD have flown out of my own head, taken my con-
sciousness up high enough to make Between a topical map
below me so that I could see Mama and Fisher and all my family
spread out below, tiny and frail, I never would have left them. But
I couldn't see the future. I couldn't see anything. Perhaps nurture
hadn't given me the ramrod will that seemed to be standard Frett
issue, but nature had certainly granted me the blinding Crabtree
temper.

I was angry with Jonno and his floppy doll who'd appeared
whining on my doorstep, furious with Mama, enraged with myself. So I got in the canary-yellow BMW convertible that was
parked in front of the house and left.

Amber DeClue tore onto 78, already breaking the speed limit.
She drove hell-bent for Athens, and beneath my anger, I worried
she would splatter us both all over the highway. Surely she
wouldn't want to show up for her wedding to my husband covered in scabs or, worse, dead. A bray of bitter laughter welled up

in my chest, and I pressed my fingers hard into my temples to keep it from escaping. I was halfway to hysteria, and I was making my husband's fiancée drive me to my divorce. There was so much wrong with that, I couldn't begin to process it.

Amber's soft hands gripped and worried the steering wheel, and she was leaning toward it with her spine rigid and straight. It was as if she believed relentless good posture made the car go faster.

The top was down. Of course it was. Amber was a top-down kind of girl. She'd pulled a scrunchy off the gearshift and secured her hair, but mine was torturing me, whipping around and getting in my eyes and mouth. By the time we got to Athens, I'd look like a fiery Medusa. Silence had swallowed up the car, except the white noise of the wind. I felt no obligation to break it.

Amber kept sneaking sideways glances at me. "Quit staring at me," she said. I didn't respond, and a few moments later, she added, "You're giving me nerves. I swear, I'm going to end up running us off the road."

I blinked twice and found it was difficult to stop watching her. I wanted to look at her, to try and get some sort of idea of what or who she was. The girl I met at the interview had been a false front, and maybe this wee virago was a false front, too. The BMW said "daddy's girl." So did the fat gold bracelet around her wrist, clunky with charms. I picked out a ballerina, a graduation cap, a key. Her nails were professionally manicured, and her glossy brown hair was streaked with caramel and gold. I'd noticed before that she looked too expensive to have a job at Bibi's, but I had been too worried about Mama to ask myself the right questions.

It finally occurred to me to check her left hand. Sure enough, she was wearing the big diamond I had seen her twirling at Bibi's. The stone had to be almost two carats, set in white gold or maybe platinum.

"Jonno gave you that?" I said, indicating the ring.

She shrugged. "It's a family ring."

"Yeah, your family's, maybe."

"It was my gramma's, okay? It's special to me, so Jonno didn't mind using it."

"I bet," I said.

She looked at me and said, "Why are you picking on me about my ring? Quit staring holes in me, you're making my stomach sick." She wobbled up onto the shoulder and jerked us back. "Shit! I told you!"

I turned to face forward, keeping my eyes deliberately off her. We were on a stretch of highway that offered nothing to look at but plowed cotton fields on either side of us. "So in Jonno's version, I'm the only one dragging my feet, huh?" This time she did not answer, but in my peripheral vision, I could see her hands still kneading the steering wheel like dough. I went on, "It doesn't seem that way to me, but maybe there's some truth to that. We could have been divorced six months ago if I'd stayed out of bed with him long enough for him to believe I meant it when I said we were finished."

She said, "Don't you bad-mouth him to me." She was very fierce, and her voice was filled with righteous conviction. She flipped on her sound system. She had a CD in, some faux-punk boy band I didn't know, and she jacked up the volume to six. She had to yell so I could hear her over the wind and the music. "If you're making me drive you so you can have some time to try to poison my mind against him, I already see through that."

"You don't want to hear about my frying pan? You want to leap straight into the fire?" I looked at her again. I couldn't help it.

"So you're trying it anyway? Fine. Trying just shows you still want him, and if he's an asshole, why would you want to keep him? And anyway, hello, he loves me. That must kill you, and I can even feel sorry for you, because if I lost him, I'd totally lie down and die. I can feel bad for you or whatever, but I am telling you up front, if you trash-talk him and pretend like he's cheating on me, I'll pull this car right over and slap you backwards. And I fight dirty. I pull hair and I bite. You don't want to start with me."

Her fingers had gone white on the wheel, but she hadn't once looked away from the road since she turned on the music. I reached over and flipped it off, then said over the whistling air, "You don't look to me like the kind of girl who's ever been in a fight."

She darted another sidelong glance at me. I saw her square her shoulders and willfully firm her trembling mouth. She said, "I told you to stop staring at me. If the question is whether or not I'm prettier than you, let me help you out. I am. Much."

A sharp bark of laughter escaped me. I sat back in my seat, looking out of the windshield at the flat expanse of the fields. "You've got a pair, as my aunt Bernese would say. How old are you, anyway?"

"Twenty," she said. She sounded as if she begrudged me the air it took to let me hear the word.

"So was I," I said. "When I married him. Ten years ago."

"That won't work, either," she said.

"Then I'll leave it at this. A man who cheats on his wife with you will cheat on you when you are his wife."

She braked, angling toward the shoulder. "Do you need me to kick your ass? Seriously?"

"Go ahead. Give it a try," I said. "I think I'd like that. But if you pull over, we'll miss the hearing."

"Dammit!" she said, and stomped on the gas again. We lurched forward until we were back up to eighty-five, and then she set cruise control. "Stop talking to me. Really."

"You don't get to decide what I do and don't do. You want me in Athens? This is what it costs you, and since you're having sex with my husband, it's pretty damn cheap."

"I didn't know he was married," she said.

"Really." I made my voice drip disbelief.

"I didn't! Well, not at first I didn't. And by the time I did, it was too late. We were in love. And it was, like, our love was bigger than that."

"Bigger than what?" I asked.

She waved one hand airily and then put it back on the wheel. "Bigger than rules. Bigger than whatever happened before it. Bigger than you." She was filled with such certainty, she sounded almost casual. She was so young, and all at once I was sorry for making her do this. She wasn't a match for me by half. Knowing that, I felt some of the anger loosen in my chest and then let go.

On a hunch, I leaned down and dug around under the seat. Sure enough, my fingers found the edge of one of Jonno's endless supply of coverless paperbacks. I pulled it out. Ken Kesey's *Sailor Song*. I paused, holding it. I had intended to read my way to Athens, but the physical presence of the book shook me. The book proclaimed, louder than anything Amber had said, louder even than the ring, that Jonno had been here.

I shoved it back under the seat. I didn't need a talisman to tell me what I already knew. Then I realized I already had one. I dug around my purse until I found my empty pill bottle. I glanced at Amber. Her eyes were on the road, so I slipped the pill bottle under the seat after the book. A message to Jonno that I had been here, too.

I sat back and stared out the window, watching the car eat the miles between me and the end of my marriage. The fields gave way to Georgia-pine wilderness, and then to townlets and suburbs that lined the path into Athens. I was content, for the moment, to be driven. I suspected that the girl beside me would drive Jonno, too, metaphorically speaking. She was so single-minded in her version of love. If he'd been using me in the role of clinging bitch-wife to buffer himself from the string bean of willful possession sitting next to me, he would not have that luxury much longer.

We pulled off 78 and headed toward downtown Athens. Amber drove directly to the courthouse. She must have been there recently, applying for a marriage license. It couldn't have gone well. We came up to the corner before the courthouse, and she pulled over, flipped on her hazards, and put the BMW in park.

"You're here," she said. She looked at her watch. "We made it. Plenty of time." She kept her gaze resolutely ahead, but as I stared at her profile, I saw another tremor hit her mouth. She pressed her lips together, stopping it. "Are you going to sit here in my car until you miss it?"

"No," I said. "You're leaving?"

She shrugged. "I'm supposed to have a dinner with my bridesmaids tonight. I have to go iron my hair. I have to dress and pretend none of this whole afternoon happened."

"How am I supposed to get back to Between?" I asked.

"Not my problem," she said. Her voice had an edge of rising hysteria. "You are a very weird person, do you know that? It's completely freakish, having me drive you here. That's not normal. You are not normal. I can't drive Jonno's wife around the night before my wedding, okay? It's making me upset."

"By the time I need the ride home, I won't be his wife," I said.

"Get. Out. Of. My. Car!" She was borderline hysterical. I suddenly felt so sorry for her that there wasn't room for feeling much else. It was a relief.

I opened the car door to get out, and that was when I saw Jonno. He was coming down the sidewalk toward us. As I climbed out of the BMW, our eyes met. He came to a halt so abruptly, he almost overbalanced. His mouth dropped open, and then he went leaping wildly to the right, off the sidewalk, flailing his arms and then dropping behind some bushes. I couldn't remember a time when I had seen him so graceless.

I looked down at Amber. She hadn't seen him. She felt my gaze and asked, "Are you ever going to close the door?"

"Good luck," I told her, and I stepped away and slammed it.

She was already driving off as I walked toward the trembling bushes, shaking my head. Funny how the world worked; the last time I'd seen Jonno, I'd been crouched in some bushes beside his house, hiding from him.

Jonno peeked out as Amber accelerated, then he crouched again. I watched until the car had safely turned the corner, and then I said to the bush, "Olly olly, oxen free."

He peered over the top. He had enough class to look the smallest bit ashamed. "Hi."

"That doesn't seem to quite cover it, does it?" I said.

"Was that . . ."

"Amber?" I said. "Sure was."

Jonno stood up and joined me on the sidewalk, brushing at his faded Levi's. The courthouse was behind us, a squatty white building with too many square pillars. There we stood in our jeans, rumpled and uncertain, quailing in front of it.

"Are you really going to marry that child?" I asked.

Jonno shrugged, embarrassed. "Are you really going to divorce me?"

"Do you want me to?" I asked.

He looked at me quizzically. "No, dumb-ass. Of course not."

"And yet. You have an Amber."

He looked down at his steel-toed boots. They were chocolate-brown lace-ups made of distressed leather, the cool-guy version of a workingman's boots. "She came after you had kicked me out."

"Oh, good," I said. "Comforting to know you aren't marrying the one who gave me syphilis."

His boots were apparently divulging unto him the untold secrets of the universe. At last he raised his head, staring past me up the street where her car had gone. He said, "Her dad works for Geffen."

"Hello, hello! Here's everyone all together!"

Jonno and I both started. Our divorce lawyer had joined us without our noticing. He was a genial little man, as pink and plump as a cherub. Every time I'd seen him, he'd been hugely and, it seemed to me, inappropriately cheerful. He stepped between us and put out a hand, ushering us toward the courthouse.

"We're running the smallest bit late," he said, urging us forward at a tidy clip. For a moment I thought my machine god might actually be him. He certainly knew how to process us through the blocky building. And it felt like we were in the clutches of a large machine as he walked us through the clots and streams of milling people. There seemed to be a pattern, as if the air had currents that shifted us and set our course.

He led us through metal detectors and stairwells to a dingy courtroom where our marriage could be unraveled in a businesslike and tidy fashion. Dismantling a marriage, it seemed, was an abrupt and definite process that involved sitting on a bench, standing when called, and watching a bored judge stamp signed papers. It felt entirely surreal.

I had expected something solemn, maybe even beautiful. Like a wedding, only backwards. Or maybe I had expected to drift into the divorce, a natural progression of one slow thing after another until there we were at an end, finished with each other.

It struck me as ironic that I'd caught Jonno cheating when we were trying to make a baby. I'd married him mostly because I'd thought we already had. We hadn't been dating even a year, and it didn't seem possible that the result of all the astounding sex we'd been having could be a pregnancy. He was my first love, and sex seemed like something we'd invented. At nineteen, I knew how reproduction worked in theory, but it had never occurred to me that there could be an application. Anyway, we'd been careful. I'd been meticulously careful. After all, I was raised a Frett. So sex with Jonno was a lot of things, but it had never seemed like a viable way to procreate until the month my period didn't show.

I told Jonno in the same way I would have told him any other mildly interesting but improbable scientific fact: An ant can live underwater for fourteen days, Jonno, and I am six days late. He had shrugged, calmly, and said, "Maybe you should pee on a stick?"

"I can't be pregnant," I said.

"Sure you can," he said, and that made it a little more real. I felt the first stirring of panic. He saw my eyes widening and grinned at me. "Don't sweat it, Gig. If the line goes pink, we'll get married. I mean, hell. I love you, right? And you love me. No big deal."

So we'd gone to Walgreens and gotten a First Response. This was back when Jonno was living with his old band in an ancient rental house that probably should have been condemned. The den smelled permanently of feet, and one of the bedrooms had a gaping hole in the floor that led into the kitchen. Jonno called it Chez Crap. It had two bathrooms, and the one Jonno used was less revolting than the other, though not what I would call clean. But we went there because I didn't want anyone in my crowded dorm to catch on to what I was doing.

The bathroom was built long and narrow, and Jonno came in with me and boosted himself onto the counter to sit by the sink. I made him close his eyes and run the water. When I was done, we set the test down by the sink and stood over it, staring, for three minutes. We watched the test line slowly fade into being, getting deeper, going almost red. The window that would indicate a pregnancy stayed purely, blankly white.

"There you go," said Jonno.

"All right, then," I said.

That might have ended it, except he added, "We could get married anyway, Gig. If you want to."

"All right, then," I said again. Even then nothing would have happened if I hadn't called my family and told them that Jonno had asked me and I had said yes. Mama kept asking if I was sure this was what I wanted, but all Bernese heard was "wedding." All three of her boys were married, but the weddings had been planned by the brides and their mothers. Lori-Anne was only eleven, a weedy-looking, sullen child who claimed she would never marry because boys were revolting.

Jonno and I were tugged bonelessly along in the huge wake of Bernese's planning. She had Pastor Gregg marry us outside by the fountain in the middle of Between's town square. My dress was a winter-white raw-silk shift, very simple. I'd worn short white gloves and a hat I now found embarrassing whenever I looked at the pictures. Genny's idea, that hat. Jonno wore a lightweight blue summer suit bought for the wedding and never worn again.

The entire town was there, Mama pressing her lips into a flat line, Genny sniffling into her hanky. Lou walked me down the aisle and Bernese sat with Isaac, presiding like the queen bee. Poor Lori-Anne was tricked out in a mint-green puffy-sleeved lace monstrosity that made her look jaundiced. She was my flower girl, and Lily Crabtree came home to be my bridesmaid, standing up with Boyd as best man.

Even Ona Crabtree came. She was alone, and she sat twitching uncomfortably in the back row, wearing an ill-fitting rayon dress. She didn't stay for the reception; it was dry.

Jonno's mother had passed, and his father and stepmother, who lived all the way up in Wisconsin, didn't make it. They sent a check for five hundred bucks inside a Hallmark card.

Had it rained, we would have gone inside the church, right beside us on the square, but we lucked out. We had a gorgeous day, not too hot, with bright yellow sunshine streaming idyllically down over everything. Bernese had farmed Azures like mad in the weeks leading up to the wedding. She had Ivy Marchant release them into the square right before the ceremony. The flower beds were thick with butterflies, and they seemed to fill the air around us, fluttering in romantic approval. While Jonno said the standard Baptist vows to me and put the ring Bernese had picked out on my finger, one of the Azures lit on his shoulder. It stayed the entire time he was speaking, opening and closing like a flower blooming and returning to bud, showing me its colors. I remember thinking it was a sign.

And now this quick and businesslike undoing seemed shameless in its speed, especially when filtered through the memory of our wedding. Jonno seemed to feel it, too. He stood with his handsome brow furrowed, stern and solemn. Or maybe he was simply adjusting his expression to suit the mood. There was no telling with Jonno. And then it was over.

Our lawyer walked us out, his jouncy, cheerful gait making his head bob like a chicken's as he all but skipped along between us. We thanked him, and he headed for the parking lot. The courthouse was closing. Jonno and I stood together at the bottom of the steps. The day was just beginning to die around us, the afternoon sunlight losing its heat and mellowing to gold.

"I can't believe you came," I said.

"I only showed up to see if you would," he said. "I still don't feel like you mean it."

I felt it, too, this open-ended unending. I said, "Maybe we need to go hit a ship with a bottle or cut a ribbon." It didn't seem possible that he could have another wedding planned for the next day. In typical Jonno fashion, he hadn't yet brought Amber back up. I didn't want to, either. It was none of my business as of fifteen minutes ago.

He said, "Do you want your keys back?"

I shook my head. "I'm not going to stay in Athens, Jonno. And you need to go by tomorrow and get Lewis. The neighbor's kid has been feeding him."

"Where are you moving?"

I didn't answer him, and after a few seconds passed, he said, "Not my business. Gotcha. Okay, I'll pick up Lewis tomorrow. Boyd hates cats, so that'll be fun. Hey, you want to go get something to eat?"

"No."

Jonno was looking at the courthouse, and I was watching the sun set over his shoulder. I waited for him to say goodbye or walk away. But he didn't, and I didn't, either. I said, "You know what, though? I could use a ride home."

"Home, the apartment? Or back to Between?"

"Between," I said.

"Yeah, okay. That would be good. If I felt like I was driving you away from me, out of town, then maybe this would feel like it was true. Because right now you still look like my Gig to me."

"That's almost charming," I said tartly.

"Don't be an asshole. I said I'll take you," he said. "But real quick, I have to go meet Boyd's friend at this warehouse and pick up our new amp, okay?"

I should have said no. But part of me didn't want to go home yet. I was still, at the core of me, so angry with my mama. So I said, "Sure. Let me give them a heads-up at home."

I got out my cell phone and called Mama's house, dialing directly instead of using the relay service. While it was ringing, I said to Jonno, "Don't talk."

He nodded, and I had a dizzying moment of déjà vu. So many times in the last year, I had called my family with Jonno hiding in the silence beside me.

I was expecting Genny, but Bernese picked up.

"It's done," I said.

"Good! You on the way back?"

"In a little," I said. "I need to do a couple of things while I'm here, and I have to work out a ride home, okay?"

"The whore can't bring you back?" Bernese asked. It was rhetorical. "Lou just called. He's closing up the shop, and then him and Fisher will be home. You took your keys off to Athens with you, so your car's still parked behind the church. Do you think Genny'll be okay with your mama, or should I stay here with them?"

"Genny's fine with Mama," I said. "How's Fisher?"

"Mad at you," said Bernese. "But you did the right thing, Nonny. She'll get over it—especially if this means you'll be around here for a good spell."

"It does. I'll have to pack up at some point, get out of my lease. But other than that, I'm not coming back here at all if I can help it." I got off the phone and clipped it back to my purse. Then I followed Jonno out to the parking lot where he'd stashed his Impala, and we got in. He negotiated his way out of the lot and paid. I flipped the radio on. He had it set to the college station, and they were spinning some weird alterna-crap. It sounded like an electric guitar backed up by a sitar and some singing mice.

Jonno had about fifteen words of directions to the warehouse scrawled on the back of a parking ticket. We set off looking for it, and before I knew it, we had slipped sideways into Jonno time. Jonno time zoomed by faster than regular time and had no set boundaries except the moment that a sacred gig began. If the band had a spot, he was there, on time, impeccably groomed, revved up, and running hot like a huge engine of charisma. But everything else was mutable and flexed and changed within the moment. After a little while, the warehouse began to seem like mythology.

He spent the next three hours running down my cell-phone battery, calling Boyd repeatedly to get new directions, yelling over the car radio and whatever music Boyd had going at the other end. At nine, we were parked in an otherwise empty lot behind yet another obviously incorrect warehouse. My cell was dead.

We waited hopelessly for a guy named either Dale or Paolo whom Boyd was sending to lead us to amp-land. We sat through half a Pink Floyd album that had been remixed by someone called DJ Peep-Peep. Meanwhile, Dale-or-Paolo was no doubt sitting at some other warehouse seven miles away, cussing us out.

I said, "This isn't going to happen."

Jonno nodded, but he didn't start the car. He sat there looking at me with his eyes half closing, becoming heavy-lidded and suggestive.

"Oh, you're kidding me," I said.

"Nuh-uh," he said, and he leaned across the gearshift to kiss me. I put my hand up between us like a stop sign.

He stopped moving forward, but he didn't sit back. He froze, waiting for me to put my hand down.

"Are you going to marry that girl?" I said.

He shrugged. "Not if you tell me not to." He dipped down and pushed his forehead into my hand, like a big dog wanting a pet, rubbing against my palm. He pushed my hand to the side with his head, and then he kissed me.

It was a typical Jonno kiss, perfect, practiced, almost endless. And wrong. Dead wrong. I tilted my head, and he moved in closer until I could feel the heat of his body. On a physical level, it was working for me—he always worked for me—but it was wrong. I willed Dale-or-Paolo to show up and interrupt us, wished Jonno would feel the wrongness and move away from me. Instead, he put one big hand on my knee, sliding it slowly up my thigh.

My purse was at my feet, stocked with the necessary condoms, and the parking lot was dark and deserted. It occurred to me that there was nothing that would come along and stop this, and he never would stop on his own. A thousand Ambers could knock on my door to demand him, and a million judges could bang gavels and call it over, but they couldn't start the credits rolling, and Jonno wouldn't.

So I broke the kiss and leaned back, tapping the back of my head against the passenger window, once, twice, hard enough to hurt. Jonno was still leaning toward me across the gearshift, his hand halfway up my leg. I swallowed, surprised.

It was only a broken kiss. I had only leaned back six inches. But I had ended us.

Right then I wanted nothing more than to be at home. I wanted to see Henry, and I needed to talk to Mama. I had to tell her, tell them both, that yes, hell yes, there was a god in the machine. But it had nothing to do with Amber. It wasn't her or even hers. The machine had been working this whole time, before I knew Amber existed. It had been the low hum underneath everything, droning in such a way that after a while I no longer heard it as it ground me toward my beautiful divorce. Maybe I had let it push me, and maybe I had gummed it up at times, but I had built it when I kicked Jonno out, and I had set it in motion when I drove us to a lawyer. The machine was mine. It had run on my time and no one else's, and the only god in it was me.

"It's no-go, huh?" he said.

"It was a good game and all, Jonno. But I'm out. Take me home, okay?"

He leaned toward me again, but I rolled the back of my head against the window until my temple rested on the cool glass. He stopped short before his kiss could land on my cheek.

"Okay, Nonny," he said. He sat back, his hand trailing away and coming to rest on the gearshift. I sat up, too. I wasn't even angry with him. I wasn't anything but longing to be home. And hungry. As my stomach growled, I realized I had never called Ona to cancel our dinner. I grabbed my cell, but of course it was dead as paint. Perfect. This was really going to help my peace negotiations.

Not speaking, Jonno drove for Between. He had the radio up loud, and we listened to whatever the too-hip-for-TV college DJ said was cool until we lost the signal. Jonno knew from experience that once we lost the college station, there was nothing but country music, preaching, or an eighties pop station that leaned heavily toward Mr. Mister. He put in a tape.

We were only a mile or two from my exit when the fire truck passed us with its siren on, lights blazing. Jonno canted right, easing toward the shoulder to let it pass. A minute later, we heard another siren. An ambulance this time. Then a state trooper and a fire marshal's car. We followed them all down 78, and it didn't even occur to me to panic until I saw they were pulling off at my exit, heading into my tiny town.

CHAPTER

18

LIVING HALF MY life in Between and half in Athens had made me an expert at finding the truth spread thin among at least three versions. I was adept at picking out key details from different narrators and combining them, interpreting through my family's bents and prejudices. But that Friday, almost nothing that mattered to me happened in the presence of my family. The only witnesses were Crabtrees, and the only Crabtree eyes I trusted were Henry's. I had to adopt his account in a single, unbroken piece, filling in blanks with nothing but my own imagination.

Henry Crabtree spent his Friday checking inventory and waiting for me. He was good at it. He didn't worry; he just waited. Around two-thirty, he saw Fisher playing in the gardens in front of the Dollhouse Store. He stepped outside and saw Lou framed in the display window, keeping an eye on her. He didn't see me, and on Fridays after school, whither Fisher went, there I went also. He went back inside and found himself humming while he restocked the travel section. If Fisher was with Lou, I was in Athens killing two birds with one stone: getting divorced and making Henry cheerful. Unless I was hiding from him. He stopped humming. As off-kilter as I'd been the last few days, he wouldn't put hiding past me. I wouldn't have put it past me, either.

He closed up at six, like always, and decided to stroll down to the end of Grace Street to see if I was home. He crossed the square on the diagonal and came to the crosswalk that led across Philbert, and like any former Boy Scout, he looked both ways.

That was when he saw them. The Alabama Crabtrees came caravanning off the interstate in two red trucks, first Teak Crabtree's old Ford, followed closely by Grif's Chevy. As they approached, Henry could see that Teak had Jimmy Crabtree in the cab with him, but he couldn't get a good look inside Grif's truck.

"Shit," he said under his breath, and walked back across the square, hoping they hadn't noticed him. He went inside his store and locked the door, then walked swiftly to the back. He paused by the sitting area in front of the office, staring at the sofa for a moment, rubbing his long fingers against his forehead.

He went upstairs to his apartment, where he spent a few minutes pacing and thinking. Grif and Teak were the only two of Ona's nephews who had the same mother. They were almost identical, with long-nosed, bony faces and scraggly red hair. They could hardly stand to be in the same room, they loathed each other so, but neither one could bear to be outdone by the other. Grif and Teak together guaranteed that any bad idea let loose in the room would be taken further and applied faster.

Jimmy, his red-gold hair razored close to the scalp to hide his receding hairline, had been easy to recognize as he sat in Teak's passenger seat. Jimmy was a good old boy when left alone, but he liked to needle Grif and Teak when he was liquored up. He was almost always liquored up.

Henry focused all his mental energy on hoping Billy hadn't been in Grif's truck. If Billy wasn't with them, they'd get drunk and trench Bernese's yard and then go smash the Dollhouse Store's front window, maybe drag off the register. Then they'd head back to Ona's, and Jimmy would needle Grif and Teak until they beat the crap out of each other. In the morning, if they hadn't been arrested, they'd convoy back to Alabama. They'd be hungover, feeling as mean as fifty snakes, but with all their venom drained. Probably nothing irrevocable would happen as long as it was just the three of them.

But if Billy had come? If it was Billy and Grif and Teak, drinking, pissed off, with Ona demanding justice and Jimmy niggling and pushing them from behind like a seedy, balding sprite? It was the working definition of trouble.

All the Crabtree boys had been in and out of jail for guns and dope, drunk and disorderly, DUI, petty larceny, and fighting. But Billy was a different animal. He'd been up on charges of arson, destruction of property, rape, and assault. He'd walked on most of them, but he had logged seven years in St. Claire after he killed a man in a bar fight. Henry needed to find me, fast, but first he needed to know if Billy was in town.

He reached up and took the leather band out of his hair, letting it fall straight and dense, two black curtains closing around his face, deepening the hollows of his eyes and cheekbones. He took off his black Bass loafers and hung them on his shoe rack, right next to his oxblood Bass loafers. He traded his ironed khakis for a pair of jeans (also ironed) and folded his starched shirt

239

neatly. He put the shirt in the bag he dropped off at the cleaners in Loganville twice a month and got a plain gray T-shirt out of his drawer.

Crabtree fashion sense ran toward shirtlessness and flip-flops. They accessorized with jailhouse tats and attitude. Henry was different, but he'd grown up around them. He was in them but not of them, and he knew how to flash their colors. He had that wicked edge in him, a suggestion of impiety that made the truckers listen to his book recommendations. He slid on this persona now, changing skins. He put on his running shoes and left the apartment to walk over to the gas station.

Grif's truck was parked in one of the six spaces in front of the country store that housed the aisles of motor oil and aging snack foods. Henry glanced in the truck's cab. It was empty, and the truck bed held nothing but a toolbox, a filthy blanket, and three rusty old gas cans. Teak's truck and Ona's blue car were nowhere to be seen.

Henry stuck his head in the front door. A Loganville kid, one of Tucker's friends, sat at the register on a stool. His name was Danny, but he had recently joined a band and was trying to make everyone call him Banger. He was tipped back to lean against the wall of cigarettes with his feet up on the counter. When the bell over the door jangled, he jerked up and clutched wildly at the racks of cigarettes to keep from toppling over. Four or five packs of Merits tumbled to the floor. When Banger saw it was Henry, he righted himself and scowled.

"Aw, come on, Henry. I don't wanna pump. Why'ncha swipe your card, man? Unless you need, like, a gum or something?"

"Is Grif here?" Henry asked him.

"Nah, it's just me, man," said Banger. "They left." The whites of his eyes glowed as pink as a lab rat's.

"Was Billy with them?" Henry asked, but Banger just shrugged. "How long ago did they leave?"

"Um . . ." Banger glanced helplessly at the clock. "It wasn't really soon ago."

Henry considered asking if he knew where they'd gone, but Banger was leaning down from atop his stool to pluck at the fallen packs of cigarettes. He missed and plummeted to the floor, landing with a meaty thud.

"Aw, man," he said. Henry withdrew, letting the door shut behind him. Ona's house was barely outside of Between's city limits, which meant he could walk there in about five minutes. He glided down Philbert, past the exit from 78 and the entrance to Country Glen, one of Between's two subdivisions. Once he got past Country Glen, he was outside of Between proper. The sidewalk ended, so he walked on the strip of dirt by the curb, woods flanking him on both sides of the street. One more block and then he took a left, up Hook Lane.

There were five or six houses there, all of them nearly hidden by a row of kudzu-choked trees and overgrown bushes and weed patches. The first two houses were empty and had most of their windows broken out. The next one was a burned-out shell. Ona's driveway was the fourth one down.

Henry started climbing the steep drive to her house. The concrete had split, and the cracks had branched and run across the drive, forking like lightning. Weeds and grass were fighting for life in the narrow spaces. He could see Teak's red truck pulled up in the dead grass beside the carport. Lobe's junky Packard was nowhere to be seen, but the ancient blue coupe Ona shared with her youngest son, Tucker, was there.

Ona Crabtree lived in a flat brick ranch built sometime in the fifties. It squatted low to the ground, and five exhausted azalea bushes stood in a line in front of the house, two of them flanking the small porch. The back door was under the carport, which was so filled with junk that for years no one had been able to do more than crack the door far enough for the cat to ooze out and slink away through the debris. Henry went up on the front porch. The doorbell had never worked in all his memory, so he gave the knocker three hard raps.

He heard Ona holler, "Come on in if you're coming."

The front door opened into the den. It was so smoky and dim that it took a few seconds for his eyes to adjust. He squinted and clocked Grif and Jimmy sitting on the sofa with their dirty bare feet lined up on the coffee table. They were slouched deep into the sofa, watching *Wheel of Fortune,* and Jimmy had a beer balanced on his stomach. Teak was sitting in an armchair to the left of them. He was ignoring the TV, leaning forward and watching Grif with a sullen gaze that told Henry the two of them were already ten feet deep into it.

"Henry!" said Jimmy. "Get yourself a beer, there, boy. Set your sorry ass down."

"Hey, Henry." Grif raised a lazy hand.

The fourth man in the room was Varner Coop, the latest in Ona's long series of common-law husbands. He was lounging in the chair opposite Teak, sucking hard on a Marlboro Red. Ona was standing in the doorway to the kitchen, drinking something pale pink out of a chipped juice glass.

Billy was nowhere to be seen, and Henry's tense shoulders relaxed a notch.

"Henry!" Ona said. She wended her way blearily from the doorway to his side and gave his arm a squeeze. "I hope you come hungry. I made the most huge roast. We're expecting Nonny, too, but there's plenty, so's you may as well stay."

"Nonny's coming?" said Henry. Grif took his feet down and sat up, lighting one of Varner's Marlboros for himself. The smoke was stinging Henry's eyes.

"Said she was," said Ona. "I invited her earlier this week. Stop letting the bugs in and come have you a beer or something." She tugged at his sleeve.

Henry closed the front door and came a step or two farther into the room. "Nonny's in Athens," he said. "Her divorce hearing was today."

"Shoot," said Ona. "That girl's not going to get a divorce. I'd put ten bucks on it. She's a sucker for a pretty man, just like her granny." She cackled and tipped Varner a wink, but he had his eyes on Vanna White and didn't notice.

Grif said, "I don't want to watch a show about your big head, Henry." Henry moved over to the couch and sat down on the end next to Varner's chair.

"Bless my balls, it's Henry." Billy was there after all. He'd been in the kitchen. He stood framed in the doorway in his almost white Levi's and a lime-green muscle shirt. He had fatty armpits and narrow shoulders. The skin of his bare arms and face was pure and creamy, so smooth it looked like it had been ironed. His red-gold hair was straight and glossy, flopping over his broad forehead. He was soft in the middle and sweet-looking, except around the eyes. They were a brown so pale they looked yellow, and they were as cool and glittery and empty as glass. "And you took my seat."

"Billy," said Henry. He started to get up, but Billy waved him back down. "Here, take this, I'll get me another." He fast-balled a Coors across the room, and Henry's hand went up automatically to catch it. It smacked into his palm, hard and perfect. Billy had deadly aim.

"What are you doing here, Billy?" Henry said. "What are all of you doing here?"

"Shit," said Billy, drawing out the I. "We come for supper. Just like you." He disappeared back into the kitchen.

Henry wasn't sure what his next move should be. If he confronted them, they'd beat the crap out of him and then go do whatever they were planning anyway. He figured nothing would happen as long as he was here. If they took it in their heads to leave, to go after my family, he couldn't physically stop all four of them. But he could play dumb and let them go and then call the cops. He could feel the smoke coating his throat, making it harder to breathe. He said to Ona, "I didn't know you were expecting all this company tonight."

Ona stared down into her glass and shrugged. She had all but promised Henry that she wouldn't call her brother until she'd talked to me, at least. "Yeah. Waren't that a nice surprise." She wasn't a very convincing liar.

"Even Billy," Henry said to her.

"Yup. Even Billy," said Teak, glaring at Grif as if Billy's presence were the fifteenth thing Grif had done wrong that day.

"Where's Tucker?" asked Henry.

Ona said, "Both my boys went into town. They's gonna shoot some pool."

Grif flared his nostrils and said, "Someplace where people know them?"

Ona said, "Oh yeah, they's regular there."

Grif opened his mouth to say something else, but then he glanced at Henry and stopped. He cleared his throat theatrically and then said to Henry, "You gonna drink that beer or hold it until it's piss-warm and poorly?"

Henry passed over the Coors, and Grif lifted it up close to his face before he popped the tab, sticking his mouth fast over the hole to catch the foam that came shooting up.

"You want me to make you one of these, Henry?" Ona said. "It's a salty dog. Got gin in it, and salt, and then red grapefruit juice for nutrition."

"Shit, no, he don't," said Jimmy. "Henry don't want some pink fluffy cocky-tail." He lifted his voice. "Billy, bring another cold one for Henry. Grif skunked him."

Billy reappeared in the doorway. Henry lifted his hand, and another beer smacked into his palm, dead center.

"I wisht Nonny would get here," said Ona. "That roast'll dry up and die."

Henry popped the tab on his beer, holding it close and catching the foam as he had seen Grif do it.

"Well, she better," said Billy from the doorway. "She sure as hell don't want to be no place but here tonight."

The foam shot out all the way to the back of Henry's throat. He tried to swallow, but it was too fast, and he choked.

"Watch it there," said Grif, and pounded him on the back.

"Shit, Henry. You're such a fucking girl," said Jimmy, sniggering. "You better feed us, Ona. Nonny'll be along."

"Come give me a hand, Henry, and you, too, Billy. We'll fix everyone a plate," said Ona.

While the Crabtrees, neutralized by Henry for the moment, ate roast beef and Ona's velvet potatoes, Fisher was lying down, stiff and sullen, in her room. Her legs were rigid, ankles flexed so her toes pointed at the ceiling. Her arms were folded across her chest, asphyxiating her stuffed monkey in an angry elbow lock.

"And you better stay in that bed," said Bernese, watching from the doorway.

Fisher kept her baleful gaze on the ceiling, praying open-eyed for God to come and explode the world. Fisher had been promised me and movies and kettle corn, and she'd gotten tuna salad and broccoli and a spanking for having a smart mouth.

"You hear me? You better not go night-walking over to next door and climbing in with Nonny."

"I wish spiders would come and eat me," Fisher said. "You'd be so sorry."

"Don't be spoiled. Nonny will be back late, and you two can have a big time tomorrow. And tonight I do not care how mad you are. If I see this bed with you not in it, I will come and I will find you and I'll paddle your butt blue."

Fisher said nothing.

"Do you hear me?" said Bernese.

"I hear you," said Fisher.

Bernese eased back from the doorway. "Did you say your prayers?"

"Yes, ma'am," said Fisher. "You want to know what I prayed?"

"No," said Bernese, and stomped off downstairs. A couple of

hours later, right before she turned in, she poked her head into Fisher's room.

All she saw was a short, squatty tube of resentment wrapped in a woolly blanket, black hair sticking out the top. "Nighty-night," Bernese whispered. Fisher did not move or answer, because Bernese was actually talking to the back of Fisher's Happenin' Hair Teresa styling head. The real Fisher had already slipped out the back door.

Bernese said, "Fine, then," and went off to bed, muttering about sulkers.

Down on the square, Trude was standing in the darkness in front of her closed diner, having a smoke before she walked to her car and headed home. She saw Fisher go to the plastic rock Bernese had in the flower bed in front of the store. Fisher opened the bottom and picked out the key. She let herself inside the store, and the door closed behind her. Trude waited, but the lights did not come on.

Trude cussed under her breath, went back inside the diner, and picked up the phone. She was four digits in when she stopped dialing and hung up to think things over. Bernese hadn't seemed herself lately. Even Trude had noticed how hard she had become with Fisher. And Trude had not forgotten Bernese's attitude just days ago, when the Bitch had taken down Genny. Trude had left her place of business and come running to help Bernese's family, bringing every paper towel she had in the place. She had very naturally been upset by all the blood and carnage. And Bernese had slapped her. Some thanks.

When she thought about it, Trude didn't much feel like calling Bernese, and anyway, Fisher was my responsibility on weekends. She rummaged around in her purse and pulled out her Day-

Timer. Sure enough, she had my cell phone number scrawled in the back. She had gotten it from Bernese a few weeks ago when I'd left a book I was reading in the diner.

She dialed me but got sent immediately to my voice mail. "Nonny? It's Trude. I saw that little gal of y'allses off on one of her night walks. She's holed up over the store. I didn't want to wake up Bernese with it. Okay, then. You might want to come by and get her little naughty bee-hind before Bernese gets wind of it. Okay, then. You call me, let me know you got this, hear?" She meant to call me again after she was home, but she was tired and forgot.

During dinner at Ona's house, Henry had gotten out Ona's tequila and tried to render everyone drunk enough to be harmless. Teak and Grif had resolutely stuck to beer and were no more than solidly buzzed. Billy had taken every shot Henry offered, though he had a legendary hollow leg and seemed all but unaffected. Jimmy and Varner and Ona, however, were flat-out worthless drunk.

"You'da thought Nonny would've called," Ona said over and over.

Henry sat on the sofa with his empty Chinet plate balanced precariously on his knee, nursing his beer and regretting the two shots he'd downed to try and get the ball rolling. Varner was already rumbling out bear snores from his chair, and Jimmy seemed close to joining him.

"S'not like her. She's a 'sponsible little thing. Most times," Ona said.

"Maybe she did go to Athens," said Henry.

"How? You think she hitched? I saw her car. It was parked behind the church all day," Ona said. "She couldn't have tooken

someone else's—the blind one don't got a car, and Bernese and
Lou Baxter don't got but one tire left between 'em." Ona let out
a snort that sounded suspiciously like a laugh. "I keep calling
Nonny's cell phone, but I just get that voice mail, blah blah.
Leave a message, beep beep beep." She took another slug of her
salty dog.

"May as well go to bed, if Nonny ain't gonna show," said Teak
to Grif, and there was a nasty edge to his voice.

"Why don't *you* go to bed," Grif said to Teak.

Teak sat up straight, leaning forward angrily. "I wanted to go
to bed, didn't I? But Nonny ain't coming, so we might as well all
go to bed."

"Henry's here," said Jimmy blearily from the depths of the
sofa. He had sunk down so low, his head was level with his feet,
which were back up on the coffee table. One of his heels was resting in a drift of velvet potatoes; Grif had put his Chinet plate
down in front of Jimmy when he was done eating.

Grif and Teak and Billy paused and looked over at Henry.
"Yeah," said Henry. "I'm here, all right."

"Henry's a Crabtree," said Billy.

"Not so's you'd notice," said Grif, and Jimmy cackled.

"Don't talk shit about his mama, you prick," said Teak. There
was some conversation between Grif and Teak that was going on
under the conversation everyone else was having. Henry couldn't
follow it, but he could sense its presence, and he wondered if he
couldn't find a way to use it. He sat up straight and leaned forward.

"Are you calling my mama a whore?" said Henry to Grif.

"Aw, Henry, don't be like that. You know she was a whore,"

said Grif. "Anyway, what you gonna do about it? I'd hand you your ass."

"Then I'll give Teak fifty bucks to hand you yours back," said Henry, playing drunker than he was.

"Shit, I'd do it for a dollar," said Teak.

"You couldn't fucking do it for a million," said Grif, and he started to get up.

"You going to take that?" said Henry to Teak.

Teak started to get up as well, but Billy glided to the center of the room, breaking Grif and Teak's eye contact. "Nonny's a Crabtree, too," said Billy.

"Not so's you'd notice." It was Teak who said it this time, snide, mimicking Grif's facial expression with eerie precision.

Henry laughed, nasty, egging them on, and he thought Grif might go leaping over the table for Teak's throat and the violence building in the room could be discharged in a Crabtree brawl, but just then Jimmy said, "Baby Jesus, but I fucking need some pie," and Grif burst out laughing in spite of himself.

Billy said to Ona, "You got any of that icebox pie?" Ona shrugged and Billy said, "Grif, go and look. If she's got any, just bring it. We can use our same plates."

Grif said, "Jimmy has his foot in my goddamn plate."

Billy shrugged. "He can eat off that plate, then. It's his own foot, so it won't bother him none."

Grif went in the kitchen, and Teak sat back, cooling. Billy was staring at Henry, who felt a flush coming up under his cheeks.

"Don't fuck with me," said Billy. "Smart boy."

"I'm not fucking with you," said Henry.

Grif came back with five beers stacked in his arms like cordwood and passed them out. "No pie."

"Thanks, bro," said Billy.

Jimmy held his loosely, unopened, but everyone else popped their tabs and took a drink, almost in unison.

Wheel of Fortune had ended some time ago, and now a Schwarzenegger flick was on. "I think I better hit the sack," said Billy, suddenly jovial. "We gotta drive home in the early A.M. Shit to do, you know. You don't mind, hey, Henry?"

"No. I don't mind," said Henry.

Ona said, "I'da thought Nonny would've called."

Billy tipped back his beer and opened his throat, chugging it, and Grif followed suit. Then Grif said, "Don't matter, Aunt Ona. You can catch up to her tomorrow. I guess I better go on and hit the sack, too." He turned toward Henry. "You gonna keep these reprobates company for a little?"

"I'll be right here," Henry answered, but his eyes were on Billy. "I'm not going anywhere."

"Good, then," said Billy.

"Good," said Grif.

"I better head on along to bed, too," Varner said. Henry hadn't noticed Varner wake up, but he was stirring, digging deep into his belly button with one thick forefinger and then rising and stretching. All four of the Alabama Crabtrees turned to look at Varner.

"You're going to bed, too?" said Grif.

"Yeah. He's going to bed," said the sinkhole on the sofa that was Jimmy. He had oozed down even farther, his chin tipped to rest on his chest. Henry didn't see how he could possibly see the TV over his feet. Especially since his eyes looked closed. "He's sleepy, Grif."

"Oh. Right," said Grif.

Varner got up and headed out of the den. Henry could hear him lumbering down the hall toward the bedrooms. Grif stood up and turned sideways, stepping over Henry's legs to get free of the coffee table.

Henry said, "You are about as covert as a stampede. You might as well tell me what's going on, because I'm not leaving."

"Nothing's going on," Grif said.

"Yeah, nothing's going on," said Teak. "It's just that Grif's retarded."

"And Teak's an asshole," said Grif, taking a step toward Teak.

"But you knew all that," Billy interjected smoothly, grasping Grif by the elbow before he could get any closer to Teak. "Say good night, boyo." He gave Grif a shove toward the doorway that led back to the bedrooms. Then he paused and smiled at Henry, all his teeth showing. His round cheeks made his expression bland and benign, but Henry felt gooseflesh break out on his arms. "You've kinda pissed me off." Before Henry could answer, Billy turned and followed Grif off to bed.

Henry stayed where he was, watching Jimmy sink into a coma and Teak sulk and Ona, who had taken over Varner's chair, get drunker and drunker. Schwarzenegger was running through a military compound, machine-gunning down men in fatigues.

"I can't believe she didn't come," said Ona. "Henry, you think she's in Athens?"

"I don't know," Henry said.

"You don't think Nonny is at her house, do you, Henry?" asked Teak.

"Why would that be bad? What do you think is going to happen at her house?" Henry said.

Teak stirred, but Ona waved a hand at him and said to Henry, "It's better if we don't know nothing, baby."

"What are you going to do, Teak?" Henry demanded.

"I'm not going to do a damn thing." Teak stared sullenly at the television.

"Shut your holes and watch the movie." Jimmy was still conscious.

But Henry had finally gotten it. If Teak wasn't doing a damn thing and was pissed off about it, it could only be because Grif was doing something. Right now.

Henry leaped up off the sofa, his Chinet plate tumbling to the floor, and went running down the hall toward the three bedrooms. The door to Tucker's room stood open, and Varner would be in the master at the end of the hall. The door to the third bedroom was shut. Before Henry could open it, Tucker's hand snaked under his arm and grabbed the knob, holding it shut.

"Let go of the door," Henry said.

"You don't want to look," Teak said. "If you don't look, then as far as you know, they're in there."

"And that was Nonny's job, right?" Henry smacked the flat of one hand against the door, hard. "You and Jimmy were supposed to keep her here late, and meanwhile, Grif and Billy go to bed and slip out the window. She thinks they're sleeping, and she's sitting right there with you guys. So when something happens to her folks, she thinks it wasn't you. And she tells the cops she was here with you guys all night. So you screw with her family, and she's the one who alibis you? That's sick."

Ona, behind Teak, said, "Them Fretts are not her folks. We're her folks."

"Get out of my way, Teak," said Henry.

"Make me," said Teak.

Henry shoved down hard on Teak's wrist, and it slipped off the knob. Henry threw open the door and stepped inside, flipping on the lights. The window was open, and a faint breeze was stirring the blinds. The twin beds were undisturbed. Henry turned back around and found Teak blocking him in. He moved toward the door anyway, and Teak reared back and popped Henry in the eye. Henry went down.

"Teak, no!" yelled Ona.

Henry got slowly back to his feet. He hadn't been in a fistfight since he was in third grade, and Teak, long-armed and tall, was in a brawl or two every month. Henry went for him, landing a solid right to Teak's belly before Teak put him on the ground again.

"Stop it! Stop it!" Ona was still cawing.

"Think it through, Teak." Henry got to his feet again. "You better let me go stop them. Nonny didn't come, and you were so transparent that even I saw through it. The cops will, too, in a lot less time than it took me. And you won't have a witness to back up your story. You're sending Billy and Grif out there with no alibi."

"Serves Grif right," said Teak.

"But not Billy," Henry replied softly. "Do you know what they're going to do?"

Teak shrugged, but Henry was still turning it around in his mind. Something was niggling at him. He took a deep breath, trying to clear his aching head. His eye and the side of his head hurt. And then he had it. Back at Crabtree Gas and Parts, he'd looked into the bed of Grif's truck and seen the toolbox and a blanket. And three gas cans. No one needed three gas cans.

"You piece of shit," said Henry. "There's a little girl living in one of those houses. There's a deaf and blind woman in the other, sleeping. What if they don't get out? If you keep me here while they light those places on fire, Billy's going to end up in trouble for felony murder."

"Fire?" said Ona.

"I ain't shifting," Teak said.

Ona clutched at Teak's arm from behind. "Teak, they can't mean to light them houses on fire with all of them sleeping?"

Teak didn't answer, and Henry said to her, "It's better if we don't know nothing, baby."

Ona said, "Teak, no. And what if my Nonny's in there?"

Henry started forward again, but Teak held up both hands. "Don't, man. You think I like beating the piss out of family?"

Ona tugged on Teak's elbow from behind. "Nonny could be sleeping in that house. She's your blood."

"Aw, crap. Lemme think," said Teak. "I better ask Jimmy what to do. Henry, sorry, man, but you ain't going nowheres until I ask Jimmy." To Ona he said, "Watch him and call me if he tries to go someplace."

Teak went back up the hall, and Ona and Henry stared at each other for a heartbeat. Then Ona cut her eyes at the open window and deliberately turned her back. Henry was moving as soon as she began to turn, climbing over the windowsill and dropping into the azalea bushes. He took off at a dead run.

He didn't bother heading back down Hook to Philbert. That was where Teak would come looking for him. Instead, he ran into the woods, cutting through the trees until he emerged in a cul-de-sac in Country Glen. He sprinted through the backyards, making a beeline for Mama's house. He got to the other side of

Country Glen and ran back into more woods, thin, filled with hiking tracks, mostly Georgia pine and some scrub.

The air was burning his lungs. His feet pounded against the ground, and he could feel the tequila and the beer and the velvet potatoes sloshing around in his gut. As he came out of the woods onto Grace Street, he slowed. He was looking from Bernese's house to Mama's, his eyes flicking back and forth. But everything there was peaceful and still. Grif's truck wasn't there, and Henry didn't see Grif or Billy anywhere.

He panted, trying to think like one of the Alabama Crabtrees, and that was when he heard the first booming explosions coming from the square. He started running again, up Grace this time. Three gas cans, three gas cans! He'd been stupid.

They'd changed their plan and gone after Bernese's store and the museum. Billy had thought it through, and maybe he didn't want to set fire to a house if I was in it. More likely, though, Billy had switched targets because the Dollhouse Store was attached to Henry's bookstore, and Henry had pissed him off.

Henry ran as fast as he could, listening to the staccato bursts. He couldn't figure out what the noise was. Something in the museum? In his mind's eye, he saw the blue velveteen drape that hid Bernese's dollhouse terrarium going up in flames. It would incinerate quickly, fusing to the melting plastic framework. He saw the glass cracking and then running down itself as it liquefied. The adult moths would flutter as they burned, and the heat would push the blackened tissue of them upward even after they had changed from animal to ash. He was seeing the plastic smile of the mommy doll peeling off and crackling as her head melted, and the flames touching the feet of the young girl doll with my face. In his mind, the popping noises were the cocoons of the luna moths, bursting in the heat, and he saw all the solid little caterpillars that Fisher loved, curling and uncurling as they burned.

He sped up, his head aching where Teak had hit him, his pulse beating so hard through his body that he could feel it even in his eyes.

As he neared the square, he could see an orange glow filling up the sky. He ran toward the center fountain. The Dollhouse Store was a mass of flames. The fire had already spread sideways to the wall of his bookstore. The bottom floor of Bernese's store was engulfed, and as he watched, the flames were reaching from the wooden trim to lick at the brick storefront. Flames were creeping up the frame side to the roof, and the windows in the apartment above bowed inward from the heat. There was no getting in there, and as far as he knew, there was no reason to try.

The museum was blazing, too. For the moment, it seemed to be mostly on the side closest to the store, but the museum house was all frame and gingerbread, so the fire was moving fast. He saw Isaac coming toward him across the square, wearing a plush burgundy robe. His pale feet were bare and veined in translucent blue. He hobbled across the grass, the light from the fire washing him in tones of rose and gold. He had a cell phone clutched to his ear.

Henry hoped to God Isaac was calling 911 and not Bernese. He stared at the burning museum, glad at least that it was empty, and then he realized it wasn't only the terrariums burning up. Almost all of my mama's original dolls were in there, on display and stored upstairs.

He turned away from Isaac and ran as fast as he could, directly toward the burning museum.

CHAPTER

19

AS JONNO EXITED the highway, I could see the lights of the fire trucks and police cars coming from the square. I was leaning forward, hands pressed into the dashboard as if I were shoving the Impala forward. From the top of my throat all the way to my stomach's pit, my body buzzed and trembled. I felt like I was full of bees.

"Pull over here," I said as we reached the turn into the parking lot behind the church. There was no getting any closer. Before the wheels stopped turning, I was out of the car and sprinting down Philbert.

The church was blocking my view of the museum and Bernese's store, but I could see the orange glow of fire, and the rising smoke was like columns of darker black against the night sky, blocking out starlight.

As I came around the corner, I could see that the museum and the Dollhouse Store were awash in flames. Half of Henry's store was blazing, too. The firemen were working to put a water wall in between Henry's store and the Sweete Shoppe; they weren't trying to put out the fire so much as contain it until it burned itself out. A second truck was working on the museum.

I looked wildly around, trying to find someone I knew. Strangers in uniforms and slick coats were bustling back and forth, anonymous and busy, and then I saw the Marchants standing by the curb in their fluffy robes and slippers. They were holding hands. Their daughter, Ivy, was beside them, her hands clamped over her mouth as if her throat were also full of bees and she had permanently committed to not letting even one escape. I heard someone calling my name in a deep, croaking voice I did not recognize.

I turned toward the sound and saw Henry. He was sitting on the floor of an ambulance parked on Philbert. His feet hung down over the back bumper. Both doors were open, and I could see an EMT behind him, digging in the equipment. Henry had an oxygen mask on, and his face and clothes were striped black with soot and ash.

I ran up to him and said, "Oh, God, Mama's dolls. Does she know? Where's my family?"

He pulled the mask off for a second and croaked out, "She's somewhere here. She knows, but—" He broke off and started choking. He sounded awful. I pressed the oxygen mask back to his face.

"I have to find her," I said, crazed.

But he grabbed my wrist. From behind the mask he said, "Listen. I was in there."

"The bookstore? Henry, I have to find Mama!" But he didn't release me, and I noticed that under the ash and grime, Henry was developing a glorious shiner. "What happened to your eye?"

He waved it off. "Teak happened. Screw it. Listen. You have to tell your mama." He started hacking, and the EMT looked up from her equipment and said in a fussy, isn't-he-cute tone, "Keep that mask on. Breathe deep."

Henry rolled his eyes.

I glanced over at the burning store, putting it together. "Teak Crabtree is here? Teak did this?"

"The animal dolls," Henry said from behind the mask.

"Wait, you mean you were in the museum?" I said. I stopped pulling away from his grip and listened.

"I got a lot of the animals out. As many as I could carry. They are sitting in rows on Isaac's sofa, creeping him right the hell out. I broke the case." He coughed. "Isaac hates that grasshopper doll."

"Henry, does Mama know you got them?" I said.

He shook his head, grinning. "Isaac was still talking with the cops." He couldn't stand not telling me, I could see it. He took a deep hit of oxygen and pulled the mask right back off. "It was like being on a movie set. I couldn't believe I was in a room that was actually on fire. I had my T-shirt tied over my mouth—"

"Fat lot of good that did you," the EMT said. She was about my age, with a glossy cap of blond curls. "Please keep that mask on."

Henry obediently put the mask on for another breath and then said, "The sprinkler system came on—"

"The insurance company made us get that," I said. "Bernese was furious. It cost a mint."

"It gave me time to get into the carousel room," Henry rasped. "All the while I was hearing this banging noise, boom, boom,

boom. No idea what that was. It sounded like they were making popcorn in hell."

"Bullets!" I said. "Bernese buys them by the case and keeps them at her store."

"Right. They scared the crap out of me, going off in long chains. I thought—" Henry's gaze shifted off me, to the left, and he stopped talking abruptly. He wasn't coughing; he simply stopped. All the animation leached out of his dirty face, and he became as bland and expressionless as a waxwork. When his eyes met mine again, it was as if whoever lived behind them had flipped a sign from OPEN to CLOSED.

I looked over my shoulder and saw that Jonno had come up behind me. "Hey, man," he said to Henry.

Henry gave him a nod, not speaking, and pointed at the mask.

"Hey, no, that's okay," said Jonno. "Keep sucking up the good stuff."

Henry nodded once, his eyes narrowing.

Jonno said, "Nonny? I found your mama. Bernese brought her to sit down over near the Marchants. She's ruined."

"I need to go talk to her," I said to Henry.

He nodded and said, "Yes, you do. Sorry I wouldn't shut up. Go."

The EMT started to say something, but I had to get to Mama. I followed Jonno a few feet, ducking around two policemen. And then I saw her. She was sitting with Genny on the curb. Genny had both her arms around Mama and was holding her so tight, and Mama was rocking back and forth. Her eyes were squashed shut and her mouth was open and she looked like she was wailing, but she was silent.

Bernese stood beside them. Her eyes blazed as brightly as her store.

As I came toward them, Bernese looked up and saw me. "This was Crabtrees," she said. "A whole slew of those Alabama Crabtrees. Henry told the cops. They already went and got two of them from over at Ona's house."

"Oh, shut the fuck up, Bernese," I said, and I sank down on Mama's other side. I drew my heart on her shoulder, and she made my name sign and then clutched at me. I rocked her, my arms wrapping around her over Genny's arms. She started signing, shaping *Gone, all gone, gone* again and again. I tried to give her my hands, to sign to her, to tell her about her animals, but she ignored my hand and kept rocking, signing almost to herself.

I realized I had forgotten to put back the head I had chosen for Bernese's buyer. I let go of Mama long enough to dig down deep into my purse. Sure enough, I found the box with Josephine's head and hands inside, carefully wrapped and labeled. I'd been so distracted that I'd been walking around for days with a museum piece worth thousands of dollars stuffed in the bottom of my handbag. I pushed the box into Mama's hands, and she clutched it, instantly recognizing the familiar size and texture of the box.

She turned it in her hands until she found the label and then ran her fingers down the Braille, her lips shaping a loose and silent word. Genny relaxed her grip and sat up straighter, staring at the box.

You forgot to put her back, Mama signed. *Josephine.*

I nodded into her hands, and while I had her attention, I signed quickly, *And Henry Crabtree got some of your animal dolls off the carousel. It isn't much, I know.*

Mama took a deep breath and clutched the lone box, shuddering. Tears were streaming unchecked down her face. I pressed close into her side and sat quietly with her while she wept, Genny leaning into her other side. Mama rocked the box as if it were a baby, her arms folding all the way around it to hold herself.

Another car was coming up Philbert. The headlights were shining our way, making me squint until they abruptly clicked off.

Bernese had stalked away while I was talking with Mama, but she reappeared out of the crowd and came over to me. "The cops say there's two more Crabtrees loose around somewhere. They got gas right across the street and torched everything in this world that matters to your mama and me. Everything that matters in this world."

I buried my head in my hands. "When is this going to stop?"

Jonno squatted down beside me on the curb and put one hand on my shoulder. I lifted my head long enough to push his hand off me. I saw Bernese note the motion, but she said nothing.

The car I'd seen was Trude's old Packard. I saw her running up Philbert toward us. Her whole face seemed composed of circles, her eyes stretched as round as quarters, her mouth open in a wide O of surprise. She was heading straight toward us.

Bernese saw her, too. "Perfect. My sister gets eaten, my other sister loses her life's work, my store burns down, and Trude gets to show up just in time to have the vapors."

Trude came clattering up, staring wildly from the blazing Dollhouse Store to my face and then back again. She leaned down and grabbed my arm so hard I felt her grip all the way to my bone. She jerked me to my feet. Her face was inches from my own.

"Ivy called my machine, said the square was on fire," she

panted. "She hung up before I could get to it. Tell me you got Fisher out of there."

"Fisher's safe at home in bed," Bernese snapped.

At the same time I said, "Got her out of where?"

"The store!" said Trude. "Bernese's store!"

"Fisher's not in there," Bernese said.

"She was," Trude said to Bernese. She yanked on my arm. "Did you get my message?"

"Message?" I said. Something black and tarry was grasping at my heart, pulling it downward in my chest.

"On your cell?" Trude said, frantic.

I turned to Bernese. "You saw Fisher at home? Right before you came down here?"

Bernese nodded. "Isaac called and told me what was going on. I was in a hurry to get down here, but I peeked in. She was snug as a bug in her bed. I left Lou at home in case she woke up."

"No," said Trude. "She was night-walking. I saw her go in the store."

My heart was swelling, and the tarry fingers on it levered it down into my gut, pressing the breath out of me. "Call Lou," I said.

Bernese, looking alarmed now, pulled her cell phone out of her bag and hit the speed dial for home. I counted through the twenty endless seconds it took Lou to pick up.

Bernese said, "Hey, it's me. Trot on down the hall and look in on Fisher." We waited another small eternity, and then the side of Bernese's mouth quirked up and she nodded. "That's what I thought." She held the phone away from her face and said to me, "Safe in bed."

Trude's death grip eased, and I wrenched my arm away from

her and grabbed the phone. "Lou?" I said. "Lou, go pull the covers back."

"I'll wake her," he said.

"Just do it." I was practically screaming. Trude was pulling at her lower lip, and Bernese's eyes were on my face.

"All righty," said Lou, and I waited what must have been a million years, an ice age, for him to cross the room. There was a moment of baffled silence, and then Lou said, "Oh my goodness." And I knew.

I couldn't know, and I didn't want to. I hurled the phone away from me and heard it clatter and crack in the road.

"Nonny?" said Bernese from very far away. She sounded both scared and uncertain. I looked at the store, and it seemed to my eyes to be a solid block of fire, but that didn't matter. It was all very easy and clear. Fisher was in there, and I had to go get Fisher. I started running, thinking this was all very simple: I would go in there and I would get Fisher, Fisher who hated to be held, and she would struggle and be irritated, so I would have to take her out on piggyback. I would bring her down the stairs and out the door and they would put an oxygen mask on her like Henry and she would say, "It was hot in there," and it would all be fine.

I could not feel my feet hitting the earth as they took me toward the store. I thought I heard someone say "Miss?" Other people were yelling things like "Hey" and "Stop" and "You can't." But I could. I would.

I came even with the fountain, flying toward Fisher, flying to reach into all that liquid flame and lift her out of there, perfect and whole and perfectly herself, and then something slammed into my side, and the ground rose up to meet me and I plowed hard into it.

"Nonny, no," croaked Henry Crabtree, and I twisted in his arms, beating at him, hitting his face where Teak had hit him. I hit him hard and again and then again, but he didn't let go of me. He was about my size but so amazingly strong. So much stronger. I couldn't understand how he could be so strong, how he could hold me down so easily when I was this mighty. I was so invincible it was obvious that I could go into the mass of flames and pluck my girl out if only he would let go of me. But he wouldn't. So I fought him, trying to scratch his eyes out of his head, and he was saying "No" to me, but there could not be a no. There could only be Fisher, and only I could go and get her.

Then we heard a crack like the spine of the world breaking, and I stopped fighting him long enough to look up at the burning store, at the place where Fisher was, and the crack was the roof falling in and smashing her, and then more cracks as the walls crumbled and fell in, folding up the store on top of her, burying her, and at last the brick front of the store tottered inward and fell whole on top of it all, like a lid closing, and Fisher was gone.

"Get off me," I said to Henry. I was limp beneath him, and he did what I said.

There was a terrible noise inside me, and I couldn't think over this terrible noise. I looked back toward Bernese and saw she had dropped to her knees, gray-faced, and Trude was beside her weeping, and I could make no sense of it over the noise in my head.

I saw Mama, too, standing with Genny by the Marchants. Genny was as white as paper, but I knew her first rule. If it happened in front of Mama, Genny never lied. Never. I saw her hands moving. I saw what she was telling Mama, telling her in a language I knew, and I could not stand to see what she was saying, as if her sign might make it so.

Mama was shaking her hands no, and no again, emphatic, absolute, but Genny wouldn't stop signing it.

And then the sound that was roaring nonstop in my head came out, and everyone could hear it. It was coming out of Mama. Mama made the sound and it was like a living siren of white noise, an unearthly keening. It wasn't bearable to have this noise both in me, radiating outward to push against my skin, and also coming from my mama to press against the shell of me. I couldn't be where this noise was. I turned and ran toward the church.

I heard someone say, "No, I'll go," and someone was with me, some blurred shape of a person. I kept running through the night, back behind the church until my car was in front of me and the outside noise was far away from me and may have stopped, but the inside noise was relentless. I put my hands against the car door and leaned on it.

The person behind me spoke, and it was Jonno. He said, "Baby," and a stranger in me reared up and said, "Get the fuck away from me. I'll kill you." And then some time went by, and time kept going. Time wouldn't stop and the world did not have Fisher in it. "Get the fuck away from me," I said again. When I turned back, there was nothing there and no one there to see.

I got in my car and made it start, and I made it be going, moving me away, but the noise was moving with me, vibrating in my chest, in my head, shaking every limb. The air in the car was made of salt and ashes, and I put the car in gear and tore toward the exit, wanting only to get far enough away so that it would be quiet. But I knew it wouldn't be. The noise was in me, going with me, and the only thing I was driving away from was Mama, who would need me.

I slammed on the brakes, and the car jerked to a halt and shuddered and died. There was a rolling thump from the backseat, the only thing I could hear over the bad sounds in my brain, and then, piping through, clear and high and sweet-pitched as a bell, Fisher's dour, small voice said, "Ow."

I sat very still, and then I turned around and got to my knees, peering over the seat. And there she was.

She was cocooned in a blanket she had taken from the rental property over the store, and a pillow was under her. All I could see of her was her round face, blinking up at me from where she had tumbled. Fisher fought the blanket until one perfect pale hand emerged to scrub at her eyes. "You got back?"

"Yeah," I said, and then I added, "Hi."

"Hi," she said. I was afraid to touch her. I was afraid she wouldn't be her solid self, real and alive. I watched as she fought and twisted her way out of the blanket, kicking free and then boosting herself back up to the backseat.

"Why are you in my car?" I said.

"I didn't want you to leave town again while I was sleeping."

"I wouldn't do that," I said.

Her lower lip poked out. "Yes, you would, too."

I shook my head and said, so careful, "Do you think you could come up here for a minute."

She stood up and leaned toward me, letting her stomach rest on the lip of the front seat, and then she slithered over, slipping down to fall into my waiting arms.

I couldn't help it. I pulled her into me so close and tight, burying my nose in her hair to breathe her in.

"You're squashing me," she said, muffled against my chest.

"I'm keeping you," I said to her. "You are mine and you should come and live with me. I am keeping you. Would you like that?"

"Yes," she said, and she relaxed into me, letting herself be squashed for once. Some time went by, and it was all right, time could go again, I would allow it, and I had a hard time not giggling as I gave the world permission to rotate on its axis.

Fisher wormed backwards, away from me, until she was sitting beside me on the seat, perfectly contained in her whole, smooth skin.

"I'm hungry," she said. "I'm practically starved."

"We can fix that," I said. I couldn't stop looking at her, at how all the pieces of her fitted together exactly to make Fisher.

She was looking down at her legs. She said, shyly, "Nonny? Is that true? About I can come live with you?"

"Yes," I said, even though I didn't yet know how to make it happen.

She said, "Because that was my secret wish. My real wish. The one that cost fifteen dollars."

"It will be true," I said, and my voice was sure. I might not know how to make it happen, but I knew how to find out. "We have to go see everyone. People are worried. No one knew where you were, and you can't ever do this again."

"Am I going to get a spanking?" she said.

"No," I said. "Not this time." And then I heard myself adding with absolute sincerity, "I will kill anyone who tries to spank you."

Fisher nodded matter-of-factly. I left the stalled car right where it was, blocking the exit from the parking lot. Fisher and I got out, and I went around and took her hand. We started walking out of the parking lot, out onto Philbert Street first and then toward the square.

"What's happening?" said Fisher, staring big-eyed down the street at all the lights and vehicles and smoke.

"Bunch of stuff," I answered. "Don't worry, everyone is okay."

I don't know who saw us coming. I didn't register it much at all. I heard the hum of joyful conversation and exclamation building as we came, but all I could see was Mama. She was sitting on the curb between Bernese and Genny. They were lined up in a row like the three monkeys, Bernese and Genny weeping into their hands and Mama between them, her hands folded quietly around the box in her lap, seeing and hearing and speaking no evil for all of them.

Genny looked up, tear-stained and trembling, and she said, "Oh, Bernese! Oh, Bernese!" Bernese looked up and her face was made of clay, a sagging death mask. Then she saw Fisher beside me as we came walking staunchly hand in hand, and she burst out crying again and turned to Isaac, who was sitting beside her, and she collapsed onto him.

Genny held her hands up, but there were no words in English or in sign for what she had to say. There was no way to tell Mama except to pick up Fisher, to swing her up into my arms and then to put her, all of her, into my mother's lap. I watched my mother's arms close around her, watched her feel and understand the shape and smell of what was being given back to her. The box with Josephine in it teetered and then tumbled off her legs into the road, and Mama let it go, hugging Fisher tight against her.

I knelt in front of her in the road and put my arms around both of them. Fisher, smashed in between us, was protesting, but I ignored her as we held her safe and living between us.

Bernese and Genny were hovering, and after a few minutes, Bernese reached in between us and dragged Fisher out to smother her in hugs while Genny patted and dabbed at any piece of Fisher she could reach.

"You people are bothering me," Fisher wailed.

I picked up the box with Josephine's head and offered it to Mama, but she pushed it away. I set it down beside us, and then I gave my mother my hands and said the best part of our love story back to her. I gave her the words she had given me so many times when she was telling me how we found each other.

I signed to her, *That baby is my baby. I know it. I don't know how to do it, how to keep her. But you do.*

My mother's searching hands reached out and found my face, stroked gently down my cheeks.

Good girl, she signed. *Good girl, good girl.* And then she nodded her hand. She would tell me how.

CHAPTER

20

I HAD TO wait for an opportunity to put Mama's plan into action. It had to arise on its own. It was easy to be patient, however, because Fisher was staying with me at Mama's house for now. Bernese was hip deep in a battle with the insurance companies over her store and the museum and engaged in a separate war with the judicial system.

Teak and Jimmy were already back in Alabama. Teak was in jail for parole violations, but Jimmy was home in Jackson's Gap; apparently, there was no law against passing out on a sofa while your half brothers try to burn up a town. Grif was in custody, but they hadn't found Billy. Billy Crabtree always seemed to land on his feet, and this time he had hit the ground running. Bernese was all over the A.D.A. who caught the file, agitating for a countrywide manhunt and trying to make sure Grif wasn't offered bail.

I used her distraction to put *Get Fit, Kid!* through her paper shredder. Fisher, let off the chain, spent three days eating herself sick, voraciously stuffing in junk until I thought she'd swell up like a tick and pop. I let her. I said nothing as she ravaged an entire bag of Doritos and licked all the frosting and sugar off half a box of donuts. I even kept my mouth shut when she threw each naked pastry back into the box, shriveled and slightly damp.

But by the time a week was out, she had settled and started asking for real food. She still agitated for Cap'n Crunch but accepted Kix, negotiated a certain number of bites of broccoli, and asked for candy twice as often as she was allowed to have it. In other words, she was acting and eating like a normal little kid.

On the square, workmen were clearing out the debris from the burned-out shells of Bernese's and Henry's stores. I went down there one day during school hours. I kicked around in the rubble from the museum, but if there had been something salvageable, how would I recognize it? I quit digging and dusted off my hands. There was nothing here I could save, nothing I could learn.

As I walked back toward Philbert, one of the workmen behind me let out a wolf whistle. I was wearing my tightest jeans and a turquoise knit top that always made me feel pretty. I grinned at the sound; I was going to see Henry Crabtree, and I needed the affirmation.

Henry had been staying down at Ona's. I hadn't talked to him since the night of the fire. Part of it was that I had Fisher all the time, and Henry was hung up with insurance companies, too. We'd waved at each other across the square a few times, but we hadn't had a single conversation. In a town as small as Between, that couldn't be coincidence.

I picked my way up the cracked driveway to the front door. I banged on the knocker, and after a few minutes, Ona Crabtree opened the door, her eyes widening when she saw my face.

"Nonny!" She seemed frozen.

"Can I come in?" I asked.

"Sure you can. Sure," said Ona. She backed out of the doorway. Henry was on the sofa, an open book in his hands. His feet were bare, and his jeans weren't ironed. His hair was down, and he looked much too rumpled and casual for Henry until I considered how recently his iron, his tailored New York clothes, and even the leather hair tie I had once pulled off of him had been converted into great filthy drifts of soot and ash.

Ona closed the door behind me. "Can I get you a cold drink? Sit down. Sit down." Her voice was eager and a little too loud for the small room.

She led me to the big chair facing the short end of the coffee table. I perched gingerly on its edge, and she said, "You want a Coke? We got Coke."

"That'd be great," I said. She scuttled off into the kitchen.

"How's it going, Nonny Jane," Henry said. He sounded noncommittal and hugely guarded, but that may have been my ears. He may have been sleepy. He rubbed at his eyes with the heels of his hands and then clasped his hands in front of him, forearms resting on his thighs.

"Good," I said. "It's good."

We fell silent as Ona came back with a can of Coke. She popped the tab theatrically and set it down in front of me on the table.

"You want some cobbler? It's peach."

"Not really," I said. I took a bracing sip of the Coke. It tasted too sweet, and I picked it up and looked at the label.

"That's that vanilla kind," Ona said. "I like that vanilla taste in there." I didn't answer, and she stood awkwardly in front of me, twisting her hands. The hungry look she always had for me was back, and I stiffened uncomfortably under it.

Henry was watching us, his eyes cool and appraising. As politely as I could, I said, "Ona? Would you mind if I had a minute alone with Henry?"

"Naw, I don't mind," she said. She stood looking around as if uncertain where to go, then chose the hallway that led to the back bedrooms. She went through the doorway, but I couldn't hear her footsteps very well on the carpet. I wasn't sure if she had gone to her room or if she was crouched right at the corner, listening.

I said, "Henry, tell me what happened last Friday. Tell me everything you know."

He nodded and then started talking, telling me what had happened at the Crabtree version of a family dinner and then at the square, filling in the parts I hadn't heard from the police and Bernese. "And that's when you showed up. And Jonno. So you know the rest," he ended.

"You shouldn't have gone in there after those animal dolls," I said. He started to wave me off, and I added, "But I'm glad you did. You'll never know what that means to my mother."

Silence fell between us, and my throat felt as if it were stuffed with grit and pebbles. I sat up straighter. I kept imagining Ona lurking in the hallway, craning her neck to try and catch what we were saying. I said, "I need to talk to you about something else. Do you think we can go to your room?"

"No," said Henry. My surprise must have shown on my face because he added, "I mean that literally. We can't. There's no place in it to be. I had to set up a work space. I got a good PC and a printer and a fax and so on. I've got deadlines."

"Crap, did you lose all your work?"

He shook his head. "I back up everything and store it in an online data bank. But that bedroom is stuffed. There's a sliver of bed I can sleep on or sit on to reach my keyboards. You want to—what? Take a walk?"

"No, this is fine," I said. I got up and came to sit beside him on the sofa so I could lower my voice. He scooted back, making a little too much room for me.

"Bernese is giving me custody of Fisher," I said.

He smiled then, a genuine expression, and he looked so much like my old friend Henry that I relaxed a notch. "I'm really glad for you, Nonny Jane."

"Well, she doesn't know it yet. But she is."

Henry's grin widened. "You're taking on Bernese? I'm not sure if I should buy a ticket or leave the state." I smiled back at him, and then we sat there looking at each other until both our smiles faded. He said, "Is that what you came to tell me?"

"Kind of. We're not going to stay here, obviously. There's no work for me. The deaf community in Between numbers one, and I can't see clear to charging my own mama. So Fisher will be moving with me. I already had the most complicated family in America, and now I'm a self-employed, divorced single mother. I guess I know I'm not the world's best prospect for a date, but your bookstore is pretty much toast, and you can write code anywhere. It occurred to me, there isn't a good reason you couldn't write code where I am." He swallowed, and I realized I was hedging, talking around what I wanted. I braced myself and said, "I want you to come after us."

He looked down at his hands, and I saw the ropy muscles of his forearms shift beneath his skin as he rubbed his palms together. When he looked back up at me, his deep-set eyes were shadowed and unreadable.

"I don't know if you noticed, but I have been coming after you. For almost a year now."

"I did notice," I said, but he shook his head.

"I've been in love with you for longer than that. I sat on it because you were married, and no matter what I thought about the guy, I had to respect that." I tried to speak again, but he kept talking. "And I know my timing has sucked. I shouldn't have kissed you. When I did, you told me loud and clear you were still married. I should have backed off after that. But I didn't get it. I didn't want to. But I get it now. I finally got it on Friday, when he showed up with you."

"I got divorced on Friday," I said.

"Yeah, I heard. It's a very small town. But nothing changed, Nonny Jane. You were still with him. You *are* still with him. I can't come after you anymore, because he's always there first."

"I'm done with Jonno," I said.

His voice was very gentle. "You've said that to me before. Then you have to go tell him you're done, and before you get through saying it, you aren't again. And I'm tired. Everything I own is either gone or stinks like the bottom floor of hell. I've had a shit week, and for the record? I've also had a shit marriage with a woman who was in love with someone else. I'm not up for it again."

"Henry," I said, "I know what I said before was—" But he was standing up.

"My friend, I don't want to have this conversation today. I am too damn tired. I don't know where I am going, Nonny Jane, but I have family here. So do you. We'll both be back. I'll see you around sometime." He turned away from me, disappearing through the doorway that led toward the bedrooms.

I heard him say, "Excuse me, Ona," in his driest voice as he stumbled over her in the hallway. Then I heard one of the bedroom doors shut. I sat there trying not to cry, and Ona Crabtree peered around the corner into the den.

"He's just stupid," she said.

"I don't want to talk about it," I said. I didn't want to talk with her about anything.

"Any man'd be lucky," she said.

I glared at her. "I said I don't want to talk about it."

"I know I shouldn't of listened in on y'all," she said. I waved it away. I got up abruptly to go, and she sidled over to block my path to the front door. "Nonny? I did want to say, I'm real sorry about what all happened."

I felt the Crabtree temper trying to rise in me. That was such a load of crap. She had instigated it, she and Bernese both, with their one-upping and retaliations and assumptions and shared inability to stop. I wanted to smack her in the head, but she looked too pitiful for that. Her yellow eyes were mapped in pink, and her skin sagged over her good high cheekbones. Cheekbones like mine.

I stared at her, and I knew I wouldn't ever love her. I couldn't love her. She was buried in every scary memory from my childhood. She'd gone balls-to-the-wall in a war with Bernese that had done too much collateral damage to my family. What my mother had lost could never be replaced.

But balanced against that, I thought of what Henry had told me, about that moment when she'd glanced at the open window and turned her back so he could go and help my family. If I put it on scales, it did not amount to much. It was a single drop of grace against a lifetime of selfishness. But the grace was there, and had been offered on my behalf.

She had something else going for her: Henry Crabtree loved her. And dammit it all to hell, I loved Henry Crabtree. I'd blown it with him. I got that. But that didn't change anything. I loved him. And he loved her.

"Oh, screw it," I said, and I went across the room and took her in my arms. It was like holding a loose sack of skin, and then the bones inside clicked to life and clamped so hard around me she was practically squeezing my guts out.

"All right, then," I said, patting her back. I couldn't love her, but I didn't understand why it had never occurred to me to simply offer kindness. "All right, then."

Eventually, I pulled away. She clutched tearfully at my arm and said, "I don't know how it all got so far away from what I thought."

"It's fine, Ona. Let's stop thinking about it. There are all kinds of things we could use to hit each other with until doomsday, or apologize for until our lips turned blue and dropped off. But let's not. Let's forget about it."

"I won't do nothing no more against Bernese, if that's what you mean," she said. "Long as she don't start fresh up with me."

"I know you won't, and I know she sure as hell won't. But that's not what I meant," I said. "I meant us." She stared at me, puzzled. "Let's start this way. Why don't you invite me to supper again."

"All right," she said. She dropped her voice and tilted her head toward the back bedrooms in a theatrical manner, saying, "Better be soon. When State Farm cuts his check, he's gone from Between."

"I know," I said. "I didn't mean him. I meant you. I'll be out of town over the weekend. Fisher and I are going house-hunting. But maybe when I come back, we could go to the diner, or you could cook me something here."

"Just us?" she said.

"Yeah, and your boys and Varner, if you want," I said.

"I reckon I could do that," she said. "Really just us?" She was looking at me suspiciously from under her scraggly brows, and I noticed for the first time that they had faded to a pure gunmetal gray, not a scrap of red left.

"Just us," I said, and smiled at her. I stood beside her as she clutched my arm, and I patted her grasping hand until the wariness faded from her yellowing fox eyes.

CHAPTER

21

FISHER AND I planned to leave town on Friday after school. We'd spend the weekend checking out Atlanta neighborhoods with good schools, maybe hit the zoo and the Coca-Cola museum. I wasn't in a hurry. I didn't want to move Fisher until school let out for the summer. I couldn't go, anyway, until I'd settled Fisher's custody with Bernese. Bernese knew I was moving to Atlanta, but she didn't yet realize I was plotting a coup.

Early that Friday morning, as Fisher was finishing her normal, human breakfast, I saw my opportunity. Lou poked his head into Mama's back door and asked if I wanted him to give Fisher a ride to kindergarten. He said, "Save her a bus ride. I've got a list this long from Bernese, so I'm heading early into town. I may still be in Loganville when it's time to pick her up, too."

"Thanks, Uncle Lou," I said. He came in and fixed himself a cup of coffee while I got Fisher's lunch money and checked to make sure her shoes were tied tight.

"Bye, Nonny," she said, giving me a quick squeeze. I hugged

her back, resisting the urge to clutch her hard to me and refuse to let her get in Lou's car. I got that way sometimes when she came to hug me goodbye or give me my good-night kiss. Ever since the Night Nothing Bad Happened to Fisher, I'd been skittish about letting her out of my line of sight.

She trotted down the steps on her sturdy legs, running along-side Lou with her green backpack flapping joyfully against her spine. As they drove away, I ran up to Genny's room, where I had a clear view of Bernese's front yard. Lou and Fisher had not been gone five minutes before Bernese came out of her front door and walked rapidly down Grace Street.

I watched her go, and then I went and found Mama and Genny in Mama's bedroom. Genny had just finished their faces and was capping her pink lipstick and closing her compact.

I drew my heart on Mama's shoulder, and she reached for me. I signed into her hand, *I think it is happening.*

She knew at once what I meant and twitched her hand in a brief nod; then, for Genny's benefit, she signed, *Yes, today is the day Genny is going to make a body and a dress for Josephine. Lou brought over Bernese's Singer.* I gave Mama's hand a squeeze, and she returned the pressure and then signed, *And I will begin to work in the garage on my new sculpture. I told you about it?* The Bones of Dogs. *You see? I am getting to be my old self again.*

I leaned in to kiss Mama and then said to Genny, "I think Josephine will be your best doll ever." I signed it for Mama and added, *And I think this new sculpture will be your best ever, too.*

"I agree," said Genny, and Mama nodded her hand solemnly.

It will have to be, she signed, and I didn't know if she meant the sculpture or this last china doll. But either way, she was right. For her it would be. My mama had learned a long time ago how to live, and live richly, within the boundaries of what was left to her.

I left and headed down Grace Street, toward the square. By the time I got there, Bernese was nowhere to be seen. No one was out and about this early, and all the shops were locked up tight. I stopped to look at the crumbled walls of what was once the museum. The rest of it would be taken out next week. They had already finished clearing the lots of Henry's and Bernese's stores, and nothing remained except an expanse of blackened concrete next to the Sweete Shoppe.

I crossed Philbert and went around to the back of Isaac Davids's Victorian. He had a fake rock just like Bernese's under his azalea bushes. I got out his spare key and let myself in, walking through his kitchen and up the back stairs. That was where I found them.

They weren't in his bedroom, and they weren't doing anything particularly damning, but the way they stood together in the hallway confirmed everything Mama had told me. Bernese was leaning in to him, her arms tucked up and bent at the elbow so she could rest her palms on his long, narrow chest. Her face was resting on his chest as well, in between her hands. He was stooped at the shoulders so he could put his arms around her thick waist, his head bent down to press his lips into her hair.

He saw me first, his eyes meeting mine over Bernese's head. To his credit, he didn't shove her away or leap back. He barely started at all, and then he straightened his back and turned her, keeping one arm firmly around her shoulders, so Bernese could see me, too.

Her eyes widened and she stiffened. She stared at me and shook her head, and then she said, "Shit." It was the first time I had ever heard her say a cussword that wasn't in the Bible.

I stopped where I was, three steps from the top, and said, "I'll wait downstairs. Come talk to me when you're ready."

I made coffee in Isaac's modern kitchen. His coffeemaker was a large black contraption that could steam and foam milk and make espresso and probably cook a chicken if I'd only known how to program it. As it was, it took me fifteen minutes to get a pot of regular coffee going.

I had fixed myself a cup and taken a seat at the butcher-block table before Bernese came down the back stairs. She was alone.

She poured herself a cup without speaking, stirring in four big spoonfuls of sugar, and then she came over and sat at the table across from me. She'd pulled herself together, and her face was unreadable.

I broke the silence. "I suppose it makes more sense to me now. Of course you wouldn't think adultery alone was a good enough reason to get a divorce."

Bernese laced her hands in front of her on the table and met my eyes, her mouth firm. "I deserved that, but that was your one shot. Hope you enjoyed it." We sat there for another minute, and her gaze dropped first. She said, "I'm in love with him, you know. This isn't some whim. I've always been in love with him."

I shook my head. "Why didn't you marry him, then?" I asked. "Just because he's Jewish?"

She snorted. "I would have married him if he worshipped Baal." She twisted in her seat, shifting as if she couldn't get comfortable. "He wouldn't marry me. And yes, it was because I wasn't. I was so mad at him for that, I came straight home and married Lou. Lou'd wanted to marry me right out of high school, and he still did. We'd stayed friends, you know. I'd see Lou when I came home summers and spring break and all, and he never lost that way of looking at me. Once I moved home after nursing school, I didn't figure I would ever see Isaac again."

I said, "You've had pretty good cover. Half the town thinks he's gay."

She wasn't listening to me. "I've been a good wife, mostly. And Isaac and I weren't really doing anything. We haven't done anything this time for over a year now. I hope you don't plan to bust up Lou's whole life this late in the game." Her eyes widened into a pleading expression I had never seen on her face before.

I heard Isaac's measured tread coming down the hall, and then he joined us, tall and elegant and self-assured. He sat down at the kitchen table in his accustomed place by her side. Bernese shifted, her body language changing almost imperceptibly, angling toward him as if he were slightly magnetic.

I took a sip of my coffee and set the cup back down. I knew from experience that Mama didn't miss a trick when it came to knowing exactly who was having what sweetheart, but I had never seen this Bernese. I couldn't quite fathom my pragmatic aunt in the role of Juliet. I tried to imagine her off at college, young, pretty, crazy in love, sporting a long, bouncing ponytail and running across campus to hold hands with Isaac Davids. I tried to imagine her having her heart broken.

It was hard to believe that she hadn't been able to stop going back to Isaac, even after forty years. I couldn't wrap my head around it until I connected her behavior with my own on-again, off-again dance with Jonno. I had assumed my inability to cut things off came from some slutty Crabtree gene. But apparently, I'd learned it by osmosis from a Frett.

It had been so hard in the car to lean back six inches and break with Jonno, even though our marriage was stone-cold dead. I tried to imagine how much harder it would have been if I'd still been at all in love with him. I probably wouldn't have managed it. I said, "How did it happen? You were back home, married to Lou."

She dropped her eyes. "I thought Isaac was married, too. I'd seen his engagement announcement in the Atlanta paper the year after I graduated. Nice Jewish girl, old family, exactly what his folks wanted. He was in practice then at his father's firm, and I needed a lawyer to look at a contract I'd been offered for your mama's dolls. I didn't know if it was fair or what half of it even meant."

Isaac reached out and took her hand. I hadn't realized that it was trembling until he stilled it. She looked at him, but he nodded for her to continue.

"So I went into town to see him. And I told myself it was because I knew that I could trust him, as a lawyer. Also, I thought if I saw him married, happy, I'd stop thinking about him all the time. But Nonny, he hadn't married that girl. He'd shied off at the last second. He couldn't forget me, either. And then that article came out in *Life* magazine, and Cordova offered us the big contract, and Isaac could afford to leave his father's firm and open up his own practice."

"And he decided to open it here," I said.

Bernese tapped the fingers of her free hand against the table and firmed her jaw. "I want you to know, we haven't gone on and on this way. We know it's wrong. We've stopped a lot of times. We're working on it."

I smiled in spite of myself, seeing Mama telling me I had to stop working on things. Saying that Fretts don't waffle. Fretts choose. Fretts do.

At last Isaac spoke. "Bernese and I would like, as a courtesy, to know what your course of action will be regarding Lou. Preferably before you take it."

I took another sip of my coffee and then said, "I guess that depends on Bernese."

Bernese's eyes narrowed, and her spine lengthened as she drew herself up. She took a quick breath, and she and Isaac exchanged a glance that spoke volumes in a language only they knew. They both realized that we were sitting at a negotiating table, probably the place Bernese and Isaac felt the most at home in all of life.

"You want peace?" Bernese said. "I can get straight with Ona on those dogs. And I know she was part and parcel of that fire, but I won't press that. I can even forgive her." She said the word "forgive" as if it were made of dry ice, so cold it made her teeth ache. But she said it.

I shook my head. "You're offering something you can't deliver." I could see now that what Henry had said was true. Ona and Bernese were more alike than I ever would have realized, and they'd never be able to stomach each other. "I'll make my own peace with Ona. I can't imagine the two of you getting past loathing. On your side, I'll settle for fake indifference, maybe even a show of good manners."

"Done." Bernese leaned forward again. "What else are you after?" I sat quietly and waited her out until she sucked in her breath and said, "You're taking Fisher."

I nodded. "I'm taking Fisher."

Isaac's hand moved to her shoulder, and I wasn't sure if he was placing it there to show support or to keep her from lunging across the table at my throat. Her nostrils flared, and her breath came faster and faster. She was almost panting. "But I love her," she said.

"I know you do, Bernese," I said, and then I added, as gently as I could in the wake of the last few weeks, "But face it. You aren't very good at it."

I could feel the huge excess of will she carried trying to rise up in her, but I sat and stared her down. And I broke her. Her shoulders sagged, and then her whole body followed in an avalanche of release. She nodded at me before she folded her arms in front of her and put her head down on the table. Isaac's hand moved to her back, and his eyes in their webbing of crow's-feet were gentle on her.

"I'll write it up," he said to me. When I started to rise, he stopped me by adding, "But not because I'm afraid of the truth, Nonny. I'll write it up because it's what's best for Fisher."

I felt a twinge of Crabtree temper, but he stared at me with eyes that were dark and deliberate. Such distinctive eyes. How had I never noticed that funny down-tilt? All at once I wondered if perhaps Isaac Davids had more rights at this table than I had realized. I pushed the thought away; I knew too much already.

I stood up, saying, "I want to be Fisher's legal guardian as soon as possible, full physical custody, and get the paperwork started for a straight-up adoption. Don't the two of you get your heads together and be cute with me. I'll get a lawyer of my own to check everything." I walked around the table and bent over to hug Bernese. "I love you so much. And you know we'll be around. Fisher and I will come to town all the time, and you can be her grandma. That's what you are, and that's what you're supposed to be. But you and I both know that baby needs a mother. And I'm it."

Bernese propped her head on her hand, clearly angry with me, but I could also see her relief. Fisher was a burden she never would have set down, but I thought she hadn't realized what a weight it was until I lifted it.

She rallied and said, "This has to stop here, though. You never say a word to Lou. No matter what. You can't hold this over me every time I work your nerves."

I nodded. "Let's get the paperwork done, and don't you start anything new with Ona Crabtree. And I swear it will be like this day never happened."

"How do I know that?" said Bernese, looking more and more like herself every second. "How do I know you won't use this on me every living minute?"

"Because I am promising I won't," I said patiently. On impulse, I leaned down and kissed her cheek. "And because I love you, dumb-ass."

She put her hand to her cheek, surprised, and then said, "Watch that mouth."

"No, ma'am," I said. "I heard you cuss like a navy boy today, and I *will* use that against you every day as long as we're both living."

I turned and left her there, rubbing at her cheek and staring after me as if not quite sure what she was seeing. I felt her gaze on my long body. I was narrow-shouldered, tall, long-waisted, curvy at the hips, with my Crabtree red hair and freckles on every inch of my hide, yet I knew that her eyes were seeing something different. She thought she was looking at a Frett.

But she was wrong. Henry had pegged it when he said Bernese and Ona were alike, but it was more than that. It was all of them. Every Frett and Crabtree with a breath in their body became dangerous, ruthless, would never bend or stop when they were protecting one of their own. This was the place where they connected, and that place was me.

I walked home and got to work, packing Fisher and me for our weekend in Atlanta. We would leave as soon as Lou brought her home from kindergarten. I was a little giddy. I had gone to the negotiating table with Bernese, of all people, and had come away with almost everything I wanted.

Almost.

I wondered where Henry would be moving, and the giddiness ran out of me as if I had been punctured. I had no one to blame about Henry but myself. And hell, why not, maybe Jonno, too. But mostly me. I scrubbed angrily at my damp eyes and went down to the garage to clutch my mother and ask her to make me one of her cakes. She felt my moist fingers and reached up to touch my cheeks, wiping them the way she used to when I was five and had scraped myself to bits falling off my bike.

She didn't ask me what was wrong, just signed, *Men can be so stupid. But cake is always good. Go pack. I'll bake.*

The comforting smell of her orange pound cake filled the house as I loaded up my Mustang with our suitcases. Fisher came running in the front door at one, full of news about the class turtle and her latest art project. She sat at the kitchen table and we all had cake, me and Mama and Genny and Fisher. It was like a preview of what the Between half of my life would be like now. And it was good. It was very good. I could be like Mama and learn to live richly in it, Henry or no Henry.

I helped Mama with the dishes, and then Fisher and I climbed into my Mustang. I backed out onto Grace Street.

"In Atlanta, will we have a yard?" said Fisher.

"I hope so," I said.

"Can we put a dog in it?"

I glanced over my shoulder. She was so earnest and so inno-cent. "A small dog, maybe," I said. "A tiny, tiny, pink-hearted, fluffy dog who is so gentle that squirrels can beat him up."

She giggled and then asked, "Can we put the top down?"

"We're already driving, Woolly-Worm. Next time ask before we take off."

We drove past the square. I saw the sheriff's car idling down near Isaac's house, right at the corner. Thig had gotten out and left his door hanging open to write a ticket to some tourist who had parked on Philbert instead of pulling into the lot behind the church.

I waved out the window to him, and as we looked ahead, I saw Henry out on the square, too, by the fountain. He lifted his hand, casual, and then let it drop. He must have thought I was waving at him. I felt my cheeks flush. I pulled my hand back in the car and kept on driving.

At the highway entrance, I turned west onto 78, heading toward Atlanta. I hadn't gone two miles before Fisher asked how long it would be before we got there. I told her, and she said, "I wish you'd've put the top down," in a grumpy voice.

I hadn't gone another mile before I saw the lights of a cop car flashing behind us. I checked my speedometer. I was my usual three miles over the limit. I waited for the cop to go around me, but he stayed doggedly right behind me, pacing me. Then the siren came on. Not a peep like a polite cough, either. The whole siren whined to life and built itself up in a rising wail usually re-served for the high-speed chases of ax murderers.

I pulled over. As soon as I stopped and got a good look at the car, I realized this wasn't some trooper. It was Thig Newell's car. I felt a huge flash of irritation that Thig was pulling us over, followed by a moment of pure nerves. Maybe Bernese was calling my bluff and had sent Thig to snatch Fisher back.

The flashing lights and the god-awful siren stayed on, and no one got out of the car. I was about to walk back and see if Thig was having a stroke when the door opened, and Henry Crabtree got out and came walking along the shoulder of the freeway toward me. My heart leaped up in my chest, and I scrambled out of my car, too.

"Nonny?" Fisher said.

"Just a sec, baby," I said, and shut the door. "Can't you turn that off?" I called, waving at the blaring car with its lights and siren.

"No," Henry yelled back. "I mean, really, really no. I wish I could."

I started laughing. I couldn't help myself. "You stole Thig's car?"

"I stole Thig's car," he said solemnly, nodding.

"And broke the siren," I said, still laughing.

"Looks like."

"Why?" I said. "Why on earth?" But I thought I hoped I maybe knew.

"You went west," he said.

"I know."

"Athens is east."

I grinned at him. "You stole a police car and broke the siren and pulled me over to tell me which way Athens is?"

"No," he said, "I didn't. I pulled you over so you could tell me that you and Fisher there are moving to Atlanta."

"That's correct," I said.

"You're not going back to Athens at all."

"Correct again."

"See, that would have been good information to have," Henry said, half laughing, half exasperated.

"Henry, what are you doing?" But I knew what he was doing, and the blaring of the siren was like church bells and choir music.

"I'm coming after you," he said. "Not right this second. I have to return this car, obviously, and get a check from the insurance company and buy a table or something. You know, to put in the moving truck. But then I'm coming after you."

I laughed so hard I had to put one hand on my car to keep from falling over. When I could speak again, I said, "Henry, we'll be back in two days. You could have told me this on Sunday."

"Nope. I couldn't." And then Henry Crabtree kissed me breathless while a car whizzed past us and Thig's siren blared un- relentingly and the flashing lights went whirling round and round like a strobe.

I felt a little hand tugging on my elbow and broke the kiss to look down at Fisher. She'd rolled down her window and stuck the top half of her body out to reach me.

"That's really loud," she yelled.

My knees were weak. Henry was holding me up. "I know," I said.

"Are you kissing Henry Crabtree?" Fisher asked.

"You bet."

"Well, but the car's stopped," Fisher said. "Can't we put the top down now?"

"Why not," I said. "Give me a hand, Henry?" He kissed me again and then reluctantly let me go. He walked around my car, and we put the top down. Henry secured the passenger's side while I did the driver's.

"Buckle back in, Woolly-Worm. We have to get on the road," I said to Fisher.

Henry said, "I better return that car. Maybe Thig can shut it off."

I couldn't stop grinning at him. "You are going to get arrested."

"Nah," Henry said. "You know my girlfriend? Her aunt pretty much owns the sheriff in this town."

He walked away into the lights and got back in his screaming stolen car. He pulled onto 78, and the wailing grew fainter and then disappeared as he exited to circle back to Between.

I got in my Mustang. Fisher was safely buckled up in back. "Ready?"

"Go!" said Fisher, and the Frett in me checked carefully for traffic just before the Crabtree peeled out, spraying gravel to make Fisher giggle. I accelerated up to the speed limit. In my rearview mirror, I could see Fisher's fists rising up against a background of blue sky. She unfolded her hands, opening them wide, her fingers spreading to catch the wind as we roared down the highway.

"Nonny?" she called. "Nonny? It's like we're flying!"

And it was.

READING GROUP GUIDE

Discussion Questions

1. According to one theory, our identity is shaped by our genes, immutable and unchanging. Others argue that our character is informed by our experiences, upbringing, and surroundings. Discuss the idea of "nature versus nurture" as it applies to Nonny and her two families in *Between, Georgia*. Which do you think played a bigger role in the formation of your own character and identity?

2. How is the setting of Jackson's book critical to the story? Could these characters exist in any small town, or are they necessarily products of *Between, Georgia*?

3. In the book the Fretts are portrayed as upstanding, churchgoing citizens and the Crabtrees as a rulebreaking bunch of scofflaws. Upon close inspection, how do their actions in these pages support or refute their reputations? What is your true definition of abusing authority and how does it compare to that of each family?

4. Nonny is drawn to Henry and Jonno for different reasons. What does each man seem to represent to her?

5. Stacia, as a deaf-blind character, calls into question the process of "knowing" others. How does Stacia replace seeing and hearing as avenues to "knowing" the people she loves and detests?

6. What does Jackson mean when she says on page 181 that Mama had "quietly found her own way to make the world tell lies, and SAY that it was safe"? Do you believe she was justified in her sur-

reptitious actions here? Which other characters engage in deception in the pages you have read? Do their ends justify their means?

7. The idea of ownership is a central theme in the book. How do each of the main characters go about staking claims on other people, things, and even Between itself? To what extent can one "own" another person? Why is it so important for the people of Between to feel they own something? How can the feeling of ownership toward another person be detrimental? How can it be positive?

8. Nonny engages in relations with Henry while technically still married to Jonno, and Bernese, while critical of these acts, is shown to have engaged in extracurricular activities as well. What is each character's view of marriage? Were you sympathetic to their perspectives throughout the book? Did you change your opinion by the end?

9. Motherhood is a key theme in *Between, Georgia*. What role do nontraditional mothers play in the story? How do the nontraditional mother-daughter relationships in the book compare to the traditional ones?

10. Years of feuding between the Frett and Crabtree families is brought to fruition through a series of violent events starting with the dog attack. Why do you think the author chooses violence to initiate healing?

11. The characters in *Between, Georgia* seem to express care and concern for each other by administering tough love. What are some examples of tough love in the book? Is this approach an effective one?

12. Discuss the ways in which Nonny and the residents of *Between, Georgia* are stuck in certain patterns of behavior. Why do they seem unable to make progress in some aspects of their lives? Is this inertia a function of who they are, or of their surroundings and circumstances?

13. In the future, what would you expect to happen to the families? Would they still be in Between? What would be the status of Henry and Nonny's relationship? Is the feud truly over?

A Door of One's Own

While I was visiting libraries and book clubs to talk about *Between, Georgia*, there was one question that always popped up: People wanted to know my writing rituals, the nuts and bolts of how I work. It always left me floundering, so I set about trying to find an answer. I began to take my own unofficial poll, posing the question to every writer I ran across. I would listen to their answers and nod and pretend to be deep in earnest thought while feeling subpar. It was all foreign to me, and at first the best I could do was figure out what I didn't need.

I feel very strongly that I don't have a muse. I find the whole concept of muses to be suspect and a little creepy. An invisible chick with the power to hit my mute button if I do something with a gerund that displeases her? And where do they go when you are in the shower, these muses? None for me, thank you.

I am not organized. I know most writers aren't rabid alphabetizers, but many of them said that they write at the same time of day, every day. I can't manage that. Organizationally speaking, I am so far beyond regulation flaky that me and regulation flaky don't even share a zip code. I can't become dependent on a writing ritual because I am not physically capable of sticking to a schedule.

I am not the sentimental sort who still has the potpourri made from her prom corsage or all her old love letters. In fact, nothing makes me happier than watching the Salvation Army driving away with a truckload of my former stuff. I have never owned a pair of lucky underpants, and when my husband, Scott, gave me an eternity ring for our tenth anniversary, I promptly lost my original wedding band.

Then it came to me: The thing I really need to have in order to write is a door between me and the husband-children-cat-television-fornicating-gerbils-telephone chaos that reigns in the rest of the house. If it shuts, even better.

Up until my daughter, Maisy, happened, we lived in a house with a wide-open floor plan. The only closed-off rooms were the three bedrooms. Scott and I had the largest room, and our son, Sam, had the room across the hall. I planted a flag and claimed the back bedroom for Virginia Woolf. I thought my house was perfect, except for the postage-stamp-size bathroom Scott and I shared. There was exactly enough floor for one person to stand in front of the sink. The toilet was directly to the left, an inch away from my knee as I brushed my teeth. A single step backward landed me squarely inside the faux-porcelain receptacle that began its career as a Barbie's Dream Tub. But otherwise, my house fit my family like a perfect shoe.

Maisy arrived just before I was ready to start writing the book that would become *Between, Georgia*. But now that my office had become a room of *her* own, I had no place to work. My house, my former perfect fit of a house, now had room in it for everything but me. I tried moving my office into a corner of our master bedroom. If I could afford a belief in feng shui, I would say that the feng shui in that room was dreadful. And I was always in it. I slept in that room, I worked in that room, and since my husband and the big TV with cable and my reading chair and the bookshelves and the GameCube and the DVD player and my computer were in there, I did most of my in-home recreating there, too. I began to feel like a mental patient, looking at the same four walls every day, all day long, let out for meals downstairs in the inmates' cafeteria.

So I stored my dining room table at my mother's and crammed three of the chairs around a smaller table I wedged into the kitchen. We ate there, Maisy's high chair backed into a corner. My office took over the room we'd affectionately nicknamed the "Dining Cabinet." It was an eight-by-eight cube that had two huge triple-doorway-wide chunks cut out of the walls. One chunk led into the family/living room and one led into the kitchen, so the downstairs was like a circle: the kitchen, then my open-walled cube, then the family room.

It was a wash. The teenage mother's helper I'd hired to come in two mornings a week came to the kitchen to get something for Maisy approximately once every four minutes. She'd tiptoe past my huge doorways with elaborate, theatrical silence that was more distracting than simply walking through the room would have been.

On the weekends, Scott kept the kids so I could work, but baby Maisy came worming straight for my desk every time she was placed on the floor. Scott would be close behind her, peeling her up and moving her back, but she would let out enraged peeping noises and begin worming her relentless way toward the gateway to mommy-land. Sam, glowing with radioactive small boy energy, went thundering through approximately every forty-five seconds, treating the circular downstairs like a racetrack. I became hypersensitive to sound, so that even the soft pads of my obese cat scuffling along the hardwood made my fingers still on the keys.

When Maisy got all the way into my "office" for the hundredth time and started gumming at my shoe while I was trying to write a pivotal love scene, I realized we had to move.

The house we live in now is less than two miles from our old house, but I fell in love with it the first time we walked in. The downstairs is very similar—the kitchen runs into a family room, which runs into a small dining room—but there's one spectacular difference. Off to one side, the previous owners walled off an extra room that was supposed to be a formal living room. They'd put in a phone line and turned it into a home office. Best of all, the abbreviated entrance was already hung with real, live, actual doors. My office-stealing girl is almost five now, and still, to this day, the way those doors close so seamlessly makes my heart go pittery-pat-pat.

My personal Room of My Own is painted crocodile green, and it has speckled window treatments my mother made for me. There's a painting hung over the desk. It's by one of my favorite surrealists and it features a melting cat who rides a woman-shaped, busty spaceship through a tranquil wasteland. All around me, random piles of my crap grow peacefully like a Crap Garden and every available surface is coated in paper piles and books and my kids' abandoned shoes and galleys and McDonald's Happy Meal toys and Target bags full of only-the-Lord-knows . . . It is my own tiny slice of heaven.

Because it turns out that writing, for me, begins with a closed door. Period. Maybe I don't have an artistic temperament; I think my lack of rituals and totems and touchstones is where my writing comes from. I've accepted that I am a destination person, not a journey person. I point, I shoot. I see, I want, I walk toward hopefully.

When I close my door and start a book, I don't know what the story is about, and if I did, there is no way I could write it. I don't think I want to know how much I am revealing while I am in the process of re-vealing it. Par for my course: I read every word of *Between, Georgia* out loud while we were taping the audiobook. Listening to it, I was shocked to realize how much of my mother's childhood had snuck into the book. There's some deeply personal stuff in there, and I have revealed things via theme about how I feel about family obligations and nature vs. nurture and how love works that I didn't even know I felt. These are things that I probably wouldn't have understood, ever, if I hadn't writ-ten that book. Not with my pragmatic, goal-oriented approach to life.

I say, truthfully, that I write primarily to entertain myself, but as a byproduct, I oftentimes and accidentally end up understanding a little more about the kind of person I want to be should I ever grow up. I think if I were a more sensitive, artsy person, a muse-haver, a deep thinker, the type who watches stones grow and then keeps the stone forever as a solid memory, I wouldn't need to write at all. But story is the only way I know to process my world, and I have a strange need to tell my tales to other people. Just give me a door to close, and I'll spin you another one.

CHAPTER

1

U NTIL THE DROWNED girl came to Laurel's bed-room, ghosts had never walked in Victorianna. The houses were only twenty years old, with no accumulated history to put creaks in the hardwood floors or rattle at the pipes. The backyards had tall fences, and there were no cracks in the white sidewalks. Victorianna had a heavy wrought-iron gate guarding its entrance. The intricately curled top looked period, but it was new as well. It ran on hydraulics, and it swung wide only for those who knew the code.

Laurel and David moved into the big house on Chapel Circle when Laurel was only nineteen, and since that day she hadn't seen so much as a glimmer of her dead uncle Marty. He was tethered to the three-bedroom brick ranch where her parents still lived, half an hour away in tiny Pace, Florida. As a girl, she had seen him often, mostly on the nights before a storm broke.

She'd be fast asleep on her old Cinderella sheets, faded and soft from a thousand washings, with *Anne of Green Gables* or a Nancy

Drew book lying open-spined on her bedside table. Then he would be there, standing on her side of the room by her bed, mournful and transparent. He didn't belong near the ruffled shade on her reading lamp, and his feet should not have been allowed to rest beside her cotton trainer bra and Thalia's dirty Keds and the abandoned issues of *Tiger Beat* left scattered on the floor. The stuffed pony she'd loved best was still allowed a place at the end of her bed, but Marty was not reflected in its glass eyes, as if her loyal pony doll refused to acknowledge his presence.

He'd smile at her, one hand tucked easy in the waistband of his faded Levi's, the other reaching out to her. He wanted to lead her away, travel her to secret scenes, her own personal ghost of Christmas Never.

A thin finger of moonlight came through the bullet hole left of his center, reaching to touch Laurel's eye and help her lids come shuddering down. She'd leave them closed and roll away. In the morning, the sun would light up dust motes in the place where he'd been standing.

He left a cold spot in the room she didn't like to walk through, and sometimes she'd see the impression his pale cowboy boots had left in the nap of the rug. Once, her sister Thalia caught her down on her knees, trying to smooth away those faint footprints.

"Are you feeling up the carpet, Jesus Bug?" Thalia asked.

Laurel only shrugged and stilled her hands. Thalia slept light, but she never saw Marty.

Laurel brought Thalia over to see the house in Victorianna a few days after she and David closed. They'd been married all of five weeks. Thalia sat in the passenger seat drawing her upper lip back from her teeth, higher and higher, while Laurel drove her slowly through the winding streets. The lip was practically touching Thalia's nose by the time they'd passed six blocks' worth of the large pastel Victorians with their gingerbread and curling gables and romantic little balconies.

"It looks like Barbie's Dream House threw up in here," Thalia said. "A bunch of times. Like, went full-on bulimic."

"I think it's beautiful," Laurel said. Her tone was mild, but low in her belly, she felt the baby flip, popping sideways like an angry brine shrimp. "Look, this one's ours."

She pulled into the driveway. Laurel and David's house was the palest blue, trimmed in deep plum and heather. Two gargoyles hidden in the eaves watched over her with fierce eyes. A weather-vane on the roof told her the wind's plans for the day.

Thalia glanced from the turret to the sloped roof and then shook her head.

"You say something nice," Laurel said, putting one hand over the swell of her abdomen. She was four months gone, and Shelby was so little, Laurel could only feel her fierce spins from the inside.

"Okay," Thalia said. "It looks clean? Like they don't even let dogs pee here."

Laurel laughed. "I think that's in our charter."

She started to get out, but Thalia put one hand on her arm, stopping her. "Seriously? This is what you want? This house, this husband, a baby at nineteen?" Laurel nodded, and Thalia let her go. But under her breath, Laurel heard her mutter, "It's like you're living inside a lobotomy."

"Oh, stop it," Laurel said. "That doesn't even make sense."

"Sure it does," Thalia said. "Lots of things live in holes. This place is a hole where your brain used to be."

But then Thalia had also said Laurel's quilts were too pretty to be art, while Laurel found her quilts and her neighborhood to be pleasing in the same way. On a single quilt, Laurel would put both sugar-cookie angels and a crimson pocket with a bleached bird's skull sewn inside. But every piece, whether beautiful or ugly or indifferent, was subject to the larger pattern.

Thirteen years now she'd lived in her blue house, and Victori-anna's pieces still made a whole that Laurel thought was lovely. Her neighbors might each have their own special favorite sin: They drank or fought, they cheated on their taxes or each other. But they washed and waxed their cars on Saturdays, and kept their hedges and their lamps trimmed. They put up neighbor-hood watch signs and kept their curtains open, ever vigilant. Old-fashioned glass lampposts lined the streets, so that even at night, a ghost would be hard put to find a shadowed path to Laurel's door.

Even so, that night the drowned girl came anyway.

A storm was gathering, so Laurel checked that the chain was on her bedroom door before climbing into bed. She was more likely to sleepwalk when the air was humid enough to hold the taste of electricity. She'd rise and undo locks, pull up windows, unpack closets and drawers. Once she'd left a puffy beaded poppy she was hand sewing sitting out on her bedside table. She fell asleep thinking that the black beads at the poppy's center were as glossy and round as mouse eyes, and then she got up in the night and picked out every stitch. Her hands liked to open and undo while she was sleeping. The chain was no challenge. Its true job was to rattle against the doorframe and wake up David so he could lead her back to bed.

Their bedroom felt like a crisper. David, whose metabolism ran so high his skin always felt slightly fevered, couldn't sleep in summer unless the thermostat was set at sixty-five. She climbed in and got under her blankets, pressing her front against his warm back. She kissed his shoulder, but he didn't stir. He was sleeping so soundly that his lanky body had solidified into something dense and hard to shift.

David was working fifteen-hour days, adapting simulator code he'd written for the Navy into a PC game for a company out in California. He'd probably spoken ten complete sentences to her in the last week. All the pieces of him that she thought of as her husband had moved down to live in his brain stem, and code took all his higher functions. She'd get him back when the math was done. She always did, and so she let him be.

She slept hard until the temperature dropped even lower. She rolled onto her back as the cold sent her rising toward the surface of her sleep. Her eyes opened. She saw the outline of a young girl, twelve or thirteen, standing by the foot of the bed.

"Shelby?" she said, and sat up. But Shelby was built like a blade of grass, her breasts only now budding and the faintest curve to her tum. This girl's puppy fat had shifted into real breasts and small hips, and she was soaked to the skin. She caught the moonlight that came in the window and glowed with it.

"Honey, aren't you freezing?" Laurel asked her, but the question came out in a strained whisper, as if Laurel had been sleeping so long and heavy that her throat had rusted shut.

The girl didn't answer. Laurel could see her body through the wet fabric, and she realized she could also see the bedroom window. The girl had gone as transparent as her dress. Then Laurel understood what she was, and she checked the corners of the room for Marty; this girl had to be one of his.

He wasn't there. It was unprecedented, but the drowned girl

had come alone. Her head was tilted down and her wet hair was a veil, strands of it clinging like lace to her nose and cheekbones. Her hair was blond or light brown, hard to tell since the water had darkened it.

"You can't be here," Laurel said, swinging her legs out of the bed. David muttered something and turned over. His long arm moved into the space where she'd been lying.

The drowned girl turned away and walked to the open curtains, as if complying. Dark water dripped from the ends of her hair and the hem of her dress, but the carpet stayed dry. Her bare feet brushed the surface, swaying the thick pile.

"I didn't mean leave," Laurel said, standing up and taking two cautious steps after her. "I meant, you can't *be* here."

The girl had reached the bedroom window, and the sound of Laurel's voice did not restrain her. She took another two steps forward, melting through the window and arching herself out, spreading her arms and drifting into the darkness without pushing off. Laurel followed, stretching a cautious hand out, but the glass was cool and solid under her fingertips. She watched gravity catch the girl's dress and her long hair, tugging it downward, but her body drifted down easy. She tilted her head up and her feet down as she sank, landing softly on the tiles by the pool.

The yard was dark, but Shelby had forgotten to turn off the underwater pool lights, so the water glowed, and the girl glowed too, as if she had her own light. She swept her right arm down in a smooth and graceful arc, like a game-show hostess modeling the water. Laurel's gaze followed the gesture and at first she couldn't make sense of what she saw. The drowned girl was now resting facedown in the center of the pool, her pale skirt opening like wings on the water. Her body was slim with long, thin legs like a pony's leg, her hair spreading in a water-darkened fan around her head. Her ghost faded to a moving shadow in Laurel's peripheral vision, blending into the darkness.

Laurel slammed her hands against the glass.

She heard David saying, "Wha—" behind her. He sounded far away.

Laurel bayed in her sleep, a long, loud howling. The noise woke her up. She stopped making it. She was standing at the window, looking down at her backyard. It didn't make sense. She was awake now, this was her real hand touching her own cool glass. The girl should be gone, but Laurel could still see her. She was facedown and the lights shone below her in the water, giving her pale edges and a shadowed back. The water rocked her still body as it floated in the middle of Laurel's pool.

Laurel heard David again, closer now, saying, "Baby, what—" but she was already pushing off the window and running to the door, scrabbling to unlatch the chain. She wrenched the door open and ran down the hall toward the stairs. Her head turned toward Shelby's room as she ran past, an involuntary movement.

Shelby wasn't there. Shelby's bed was still made up.

Laurel kept running for the stairs, even though her mind was telling her that Shelby had to be in bed. Her mind wanted to go back and look, to look a hundred times until the bed stopped being empty and her eyes saw Shelby, safe and sleeping where she belonged. Her heart felt like it was swelling, taking up too much room in her chest, compressing her lungs so that she couldn't get a breath as she ran down the stairs. Shelby had been reading in the keeping room when Laurel went to bed, but now the sofa was as empty as the bed had been, a hunter-green throw puddled on the floor.

Laurel flipped the lock on the sliding-glass door and shoved it sideways along its track. The alarm began its prehowl beeping, an electronic drumbeat of sound, heartless and high, that drove her forward across the patio. All at once she was too close to the low fence encircling the patio. She'd installed that fence back when Shelby was a toddler whose only goal was to walk straight into the pool and sink like a beautiful, stupid lemming. David, whose gaze turned inward toward his own brain most times, had barked his shin on it so often when it was new that Shelby had thought the fence was called a "dammit."

Now Laurel stumbled on it and went skidding across the damp lawn. She fell to one knee and then was up again, running to the higher fence that encircled the pool. She was praying, a wordless call to God. The gate was unlatched, and Laurel shoved it open and ran across the tiles, straight down the steps into the water.

The cold shocked her legs and shot up through her spine. It was as if she had been wearing a second set of eyelids, sheer as membrane. The cold snapped them open, and she saw that the girl wasn't Shelby. She knew Shelby's every molecule, and the delicate set of the shoulder blades and the contours of the head were not the same.

A wash of red joy bubbled and crashed its way through her every vein, as if her blood had suddenly been carbonated. Her whole body sang with a sick gladness that this was any child but hers. It was as immediate and involuntary as her heartbeat, and in her next breath, shame crept in: not Shelby, thank God, thank God, but this girl was *someone's*.

The water forced her into that slow, sodden running she was always doing in her dreams. She waded in up to her chest before she was close enough to grab the girl's ankle. She pulled her back, and a reasoning piece of her took note of how cool the girl's skin felt, dead and pliable under her fingers.

Bet Clemmens? She'd forgotten Bet was staying at the house; she'd forgotten Bet existed in the last long minute. But now her mind was seeking possibilities. Not Bet. She was taller than this, and her hair was a single toned red with an inch of brown at the roots.

The house alarm began blaring. Laurel reached the steps and tried to roll the girl, to get her face into the air, but she folded instead of turning. Then it was as if the girl's body pulled itself upward, levitating. For one crazy second Laurel clung to her, not understanding, but then she saw David's hands. He was on the pool steps, bare chested, the water soaking the legs of his pajama bottoms, lifting the girl out.

Laurel grabbed the silver rail and hauled herself up the steps. Her heart still felt swollen, taking up all the room in her chest, banging itself against her rib cage. David laid the girl out on the tile, and he'd gone to that burny-eyed place he went to in a crisis, his movements precise and spare.

He said, "Start CPR. I'm calling nine-one-one."

Laurel dropped to her knees, facing the house. She cupped the back of the girl's neck and pulled upward, tilting the head back, using her other hand to push the heavy strands of long hair away. She saw a heart-shaped face, pug nose, and round blue eyes half open under straight blond brows.

She recognized her. More than that: She knew her. It was Molly, and Laurel knew her high giggle and the way she walked in quick, small steps with her toes turned in. Just last October, she'd sent Molly off with Shelby, both of them in red lipstick and the ragged pirate miniskirts she'd made for them. She had wondered if this was the last Halloween they would want costumes and trick-or-treating. They'd refused to ruin their look with jackets, and they'd run off with their skinny, bare arms linked at the elbow and prickling with gooseflesh in the mild chill. This was Molly's face. It was Molly Dufresne.

Laurel felt like something huge and heavy was rolling fast over her, flattening her and pressing out her breath. There was a film over Molly's pale, familiar eyes. Laurel wanted to stand up and walk inside the house, to slip lightly into a peaceful room where none of this was true. She had to make herself keep doing necessary things, thrusting two fingers into Molly's slack mouth to clear it. She put her mouth on Molly's and pushed air, hard, meeting resistance.

Bent over, all she could see was the cheerful pebbled tile, and beyond that a small part of the lawn and David's bare feet running for the house. As she sat up she yelled after him, "David? Where's Shelby? You have to find Shelby."